Praise for *Magic to the Bone*

"Loved it. Fiendishly original . . . a stay-up-all-night read. We're going to be hearing a lot more of Devon Monk."
—Patricia Briggs, #1 *New York Times* bestselling author of *Bone Crossed*

"[A] gritty setting, compelling, fully realized characters, and a frightening system of magic-with-a-price that left me awed. Devon Monk's writing is addictive, and the only cure is more, more, more."
—Rachel Vincent, *New York Times* bestselling author of *Rogue*

"Highly original and compulsively readable. Don't pick this one up before going to bed unless you want to be up all night!" —Jenna Black, author of *The Devil's Due*

"*Magic to the Bone* is an exciting new addition to the urban fantasy genre. It's got a truly fresh take on magic, and Allie Beckstrom is one kick-ass protagonist!"
—Jeanne C. Stein, national bestselling author of *Legacy*

"The prose is gritty and urban, the characters mysterious and marvelous, and Monk creates a fantastic and original magic system that intrigues and excites. A promising beginning to a new series. I'm looking forward to more!"
—Nina Kiriki Hoffman, Bram Stoker Award–winning author of *Spirits That Walk in Shadow*

"Monk's reimagined Portland is at once recognizable and exotic, suffused with her special take on magic, and her characters are vividly rendered. The plot pulled me in for a very enjoyable ride!" —Lynn Flewelling, author of *Shadows Return*

"Clever and compulsively readable. . . . Allie's internal and external struggles are brilliantly and tightly written, creating a multifaceted character who will surprise, amuse, amaze, and absorb readers." —*Publishers Weekly* (starred review)

continued . . .

"Devon Monk has created a cool new heroine in Allie Beckstrom.... She has developed a system of magic that is intriguing and distinct from those filling urban fantasies by the score.... With a strong heroine, a great setting, and an interesting new system of magic, *Magic to the Bone* is likely to give urban fantasy readers more of what they want: a worthy read. Recommended." —SFRevu

"Devon Monk is casting a spell on the fantasy world.... Allie is a convincing, street-smart heroine.... Monk has done an outstanding job creating a gritty, authentic-feeling urban fantasy on par with Rob Thurman or John Levitt; it should be interesting to watch how this series develops." —Monsters and Critics

"With style and a magical world that is quite fresh, Monk explodes on the scene and makes a few waves.... For sheer guts, stubbornness, and determination, they don't come much feistier than Allie." —*Romantic Times*

"Monk makes a grand entrance with her debut novel, captivating readers with a well-imagined tale of magic and suspense. *Magic to the Bone* delves into a dark-edged magic and adds a touch of romance that keeps the heroine more human than those around her. I'm looking forward to seeing where the next portion of Allie's journey takes her."
—Darque Reviews

"An intelligent, entertaining mystery. The kick-butt heroine is strong and independent.... Exciting fun; readers will look forward to more adventures of Allie."
—Genre Go Round Reviews

"This book is fresh, original, and so totally captivating that I could barely look away from the pages."
—Errant Dreams Reviews

"A solid and pleasing mystery story ... engaging ... impressive.... [*Magic to the Bone*] introduced enough interesting concepts and potential story arcs to propel the series for some time to come. I expect big things from the next installment, *Magic in the Blood*." —SciFiGuy.ca

"*Magic to the Bone* is a breath of fresh air in the urban fantasy genre, in much the same way that Ilóna Andrews's Kate Daniels series is a breath of fresh air. Instead of the same tired werewolf/vampire soap opera that so many novels perpetuate, *Magic to the Bone* is more concerned with the ramifications of adding magic to modern society and exploring the realistic consequences . . . an exciting and often poignant story. . . . Devon Monk shows the potential to be a standout writer in the subgenre. Most important, I could not put this book down; I read it in two nights, with only work and sleep coming between me and the pages. Well-done." —Fantasy Literature

"A unique character, her interior quips are humorous. . . . The humor blends with the drama to make it stronger. Devon Monk has created some fantastic characters to inhabit her suspenseful story. The ending indicates this might be the beginning of a series, which is wonderful, because the story is as addictive as the use of magic, earning *Magic to the Bone* a Perfect 10." —Romance Reviews Today

"A thrilling, magical ride that will leave you breathless for more. Toss in a bit of romance with gritty characters, a magical world, and a mysterious plot, and you have a superb adventure. Devon Monk is original and exciting and I can't wait for more." —Romance Junkies

"The magic system created by Devon Monk is inventive. . . . [She] is a fine writer and moves the plot along at a good pace. . . . If you like urban fantasy with a touch of romance, then you will thoroughly enjoy this novel."

—Robots and Vamps

"*Magic to the Bone* is a good mystery/adventure with a likable heroine, a mysterious hero, and cute supporting characters."

—The Good, the Bad, the Unread

Also by Devon Monk

Magic to the Bone
Magic in the Blood

Magic in the Shadows

Devon Monk

A ROC BOOK

ROC
Published by New American Library, a division of
Penguin Group (USA) Inc., 375 Hudson Street,
New York, New York 10014, USA
Penguin Group (Canada), 90 Eglinton Avenue East, Suite 700, Toronto,
Ontario M4P 2Y3, Canada (a division of Pearson Penguin Canada Inc.)
Penguin Books Ltd., 80 Strand, London WC2R 0RL, England
Penguin Ireland, 25 St. Stephen's Green, Dublin 2,
Ireland (a division of Penguin Books Ltd.)
Penguin Group (Australia), 250 Camberwell Road, Camberwell, Victoria 3124,
Australia (a division of Pearson Australia Group Pty. Ltd.)
Penguin Books India Pvt. Ltd., 11 Community Centre, Panchsheel Park,
New Delhi - 110 017, India
Penguin Group (NZ), 67 Apollo Drive, Rosedale, North Shore 0632,
New Zealand (a division of Pearson New Zealand Ltd.)
Penguin Books (South Africa) (Pty.) Ltd., 24 Sturdee Avenue,
Rosebank, Johannesburg 2196, South Africa

Penguin Books Ltd., Registered Offices:
80 Strand, London WC2R 0RL, England

First published by Roc, an imprint of New American Library,
a division of Penguin Group (USA) Inc.

First printing, November 2009
10 9 8 7 6 5 4 3 2

Printed in the United States of America

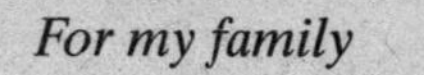

For my family

Acknowledgments

Writing is only part of what brings a story to its final form. Without the many people who contributed time and energy along the way, this book would not have come to fruition. Thank you to my agent, Miriam Kriss, and my editor, Anne Sowards, two consummate professionals and awesome people who make my job easy. Thanks also to Cameron Dufty, Ray Lundgren, and artist Larry Rostant, who have each contributed their remarkable skills to make this book what it is today.

My love and gratitude to my amazing first readers, Dean Woods, Dejsha Knight, and Dianna Rodgers. Your support and willingness to tell me what I got wrong and what I got right made this story shine. That said, any errors in this book are my fault alone.

To my sister Deanne Hicks and friend Sharon Thompson, thank you for your unfailing encouragement. An additional huge thank-you goes out to my wonderful sisters, brothers, aunts, uncles, nieces, nephews, and distant relations who have cheered for me along the way.

All my love to my husband, Russ, and my sons, Kameron and Konner. You are, as always, the very best part of my life.

And perhaps most important of all: Thank you, dear reader, for letting me share this story with you.

Chapter One

Rush hour traffic below my apartment window breathed a deep note behind the rise and fall of winter wind. Rain tapped like pinpricks against glass. The only noise besides my rapid breathing was the cold water pouring into the bathroom sink.

That, and my dead father's voice.

"Allison." My father's voice again. Distant, as if he strained to pitch it across a crowded room, a crowded street, a crowded city.

I was the only one in my apartment. And my father was really dead this time.

I'd gone to his funeral that morning and seen him buried—literally watched as his body was lowered into the grave. There was no mistake, no corpse stealing, no weird magical rituals this time. This time, he didn't have a second chance, third chance. He was well and truly gone.

"Allison."

"Oh, for cripes' sake," I said—yes, out loud—to my empty apartment. "You have got to be kidding me. What the hell, Dad?"

The bathroom mirror in front of me showed my panic. I was still a little too pale from the recent hospital stay, which made the opalescent mark of magic look even brighter where it wrapped from my fingertips up my right arm, shoulder, and onto the edges of my collarbone, jaw, and temple. My dark hair was mussed from kissing Zayvion Jones a few minutes before in the kitchen, but even though one eye was obscured by hair, a shadow stained my eyes. That shadow, I knew, was my father.

He wasn't in the room. He was in me.

This was going to put a crimp in my date tonight.

You must, my dead father said in my ear, less than a whisper, more than a thought.

Must nothing. Not this time. Not ever again.

"No. No way," I said. "No to whatever you were about to tell me. Listen," I said, cool as a 911 operator talking someone down from a ledge, "you're dead. I'm sorry about that, but I am not going to let you possess me. So follow the light, or go to the other side, or hang around your own house and haunt your accounting ledgers or something. You do not get to stay in my head."

Nothing.

But I knew my dad. Nothing was not a guarantee he was gone.

How did one dispossess oneself, preferably before one's hot date in a few hours? The only thing that came to mind was vampires and thresholds and not inviting them across. I doubted vampire stuff would work on my disembodied father. He might have been a soulless bastard, but he was not an actual vampire, since vampires, as far as I knew, did not actually exist.

And even though I was putting up a brave front, it was hard to ignore the fist-hard thump of my heart against my ribs, the salt of cold sweat on my lips.

"Daniel Beckstrom," I said, putting all my focus and concentration on the words, giving them the weight of my will, "leave my mind, leave my body, and leave me alone. I do not give you permission to be a part of me."

Sweat ran a line down my temple. I watched my eyes. Watched as the shadow drew away from my pinprick pupils, dissolving outward like clouds retreating from the sun, until a thick ring of night edged my familiar pale emerald irises.

I blinked, and even the ring of darkness was gone.

Gone.

I exhaled to slow my breathing. In through the nose, out through the mouth. I was fine until I swallowed. The taste of wintergreen and leather rolled down the back of my throat. My father's scents. In my mouth. In me.

He wasn't gone. Not at all. He was still there somewhere, a moth-wing flutter, soft and fast, behind my eyes.

I had thought that flutter was just another side effect from all the magic I'd used lately, another price to pay for trying to save those kidnapped girls and trying to save Anthony.

Bloody memories came to me unbidden: the warehouse with the abducted girls tied down by knotted spells; the kid, Anthony, broken and bloody on the floor. My friend Pike's mutilated face, his remaining eye fever-bright as he held my hand and made me promise, made me swear to look after the ragtag group of Hounds he called family. Just like he called me family. And my father's corpse . . .

I pushed that memory away. The girls were dead or returned to their families. Anthony was back with his mom, or maybe in juvie; I wasn't sure. Pike was gone. Dead.

Just like my father should be.

My hands had been under the rush of cold water for so long, they'd gone numb. I pulled them out of the water, fumbled the vase and rose I'd been holding. The vase clattered into the sink. I turned off the water and scrubbed my forehead with cold, wet fingers, trying to stop the flutter in my skull.

"We didn't like each other when you were alive," I muttered to my father. "You think living in my head is going to change that?"

Find the disks, my father said from the far side of my head.

I resisted the urge to pour mouthwash in my brain.

"Forget about the damn disks. You're dead, Violet said the police are looking for the disks, and I don't want you in my head. Go away."

The flutter scurried off to the back of my brain, so far from my conscious thought that I couldn't feel it anymore.

And there it was: the official least-comforting thing that had happened all day. Dad was not only in my head, but he could speak to me, understand me, *and* hide from me.

How fabulous was that?

The only bright side? My father, the most powerful magic user I'd ever known, had actually done something I'd ask him to do. Which was a first. But the thought of him curling up cozy in my brain made me want to stab a hot spork through my head.

Since I didn't have a spork handy, I leaned over the sink and scooped up a palmful of cold water and pressed it against my face. There had to be a better option than a violent sporking. There had to be a way to get rid of my dad.

Think, Allie. There has to be someone who can figure this out.

I was going to see Maeve Flynn tomorrow so she could start teaching me the things about magic the Authority didn't like regular people to know about. Secret things, like there was a secret group of magic users—the Authority—who ran their own kind of justice in this city and went around deciding who would and wouldn't be allowed to use magic. Secret things my father had been involved with—including the disks that made magic portable and nearly painless. Dad had been a part of the Authority, and he had been killed because there was some sort of magical war brewing among them.

And Zayvion, who was most definitely a part of the Authority, had lobbied to get me admitted into the group for training with Maeve. I wasn't convinced it was the best option, but since my choice had been join or have all my memories of how to use magic taken away from me, I'd joined.

Being possessed by a dead relative sounded like something right up Maeve's alley.

Okay, so I'd talk to her about it and see what she could do.

Now I just needed to get through my date with Zayvion Jones. I so did not want my dad in my head on my first real date with the man I was pretty sure I might love.

Maybe I should cancel.

Zayvion didn't carry a cell, and I didn't know his home number. That's the problem with dating a secret magic assassin, a Closer: you don't call them, they call you.

So, the date was on. I'd tell Zayvion I had a chaperone. Maybe he could help me figure it out.

Step one: shower. Would my dad feel me naked? Don't think about that.

Step two: dress. Would my dad see me naked? Really don't think about that.

And step three: go on a date with Zayvion. Would my dad know what I felt about Zayvion? Would he hear what I thought about him? Would he feel me hot and needful for him?

Probably. 'Cause I'm just lucky that way.

A knock on the door rang out so loud, I yelled and spun, fingers poised to draw a Hold spell. No one in my bathroom. The knock had come from my front door, not my bathroom door.

Magic flared through my bones, my hold on it slipping. The sensuous heat of magic pushed against my skin, stretching me, straining to get free, and I had to exhale to make room for it to move. It pressed heavy in me, a sweet pain, promising anything, everything, so long as I was willing to pay the price for it.

I felt the moth-wing flutter of my dad in my head, his curiosity at the magic inside me.

"You touch it, and I'll use it to end you," I said through my teeth.

The curious little moth became very, very still.

Good. At least he could tell when I was not kidding around.

I very carefully spread my fingers apart and then closed them into fists, consciously resisting the temptation to draw the Hold glyph, to cast magic. Because no matter what magic promised, every time I lost control of it, magic used me like a disposable glove at a proctology exam.

I am a river, I thought. *Magic flows through me but it does not touch me.*

I took another good breath or two, and magic retreated into a more normal rhythm of flowing up from the cisterns deep beneath the city, into me, and, unused, out of me back into the ground.

The knock at the front door rapped out louder.

I fished the vase and rose out of the sink and put them on the little shelf above the towel rack. The pink rose Zayvion had given me looked a little worse for the wear, but it wasn't dead yet. Tough flowers, roses. All that sweet beauty with the thorns to back it up. I appreciated that.

I dried my hands on my jeans and strode out of the bathroom. I wasn't expecting company. Well, except for Zayvion. But he said he'd be back in at seven. We had dinner plans. First-date plans. Let's-be-normal-like-other-normal-people plans.

The knock rattled out again.

There is one thing I can say about living in the city. There isn't a Ward or Alarm spell on the market strong enough to keep someone from breaking down your door if they have the will, the way, and a strong enough shoulder.

My baseball bat was under the bed, but I always left a hammer on the bookshelf.

Hammers can do all kinds of damage if they are swung low enough.

Yes, it had been that kind of week.

And the knocking just kept coming.

I stopped in front of the door, took a breath, and held still both it and magic in me for a second. I recited my little mantra: *Miss Mary Mack, Mack, Mack, all dressed in black, black, black* . . . until the order of those words calmed my racing thoughts.

It took about five seconds. My mind, my thoughts, cleared.

Using magic wasn't as easy as the actors made it look in the movies. It can't be cast in states of high emotion—like anger or, say, while freaking out because your freaking dead dad is in your freaking head. Every time you use magic, it uses you back. Sure, you could magic yourself a photographic memory for that big test, for that big interview, for that big stock market job. And all it cost you was a nice case of liver failure.

Or the memory of your lover's name.

Exhale. Good. Calm? Check. I leaned against the doorframe and sniffed. I didn't draw magic up into my sense of smell, though I was good at that too. Smelling, tracing, tracking, Hounding the burnt lines of spells back to their casters was how I made my living. But I couldn't smell anything over the oily tang of WD-40 I'd sprayed on the lock the other day.

I peeked through the peephole.

The woman in the hall was dressed in jeans, a knitted vest, button-down blouse, and a full-length coat. Blond, about eight inches shorter than my own six feet, she was a little wet. Portland's good at wet. The best. But even in the unglamorous warp of the peephole, she looked like a million sunny days to me.

Nola Robbins, my best friend in all the world.

I slipped the locks, which slid smoothly—thank you, WD-40—and threw open the door.

"Oh, thank God," she said. "I thought I heard you yell."

"I did. I'm fine. It's so good to see you!" I practically flew out of my apartment and into her arms.

Nola hugged me, and I caught the scent of honey and warm summer grass even though it was the middle of winter. The familiar comforting scents of her brought up memories of her nonmagical alfalfa farm and old nonmagical farmhouse. I inhaled, filling myself with the scents and memories of pleasant days. I did not want to let her go.

She patted my back, and I gave her one last squeeze.

"What are you doing here?" I asked. "Is something wrong?"

"I don't think so," she hedged. "What's up with the hammer?"

I dropped it on the little table by the door. "Just, you know. It's the city."

She shook her head. "You could get a dog."

"Don't start with me. Come on in." I belatedly noticed she had a suitcase with her. "Let me help."

"I got it." She strolled into my apartment, wheeling the suitcase behind her.

Out of habit, I looked up and down the hall. No one. Not even a shadow on the wall, watching us. I hoped. I wasn't the only Hound in the city, and Hounds knew how to be quiet when they wanted to be.

I relocked the door.

"Allie," she said, scanning my overcrowded bookshelves and my undercrowded everything else. "Have you even unpacked since you moved?"

"Pretty much," I said. "This is all that's left." Or at least it was all I could stand having. Whoever broke into my old apartment had not only tossed everything I owned; he or she had left a scent on it. The stink of iron and minerals, like old vitamins, not only kicked up half-remembered pain, but was also a bitch to scrub out of the upholstery.

And underwear. Not that I tried for long. Some things aren't worth saving.

Nola shook her head. "What am I going to do with you?" She gave me that sisterly smile that made her look ten years older than me, instead of my age. "How are you feeling? Are those bruises on your neck?"

"Good, and no. Not really. It's . . ." I was going to say nothing, but Nola could see right through my lies. "Well, maybe not fine, but . . . you know." I waved at her to sit on my ratty couch, which she did, and I sat on one of the chairs by the little round table at the window. "What are you doing here?" I asked again.

"You know I'm trying to get custody of Cody Miller?"

I laced my fingers together and rubbed my thumbs over the marks on my right and left hands. Marks put there in part, I was told, by Cody using me as a conduit for magic. A lot of magic.

"Is that his last name?" I asked.

"Yes. I'm running into a little bit of trouble getting him released. He was put in the state mental health hospital for criminal use of magic—forging signatures with magic." She shook her head. "He must have been eighteen when that happened. They said he suffered a mental break during his trial and has never been the same. But now it's been determined he needs to undergo more psychological exams." She shook her head. "They've had him for two years; I don't know what they haven't tested by now."

"Wait, Cody's twenty?"

"Right." Nola dug in her purse, pulled out a photo of a young man with delicate, almost fragile features. He was smiling, but his blue, blue eyes held the kind of simple intelligence I'd expect from a child.

"He's twenty on the outside, but not mentally," Nola said. "I decided I might be able to talk to some people personally, and find out why he hasn't been released into my custody yet. I'm hoping to take him home with me in the next few days."

"Want me to see if I can pull some strings for you?"

"Can you?"

I shrugged. "Maybe. I still haven't talked much with my dad's lawyers. But Violet basically told me the fate of Beckstrom Enterprises is mine to decide. And I'm sure Beckstrom Enterprises has string-pulling capabilities." I grinned. "Power in the palm of my hand. Pretty cool, huh?"

"Mmm," she agreed. "How are you doing with that?"

I opened my mouth to say I was fine, I could handle it, it was no big deal. But there was something about Nola that negated my bullshit ability. I'd never been able to lie to her, so I didn't even try.

"I'm worried. I'm not sure what I should do. Violet has done a really good job running the business since his, uh . . . death. She's still working on developing magic-technology integrations. She . . . she has reasons to keep things running."

I didn't tell her Violet was pregnant with the child of my powerful and not-nearly-dead-enough father. My one and only sibling. Violet said Dad didn't know about the baby before he died. I didn't know whether he'd hear me if I said it out loud. The idea of having to deal with his ghostly fit when he found out sounded like a joy I wanted to save for later.

The flutter started up in the back of my head and I rubbed my forehead until it stopped.

"Allie?" Nola asked.

"I'm fine. My head still feels weird after everything."

"Pike?" she asked.

I nodded. And before her concern could turn to pity, I said, "I don't have the training to run Beckstrom Enterprises the way it should be run. I've hated it for so long.

Still, there might be someone there who could help with Cody. I can call Violet and find out who I should talk to."

"Are you and she getting along okay?" she asked. "It must be really hard to work together with your dad's business and money, so close to his death."

Oh, she had no idea how close to his death I was. Time to change the subject.

"You didn't get a hotel, did you?" I asked. "You should stay here with me."

"I did make reservations, just in case." She glanced over at my answering machine. "I called, but you never answered."

I looked over at the machine too. The light was green. No messages waiting. "Maybe I forgot."

She nodded. "Still keeping your journal, honey?"

"Yes. But I've been having some problems with phones and stuff."

"And your computer?" she asked.

"No, that's been fine. But anything electric I keep on me—cell phone, watch—wears out fast."

"So your landline is okay?" she pressed.

"Yes."

"I thought you and I had a deal about your checking in every day for a little while. I even had a phone installed for you."

"What are you, my mom?"

"No, I'm your extra memory, remember? You, my friend, have holes in your head." She held up a finger at my faked shock. "If you want me to tell you what's been happening in your life when magic eats up your memory, then you need to tell me what's going on. So, what's been going on?"

I glanced at the clock on the wall.

"Well, for one thing, I have a date tonight."

She didn't even fight the smile that made her face light up like she was made of sunshine.

"With Zayvion?"

I nodded. "We haven't had much of a chance to really talk since I came back to town. Or at least not about normal things. Not about us. He remembers . . . things about us

I don't remember. Which is weird. So we're going to try a date—a real date. Get to know each other a little better."

"When is he supposed to be here?" She stood and looked me up and down, obviously not impressed by my wet-cuffed jeans and sweater. "Are you going to dinner? How fancy is the restaurant?"

"Less than an hour. And yes, superfancy. He made reservations at the Gargoyle."

"Tell me you're not wearing that."

"Excuse me? Did I just hear fashion attitude from a woman who wears overalls and men's boots every day?"

She made a face at me. "Only on the farm. Do you even own girl clothes?"

"These are girl clothes."

"Dress? Skirt? Heels?" She said each word slowly, as if I'd never heard them before.

"Maybe. I think so. I haven't really looked through my closet. There's a couple boxes of stuff I haven't unpacked."

"Oh my God, Allie. Your date is in an hour and you haven't even started to look through your clothes?"

"It's been a weird day," I drawled.

She laughed. "All your days are weird. Let me help. You go take a shower. Want me to dig through your closet or make coffee?"

"Coffee. You are staying with me, right?"

She was already moving toward my kitchen. "If I'm not in the way."

I got as far as the bathroom door before I heard, "Oh, Allie!"

"What?" I yelled.

"Roses. Everywhere." She came out of the kitchen, a single pink long-stemmed rose in her hand. "You do know your kitchen is filled with them, right?"

I smiled. "There are a few irises in there too."

"Bargain at the flower shop?"

"Nope."

"Secret admirer?"

"No."

"Spill."

"Zayvion."

The sunshine smile was back, and she got that goo-goo softy look. "Then you definitely need to put on girl clothes. Go. Shower." She waved her hand at me. "I'll arrange the flowers too."

I grinned. Nola never asked; she always just told me what she was going to do for me. I'd gotten pretty used to it, and she'd gotten used to my telling her if I didn't want her to boss me around.

I walked into the bathroom and shut the door. The flutter winged behind my eyes again. Dad.

Find the disks, my father's voice breathed. *Find my killer.*

I cupped my hands over my ears. "No, no, no. Get out. Get dead."

I squeezed my eyes shut and the flutter, the voice, was gone.

Sweet hells. What was I thinking, going on a date? My father was alive in me. Aware.

Or maybe he wasn't. Maybe I was just imagining him, his voice, the flutter of his thoughts in my mind. Maybe I was going crazy.

A chill washed down my arms, and I took a deep, shaky breath. It was possible. Possible I was going insane. I'd used a lot of magic lately. Enough to do damage to my body and mind.

And sure, I liked to think of myself as someone who met any bad situation—like insanity and ghostly possession—straight on. But not tonight.

For just a few hours, for just this one date, I was going to ignore my father in my mind, ignore the state of my sanity, and ignore the entire city lousy with secrets and magic and brewing wars. Even if it killed me.

Chapter Two

I ducked under the warm stream of the shower and couldn't believe that this morning I'd been at my father's grave. Only Violet, his newest—well, his last—wife had cried. I didn't know how I felt about his death. Sad, I think.

But it was getting pretty hard to grieve someone who wouldn't just get on with the dying.

The disks, my dad whispered in my head, *must be found. The disks. My killer must be found. . . .*

"La la la," I said. "I'm not listening to you."

I rubbed soap over the burn marks left from the Veiled, the incorporeal bits of dead magic users who had gotten a taste of me they couldn't resist. The burn marks still itched in a sore kind of way, but the bruised-fingerprint look had faded. I checked my legs. Pale, long, a little bruised and scratched, but worth shaving. If I wore nylons I could probably even try a skirt above my knees.

Nola opened the bathroom door. "I'm going out. Need anything?"

"No. Wait . . . nylons."

"Anything else?"

"Is there something I'm forgetting?" Open mouth, exhale dumb question. Nola, of all people, knew there were probably a million things I was forgetting. And not just about how to get ready for a date.

"Do you have a nice bra?"

"Of course I have a nice bra." At least I thought I did. Cotton counted as nice if it had lace on it, right?

"Not cotton," she said.

"I own a bra that isn't cotton, not that it is any of your business."

She smiled. "I'll be back soon."

I rinsed, got out of the shower, and spent some time looking for remnants from my college dating days. Things such as hair spray, gel, and makeup.

The drawers under my bathroom sink gave up a few useful items. A tube of mascara, lip gloss, cover makeup, blush, and some goo I used to think made my hair look sexy. I applied everything with some degree of caution and stared at myself in the mirror for longer than I wanted to admit.

I looked . . . well, if not soft, much more feminine. It was strange to see myself that way, as a woman out on the prowl for sex instead of a Hound out on the prowl for the scent of illegal magic.

I dug my fingers at the roots of my hair again, letting dark strands slide down the side of my face, covering the marks of magic along my jaw and catching on the corner of my lips. This was who I was. At least for tonight. No, this was who I always was, whom I hid behind the lack of makeup, behind the hard edge of being a street Hound, behind the torn blue jeans and T-shirts. This was the woman who had been hurt, betrayed, loved, dumped. This was the woman who hadn't found a man who could look her in the eye. A woman who didn't like to admit her own power. This was the me even I didn't know how to deal with.

It was going to be interesting to see what Zayvion, the unflappable master of Zen calm, was going to do about it. Maybe he'd do nothing.

Maybe that worried me most of all.

I tucked the corner of the towel tighter around me, then bare-footed it out into my bedroom across the hall. My closet wasn't exactly full. Unpacked boxes took up half the closet, and the other half held a couple suit jackets, some slacks, more sweaters, and not a lot else. I didn't see my red dress. For all I knew I gave it away, burned it, lost it in a wild night of magical abandon. That subtle reminder that magic had burned holes through my memories made me angry. But it was a familiar anger, and one I knew I could do nothing about.

All I could do was go forward. That's all I'd been doing my entire life. Let go of the past, of the things I wanted, of the people I loved, and move forward.

I glanced at the clock. Still forty minutes before Zayvion showed up. I could put together something suitable for a French restaurant by then.

Maybe a nice pair of slacks. I pushed hangers around again, looking for my gray tweed pair. Found them, considered my nice jade jacket. Even though it was silk, it looked far too much like business wear. I wanted to date Zayvion, not interview him for a job. I fingered the inside of the jacket collar and a flash of red caught my eye.

My dress?

I unhooked the hanger. Beneath the jade jacket, red shone like a winter fire. My dress.

I shucked out of the towel, put on my good bra (silk, lace, black) and panties, then slicked into the dress. It fit me a little looser than the last time I'd worn it and I made a mental note to eat three meals once in a while. I smoothed my hands over the silky fabric—what there was of it—but stopped that pretty quick. My hands sounded like industrial sandpaper over the silk, and I didn't want to snag it up.

Shoes next. I found my high-heel black boots, sexy if you were into the straps and well-placed buckles look. I wondered how stupid they'd look with the dress, waffled when I came across a nice pair of high-heel sandals, and went back to the boots because it was January in the Pacific Northwest. Icy rain out there. Lots of wet. Sandals just weren't going to cut it.

Nola hadn't returned with the nylons yet, so I carried the boots back into the bathroom to get a look at myself in the full-length mirror.

What do you know. I was still a girl.

The dress slipped low and wide in the front, giving off a maximum view of my collarbone, and the whorls of magic that painted down to my right breast, but mostly covered my cleavage, and the shiny pink bullet scar over my left breast. The sleeves were short and the skirt was shorter, body hugging but with a little swing at the hem.

The whole look, from dark, messy hair that I tucked behind my ear on the left side and left loose on my right, pale skin beneath bloodred curves, painted a version of myself I hadn't seen in years.

Standing there in front of the mirror, in a dress—in a sexy dress—made me feel more naked than I'd been in the shower. For a second—just that long—I wanted to crawl back into my jeans and heavy sweater and leave the whole femme fatale stuff to girls who liked dressing up and didn't get dumped every time they tried to fall in love.

The door opened. "I'm back," Nola called out over the rustling of plastic bags. "Are you in the bedroom?"

"Bathroom," I yelled.

More rustling as she neared. "I wasn't sure what color for your nylons. Decided nude would be best . . ." She stopped at the open bathroom door.

"What do you think?" I asked when she didn't say anything. "Too much skin? Maybe it needs a sweater? Or a parka?"

"Turn around," she said.

I did.

"Are you wearing those with it?" She pointed to the boots in my hand.

"I love my boots."

"Hmm." She handed me the nylons, and I surprised myself by remembering not only how to get into a pair of panty hose, but also how weird they felt against my skin.

I stuffed my feet in the boots and propped my heels on the edge of the toilet so I could zip the leather to just below my knees.

"Well?" I turned, arms out.

"Heels might be prettier," she said.

"These have heels—over three inches of heels."

"I mean dress heels. Sexy shoes."

"These are sexy."

"Girl shoes," Nola said like it was a foreign language. "You have enough money to own a hundred Jimmy Choos if you wanted."

"First of all, when did you start paying attention to designer shoes? And second of all, it's raining out there. And cold. Portland is boot weather. Sexy-boot weather." I gave her a grin. "How about the dress?"

Nola nodded. "Gorgeous. Really. Even with the boots. Plus your, um . . . The marks on your hand and arm make it look like you're wearing jewelry down your arm."

I looked down at both my hands. Sure, my right hand was covered in swirls of metallic colors that wove all the way up my arm, over my shoulder, and licked up to the corner of my eye. But my left hand had only thick black bands at each knuckle, wrist, and elbow from where I had denied magic's use of me. Those black rings were stark against my white skin. Prison bars against moonlight. That, I realized, was a good deal of why I was feeling so exposed. My hands, my scars, my mistakes—and for the few who might really understand this stuff—my power was showing.

It made me feel all twitchy and vulnerable.

"Maybe I should wear a jacket. Real sleeves."

Nola stepped into the bathroom and turned me back toward the mirror, standing next to me so we were both in the reflection. Wow. I looked good. The dress clung in all the right places and made my modest curves look much fuller. The skirt hit high enough above the knees that even with those boots taking up all of my calf, it looked like my legs never stopped.

"You look beautiful," she said in a deal-with-it tone. "Wear your coat out. But don't wear it in the restaurant. You're on a date, not a job, okay?"

"It is pitiful you think you need to remind me of that," I said.

Nola stared at me in the mirror and gently touched one of the fading fingertip burns on my shoulder. "What happened?"

"It's a long story."

"Does it involve magic?"

"Everything in my life involves magic right now," I groused.

Nola stepped back. "So do something unmagical tonight. I recommend sex."

I laughed. "Shocking. Where's the prim and proper widow from the country?"

"I never said I was prim or proper." Nola grinned. "Just because I live in the sticks doesn't mean I don't know how to live."

The doorbell chimed.

"Think it's Zayvion?" she asked.

"Unless you invited a boyfriend over," I said.

"Stop it. I don't have a boyfriend. Do you want me to get it?"

I shook my head and tucked my hair behind my left ear again. One last muss with the right side so it better covered the marks along my jaw, and that was as good as I was going to get. Not that hiding the edge of my face would matter much. My hands and arms were covered in marks from magic.

"The boots?" I asked. "Honestly?"

"Tough," Nola said. "Unexpected. Sexy. You." She smiled. "Call me if you want the apartment to yourself tonight. I can get a hotel room for the night."

"Oh, I'll be home," I said.

"I'm not so sure about that. I know you."

I made a face at her, but she was right. I hadn't even been good at dating back in college. One-night stands, yes. Seven-course meals, no.

"Yeah?" I said. "Well, Zayvion has some idea in his head that I jump into bed too quickly with men and then push them away. Shut up and stop grinning. He wants us to take it slow. To know I really want this, want him."

"Gotta love a patient man," she said. "Rarest of them all. Go. Date."

She moved out of the way so I could walk out of the bathroom. It's amazing how little time it takes to get back into the swing of wearing heels again.

I strolled to the door and looked out the peephole. Zayvion's back was to me. He had traded his ratty blue ski coat for a black leather jacket that did worlds of good for showing the width of his shoulders. Well, well.

I opened the door.

Zayvion turned.

We stood there, caught in a breathless moment.

He looked amazing. Leather jacket, open to reveal a black sweater thin enough it showed the definition of his chest he always hid under sweatshirts. Black slacks. Black shoes. Handsome as hell, with those deep brown eyes, wide lips, and dark, tight-curled hair. He looked a little surprised. Maybe a lot surprised.

That made two of us.

"Allie," he exhaled.

"Zayvion." I licked my bottom lip, tasted the unfamiliar gloss—vanilla—and gave him a slow smile. "Don't you clean up nice? Come on in. I'm almost ready." I turned away from the hunger in his eyes and walked into the apartment. I had two reasons for turning my back on him. One, I had to stop looking at him before I just grabbed him and dragged him off to bed; I was trying to prove I wasn't that kind of a girl tonight.

Two, I wanted to see how the going-away view of my getup worked for him.

"Nola, you remember Zayvion Jones?" I looked over my shoulder at Zayvion.

Even though I'd gotten halfway across the room, Mr. Master of Zen had frozen, only one step into the apartment. He wasn't looking at my apartment. I'd lay money he didn't even notice Nola standing in the living room, watching us this whole time. His gaze slipped up the back of my boots, thighs, ass, and finally slid along the edge of my breast to my face.

Sweet loves. If he didn't stop looking at me like that, I wasn't going to make it to the door, much less the first course.

"Hello, Zayvion," Nola said.

He looked away, suddenly in motion again as if her voice had freed him. Freed us. I inhaled and realized I had stopped breathing. I had also, unknowingly, taken a step toward him.

Like metal to a magnet. That man was a force I could not resist.

"Good evening, Nola," he said as he shut the door. "I didn't know you were coming to visit." But the way he said it, the subtle tightening of his shoulders, the carefully neutral tone, sent warning bells off in my head. He was lying. He knew Nola was going to be here.

Did he know something about Cody? Something that would help Nola gain custody of him? Or was he spying on Nola? I didn't like that idea. Zayvion worked for people who gave me nightmares.

"Well, it wasn't a planned trip," she said. "I have some business in town that needs my attention."

"It is nice to see you again," he said.

Nola raised one eyebrow, obviously not buying it. I wasn't getting a good read on either of them. Partly because all I could think about was Zayvion's hands touching me, his body pressing against every inch of me. Partly because I had no idea how much they knew each other since I'd lost those memories. I suddenly felt the desire to keep Nola safe from the kind of people Zayvion associated with.

People like you, a whisper said in the back of my head.

Oh, just thanks so much for adding a little extra creepy to my night, Dad, I thought. *Now go away.*

I couldn't be sure that he listened, but I didn't hear him, didn't feel him anymore.

One thing was for sure: I trusted Zayvion—hells, trusted just about anyone in this city—more than I trusted my father.

Nola told me Zayvion had sat with me out at her farm for two weeks when I was in the coma. They would have had some time to talk then, to get to know each other. She also just said she liked him.

Good enough.

"It's nice to see you too," Nola said, and I was pretty sure she meant it. "Allie, before you go, I have something for you." She knelt beside her suitcase propped next to the couch and unzipped one of the outer pockets. "I was going to give it to you later, but I think it might come in handy tonight."

She stood and held something black and knitted in her hands.

I took the soft and supple hand-knitted lace, held it up, and discovered it wasn't just lace, it was gloves. Long enough they would rise up to my elbows where they tied off with a delicate black ribbon woven through eyelets.

"Oh, Nola. You made these, didn't you?"

She shrugged. "I had some time on my hands."

"They're beautiful. Thank you." I pulled them on. They fit perfectly. A lot of skin showed through the lace, but they did a nice job of making both of my arms look like they belonged on the same body. Plus, I thought they might be kind of sexy. I glanced over at Zayvion.

He had put both his hands in his pockets, same way I did when I was trying to keep my hands off the artwork in a museum. His gaze flowed down my body, then traced back up until his warm brown eyes met mine.

"Stunning." Deep and soft, husky with need. A wash of warmth flushed under my skin. I was blushing. Fabo. So much for femme fatale.

Sweet loves, this was going to be a long night. Maybe Nola should get that hotel room.

"Thanks."

We stood there, looking but not touching, wanting each other but doing nothing about it, until he finally tipped his head down and stared at his shoes. "So, your coat?"

"Right." I walked past him, and inhaled the warm pine and sweet spice scent of him—a new cologne? I liked it. He didn't touch me as I walked by. I kept my back to him until I had my long wool coat securely on and buttoned.

Then I turned.

He was looking at me, his shoulders tipped slightly down, body language visibly tense, as if a fire burned beneath his skin.

I knew the feeling.

"Ready?" I asked.

"I am. Are you?" He smiled, just a curve of his lips, and I wanted to kiss him, to open his mouth with my own and taste him.

I'd show him who was ready.

"Sure." It came out a little breathless, and I cleared my throat to get my volume back. "Bye, Nola. See you in a few hours."

"Or, you know, call," she said.

I gave her a look, then walked past Zayvion and out into the hall. He followed, pausing near enough that even with his hands in his pockets, I could feel the heat of him behind me as I turned to lock the door.

I took a step backward, hoping to feel the press of his body. Instead, he stepped in time with me, moving backward as if we were dancing, as if he had an instinctive knowledge of my body and his moving as one. As if he remembered very well that we had been lovers, even though I did not.

I held still, waiting, wishing he would touch me. Instead, he walked around and stood next to me.

Damn.

"You are hungry, aren't you?"

"Starving," I said.

He tipped his head toward the end of the hallway and the stairs that led down. "Good. Let's not lose our reservation."

"Right." I strolled over to the stairs.

He walked with me. "If I knew you had that dress in your closet," he said while looking straight ahead, "I would have taken you out somewhere nice a long time ago."

"Really? Before or after the psychopath tried to kill me?"

"Which psychopath?"

And seriously, if he had to ask that question—and he did—how crazy had my life been lately?

"Allie?" Zayvion asked.

"Minute. I'm thinking." How many psychopaths had I been dealing with? There was Bonnie, who had tried to shoot me. James, who was in jail now for trying to kill Zayvion, Cody, and me. Then there was the gunman I couldn't remember who left a bullet scar across my ribs.

"It wasn't a serious question," Zayvion said.

"I know."

And just a couple weeks ago, a whole slew of new psychopaths who also liked mixing a little blood magic in with their gunplay showed up in my life: Lon Trager's men. And to top it all off, the crazy death-magic doctor, Frank Gordon, had not only tried to kill me, he'd also dug up my dad's corpse to try to re-kill him.

"Forget I asked," Zayvion said.

"No, that's okay," I said. "Let's just say all of them."

"Mmm." He gestured to the stairs, indicating I walk in front of him. "I would have asked you out somewhere nice before all of the psychopaths. I don't like fighting on an empty stomach."

"That's so romantic."

I started down the stairs, ready to drop the psychopath train of thought, and pretty darned pleased with my continued grace in heels.

We made it across the lobby to the door. He held the door open for me. As I brushed past him, my leg slid against his. I caught my breath at the thrill of electricity that washed through me. Sweet loves, I wanted him. Even with all the psychopath talk.

I paused. Thanks to the heels, I was maybe half an inch taller than him. And close.

So close, all I'd have to do was lean forward to kiss him. Half in, half out of the doorway, his left arm extended to keep the door open, Zayvion would have nowhere to go if I did exactly that. I searched his face, wondering just how that would play out.

Silent, still, he relaxed backward into the doorframe and smiled softly. Inviting me. No, daring me. He knew exactly what the slightest brush of his body did to me. And he was enjoying every minute of it.

"Yes?" he murmured.

Keep smiling, Jones, I thought. *Two can play this game.*

"I think my boot's stuck," I said. "Hold on." I pressed the heel of my palm against his hip bone, for balance I really didn't need, and bent. I reached across my body, swaying my hip away from him as I lowered my head. My face skimmed just inches above his stomach, belt, and thigh as I bent to inspect my shin.

I messed with one of the perfectly not-stuck buckles on my boot and noted that Mr. Jones sure was breathing a lot faster than he had been a moment ago. Luckily, my hair swung forward to cover my grin.

Round one, I thought. *Bring it on, baby.*

I wiped the grin off my face and straightened, my fingers digging into his hip just a little. I let my hand drop, but not before dragging my thumb along the edge of his front pocket. I met his gaze.

He blinked, once, slowly. Couldn't seem to get his Zen

attitude working. Had to blink again before he managed the calm, unaffected front. I was ridiculously proud of that.

"Everything check out?" he finally drawled.

"Looks good so far." I flashed him a smile and stepped out into the cold, foggy night. "Reservations?"

"Plenty," he said behind me. "Oh, were you talking about dinner?"

"Ha-ha. When do we need to be there?"

"In about an hour. We have time."

"That's good to hear."

The night was cold. I kind of wished it were raining. I could use a little cold-shower action right now. My body, my senses, my nerves were focused on one thing only: Zayvion Jones.

Well, two things: Zayvion Jones, and keeping my hands off him.

Okay, three things: Zayvion Jones, keeping my hands off him, and not snapping my ankles in my boots.

Zayvion strolled up alongside me, and wonders of wonders, I heard the heel of his shoes thunk against the sidewalk, a hollow heartbeat in the fog. I didn't think I'd ever heard his footsteps before. He was Mr. Zen, Mr. Silent, Mr. Invisible. Which I supposed came in handy for a Closer.

But I liked the sound, liked experiencing the auditory weight of him beside me.

"The car's this way," he said.

We crossed the street. Traffic hushed and growled through the fog, an ocean of metal and steam and oil, the rasping croon of the city. We walked uphill in silence. Pale yellow and blue streetlights caught moonlike in the fog to diffuse light and deepen shadow. I took some time to breathe in the cold air, think calm thoughts, and rein in my heartbeat.

The car was parked at the end of the block. Zayvion, always a gentleman, unlocked the door for me while I scanned the shadows for Davy Silvers, or any of the other Hounds who might be following me.

I didn't see anyone, hear anyone, smell anyone, and it wasn't worth the pain of drawing on magic to sense them in any other manner.

If it were any other day I'd figure I was just upwind and too distracted to spot the Hounds in the night. And that still might be the case. Except every Hound in the city had been at the pub this afternoon to pay their respects to Pike. To say their good-byes. To mourn.

There hadn't been a sober body in that room by the time I'd gotten there. And I'd left long before the party ended. I figured there wasn't a Hound in the city sober enough to walk, much less track magic or follow me.

Still, something made me pause. A shift in the gray and yellow fog. A man-sized shadow across the street held still for too long. There, in the alley between the single-floor antique and notions shop and the condemned, hollow and broken ten-story apartment building, something waited. Something watched.

The wind picked up, pulled the scent of the watcher to me. Blackberry, burnt, all the sugars used up so only the bitter, thick tar of it remained, sweetness burned down to ash. And with that, the stink of animal defecation, sweat, and pain.

The shadow shifted again, and eyes, now low to the ground, flashed ghost green.

The thing growled, whimpered in pain. A car drove past, blocking my view and covering the sound. Once it had gone by, I heard a sucking-smacking from across the street, like something, or someone, was making messy work of a spaghetti dinner.

"Allie?"

I jumped at Zayvion's soft voice. He was standing in the open door on the driver's side, leaning one elbow on the roof of the car. Watching me.

"Sorry," I said before he asked me what was wrong. "I saw . . . something."

"Something?"

At least he didn't brush me off or say it was just fog. I guess being an assassin makes you pay attention to subtle things.

"Over there." I tipped my head toward the buildings across the street. "Do you see anything? A dog, maybe?"

Zay tipped his head down, and his body language looked

like he'd just heard something funny or embarrassing. Nice act. With his face at that angle, he could look across the street without whoever was over there knowing.

After a moment, he said, "No. Do you?"

I didn't even try for discreet. I stared across the street. No shadow. No one. Nothing.

A chill plucked down my arms and magic stretched in me, pushed at my skin, heating my right hand and chilling my left.

Just what I didn't need to deal with right now.

I took a breath, cleared my mind, and relaxed, letting the magic move through me, up through the ground, back out of me to fall into the ground again, an invisible, silent loop.

"Someone was there," I said. "Something. Maybe hurt." And the image of Davy or one of the other Hounds, too drunk to think straight, maybe stabbed, mugged, or, hell, chewed on by a stray dog flashed in front of my eyes.

My heart started beating faster. There was no way I could drive off and leave one of my Hounds in danger. I started around the front of the car.

"What are you doing?" Zayvion asked.

"We're close enough to my house; we can call 911 if someone needs help."

"Allie," he warned.

"It will just take a second." It came out like I didn't care if he followed me or not, and the truth was I didn't care. If one of my people was hurt, I wasn't going to stand by and leave him on his own.

I wondered if this was what a mother felt like and quickly pushed that away. Didn't matter. What mattered was making sure whoever was over here was okay.

Zayvion shut up and followed me. I only knew he paced next to me because I could see him out of the corner of my eye. He was walking, breathing, moving, like an assassin again. Silent.

I was not nearly so smooth. I stomped over in my boots, making noise on purpose.

Grunts accompanied the smacking and slurping, and I had a weird feeling there was more than one person back there.

I almost turned back, because, seriously, I had no desire to walk in on some dirty lovin' going on in the alley. But the whimper, the stink of pain, drew me forward.

"Hey," I called out once I stepped up on the sidewalk. "Everything okay over here?"

Silence.

The fog in the alley did not stir. There were no lights down the narrow passage, just two buildings standing so close together I didn't think Zayvion could walk in there without losing jacket, shirt, and an inch of skin off both shoulders. Plus, the brick foundation of the apartment bulged outward at the bottom, sagging under the weight of years and making the alley even narrower.

I could see maybe ten feet into the alley. Something shifted back there. Then an almost-human moan rose to a keen, was muffled, silenced.

The familiar smell of strawberry bubble gum and cheap wine hit my nose. Those scents belonged to Tomi Nowlan. Tough girl, cutter chick, she was a Hound who didn't like me stepping into the boss job now that Pike was gone.

I didn't care how much she hated me. She was one of Pike's pack, my pack, and that meant I looked out for her. Especially when it involved a dark night and a dark alley.

"Tomi?" I called out a little more quietly.

Okay, dark night, dark alley, me with no gun—not that I ever carried one—and Zayvion with no gun, or at least I didn't think he carried one. All systems go for getting hurt or killed.

Except we both had magic.

I recited a quick mantra, just the first lines of a Beatles' song, set a Disbursement to choose how I'd pay for the magic—I was going with the tried-and-true headache in a day or so—and drew a glyph so I could pull magic up into my senses of sight and smell. Magic licked across my bones, warm, heavy, and poured out of my skin, filling the glyph.

The world burst into layers of old magic, caught and tangled like slowly dissolving spiderwebs. The ashy macramé hung in the air, snagged on the building fronts, smudged in pastel luminescence among the piles of garbage leaning farther down the alley.

Scents came at me too quickly, bubble gum and booze: Tomi; pine and spice: Zayvion; Diesel, mold, algae, moss, grilled meat, and soap from a nearby dry cleaner: the city.

The other scents were harder to sort from the stink of dog shit that permeated the entire alley. Burnt blackberry, licorice, the chemical taint of formaldehyde, and a burn of copper that tasted like hot pennies on the back of my tongue.

And among it all fear. Pain. Death.

I noted it all with detached interest, not wanting to let my emotions get in the way of casting magic.

I drew one of the most simple glyphs for Light, thinking *small, orb,* and *glow*, as I poured magic out through my fingertips to fill the ribbon and promise of the glyph.

An orb of light the size of a grapefruit appeared in front of my hand and flooded the alley with white light.

Probably should have used a lot less magic. The orb blazed like a searchlight, reflecting off the fog instead of piercing it. Blinded by the brightness, I caught only a vague outline of the figure crouching in the alley.

Hunched over, the size of a thin man or a big dog, the figure was gravestone white. Its head swiveled toward me and was too wide for a man, unless he was wearing a hood. Eyes shone animal green. Human eyes, I thought, but everything else about him was wrong.

He lifted away from the other, crumpled form on the ground. Then he lunged at us.

Fast.

Zayvion grabbed my arm.

The thing's blood-covered mouth opened on a yell, revealing fangs thick as my thumb on both the top and bottom of his jaw.

My back hit the rough stucco of the antique shop. I exhaled at the impact. Zayvion spun, pressed his back full-body against me. He blocked my view of the thing.

He whispered something that sounded like "Dead" and threw his arms out to both sides.

The smell of butterscotch and rum assaulted my nostrils, filled my mouth and lungs. A second ago, I couldn't see around Zayvion. Now that he had cast this spell over us,

I couldn't see Zayvion at all. I still felt him, his wide back pressed against me, his hip leaning against mine. Through a wavering, watery curtain around me, I could make out the buildings. But I looked right through where Zayvion should be, where I felt him, and saw only the sagging bricks across the alley in front of me,

Weird, weird, weird.

It was a Shield spell I'd never seen before. Some kind of camouflage.

Zay didn't move. I could feel his breathing, even and labored, like he was jogging or lifting weights. I got the feeling he wanted me to be quiet and still, so I did my best not to freak out while my claustrophobia stuck fingers down my throat and made me want to scream.

Just because I couldn't see any living thing didn't mean I couldn't hear.

The thing yelled again, a nerve-burning sound that was half human and wholly something else. The muscles down Zayvion's back flexed, and he leaned forward a fraction, as if pushing against an unmovable wall.

Sweat poured down my back, trickled between my breasts. I wanted to run, run, like a child from a nightmare, like an adult from a gunman, a killer, death. Instinct told me that thing out there was death. My death. Zayvion's death. And death to whatever it had been feasting on before we interrupted it.

And then it wasn't yelling anymore.

It was talking.

"Fear me."

Its voice was low—a man's—words mangled by fangs. Those two words crawled under my skin, and I wished he'd go back to yelling.

Okay, yes, I was afraid. Yes, I was comforted knowing Zayvion would stand in front of me and put himself in the way of danger. But I was done being smashed against a wall, unable to move my hands, and therefore more helpless than if I were free and standing beside my knight in leather coat armor.

I drew my hand up Zayvion's back, felt the tension in his muscles. It occurred to me that with his hands stretched out on either side, holding this spell in place like a curtain over a window, his hands were not free to draw glyphs. He couldn't cast.

Not a problem. Because I sure as hell could.

I pulled magic up from the stores deep within the earth and it poured into me, filling me, jumping to my call until I burned with the strength of it.

I set a new Disbursement—a little more pain to that headache—and stepped out from behind Zayvion, outside his reach. I stood next to him.

"No!" Zayvion yelled. The spell he cast broke. Butterscotch and rum magic rained big, warm, slippery drops around us.

"Fear this," I growled at the thing in front of us. I traced the glyph for Impact and poured all the magic I had in me into it.

The thing was a man, I think—heavily modified or disfigured, his arms too long, skin too white, and covered in blood. His legs bones were wrapped in sinew and bent wrong at the knees. He pivoted so damn fast, I didn't even have time to swear.

He dropped to all fours, dodging my spell. The spell bashed into the brick wall behind him, blowing a hole into the building and sending brick and dust everywhere. Something farther down the alley skittered and ran—the very human sound of footfalls.

A siren called out in the distance.

Then the thing, still on all fours, ran. Long legs and hands stretched out into a strange liquid lope. He covered twice as much ground as anything I'd ever seen—man, animal, or nightmare—a blur of white against shadow that crossed the street and disappeared, like a ghost into the foggy night.

Chapter Three

"What the hell do you think you're doing?" Zayvion yelled.

I rubbed at my neck, which already hurt, and worked on letting go of the magic, my panic, and the push of adrenaline that made me want to yell back at him.

"So, you do lose your cool," I said. "Who knew?"

"Do you know how stupid that was?" he asked.

"I don't even know what kind of man? Creature . . . ?" I glanced at Zayvion, whose locked-jaw anger flickered at that guess. "Creature," I confirmed, "that was. Do you?"

"Yes."

"Good, because I don't. Want to see if it's still in fighting range?"

I wiped my hands on my coat, because I felt dirty, covered in shit and blood even though I hadn't touched anything in the alley. I strode over to where the creature had been eating.

Zayvion swore, and I mean he pulled out a raft of curses that made me rethink his upbringing. He stormed out of the alley and onto the sidewalk, six feet and then some of pissed-off assassin.

Me, I could hold my calm in high-stress situations. I was good at denial—had plenty of practice. I simply blocked out the fear, terror; shoved a metaphorical sock into the mouth of the little girl's screaming panic in my mind; and took it one thing at a time. First thing was to see whether anything else was still alive back here.

I took the time to recast Light, got the glow down to a

tolerable level, and left the hovering orb behind me as I walked forward slowly and quietly. If something was alive, it was probably also hurt. Sometimes injured people and animals attacked when someone was trying to help them.

I drew a circle in the air with the index fingers of both hands, pinching the point where the circles closed between my index finger and thumb. Containment spells, the basics of Hold, that I could quickly fill with magic and toss at whatever was back there.

After a few steps, I was walking in a thin trail of blood; a few steps more and the blood thickened with gore.

And Nola had wanted me to wear my strappy sandals. Shows you what a country girl knew about city dating.

About twenty feet into the alley, I spotted the mess. It wasn't moving, wasn't breathing. I dropped the glyph in my left hand and put my palm over my nose to try to block the stink of death, defecation, and rotted magic.

Large enough to be another person, the poor thing was spread across the entire width of the alley. From the bits I could recognize—a muzzle, tail, a paw attached to half a leg—I knew it was a dog. Had been a dog.

Shit.

That thing hadn't just killed it, it had ravaged it. There were bloody bits everywhere, but the inside gore—heart, intestine, lungs—none of that was left. Just skin and bits of bone.

Bile rose up in my throat and I swallowed to keep from puking. My eyes watered, and I started coughing.

I scanned the mess one last time, looking for a collar. I couldn't see any, and I just didn't have it in me to touch the poor thing's remains. I backed away from the corpse, blinking back tears.

Zayvion made some noise striding toward me. Probably so I wouldn't be surprised.

I turned my back on the mess and headed toward him, trying to hold it together.

"What's back there?" he asked.

"A d-dog," I stuttered. *Way to sound tough, Beckstrom*, I thought.

Zayvion took a deep breath, filling his chest and making

him look even bigger than he was. But when he exhaled, some of the anger was gone, replaced by his familiar, and at the moment much-appreciated, Zen.

He placed his hand gently but firmly on my right arm. "If you ever do that again, if you ever break a protection spell, I will knock you down and drag you to safety. Do you understand me?"

"Not really."

He closed his eyes and shook his head. Okay, so maybe he really was still angry.

"Hey, it's not like anyone taught me about protection spells like that, that—"

"Camouflage," he said.

"Camouflage you did. You want me to stay out of your way, then I will." I took a step, but he pulled me against him so quickly, my boot slipped down the side of his shoe, probably smearing blood and gunk all over the outside of his leather loafers.

His arms closed around me and I could feel the heat of his body, smell the sweet pine and spice of his cologne over the sharp bite of his fear and sweat, could feel the pounding of his heart—strong. Fast.

But it was not a loving embrace.

"Let me go," I said.

"Not until you understand me." Zayvion searched my face. "You could have been hurt. Killed. It had fed—was feeding—and you have too much magic it wants. It could have killed you."

"Got it. Big scary monster is not my friend. Now let go."

He didn't loosen his grip. The stomach-dropping panic of claustrophobia licked across my skin. I didn't do tight spaces—not even someone's arms—very well. "Zayvion, let go." My voice was a little higher than I liked.

"Never storm into a dark alley. Never jump out when someone's trying to protect you. Never throw magic blind at something and expect it will go away."

"You better let go," I said. Panic and gore on an empty stomach were a bad combination.

"There are things in this city, Allie," he continued like I

hadn't said anything. "Things that will kill you in a second. And if you don't show some caution you'll never learn how to defend yourself—"

"I'm going to barf."

That got his attention.

I was out of his arms in a flash. Maybe a little too fast. I stumbled back a step or two. His hand on my arm kept me from falling, which was nice. I pressed my hand against the wall and just stood there a second, breathing the cold and fog down into my lungs so it could cool the hot panic in the pit of my stomach.

It took some time, maybe two minutes, for the nausea to pass. Zayvion was silent, waiting, one hand pressed between my shoulder blades. Touch, his touch, felt good. I stood away from the wall. And grinned at the look on Zayvion's face—something between worry and confusion.

"What? Never seen a girl get sick before?"

"Are you okay?" he asked. "Did it touch you?"

"The dog thing? No. It's just . . ." I swallowed. "Don't pin me down like that, Zay. I hate not being able to move."

"I know." That surprised me. But then, he probably knew lots of things about me I didn't remember telling him. "I . . . wasn't thinking," he said. "But you should never break a Camouflage spell, and never assume attack is the best action. Did I make that clear?"

"Loud and," I said.

The wind stirred the fog just enough to revive the stink of the alley.

"Is that thing out there?" I asked.

"No. But I've called some friends. They're looking for it."

"Are you going to tell me what it is?" I started toward the street.

"I could. Would you rather I take you home?" Zayvion asked.

Every logical bone in my body said yes. I was a little sweaty, a little spooked, and my boots had blood on them. But, damn it, I wanted a normal date and I was determined to get it.

"No," I said. "I'd like to try dinner. We have reservations, remember?"

We waited for traffic to slide by, then crossed the street to the car. Zayvion walked around to the passenger's side with me even though the car was still unlocked.

"Hold on," I said. I took a few steps away and wiped my boots on the patch of grass near the sidewalk before getting in the car. Zayvion shut the door behind me before walking around to the driver's door. He got in, started the engine, and pulled out into the street.

After we'd driven a while in silence, I finally spoke. "Should we call the police?"

"I already did."

"Really?" I turned in my seat so I could better see him. "I didn't think you much liked the police."

Zayvion shrugged one shoulder. "I have no problem with the law."

"What did you tell them? A mutant man-dog was on the loose?"

"I told them there was a mess in the alley. Animal cruelty, criminal mischief, and magic. Stotts' people will deal with it, make sure there are no magical contaminants in the conduits and cisterns. Make sure there aren't any hot spots."

"That makes sense," I said. Hot spots of too much or too little magic disrupted the power grid and caused problems with city services that rely on a steady flow—places like hospitals and penitentiaries.

"So what was that thing?"

He frowned as if trying to decide how much he should say.

I gave him my best I-can-take-it look.

"It's a problem," he said.

"I got that part."

"The stolen disks—the ones Violet and your father were developing so that magic could become portable?" He paused.

"Yes." I still had my memories about the disks. It was one of the magic-technology integrations inventions Violet had been working on for my father's company. A portable way to carry magic. And once carried like that, magic had much less price to pay. It would revolutionize how magic was channeled, networked, piped. Like a wireless phone, it would make magic more mobile. There would no longer be dead zones. Magic could be taken where technology could not, and the theory was, great good would be the result.

It would also put magic, literally, into the pockets of any person who wanted it—and let them use it with hardly a price to pay. Unfortunately, it was becoming apparent great bad could be the result of that.

"The disks can be used for changing the boundaries of what magic can do." At my blank look, he added, "Allie, those disks can make magic break its own laws."

"That is a problem," I said. It explained a few things—like how Bonnie the Hound had teleported herself and Cody off Nola's farm. Not that I remember that happening, but Nola had told me about it. "So, the thing back there?"

"We think it's a Necromorph—a magic user who has used some kind of magic, blood magic, death magic, to transform their natural state into something . . . dark."

"Think? I thought you Authority people were good at this secret magic stuff."

"We are." He flashed me a half smile. I liked what it did to his eyes. "But we haven't caught it—him. We don't know who he is, or who he may be working with. We are certain he has access to the disk technology. If he were Proxying the price to hold his body in such a mutated state, we'd know about it."

"Why would anyone do that? He didn't even look human."

"He's not."

It felt like the temperature in the car fell ten degrees. I mean, sure, I use magic. We all use magic. But this was like something out of a horror movie. Some person was using magic to make himself inhuman. On purpose. And it scared the hell out of me to think about what he could do if he could make magic break its own laws. I rubbed at my arms, trying to dispel the chill.

"Why did he kill the dog?" I asked.

Zayvion drove a little while. The tension in his shoulders, the tightness at the corners of his eyes told me the answer was not pretty.

"Transmutation. He was either trying to use magic and the life force of the dog to change himself, or he was trying to use magic and his own life force to change the dog."

"Into what?"

"I don't know. Whatever he's trying to do, he hasn't been successful yet. We've only found his . . . failed attempts."

"And how long has this been going on?"

"A few months."

"Months?"

He shrugged again. "Things are on the brink in the Authority. A very dangerous brink. Light and dark magic." He shook his head. "We've been busy."

"Chasing him?"

"And . . . other things."

"Don't tell me there are more things like that on the streets."

"Okay," he said.

I thunked my head against the headrest and watched the foggy city go by.

He glanced over at me. "Not exactly the kind of conversation I planned to have tonight. I was leaning toward suave and mysterious." He said it quietly, with a smile.

I rubbed at my eyes with the fingertips of my gloves, remembered I was on a date and wearing makeup, and placed both hands in my lap. "I'd be on for a change of subject."

"We're almost there. Have you ever eaten at the Gargoyle?"

"No. It was made into a restaurant while I was under my dad's thumb in college. Have you?"

"Been in college or eaten at the Gargoyle?"

"The last thing."

"I've been there."

"Waiting tables?"

"Nothing wrong with waiting tables."

"Good for spying on people?"

"Do I look like a spy?"

"No. You don't look like a waiter either. Perfect for a spy."

"Perfect for a lot of things," he said.

"Is that the suave or mysterious part?" I asked.

"Both."

The fog got thicker as we wound our way up the West Hills. Wooded neighborhoods wherein mansions lurked passed by to the left until there, up ahead on the crown of the hill, the flickering lights of the Gargoyle, which was once one of the grandest mansions in Portland, pulsed through the fog.

Sweet hells. Even from this distance, I could feel the massive amounts of magic being drawn upon and used by the restaurant. Those lights glowing up the road ahead of us flickered lavender, midnight blue, then slid to red, copper, and on to plum. Not electric. Not neon. Magic. So much magic that even in the enclosed car, I could smell it—deep, rich notes of vanilla and caramel. My mouth watered, and my stomach rumbled. Whoever set the spells on this place was good. Very good. I was already hungry, and we still had half a mile to go.

Three more blocks and the magic shifted, becoming less sweet, more savory. The scents tempted with salt and spice and thick cream sauces. I shook my head.

"How do they afford that kind of Proxy?" I asked.

"Wait until you're inside."

He turned the car down the winding driveway. Waterfalls flowed over stones carved into mythic creatures, some as small as my hand, delicate insects with batlike wings, and wide, scowling features. Some the size of dogs, hunched, muscled beasts with too many teeth to fit in a comforting smile. The creatures grew larger and larger, three feet, six feet, twelve feet tall, Gargoyles carved out of slick marble in blacks, grays, whites, and bloodreds, looming behind and hunched beneath the rushing fall of water.

The gargoyles were strangely lifelike—or maybe not so strangely, considering how much magic was being consumed at this place. Even through the veil of fog, the creatures' eyes followed us, glittering like precious stones; wide batlike wings stretched, flicked, catching and shifting the flow of the waterfalls to reveal glimpses of faces. Taloned hands reached out; heads swiveled; mouths opened and closed; eyes narrowed, went too wide, blinked. Creatures shuffled, moving in the moonlight as if chained down by one ankle, a slow, swaying dark dance of bodies, of wings.

I could smell the magic on them, dank and earthen, cold as a grave. I could smell their hunger, their fear.

I shivered.

"Cold?" Zayvion asked.

"No. Just . . . those statues. After the alley. Just a little too real."

"They are meant to look real, but they're not," he said. "The stones are chosen for their ability to foster the magic they are infused with."

"Huh?"

"A master Hand carved them. A Savant of art and magic combined. Lead and iron and glass are worked into the stone, carrying, supporting the magic. The glyphs worked in the stone with the lead and glass resonate with the naturally occurring magic pooled beneath the hill like two strings tuned an octave apart. It takes very little magic, and really no spells, to give them that sense of . . . life."

Looking at the gargoyles, arms stretched upward and faces tipped to a sky they would never reach, made me think they weren't too happy about being tied to the magic that made them never quite real enough. Not that I thought statues had feelings. I'm not that crazy. But every line and edge of the stone beasts spoke of a captured melancholy. Power denied, hopes quenched.

I wondered if they'd look happier in the sunlight.

Doubtful.

We reached the front of the restaurant and Zayvion slowed the car. A valet wearing black and gray from head to foot appeared out of the fog, and opened his door.

"Ready?" Zayvion asked.

"I am if you are," I said.

My door also opened, another black and gray held his hand down for me, and I took it, even though I didn't really need any help getting out of the car.

Except my skirt bunched up beneath my long trench when I pivoted in my seat to get out. I got one boot heel on the pavement, and flashed calf, knee, and a hell of a lot of thigh.

The valet, male-model handsome, let just the corner of his mouth rise in appreciation. But when he looked away from my thigh back at me, I gave him a glare that would freeze his keys.

Undeterred, he bowed his head slightly and stepped back, allowing me to move and actually stand.

And right there, behind the valet, stood Zayvion. The man was darkness against stone-gray fog, his gaze burning with a heat that seemed impossible for anyone to contain.

Never looking away from my face, he offered me his hand.

I took it, and the moment we touched, everything else faded. I did not notice the valets, did not hear the car being driven away, did not even hear my own footsteps as we crossed the remaining few feet to the wide, carpeted entrance to the Gargoyle.

The two-story-tall doors, glass, gold, and rare imported hardwoods, opened at our approach. I briefly noted the attendants at the doors, black and gray with a touch of bloodred. And then the magic of the place surrounded and overwhelmed me.

Unlike the heavy scents that wafted to me in the car, the magic here was designed to stimulate every sense.

The dining area was huge, at least three stories high, with a domed ceiling where winged figures wheeled in the ever-shifting lights. I blinked, and the room seemed smaller, intimate, as if the restaurant ended a comfortable few yards ahead of me. We stepped in, and I was suddenly very glad to have a hold on Zayvion's hand.

Magic pressed like soft hands against my boots, then up my thighs, my hips, my stomach, feathering out at my breasts with just the softest breath across my cheeks. Intimate, but unintentionally so, like a lazy summer breeze following the music that played, low and soft, the rise and fall of sweet strings over the haunting, distant rhythm of drums.

A woman framed by an arch of gold and colored glass smiled and stepped forward.

"Good evening," she said, in a voice I was sure was either classically trained or had an Enhancement spell that made her sound like the lead alto from a choir of angels. "How may I help you?"

Zayvion, who seemed a lot less dazzled by the overload of magic, said, "Reservations for two. Jones."

She blinked, and her eyes shifted from green to blue, then settled on a hazel too bright to be natural. Her hair shaded a little darker as she smiled up at him "Our pleasure, Mr. Jones. Ms. Beckstrom. Please, follow me." When she motioned with her hands for us to follow her, she held herself taller. She was wearing boots a lot like mine.

Illusion, Glamour, Enhancement. Seemed like a hell of a lot of pain to pay for this woman to undergo subtle, and what she must assume were pleasing, transformations for her customers.

We followed the woman, who looked more like me than she had just a minute ago. I watched Zayvion's body language to see if he noticed. If he did, he didn't look impressed.

Good.

She led us between candlelit booths with subtle Shield spells that obscured the occupants as if a sheer curtain had been pulled. It begged the question: why didn't they just curtain off the booths? Why make someone pay for the illusion of privacy?

Answer: decadence. This blatant overuse of magic was obscene, unattainable, forbidden. For every spell used, someone was paying the price for it in pain. In the approved penitentiaries, or maybe in the lucrative Proxy pits, where people hired themselves out to bear the pain of others' magic use. And the only thing the diners had to do to enjoy this magical excess was pay a fortune in money.

The angel took us up half a dozen steps, and finally stopped in front of a booth decorated in natural woods, with silver, or perhaps lead and iron, worked in subtle glyphs that looked more like art.

"Is this agreeable, Mr. Jones?" the angel asked.

"It should be fine."

The lady offered to take my coat, but I decided to hold on to it. My journal was in the pocket, and I didn't want to lose it. I took off my coat, folded it, and placed it on the small bench along the back wall beneath the window.

I sat. Once in the chair, the level of magic went down about a hundred notches, and I exhaled.

"Too much?" Zayvion asked.

There was some kind of Shield spell on our booth too, but it had the added benefit of filtering out some of the magic overload. Maybe that was why they didn't just hang curtains.

I took a drink of water so I wouldn't scratch my gloves off. Magic pushed and rolled in me and made me itch. "It's a lot," I said. "But not too much." *Yet*, I thought.

He nodded, and I realized he was worried about it.

"Do you like it?" I asked.

"The food is superb. Not magic. Excellent chef. Makes it worth the glitz. Plus the view . . ."

I looked out the window next to us and the tension in my shoulders drained away.

A castle atop a mountain, the restaurant took up the expanse of the hilltop. The lights of Portland, electric gold and baby blue, spilled down the hill to gather like a tumble of diamonds on the valley floor, thickest along the winding cut of the river and the star-spray grid of downtown.

"Oh," I said. "Gorgeous."

"I thought you might like it. From this high up, all you can see is the beauty."

He studied the city below us, the corners of his thick lips drawn downward. I wondered how much pain this man had seen. Being a Closer, someone who could take away a magic user's memories or life, and being a secret part of a secret society of magic users that casually dealt with horrors like that thing back in the alley, must come at a high cost.

An echo of a memory—just the emotional wash of being in danger and knowing Zayvion was there, doing something to make that danger, that fear and pain, stop—pushed up from deep inside me.

That moment was broken by the polite throat clearing of our waiter.

He recited the chef's specials of the evening for us, and we both turned our attention to ordering food and wine.

The waiter made approving sounds and melted into the swirl of magic and noise outside our booth. He reappeared within seconds with our sweet black currant liquor and canapés.

"Earlier today," I said, after our waiter had left and I'd had a chance to let the sweet and dry Kir fill my mouth with the dark berry taste of autumn, "when I asked you if Violet hired you to body guard me. You didn't answer."

Zayvion finished a canapé and took a sip of his wine. "I am not working for Violet. Not anymore. But if I were body guarding, you'd be at the top of my list."

I opened my mouth.

"You," he said before I could get any words out, "are rich. So at least you'd pay me well. Besides that, your father made enemies in both his public and private lives, and you seem to have inherited his knack for that, though you've mostly made your enemies through Hounding. So I certainly wouldn't be bored. What?" he said to my glare. "Didn't think I'd be honest? You carry more magic in your body than half of Portland's cisterns combined, and you are the leader of a pack of Hounds, half of whom don't like you, and all of whom are unpredictable addicts."

"Whom?"

"I went to school. You Hounded for Detective Stotts, who has logged more Hound deaths than any other law enforcer on record, *and* I know you'd do it again in a hot minute. Plus, for some reason, your father refused to bring you into the Authority back when you were young—"

"Watch it," I growled.

He grinned. "—younger, to train you in the less standard and more useful ways of magic that you, of all people, should know. On top of all that, you tend to stroll into the middle of situations that can kill you, and you have no formal self-defense training."

"Is that all you got?"

He put both elbows on the table and rested his mouth against his fingers, covering his smile. "Well, I've only known you a few months."

"Might just stay that way."

He watched me a moment while I sipped my water. "I don't think so."

I gave him a noncommittal nod. "Never know. You left out a few things, though."

"Oh?"

"For one, I can read you like yesterday's want ad."

"Is that so?"

"Absolutely."

He leaned back. "Well, then. Get on with it."

"Reading you?" I rested one elbow on the table and folded my fingers under my chin. What did I really know about Zayvion Jones? Not a hell of a lot. He had the advantage of a complete memory, and time spent following me around for my father.

But I had instincts. Good instincts.

"You aren't as patient and calm as you look. As a matter of fact, you have a short temper, which is why you put on the Zen Maseter bit all the time."

He raised one eyebrow but didn't say anything.

"You have a lot more money than you'd like people to know, but you don't spend it because you don't have a life outside your work. You don't have any friends, and you never speak to your family anymore. You are a total loner, Mr. Jones."

He gave me a blank look and took a sip of his wine.

"You can pour on the charm and get any woman in a room to go home with you, but it's always a one-night stand, which suits you just fine. And even though you like to pretend you're deeply moral and just, you'd willingly break the law, lie, and cheat if it's for something you believe in."

"Is that it?" he asked.

"Almost. Your favorite color is blue."

"Green," he said, looking straight into my pale green eyes.

Oh. Nice.

"Okay," I said. "Green. Am I right?"

"You're not all wrong." He took another bite of his appetizer. "Not a big fan of one-night stands, though."

Just what I needed—a rundown of his love life. "Really. So you've had multiple long-term relationships?"

"Want to see the scars?"

"Depends on where they are."

He flashed me a smile. "On my . . . heart, of course."

"Of course," I said.

The waiter interrupted our conversation, and we got busy ordering. We both chose the onion soup au gratin for our appetizer. Zayvion ordered lamb medallions with garlic for his main course, and I ordered the duck with apples and porto sauce.

"So tell me about Maeve Flynn," I said once the waiter had left.

"What do you want to know?"

"Anything. It would be nice to have a clue about what I'm getting into."

"She's a good teacher. A master in her chosen magic—blood magic. She will teach you how to access and control magic in the ancient ways. The hidden ways. She won't be easy on you. Maybe much harder now . . ." He shook his head and gazed out the window again. Nothing out there but darkness and stars fallen to earth.

"Harder now?" I prompted.

"She lost her husband a few years ago. It . . . changed her."

Oh. I took a drink of my water. "How did he die?"

"The death certificate says heart failure." He looked away from the window. Waited. Waited for me to ask.

"Okay. Now tell me how he really died."

"Your father killed him."

"Shit." I sat back and tucked my hair behind my ear. "Terrific. My teacher hates me."

"I don't know that she hates you. Maeve has always been fair-minded. Kind, in her way. She's not . . . or at least she hasn't been . . . the kind of person to punish someone for their blood relations. There's a chance she'll very much enjoy teaching you the things your father didn't want you to know."

"And there's a chance she'll want me to fail spectacularly."

"Maybe. Will that stop you?"

"No. I want to learn. Holding all this magic isn't easy, you know? Plus, I can be pretty stubborn when I put my mind to it."

"Really? I did not know that."

"Ha-ha. You can stop trying to look so surprised."

The waiter swooped down upon our table and placed the soup in front of us, then refilled our wine before disappearing back into the swirl of color and light beyond our booth.

"Stubborn might help," Zayvion conceded.

"At least I have one family trait going for me." Speaking of family, I might need to talk to Zayvion about my dad.

Did I know how to do romantic dinner conversation or what? How did one casually bring up possession?

I thought about it while I ate the soup. Zayvion was right about the food. It was spectacular.

"Um, I had a weird thing happen today," I said.

Okay, that was dumb. The day had been filled with weird things, starting with attending my father's second funeral.

"Yes?" Zay asked.

"I thought I heard my father call my name. Twice."

Zayvion wiped his mouth with his napkin. "When? Where?"

"In my bathroom—well, in my head. After you left this afternoon."

He frowned. "What did he say?"

"My name. Told me to find the disks. Find his killer. Aren't you even a little freaked out by this?"

He took a drink and shrugged one shoulder. "I'm not thrilled by the idea, if that's what you're asking."

And I guess if he could deal with that thing that jumped us on the street with relative calm, a dead magic user in my head probably didn't seem like all that big a deal.

"He is dead, isn't he?" I asked.

"Very."

"Do you think he could be dead and in my head? When Maeve came to see me, right after I got out of the hospital, she was worried about that." I took another drink of wine. My glass was almost empty. How had that happened? I was starting to feel it despite the heavy soup. It was probably time to slow down with the wine.

"Possession—full possession after death—is not well documented." Zayvion refilled my glass. "Your father had enough mental strength after he was dead to step into you in spirit form and wield magic through you." He lifted his glass in a subtle toast.

"That threw some rocks at the theory that no one can possess the living after death. But then, your father's spirit was being . . . supported . . . by Frank Gordon and dark magic. What he did was uncharted territory. Forbidden."

"Which he? Dad or Frank?"

"Both. It's a problem."

"A problem," I repeated. "So that list? The one I just made about you? I'd like to add *master of the understatement.*"

The waiter appeared, whisked away our bowls, and replaced them with the main course. It smelled delicious, and we both took some time to eat.

"It is possible you have his memories in your mind," Zayvion said.

"Is it possible he's actually alive?" I asked again.

"I don't . . . We don't know," he finally said. "Sometimes I think anything is possible with you. Maeve is going to do a more thorough search when you see her."

"Wait. You've talked to Maeve about me?"

"Maeve was my teacher for a short time. We see each other fairly often. She'll know what to do."

"Are you sure you can't just look for me?" It came out smaller than I expected. No matter how little I knew Zayvion, I knew Maeve even less. I could let her be my teacher, but I was not ready to let her mess with my brain.

Zayvion reached across the table and caught the fingers of my hand. "If I could, I would. We are Complements, Allie. More than that, we are Soul Complements. Lightning and steel. We can . . . manipulate magic together, as if we were one person. That's . . . amazing. But there are things we should never do, lines we should not cross. Using magic together is one thing. Powerful. Stepping into each other's minds . . . even with the best intentions, the clearest need . . . that never ends well."

"I suppose that's documented somewhere?"

"Soul Complements are rare."

"That's not an answer."

He took a moment to study me. I was not as drunk as he might think I was.

He sighed. "This isn't what I wanted to talk about tonight either. I don't suppose you'd like to discuss the weather?"

"Foggy," I noted. "Tell me the truth. I can take it; I've had plenty of wine to soften the blow."

He smiled, but it didn't make it to his eyes. "The truth? The few Soul Complements that are documented read like a tragedy. It has never ended well. For any of them."

"Hold on, let me get this straight. Soul Complements are just two people who can cast magic together without blowing themselves up, right?"

"No, you're thinking of Complements—two magic users who handle magic so similarly, they can, on occasion, cast magic together. There are also Contrasts—magic users who handle magic in opposite ways, and can, on occasion, cancel or enhance certain affects of each other's spells."

"So Soul Complements are?"

"Two people who can cast magic as if they are one person. Two people whose minds and souls fit each other perfectly. Two people who could become so close they feel each other's emotions, hear each other's thoughts, feel each other's pain. Two people who can take magic to levels otherwise unattainable."

I know that should sound wonderful, being so close to someone you could share their thoughts. But I was nothing if not the queen of trust issues. Letting someone know everything I was feeling and thinking sounded like my own little corner room in hell.

I finished off my wine. "So tell me the downside."

"Those Soul Complements who have become too close stop being who and what they are. Lost in the shared magic, shared emotions, shared thoughts, they lose control of their magic, or use it in ways . . . in horrible ways. And if they are not broken apart, then, insanity results."

I took a minute to absorb all that. "You and I are Soul Complements?"

He nodded.

"We're going to drive each other insane?"

"Probably."

"I'm serious."

"All right. We won't go insane if we just use magic together, and we won't go insane if we are with each other in all other intimate ways."

"Sex?" I asked.

He grinned. "I wasn't talking about water-skiing. There are boundaries—how close we can be with each other mentally, soul to soul. Boundaries that must be obeyed so that we can be together, closer than anyone else on Earth, but not so close that we lose ourselves."

"So, the shared thoughts and feelings are out?"

"It's better that way."

Well, I for one wasn't seeing a downside.

"I could look in your mind to see if your father's memories are still there," he said. "I have the training. Should I? Once in your mind, once that close to you, I may not be able to step away."

I blushed. No, I don't know why. Okay, yes, I did. Zayvion was looking at me like I was something beautiful he wanted and could not have.

"I could make you leave my mind," I said uncertainly.

"I don't think so." He let go of my hand and pushed his plate to one side so he could rest his arm in front of him. "You aren't the only stubborn person at the table."

I smiled. "Speaking of which, about that other thing."

"Which other thing?"

"All those long-term scar-filled relationships you were talking about."

"You aren't the first woman I've dated."

Yeah, well, I knew that. "Go on."

He leaned both arms on the table. The table was small, intimate. We were close enough that if I stretched just a little more, I could touch him, kiss him. His gaze held me exactly where I was. "You just might be the last I'll survive."

The blush rushed up my neck and washed hot across my face. *Slow*, I told myself. *We said we'd go slow.*

To hell with slow. I leaned forward, my wineglass still in one hand. Zayvion had both hands free, and drew his fingers down the side of my face, fingertips stroking the length of my bare neck. He bent toward me, his fingers slipping up to cup the edge of my jaw, as if he wanted to make sure I wouldn't disappear, as if he wanted to draw my mouth to his. I opened my lips and inhaled.

My heart beat harder. I wanted to taste the wine on his lips, wanted to savor the pine scent of him against the tip of my tongue.

But instead of pulling me closer, instead of kissing me, his fingertips clenched gently beneath my ear. He ran his tongue across his bottom lip and then slowly, mechanically leaned back, away, shoulders squared against the back of his chair, fingertips splayed wide against the tablecloth, brown eyes filled with fire that had nothing to do with magic.

He didn't say anything. He didn't have to. But I did.

"This isn't going to be easy," I said.

He held very still, watching me. "The best things never are."

Our waiter of impeccable timing returned, cleared away our plates, and brought burgundy and cheeses.

I nibbled on the cheese, but mostly drank the burgundy and thought about Zayvion's lips. Well, thought about his lips, and tried to pull up even the smallest memory of his naked body. No luck.

For his part, Zayvion finished his food, gave me a few smiles, and moved on to lighter subjects. The weather again—still foggy. The view—still sparkly. The time—late. As a matter of fact, it was past midnight, and the warm glow from all the wine was making me yawn.

"How about we skip dessert?" he asked after I'd hidden yet another yawn behind my hand.

I nodded. "I'm sorry. It's been long. The day, not the dinner. I think I'm a lot more tired than I thought I thought." Wait, what had I just said?

Zayvion grinned. "We'll save dessert for next time."

"Next time?"

"You didn't think this was the only date I was going to take you on, did you?"

"Uh . . . no?"

The waiter appeared like magic, took Zayvion's credit card, and returned just as quickly.

"So," Zayvion said as we both stood and pulled on our coats. "That list of things you said about me earlier?"

"Yes?"

"You forgot *determined*."

He helped me with the sleeve I wasn't having any luck getting into on my own. Damn. Too much wine. Especially now that I was standing, my head was a little muzzy. "And *old-fashioned*," I said, as he offered me his arm.

"Old-fashioned?" He actually looked offended. "I don't know what you're talking about." He placed his hand over mine on his arm and stepped closer to me. "May I have the honor of escorting you home, Ms. Beckstrom?"

I giggled. Seriously. Giggled. Bad sign. "Maybe that wine was more than I thought I drank." Smooth, Beckstrom.

"Just try to relax when we walk out into the main flow of the restaurant."

I was going to ask him what he meant by that, but then we took two steps away from the table and I got my answer. Like a hammer. A great big answer hammer over the head.

Magic pressed in around me, pushed up through my feet, sunk needle-deep into my skin. The spell that veiled our table had done more than offer us privacy from other diners. It had kept the thick crosscurrents of the restaurant's long-standing and short-term spells from being so overwhelming. But now, out here, I was most certainly whelmed.

Magic sparked within me, a fire rushing up my bones, urging me to release it, to cast, to use.

I gritted my teeth and exhaled through my nose, resisting the urge to use magic. Not easy after a couple glasses of wine.

"Zayvion?" I said. He must have caught the urgency in my voice.

He didn't talk, didn't ask me if I was okay. He set a quick but not rushed pace and guided me out between the tables that roiled with clouds of magic, thick ribbons of it in jewel tones, so strong I could see it shifting like currents of rainbow oil through the air, even without drawing Sight.

Magic prickled beneath my skin, grew hot, hotter, until my entire body was one big sunburn.

I tried to concentrate. Sang a mantra to clear my head.

Miss Mary Mack, Mack, Mack, all dressed in black, black, black . . .

Magic swelled, pressed, begged to be used. And my mental hold on it slipped. Oh, hells.

Mint washed over me, cool, sweet, soothing all the places where magic burned in me. Zayvion, my lightning rod, Grounding me.

The restaurant was behind me now, glowing with so much magic, I could feel the heat of it like a bonfire at my back. We were in the parking lot, in the cold air, the wet air. I took a deep breath, let it out.

My head was no longer muzzy. The magic, and Zayvion Grounding me, had the side effect of making me stone sober. And right now, I was really glad.

"Better?" he asked.

I nodded.

He walked around in front of me, his hand sliding down my arm. "Wait here while I tell the valet to get our car."

I thought I said okay, but he bent a little to make eye contact. "Okay?" he asked.

"I'm good," I said. "Fine."

He didn't look convinced, but turned and walked away.

Absent his touch, magic pushed in me again. The ground swayed a little beneath my feet, and I decided pacing might help. Taking even breaths, I strolled down the brick pathway that lined the front of the restaurant. The cold air did some good keeping my head clear, and I recited a jingle to stay calm and to keep the magic in me easy.

A movement in the landscaped flower bed to my left caught my attention. I stopped and peered into the brush and ferns. Two yellow eyes as big as my fist stared at me from the bushes. For a second, I thought it was alive, a dog, a cat, or—shudder—that thing from the alley, but the eyes were too large and too perfectly round. Then the wind shifted, brushing through the bushes. I caught a whiff of stone—just damp stone—and I knew what it was. A gargoyle statue.

I leaned forward and pushed a branch out of the way so I could see the gargoyle's face better.

The statue's head swiveled, following my hand like a snake follows heat. Magic. Just magic, nothing strange about it. There was enough light that I could make out the creature's body—big as a Saint Bernard's, haunches in the back like a dog, longer human arms and human hands with wide, extralong fingers. Its broad face wrinkled back from a generous fanged and smiling mouth along a doglike snout. The huge eyes were almost comical beneath a heavy brow, and pointed ears perked up from its rounded skull. Behind its shoulders, batlike wings spread out and trembled. It looked worried but happy, as if confused at being noticed.

It looked vulnerable. Lonely. It looked too damn life-like.

Zayvion wasn't kidding about the artist being a master Hand.

The wind pushed again, stirring leaves, and I let the branches I'd been holding fall back into place.

Just as I pulled my hand away, cool stone fingers reached out and touched my wrist.

Holy shit.

A chill ran down my spine. I looked down, and the creature, no, the *statue* was looking up at me. Huge eyes wide. Pleading. It was frozen in place, hand on my wrist, head tipped at a beseeching angle.

I knew there were spells on this thing; I could smell them. But I could smell something else too, a bitter scent of sorrow. Without wanting to, I also held still and looked at the creature again, trying to convince myself that it was not alive, but just a very clever infusion of magic and art. A chain collar dug into the creature's neck, the chain spilling down its chest to somewhere at its feet.

I pulled my hand away from the creature and it did not move, did not change position.

I touched the chain at its neck. Stone. Stone and magic. The chain cuffed the creature's other hand and linked to an iron rod driven into the soil.

It was irresistible, the magic that infused the stone and chain. I drew my finger along the links, marveling at the spell that ran through the iron and stone, a constant conduit to the magic that pooled in the channels that had been laid deep beneath the soil here to feed and maintain the spells on the statues.

At my touch, magic flared along the chain in a sudden wash of heat. I pulled my fingers away, not wanting to interfere with the spell, but it was too late. Magic twisted along the carved glyphs and—I am not kidding—sort of jumped the carved route it should have taken. Like a freak electric arc, magic stalled for a moment and poured through my hand, making the whorls of color on my skin flash neon bright as the magic completed the arc.

The creature jerked, shuddered. Wings flapping, it pulled against the chain.

I pulled my hand away.

I heard the grinding groan, low like a dog's growl, as metal and stone strained, snapped.

I took a step back, my hands up in a warding position.

But there was no movement in the bushes. Only darkness. Only silence.

The statue was not moving. Its wide round eyes looked at me, blank, unfocused, no longer lifelike. I looked closer and realized the chain had broken at its neck, and now lay upon the ground in front of it, glowing softly blue with unspent magic.

Hells. I broke their statue. Broke the feed of magic to the spells that bound it. Great. I was sure they had monitoring devices on the things for just this sort of problem. Any minute a gardener, sculptor, magic user, or security guard would be out here re-chaining the beast and writing me a fine.

"Allie?"

I looked away from the gargoyle. Zayvion walked my way. "Are you ready to go?"

"Yes." I walked over to him. When I was near enough: "I think I might have broken the statue."

Zayvion gave me a long look, decided I wasn't lying, and followed me back to where I had been standing. He brushed the bushes away and peered into the darkness. "What statue?"

I moved up beside him and looked. Bushes, dirt, iron rod, broken chain. No statue. The soil where it had crouched just a moment ago looked scraped clean, tended, as if someone had run a rake over it. Or claws.

"There was a gargoyle," I said. "Right there."

"And you broke it?"

"I interrupted the feed of magic, I think. Through the chain."

Zayvion touched the chain, frowned. "There is no magic here. Are you sure there was a statue?"

"Well, I touched it. And it touched me, so yeah, I'm pretty clear on that."

He made an isn't-that-interesting sound and brushed off his hands. "They'll probably charge you for it," he said. "I bet you reach over the velvet ropes at museums and fondle the statues there too."

"Zayvion, this is serious."

"Really? Why?"

"What if it's loose?"

"Allie, they're statues. Magic and art, yes. Alive, no. There's probably a hydraulic lift under each statue so they can take them underground to do maintenance on them. I don't think touching the chain could break the magic or the chain. Unless you have bare-handed stone-crushing abilities you haven't told me about? No? Then I think it's more a strange sense of timing."

"Are you sure?" I asked.

"No." He smiled at my look. "But if there's a gargoyle loose in the city, I'm sure we'll hear about it."

"Ha-ha. Funny."

He caught my hand. "Thank you. And for my encore, I'm going to take you home before you cause more trouble."

"You call this trouble?"

"Yes. Yes, I do." He put his arm around me, and I wrapped my arm around his waist.

"Then I'm not sure you're going to be able to handle our second date," I said.

"We'll see, won't we?" He pressed the palm of his hand against my lower back, and the warmth of mint spread out from where we touched.

I leaned into him a little more, enjoying him. Enjoying us. For as long as I could.

Chapter Four

Zayvion walked me to my apartment door. We paused there, caught in the proverbial unspoken question of first dates: to kiss or not to kiss?

"I have company," I said.

He nodded. "Would you like me to come by and take you to class tomorrow?"

"How very college of you, Jones. Does this mean we're going steady?"

"Now who's old-fashioned? And yes. Say, around five?" he asked.

I thought about it. I hadn't told Maeve when I would stop by her place, but if she could do something about my dad in my head, then the sooner, the better. I pulled my journal out of my pocket and made a note.

"Make it one o'clock," I said. I tucked the journal back in my pocket.

"I will." He held both my hands in his. "So, this is good night, then."

I switched my hold, my fingers around each of his, and leaned against my door. I tugged him close, until our bodies were almost touching. I didn't let go of his hands.

"This," I said, "maybe this doesn't have to be good night."

But Zayvion, damn him, eased back. He let go, took a step, out of sheer willpower or the knowledge that I would have gladly dragged him back, kissed him, taken him into my apartment and into my bed.

"Good night, Allie," he said evenly.

I swallowed, finally found my voice. Maybe I was acting like an idiot. Pushing him away and trying to pull him close at the same time. "Night."

He moved off a couple paces, walked toward the stairs, silent and sexy as always. Halfway down the hall, he paused. "Lose the key?"

Right. I was supposed to be going home. Not watching his very fine ass.

"No, no," I said. "Found it." I dug it out of my coat pocket and unlocked the door. Zayvion waited until I opened the door.

"See you tomorrow," he said.

I didn't trust my voice, so I opted to wave and just shut the door.

I glanced into the living room and guessed that Nola was on my couch, since her luggage was still leaning against one side of it.

I unzipped my boots, wanting to be out of the heels, and then padded off toward my bedroom.

"You should have invited him in," Nola's sleepy voice said from across the room.

"Trust me," I said. "I tried."

"You make falling in love look hard," she muttered as she rolled over.

"Give it a whirl again one of these days," I said. "Show me how easy it is."

Nola snorted. "I already did it once. The right way. I don't have to prove anything to you."

I smiled. She couldn't fool me. She and John had been crazy in love all through high school, and through the few years they had together before cancer took him. And even though I knew she loved her husband with unwavering devotion, it had been years since his death, and Nola was my age. She had plenty of life ahead of her.

Her answer, I noted, was not a no. Maybe she was ready to open her heart again, to love again. For no reason I could put my finger on, that made me really happy. After all, if I had to trust, love, and be vulnerable with someone, she could do it too. Misery loved a crowd, and all that.

I yawned my way into the bedroom, stripped, and fell asleep almost before I could pull the covers over me.

I drifted, not dreaming, aware of the warmth of my blankets, the curve of my pillows, the rhythm of my breath.

"Allison?" My father stood just outside my open bedroom door, one hand on the doorjamb. Something was wrong about this. I was in my old bedroom, the one I used to have when I lived with him in the condo, but I was not a little girl, I was an adult.

A part of my mind realized this was just a dream. Nightmare, more like it, since my father was a part of it. The rest of me was too tired to care.

I put the book I'd been reading aside, and my dad took that as an invitation to come into my room.

He rubbed his hand over his hair, grayer than I remembered, messing it up in a way I'd never seen him do in real life. *Dream* . . . my mind whispered. Right. Got it.

He sat on the bed next to me.

"I need your help." He looked uncomfortable saying it. As well he should. Because he'd been mean . . . treated me badly . . . done something bad to me recently. I couldn't remember what, but I knew I was angry with him. I knew I had every right to be angry with him.

"This hasn't gone the way I expected."

"What?"

"Everything." He laughed, one short sound that was almost a sob. He stared down at his shiny black shoes. "My life. Your life. My death." He nodded, as if thinking that through for the first time. "Not at all what I'd planned."

"I don't think I want to be here." I stood.

"Please," he said. "Hear me out, Allison." He softened his tone by holding one hand out toward me. "This is only a dream," he soothed. "What harm in a dream?"

And I could taste it, the familiar honey of his words. When he spoke like that, with magic behind his words, I knew he was trying to make me do as he said, trying to Influence me.

"Please. Sit."

I sat so quickly, the springs of my bed squeaked.

"Don't," I said. "Don't do that."

He looked surprised. "Do what?"

"Push me, Influence me, touch me like that. This is my . . . dream," I managed to say. "You can't push me around here."

His surprise melted quickly away. He scowled. "This is no longer about you. No longer about what you want. This is about making sure the right things happen. Making sure magic is in the right hands and used correctly. By the right people, for the right thing. You can't tell me you don't want to keep the people you care about safe."

Here he stopped, his eyes flicking from side to side, as if he were reading words printed on my forehead. "You do want the people you care for—Nola and Zayvion and . . . Violet?" He frowned, but continued, "You do want them safe, don't you? And now those Hounds. You have the entire . . ."

Dirty, useless, worthless. He didn't have to say the words. He wasn't the only one who could read thoughts. Dreaming allowed us both to peer in each other's minds.

How fabulous was that? Just what I always wanted, a breathing-room-only front-row-seat look into my father's innermost thoughts. Like I hadn't gotten enough of that when he was alive.

"Yes?" I challenged.

"The entire pack," he said, skipping over all the less charitable things he was thinking, "of Hounds looking up to you. Idolizing you after that man's death." He looked for his name, found it in my head. "Martin Pike's death. Trusting you to keep them safe and sane now, something even he could not do."

"Yeah, so?" Well, there was a choice retort. Apparently, I reverted to a ten-year-old when facing down my father.

Neat.

"You are strong enough to lead them," he said. "Stronger than Martin Pike. Strong enough to keep them, the Hounds and all whom you . . . love"—he said the last word like it was made of hot peppers—"safe. That, I am sure of. And I can help you."

That, I did not want to hear. Not from him. Because there wasn't a favor my father wouldn't play to his advantage.

"What do you get out of helping me? You're dead. Why do you care?"

His hands clenched together, the knuckles yellow beneath his skin. Anger sat in every tight muscle of his body. He did not touch me, though it looked like it hurt him not to.

"I have always cared."

"Controlling someone isn't the same as caring."

He unclenched his hands and closed his eyes. I'd seen him look like that. Right before he was going to blow.

But when he spoke, his words were soft. "The Authority is crumbling. From within. There are those, like Frank Gordon, who seek to bring back Mikhail. People who are convinced his return is foretold."

"Who is Mikhail, and where did he go?" I asked.

Dad opened his eyes. "He was the leader of the Authority. And he is dead."

"Oh, could you guys get any creepier? I mean, seriously. Why would anyone think raising the dead is a good idea?"

"I can only guess."

"Then guess."

"If he is the one foretold in legends, then his crossover into death will only make him more powerful when he returns to life. He will bring the magic from the other side with him. He will wield the magic of both life and death. Dark magic, light magic, as one. It will be a new era of power in the world. Magic will become something much more than a billable commodity."

I rubbed at my forehead. "Crazy. Crazy living people trying to raise crazy dead people. And you call these people your friends?"

"No. They were my equals. In everything, Allison. In the drive to dominate. To succeed. To own magic and those who use it. And you are willingly putting yourself into their hands." He shook his head.

"I'm not listening," I said. "I have a rule to never take advice from dead people."

"Since when?"

"Since three seconds ago."

"Allison, stop being childish. Maeve will test you. The

Authority will test you, push you. When that time comes, you must not hesitate to use everything at your disposal to win. To survive what they will do to you. You must use everything available to you. Including me."

"Whoa, wait." If he had told me he was the king of Mars, I wouldn't have been more surprised. "What the hell? You don't let anyone . . ." I didn't know what I was going to say, but the words *care* and *love* crossed my mind. His eyes widened slightly. I swore and pushed them away. This was worse than that damn blood-to-blood truth spell we'd shared before he died.

"You don't let anyone so much as *touch* you, much less *use* you. What do you get out of this? Out of me passing those tests?"

"I will live on."

Immortality. What every egotistic narcissist wanted.

And it was the blunt truth that was both exactly what he was thinking and exactly what he meant, that stopped me cold.

"Listen to me, Allison. The Authority fears you. Fears what I . . . what you can become. You are a threat to them. You have always been a threat." *To us*, he thought, before he pushed that too away. "It is why I have kept you away from them. Hidden. But now that they know what you are, you must not hesitate. When you are tested, you must be willing to kill to survive."

"I'm not going to kill anyone," I said evenly. "I am not a killer."

"Yes," he said over the top of my unspoken protest, "you are."

I don't know if he or if I drew up the memory of Lon Trager, full of bullets, his knife in my leg, my knife sunk so deep in his chest I could feel his heart beating out blood over my knuckles under his skin. Blood poured down the knife, over my body. Trager crumpled to my feet, dead because Martin Pike had shot him. Dead because I had stabbed him. It was real, so real I could smell the blood and sweat again. Bile rose up my throat and I wanted to puke.

"You have killed." My father's voice pushed at me. "And you will kill again."

I could not look away from his eyes, darker than mine, hollowed by a death he would not accept. His own death. There was madness in him, burning with a frenetic hope I had never seen in life.

Life, I suddenly realized, had limited my father's options and ambition. It had forced him to deal with the all-too-human boundaries of day-to-day minutiae, such as running a business, being married, or other minor irritants like eating and sleeping. But now that he was dead . . . -ish, those boundaries no longer applied to him. He was free to do anything his dark, hungry heart desired.

The intensity burned in him like an unholy fire, and I could not look away. It scared the hell out of me.

"To survive, Allison Beckstrom," he said calmly, in the sort of tone one uses to cast spells. No, in the sort of tone he always used to cast spells on me. "You will do anything. You will use anything at your disposal." The weight of his words was physical. Each word fell heavier upon me until I couldn't stand. Could do nothing more than sit there and sweat.

"You will use any magic. Any person. Anything to survive. Even if it means killing. Again."

He traced a spell with his fingers so quickly, I could not read what it was.

I pulled my hands up and began a Shield spell. Began. I could not remember the correct glyph for Shield. The spell, being half finished and empty of magic, was as effective as if I had waved my hands to stop a hurricane.

My father did not have the same problem. Magic, cold as winter's caress, followed the glyph he drew and wrapped around my body. The spell tightened, bit into my skin, burned cold like frozen wire twisting around my arms, my stomach, my legs. Everywhere the magic touched went numb.

Binding.

"You," my father said calmly, "will survive. You will listen to me. You will do as I advise you to do."

With each short command, the Binding tightened, cutting its own glyph into me. I couldn't breathe. I couldn't move. But damn it, this was still a dream—my dream. And I was not going to let my father pin me down.

"Go," I exhaled. "To." Pause. "Hell." I pushed hard against the Binding, straining to move my hands, my arms, to push up to my feet, to slap him, to slap myself, to do anything to end this dream.

As easy as pushing aside a mountain, I finally managed to spread my fingers. Then I made a fist. Magic wasn't the only way to do someone harm. Hells, it wasn't even the easiest way.

Dad had gone red in the face. Sweat beaded his forehead—it was an effort to keep me Bound—and I took no end of delight in that. This wasn't as easy for him as he would have me believe.

Boo-ya for me.

I cocked back my elbow and punched my fist forward with every ounce of strength in me, breaking the Binding and aiming for my father's face.

"You will not—" His command cut off, replaced by the mechanical buzz of my alarm clock.

I rolled over, turned off the alarm, and lay there, staring through the darkness at the ceiling. The clock said it was morning—ten o'clock, to be exact, but I didn't feel like I'd gotten any sleep at all. I pressed my fingers over my eyes and concentrated on my father. Was he there in my mind? Or had he retreated into the territory of my nightmares?

The moth-wing flutter behind my eyes flickered. An electric snap of pain stabbed at my eyes. Ow. He was still there. And he was angry.

"Enjoy it while you can," I said. "First chance I get, you are so out of my head." I didn't know if he could read my thoughts while I was awake, but the fluttering stopped and that feeling of otherness, of someone else's awareness hovering behind mine, grew quiet and distant.

I sat and stretched. The Binding he had cast in my dream had felt too damn real. My muscles twitched, sore as if I really had been straining against ropes. I rubbed my hands over my bare arms. That was no memory of my father. That was him. His mind. First thing I'd ask Maeve was how to dig my dad out of my brain.

The warm smell of freshly brewed coffee floated into my bedroom. Nola must already be wake. I swear she was half rooster—always up before the sun. Of course, running a farm required early rising. The great thing about her visiting was since she was up earlier than me, I didn't have to wait for the coffee to brew.

I heard her voice, and another voice. A man. Radio? TV?

I pulled on my robe and shuffled out into the living room. Nola was at the small table by the window, drinking coffee. That, I had expected. What I had not expected was the man sitting across from her.

Gray trench coat with a nice maroon scarf at the collar, slacks, and loafers, Detective Paul Stotts looked like he was at the end instead of the beginning of his day.

"Morning?" I asked.

They both looked over at me. Nola gave me a bright smile. "I wondered if I was going to have to come in there and get you. Let me pour you some coffee." She stood and bustled past me toward the kitchen. I couldn't quite place the twinkle in her eye. Something was making her very happy. And I was pretty sure it wasn't the coffee.

"Sorry to catch you so early," Stotts said, his gaze lingering just a little too long on Nola. "I thought you'd be up by now."

I crossed my arms over my robe and tipped my head to one side. Something looked different about him too. He raised one eyebrow, and I realized what it was. He hadn't shaved in a while and his five o'clock shadow gave him that just-rolled-out-of-bed, sexy-cologne-ad look. But more than that, he looked comfortable. In my living room. What was wrong with this picture?

"Okay, I give up," I said. "Why are you here?" Stotts and I weren't exactly buddies. I'd Hounded for him. Once. The kidnapping case that had nearly gotten me killed more than once and had left me with new scars and my angry father lurking in my brain.

Stotts told me he ran the MERCs, Magical Enforcement Response Corps, an undercover branch of law enforcement that handles magical crimes. Other than that, we barely knew each other. Or at least didn't know each other well enough to have breakfast. In my living room.

He leaned back a little, looking too damn at home. "I called. Ms. Robbins told me to come by. "

"This, whatever this is, couldn't wait for me to shower?"

Nola breezed back into the living room, a cup of coffee and a plate of something that looked a lot like homemade coffee cake in her hands.

"Hope you don't mind me getting comfortable in the kitchen."

I took the cake and cup she offered and glanced at Stotts.

He was not watching me. He was all eyes on Nola. And, I noticed, Nola was pointedly not looking at him, all the while hiding a smile.

"I could wait for you to take a shower," Stotts offered amiably. "Is there a chance I could get a piece of that coffee cake?"

"Sure," Nola said. "I'll get us both a slice." Nola tucked her hair—unbraided, which was weird; she always wore it braided—behind her ears and gave me an innocent look. "Shower. Take your time. We'll wait." And then she was off to the kitchen again.

I scowled at Stotts. "Are you hitting on my friend?" Have I mentioned that I am not known for my tact? Especially in the morning?

"If that's how you define a cup of coffee and friendly conversation, I suppose I am."

"Listen, Wedding Ring," I growled. "She's my best friend. And I won't let her be hurt by anyone."

Stotts, who was in midswallow of his coffee, choked and coughed into his fist. He wiped at his eyes. "What did you just call me?"

"You heard me." I raised my eyebrows and stared at his left hand and the gold band on his ring finger. "As far as I'm concerned, this will only ever be a friendly conversation between the two of you. You got that?"

"I don't think I could miss it," he said. "It was a threat, right?"

Since I could hear Nola heading back our way, I smiled sweetly. "Yes, it was."

"Are you going to eat that standing?" Nola asked as she

passed me to sit back at the table in front of Stotts. She placed a coffee carafe—the one she'd given me a few years ago—in the center of the table.

"No. Save me a seat. I'll be right back." I put the plate on the table (yes, between their plates) but couldn't bring myself to leave my coffee behind. With one last warning look at Stotts, I took a drink of coffee and headed to the shower.

I wasn't going to linger in the shower, but the heat and steam made me realize that I really was stiff from my dream. Or maybe I was just stiff from running around in four-inch heels all night.

Whatever, the water and warmth felt great. I eventually got around to washing with the mild soap that seemed to be helping the fingertip burn marks on my skin, left there by the bits of dead magic users, the Veiled. And even though I didn't want to, I found myself drawing my fingers over my newest permanent scars. The thumb-sized circle beneath my collarbone—a bullet I did not remember taking. The thicker palm-sized scar beneath my left rib cage that was still numb to the touch. And the spread-hand scar on my thigh where I'd made a mess trying to cut out the blood magic Lon Trager had worked on me.

I wondered if the scars would bother Zayvion. Wondered if they would remind him that my life seemed to be one long series of screwing up and trying to fix it, with and without magic.

Not anymore, I told myself. That was why I was going to learn from Maeve. So I could stop screwing up. So I could understand how to use magic. The right way. No matter what.

A chill snaked down my spine. That thought, those words, did not sound like me. They sounded like my father. They sounded like what he'd said in my dream.

Sweet hells, but I wanted to be rid of him.

I scrubbed a little harder, wishing I could wash free of him, and knowing I couldn't. *One thing at a time*, I thought. First, find out why Stotts wanted to talk to me, and make sure he wasn't gunning to break my best friend's heart. I wondered if he had found out about the gargoyle statue.

Technically, that was a magic problem—or crime, I guess. Criminal mischief? Tampering with other people's property? Stealing? Well, no, not stealing, since I hadn't actually taken the statue, I'd just sort of broken it or set it free or something.

I got out of the shower, toweled off, and brushed my hair, slicking it back, then messing it up with my fingertips so it dried halfway decently. No, I did not look in the mirror to see if my father was behind my eyes. I knew he was. But his occupying my brain was a limited-time offer, and it was about to expire.

I dressed in my bedroom, tugging on a pair of jeans, T-shirt, and heavy brown sweater that I'd picked up at a thrift store and loved down to holes. I took the time to put on my tennis shoes. Stotts might be here to ask me to Hound for him. I didn't often contract out to the cops, but now that Pike was dead, I guessed his job had some need of filling.

Laughter rolled through the apartment—Nola and Stotts having a good ol' time. That was my cue to lay on some wet-blanket action.

I strolled into the living room. They were still sitting at the table. I'd caught them just as they were both lifting their coffee cups to drink. I hated to admit it, but they looked pretty good together. Nola was shorter than me, compact, blond as summer, and freckled. She looked like the country, honey and wheat fields. Stotts was her opposite. Dark hair, wide shoulders, unconsciously intense and strong in that way cops always are, and he took after his Latino heritage, with a square face, heavy brows, and amazing eyes. When he smiled, or when he looked at Nola like *that*, the cop intensity melted away into something else. If she was sunlight and the country, he was sunset against the mountains, strong, vibrant, dangerous, and yet somehow sheltering, protective.

And married.

Picnic, meet rain.

"So," I said as I pulled up an extra chair and sat down so close, both of them had to scoot back to make room for me. "What brings you by, Detective?"

If he was annoyed by my intrusion, he didn't show it.

"There's a job I'd like you to Hound."

"Today?"

"While the trail's fresh."

I thought over what I had to do today. Go see Maeve, but that wasn't until one o'clock. It was only ten thirty. I had time. Except I had promised to help Nola with the Cody situation. I didn't know how I was going to fit both those things in, but I'd try.

"That works okay for me." I took a drink of coffee, and put my fork to use to wolf down half my cake. I hoped there was more in the kitchen. "This is fantastic," I said to Nola.

"Thank you," she said.

"Do you mind if we catch up a little later today?" I asked her.

"That's fine," she said.

To Stotts, I said, "I was going to contact you about Nola anyway." Wait, that didn't sound good.

"Oh?" Stotts said.

"Nola has been working to get custody of Cody Miller."

"The Hand?"

I frowned. "You know him?"

He took a drink of coffee before answering. "I know his case." And his gaze said more than his words. He had probably been a part of that case. After all, Stotts dealt with all the magical crime in the city. And Cody, Nola had told me, had once been involved with some shady characters and forgery. But if Nola had made her mind up to look after him, nothing and no one would get in her way.

"She's working to get him out on her farm," I said.

Stotts looked over at Nola. "Isn't he in the state hospital?"

"My farm is in Burns," she said. "No magic for miles. We're completely off the grid."

Stotts grunted. "And you decided to put it upon yourself to do this because . . . ?"

"Because," Nola said, "I do not give up on the people I care about. And I think Cody is a good young man who should have the chance to live a good life without the push and pull of magic, or the people who would use him for it."

Oh, that did it. If Stotts had been looking at her with barely disguised interest before, he gave her a short but clear look of admiration.

"I don't hear that every day," he said, switching admiration for the more standard police skepticism. "Not in my line of work."

Nola couldn't hide it. She beamed. What was it with these two? They were getting along better than ice cream and spoons.

"What I was saying," I said, "is Nola needs some help making sure she contacts the right people who can see that Cody can be released into her care."

"Were you running into trouble with that?" he asked.

"Not at first. But about two weeks ago, I suddenly stopped hearing from anyone. I've mailed, called, e-mailed. I was told there was something about additional psychological testing needed. Is that something you could help me with?"

"I could at least look into it for you. Find out where they're at in the process. How long are you going to be in town?"

"I could stay awhile. A few weeks, if I need to. I wasn't sure how long this would take, so I have someone looking after the farm and animals for me."

"Your husband?" he asked over the top of his coffee cup.

"No." The light in her dimmed a little, like it always did when she spoke of John. "He's been gone for several years now." She tried to smile the light back up, but any fool could see the old pain in her eyes.

"I'm sorry," Stotts said. "I lost my wife, Aryanna, just a year ago."

Me? I felt like an idiot. And a jerk. A jerkiot. I didn't know his wife was dead. Or maybe divorced? I glanced up at him. From the look in his eyes, it wasn't divorce. Well, hells. I'd called that wrong.

"I'm sorry," Nola said. Her gaze shifted to the ring on his left hand. She had noticed it, just like me, but unlike me, she had given him the benefit of the doubt.

"I would really appreciate any help you could offer to Cody and me," she said. "I thought I'd go downtown today and see who I could talk to. Would you have time to meet with me?"

"I should. Well." He stopped, like he suddenly remembered there was someone else in the room with them—me. "If you don't think the job will take too long."

"You haven't told me what the job is," I said.

"I'd rather discuss it with you in private. . . ."

Nola caught the hint and stood. "Let me clean up the dishes. You two take your time. There's coffee in the carafe, if you want. I'll be in the kitchen."

She walked off, and I finished my cake. I watched Stotts out of the corner of my eye.

"You like her," I said, pressing the moist crumbs on the plate together with the tines of my fork.

He held his breath for a second, the only indication of strong emotion I could feel off him.

"I don't really know her," he said, "yet." Calm, cool, coplike.

"She's my best friend," I said.

"I got that."

"And I will go to no ends to keep her safe. From anything. And anyone." It came out cold. Matter-of-fact. A lot like my father. Except it was all me.

"Do you really think she needs your protection?"

I stuck the fork in my mouth and pulled the cake crumbs off with my teeth. "In this city? Yes."

He made a sound in the back of his throat. At least on that point, he and I agreed.

"What do you want me to Hound?"

"I'll take you there and you can see for yourself."

"Illusion?" I asked. "Dead body?" I shuddered, really hoping it wasn't a dead body. "Illegal Offload?"

He just gave me a level stare. That was the problem with cops, especially the ones who dealt with magical crimes. They wouldn't tell you a damn thing for fear of contaminating your opinion before you Hounded the spell.

"Right," I said. "So how long do we have before whatever it is fades?"

He shifted in his chair and rubbed his palms over his slacks. "I'd like to get to it as soon as possible."

"Then let's go." He stood and so did I. We were of a height. I headed across the living room.

"What if I hadn't been available?" I asked.

"I would have asked someone else to Hound it."

"Do you keep a list?"

"Usually Pike—" He stopped, probably aware that Pike had been my friend and he was very recently dead.

I looked over my shoulder at him. "What about him?" It came out relaxed and easy. Not at all how I was feeling inside. Every time I heard Pike's name, it felt like there was a fist behind it. I wondered if that would ever fade.

"Pike used to keep me up-to-date on which Hounds were available for jobs. Even though he took most of the jobs himself."

I figured that's what Pike had been doing all those years. Hounds had always worked for the police, the nonmagical police, but I'd just heard about Stotts' particular branch of magic law enforcement this month.

It was true that magic cannot be used in high-stress emotions, so people generally believed it wasn't that common to find magic at crime scenes. But I had seen enough with my own eyes and heard enough from other Hounds, and Zayvion, to know there was more dirty magic being used in this city than any sane person would feel comfortable knowing about.

And it was Stotts' job to make sure any sane person didn't have to worry about it.

Maybe it was my job to do that now too.

My only problem suggesting other Hounds work with Stotts was that he was cursed.

And the last thing I needed right now was a curse. On me or on the Hounds I had sworn to look after.

I pulled my coat off the back of the door. There was a half wall separating the kitchen from the entry hall. Nola, true to her word, was at the sink, washing dishes.

"Nola?"

She glanced over, caught sight of me shrugging into my heavy coat. She turned off the water and dried her soapy hands on the kitchen towel she'd wrapped around her waist in a double V. She even made a dish towel look cute.

"I'm going to Hound a job. I'll try to be back in a few hours. Before one o'clock, for sure. If you need me . . ." I was going to tell her to call my cell, but it had died over a week ago and I hadn't gotten a new one to replace it yet.

Stotts picked up where I left off. "You can call me. Here's my number." He walked around the edge of the half wall and stood a little closer to her than I thought absolutely necessary. He handed her his card.

Smooth.

Nola took it, looked it over, and tucked it in her back pocket. "Thank you. I will."

I made some noise opening the door.

I held the door open for Stotts so he could walk through, which he did.

"Bye, Nola," I said. "Lock the door behind me, okay?"

"I will. Allie?"

"Yes?"

"Be safe."

I gave her my best invincible smile. "Where's the fun in that?"

Chapter Five

The fun in being safe was that it didn't hurt.

Driving over to the job Stotts wanted me to Hound had been a mostly comfortable-silence sort of thing. He didn't dare ask me anything about Nola—he probably knew I was not about to give up my best friend's secrets. And I couldn't ask him anything about the job without getting more than a noncommittal grunt out of him.

So I pulled my journal out of my coat pocket and caught up on the last day or so of things that had happened. Even with my quick note-taking ability, I filled three pages, covering my dad's funeral, Pike's wake with the Hounds, my dad in my head, Nola showing up, and eventually the date with Zayvion. I noted the Necromorph in the alley and my nightmare with Dad too.

Stotts didn't ask me what I was doing. He just drove and kept his mouth shut. Maybe he thought I was taking notes for the Hounding job.

The rhythmic sway of the rosary on his rearview mirror seemed less ominous in the daylight, although the chatter and static from the police radio set in the dash reminded me of just how serious working with Stotts could be.

He turned a corner, stopped at a light. "I heard your father's body was buried yesterday," he said.

Wow. Now that was a conversation starter.

"He . . . it . . . yeah," I said, giving up on how to classify the dead-undead body of the man still very much alive in my head and dreams.

"Private ceremony?" he asked.

"The news channels weren't invited."

"Were there a lot of people there? His friends, business acquaintances? Wives?"

It sounded like a fairly innocent question. I hadn't been there to see my dad buried the first time. From what Nola had told me, it was a pretty big event. Flowers, lots of people, the media, all his ex-wives except for my mother, in attendance.

The second, final burial had been quite a different thing. No flowers, no weeping widows except for Mrs. Beckstrom the Last—Violet. Everyone else seemed to be a part of his other, hidden life. Members of the Authority, including people who were a part of his public life and Beckstrom Enterprises. And all of them seemed to exhibit something between grim satisfaction and outright pleasure to see him thrown in a hole and covered with dirt.

And now that I thought about it, it was a little strange that the media had not picked up on the funeral. At all. Nothing on the news about the body being stolen in the first place, nothing about him being reburied. The only people in the city who seemed to be aware of it happening were the people who were there, graveside.

And, apparently, Detective Stotts.

Wasn't that interesting?

"How did you know there was a burial? I didn't see you or any of the police there."

"It wasn't a secret," he said. "I was at the warehouse. I saw your father's body there, watched the coroners take it away. I wasn't invited to the burial, but it's not a big stretch to think his body would be laid to rest."

Oh, right, he'd been at the warehouse. I'd forgotten most of what had happened there—thanks to magic eating through my memories.

"I just wondered if you were alone," he said.

"I didn't know most of the people at the burial," I said, which was true. "Violet was there. I think some of the people who worked for him—for Beckstrom Enterprises—were there."

"People who work for you, now, right?"

And that was one of the questions I'd been trying not to

think about for days. I was the heir to the Beckstrom fortune, which meant I had the final say about who was going to run the business and what was going to be done with the money. I was under no illusion that my father had run a clean operation. As far as I was concerned, that money had blood all over it.

"I guess," I said.

I'd been thinking about setting up a charity. And maybe setting up a medical fund for the Hounds. It bugged me that I wanted to use my father's money after pushing it away all of these years.

The flutter at the back of my eyes started up again, sparking little pricks of pain.

I so did not want to know his opinion on this. If I wanted to use his dirty money for a good cause, I would. Even though I'd been telling my father to stick that money up his assets for my entire adult life.

The flutter grew stronger, and I pressed at one temple.

I took a moment to envision disbanding his company. Lobbing a financial bomb at it and watching it sink for good.

The flutter quieted. So maybe he was paying attention to what I was thinking. Good.

And bad. My thoughts quickly turned to Violet, to her being pregnant with my dad's child, my one and only sibling. I pushed that thought away and la-la-la'd like crazy. I didn't want to tear Violet's world apart. And destroying Beckstrom Enterprises would do just that. I'd never make a good day-to-day sort of manager of my father's empire, not because I couldn't do the work, but because I hated the company.

Almost as much as I hated him.

Okay, and yeah, I hated the paperwork and boardroom bullshit too. There was a reason I chose Hounding for a career.

Stotts stopped next to the curb, a park behind hedges and trees to my right.

"Is this it?" I asked.

"This is it."

It looked innocent enough. Winter in Oregon meant the

sky was stacked in layers of gray, sunlight filtered to a dim bluish cast that wouldn't change much until May. It also meant the park next to us was soggy, the grass still green even in the grip of winter, Douglas fir and cedar trees dark needled and heavy with rain.

I got out of the car, inhaled the clean scent of rain and growing things. And the boiled-vinegar stink of used magic.

I turned my face into the wind, inhaled again. I took a few steps across the sidewalk and into the park itself, following the scent of magic. Stotts paced me, his hands in his pockets. He didn't tell me what he wanted me to Hound. He didn't have to.

I set a Disbursement, deciding sore muscles for a day should do the trick, then drew a glyph for Sight, pulled magic up through my body and out into the spell. The world sharpened under the cast of Sight, colors brightened, shadows deepened, as if the sun had broken through the clouds.

Sight showed me a trail of magic like ashes in the air, gray and green, snaking toward a gazebo, where the spell hung like a bloody handprint.

I made my way along a trail to the gazebo. At the corners of my vision, ghostly people swayed. I glanced over at one of them, a woman made of pastel watercolors, eyes black, hollow, hungry, as she shuffled my way.

Great. Ever since my dad's ghost had smacked me in the head, every time I used magic I could see the Veiled—the ghostly remainders of dead magic users who wandered the world. Worse, they could see me.

Well, except for in the alley. The Veiled hadn't shown up then. But maybe that had something to do with the spells Zayvion was throwing around, or the fact that I had used magic for only a second or two.

I picked up my pace. I needed to get to the spell, Hound it, and release the magic I was using before the Veiled swarmed me and added to my collection of fingertip burn marks.

The flutter behind my eyes started up again, my dad pushing at me. Exactly what I didn't need right now.

Shut up, I thought. And to myself: *Focus.* I recited my favorite jingle under my breath: *Miss Mary Mack, Mack, Mack, all dressed in black, black, black . . .*

I was almost up to the *buttons, buttons, buttons* part when I finally reached the gazebo and spell.

Sure, I knew the watercolor people, a half dozen of them, were headed my way. Sure, I felt the flutter of my father's awareness like a second pulse behind my eyes. Sure, I felt Stotts stop behind me, far enough to be out of my way; close enough I could smell his anger and his fear.

But it was the spell, hovering in the air inside the gazebo, that held me fixed, like a hot palm against my throat.

It wasn't a spell I knew the name of; didn't look quite like anything I'd Hounded before. Blood magic was involved; the sweet cherry stink of that particular magic was undeniable. But this spell seemed to be more of a sealing off or a trading off of something.

Transmutation. My father's voice was so clear in my mind, I jerked back as if he had been standing next to me. Along with that word came his knowledge of what the spell was.

A complex knot work that links the caster and the victim through dark magic. A bastardization of death magic, wherein the soul and spirit are bled from the living to the dying, or the dying to the living. A spell that can be molded to the will of the caster to break the rules of life and death. A dangerous way to make magic break its natural laws.

Deadly to the caster. Forbidden.

Holy crap. I didn't want to touch it. If it had been created by magic jumping its tracks, dark magic messing with life and death, I was not about to poke it with a stick. And I was doubly freaked out because all of a sudden my father was working hard to make sure I got the information behind this spell. I didn't know if that meant he was trying to help me or screw me up.

The Veiled were coming, still walking slowly. I knew any minute they'd rush supernaturally fast. If I didn't do this quickly, they'd be on me, pulling magic out of me, and shoving it in their mouths like taffy. Then I wouldn't be good for any kind of magic use.

I decided to take my father's information as a freak accident of helpfulness. It was good to know what the spell was, but what I was really here for was to find out who had cast it and why. And why the police would want to know about it.

I leaned in, the fingertips of my right hand spread out toward the green and gray scaled center of the spell.

Magic still burned in the spell. It licked against my fingertips with a disturbing sentience, tasting me.

It's not alive, my father's voice answered my unspoken question. *It is . . . aware of the power you carry within you. Much like the Veiled.*

"Who did this?" Oops. I said that out loud.

"What?" Stotts asked.

I shook my head and inhaled, my mouth open, trying to taste the signature on the spell. Only the faintest taste of something sweet and burnt, like berries scorched on the vine. I had smelled that before. Outside my apartment with Zayvion. Last night.

But other than that, the signature was not familiar to me. I did not know who cast this spell or what it was really for.

Transmutation, my father said again, frustrated at me being so dense. *It changes one thing, one energy, into another, suspends the state of one thing into another.*

That was the spell Zayvion said the man-dog thing in the alley was using.

Do you know who was using it? I asked my dad. *Do you know why?*

Nothing.

I blinked, realized my fist was stuck straight in the middle of the spell. I did not remember putting it there. I was not only tampering with evidence, I was also pretty much destroying it.

Dad? I asked.

He did not respond. Or if he did, I did not hear him. Because the Veiled chose that moment to snap out of their slow motion and race at me faster than any living thing.

I threw my hands up to protect my face from their clawing fingers. My hand in the spell tore up through it and magic within me sparked, like steel to flint. My magic caught the spell, ashes and all, on fire, and burned hot, clean, fast.

Just as Veiled fingers should have hit me, stabbed into me, dug under my skin, a spell rose around me, pouring like cool oil from my head to the soles of my feet, covering my skin, cloaking me. I could no longer see the Veiled. Could not feel them, smell them, or sense them in any way.

And I was pretty damn sure they could not see me.

Holy shit.

Dad? I thought again. *Did you do that?*

Yes. You cast too loudly when you Hound, Allison. Learn some control and maybe the Veiled won't be able to track you so easily.

Yeah, that, or maybe if I got the dead guy out of my head, they wouldn't notice me so much.

"That was impressive," Stotts said, walking up beside me. "Destructive. But impressive."

I turned to look at the spell that only moments ago had hovered in the air. Even though I still carried Sight, the spell, ashes and all, was gone.

"You have some answers for me?" he asked.

"What was the question?"

"How about we start with what kind of spell that was."

Huh. He didn't know. Just like I hadn't known. So this had to be either a secret thing or a very secret thing.

I wasn't sure what I should tell him. If I suddenly started spouting off the properties of a spell neither of us had ever seen before, I was pretty sure he would question where I'd gotten that information.

"That's odd," Stotts said. He walked away from me, making a wide circle around the center of the gazebo.

I looked down at what held his attention.

A perfect circle of black ash, glossy as crow feathers, lay against the floor. And yes, that's weird, because magic doesn't usually leave something quite so physical behind. Especially when the spell is gone.

I'd seen that kind of circle before. I knew I had. I dug around in my head, searching for the memory.

Stotts knelt on the other side of the circle and stuck his fingers out toward the ash.

"Wait!" I warned at the same time my father's voice echoed in my mind, *Don't touch it.*

Stotts' eyebrows lifted. He pulled his hand back and rested both elbows across his knees. "What is it?"

"I've seen it. I know I have. Give me a sec." I took a deep breath and stared off into the mist and the green, clearing my mind before I pulled out my journal. It was starting to rain, just an intermittent tapping like distant drumming.

I'd been taking notes of my life for long enough I had a pretty good coding system worked out. Anything dealing with spells was marked in the upper right corner of the page and underlined in text. I flipped through the pages. Even though I'd had this notebook for almost a year, and had noted several Hounding jobs and other spells, I didn't see anything in it about circles of burned-out magic.

So what is it? I asked my dad. Just because I didn't have the memory didn't mean I couldn't get the information out of him.

I sensed his hesitance. I could tell he was weighing something. Probably his options and whether or not telling me would work to his advantage. For just a second I wished I were dreaming because at least then I could tell exactly what he was thinking. Of course, he could tell what I was thinking too, so it wasn't all good.

The disks, he said, his voice stronger and clearer, just as if I were wearing an earbud and he was a tune. Yes, it worried me that I could already hear him clearer than I could just a day ago, and that he was interacting with me easier too. I tried not to think about how if he kept getting stronger, more comfortable, more active, maybe he would just keep going until he took me over completely.

Heck, why panic about that when I could panic about this illegal, possibly unknown, certainly forbidden spell that I had completely destroyed?

What about the disks? Oh. That was it. I remembered, or, hell, maybe Dad gave that info a nudge toward my consciousness. There was no trail left behind from magic used through the disks. When the disks were used, all that was left behind of the spell was a burned black circle of ash.

Holy shit.

"I think we need to talk to Violet," I finally said.

"Beckstrom?" Stotts asked.

I nodded. "I think that circle is the residue of a spell cast using the disks that were stolen from her lab."

Stotts looked back down at the ashes, then shook his head. "Is that why you destroyed the spell?" he asked.

"Yes," I said, needing an easy out right now in the worst way. "Can I use your cell phone? We need Violet to confirm this."

He exhaled and brushed his hands over his thighs before standing. He dug his cell out of his pocket. "I'll get it," he said. He pushed one button and waited for the person on the other line to pick up. Violet Beckstrom was on the magic cop's speed dial. Wasn't that an interesting thing?

While Stotts asked her to come on out to the park, I walked around the circle of ash, trying to get a scent off it. Just a slight greasy tang. I remembered that too, though the familiar smell did not bring any more of my memory back to me.

Dad was no help in that area either.

I tried to decide what I should tell Stotts. Just because the spell was gone didn't mean I hadn't seen exactly what it was. There was no trail to be traced back to a user. I could honestly tell him that I had no idea who cast it. But should I tell him that it was Transmutation?

I walked down the gazebo steps while Stotts talked to Kevin, Violet's bodyguard, on the phone. My sneakers and cuffs of my jeans got soaked while I made a slow circle around the structure. I set a Disbursement—those sore muscles were going to last for more than a few hours—and cast Enhancement to my sense of smell. The world broke open in a bouquet of odors, rich loamy grass, wet pine sap, musky hints of small animals who had been through the park recently, rotting wood and molds.

Lighter, but still present, were the smells of burnt blackberry, licorice, the chemical taint of formaldehyde, a burn of copper, and more. Strawberries, candy sweet, like bubble gum and booze. Tomi's scents.

Holy crap. I followed my nose, heading toward the stink of fear, pain, and death.

A hedge of bushes overgrown by ivy and tangled, dry blackberry vines filled the space beneath a small copse of trees.

I peered into the shadows there. I didn't even have to wait for my eyes to adjust to the low light to know what was spread out beneath the trees: the remains of an animal, maybe a dog or a small deer. There wasn't enough of it left to tell. There was, however, a lot of blood.

Fresh enough, everything was still wet, and the flies hadn't found it yet.

Hells.

"Tomi?" I called. There was no answer and no movement in those shadows. I inhaled again. Her scent was faint. She had certainly been here, but she was not here now.

I let go of the Enhancement and backed away until I could breathe clean air.

The wind lifted, reluctant and lazy, and I smelled warm cedar and lemons, soured by sweat and booze. Davy Silvers, a Hound and Tomi's ex-boyfriend, was here somewhere. Upwind, which was where he would be if he wanted me to notice him.

I scanned the park, finally spotted him leaning against a tree closer to the street. He had on a rain jacket with the hood up. He wasn't looking my way, but he wasn't trying to hide either.

After that bender at Pike's wake yesterday, I was impressed he was walking. But, damn, that boy needed to stop following me.

I walked back up to the gazebo. Stotts pocketed the phone.

"She's on her way," he said. "Want to fill me in on that?" He nodded toward the circle of ash.

"I'm not really sure what kind of spell it was," I started. Something was niggling at the back of my mind. I frowned, thinking. Then it came to me. I'd just pulled on magic, cast an Enhancement so I could smell out traces of magic in the air, and I had not seen the Veiled, had not been touched by the Veiled, had not been hurt by the Veiled. Not one painful burning fingertip bruise.

That was the first time I'd pulled on magic and hadn't

had to fight them off since I'd first seen my dad's ghost several weeks ago. What did that mean?

A smug satisfaction filled my mind.

You're still protecting me from them, aren't you? I asked my dad.

We can work together, daughter, he coaxed. *We could help each other through these trials. My knowledge, your power.*

"Allie?" A hand landed on my upper arm, and I literally jumped.

Stotts raised his eyebrows. "Are you still with me?" he asked.

I blinked a few times, clearing my mind. Talking to my dad was a bad idea. Too distracting, for one thing. For another, I had the very bad feeling that given the chance and my own inattention, Dad could actually Influence me to do what he wanted. From inside my head.

A chill ran down my shoulders and arms, and I shuddered.

"Okay," Stotts said, "why don't you come over here and sit down?"

I let him lead me over to the bench that ringed the outer edge of the gazebo's covered area. He probably thought I'd set an immediate Disbursement, and was bearing the price of using magic already. That wasn't true, but the truth—that I was dealing with the growing horror of my father living in my mind—wasn't something I cared to share with him. He'd take me in for a psych review.

And who had the time for that?

"Do you need some water?" he asked. "Some pain killers?"

I looked up at him. In the blue-gray light, his skin took on a dusky forest look, his thick black lashes almost covering his eyes as he squinted from the low glare, giving him lines that etched the knowledge of pain on his face. Even scruffy from not shaving, his eyes a little bloodshot and yellow from lack of sleep, and his hair messed up and wet, he looked worried for me. And willing to serve and protect, just like every nice, cursed magic police officer should be. I found myself thinking Nola could do a lot worse than be with him.

Then I pushed that thought away because, really, did a girl need more than a thousand things to worry about all at once?

"I'm just a little cold is all," I said. "That spell isn't anything I've ever seen before." Hey, that was the truth. Go me. Maybe I'd just tell Stotts everything I knew, including the whole secret society of the Authority with their secret magical spells, secret magical tests, and weird-ass secret magical backstabbing, and let him figure it all out.

My dad fidgeted and fluttered in my head, like a bird in a box. He obviously did not like that idea.

Then stop trying to Influence me, I thought at him. *Or so help me, I will spill it all.*

The hot wash of surprise flashed over my face—his surprise, not mine. And while I wanted to gag a little that his emotions had actually triggered a physical reaction in my body, I was too angry to stop yelling at him now.

What, don't think I can play with the big boys? I am not going to play your game by your rules. This is my game now.

Silence. And I mean a dead, empty silence. If my dad was still in my head, I could not feel him. Not one leathery spec of him.

Good.

Stotts was waiting, looking between me and the treed area where I assumed Davy Silvers still lingered. It begged the question of why Davy was following me so obviously. He had proved he was a very, very good Hound and knew how to stay unseen when he wanted to.

But before I dealt with Davy, I needed to finish with Stotts.

"I did get a feel for what the spell might have been used for," I said.

"Okay," he encouraged.

"I think whoever cast that spell used a disk to access and carry the magic. There was no trail left behind, so I can't trace it back—the magic did not come from the cisterns or networked conduits. I couldn't make out the signature."

"Because of the disk, or because you don't know the caster?"

"I don't know. I'm thinking mostly because of the disk." I looked past him at the black circle of ash spread across the concrete gazebo floor. The ring of fragile crow-feather ash reflected blue and green in the low light. "It could be I just haven't ever Hounded or studied the caster."

Which meant it had to be someone from outside the Northwest. Hounds do not just run around sniffing magical signatures and immediately know who they come from. There is a lot of study that goes into it, and books and books and electronic slides of recorded signatures to go through. As a matter of fact, every citizen is required to register a state-Proxied spell cast with city hall—much like applying for a gun license or having your fingerprints added to the record—so every magical signature was, theoretically, on record.

I had studied every signature in the Northwest, and thousands more beyond that. Plus, I'd spent years on the street actually applying my knowledge, and building my own list of quirks and signatures. And yes, I kept notes.

I was good at things when I put my mind to it. After I failed business magic in college, I threw myself into Hounding.

Obsession doesn't always work against a person, you know.

"I think the spell was a form of Conversion."

"Huh," he said, thinking that over. I didn't blame him. Conversion was a spell most often used in medical procedures. It was a central part of the Siphon glyphs, which were vital to draining away magic-induced pain and wounds. But out here, in a gazebo, the idea of using Conversion didn't make a lot of sense.

"Could you tell what the spell was cast for? Or who it was for?"

I shook my head. "But over there in the bushes might be another good place to look for clues. I think I smelled a Hound, Tomi Nowlan, in the area. Did you have her look at this site before me?"

"No."

Well, crap. Sorry, Tomi. But Stotts was a police officer. The law. And if some kind of mutated man was still out on the street, eating larger and larger animals, I figured it was good to let the law know about it before anyone, including Tomi, got hurt, if she was indeed mixed up in this.

He walked off, and returned in a short time. He didn't look happy, but he didn't look nearly half as sick as I felt.

"What do you know about that?" he asked.

"There was another animal, smaller, a dog, torn apart like that in an alley near my house."

"It was reported last night. Were you the one who reported it?"

"No. But I saw it. I was going out on a date. And the car was parked close to the alley. I thought I heard something, so I went back there. Zayvion was with me. He reported it."

I didn't know how much of this kind of magic he knew about, or how much of this the Authority wanted to keep under wraps. Since I didn't know what I could or could not say, I stuck with the truth. It was easier that way.

"I think there was magic involved. It smelled exactly like that mess over there."

"Do you know if the disks are involved in that?" he asked. "Was there a ring of ash left behind?"

I thought about it. "Not that I could see. It was dark. And foggy."

He strolled to the edge of the gazebo railing next to me and my bench and leaned his forearms against the wooden edge, staring out at the rain.

"Looks to me like some sort of Drain or Siphon was worked on it. Sucking all the life out before mangling the body." His eyes narrowed at the corners. "Maybe someone screwing around with blood magic who thinks they're a goddamn vampire."

"So you've seen this sort of thing before?"

He nodded. "Do you think this might have anything to do with Mr. Silvers out there?"

It surprised me he knew Davy, but of course he did. Davy was one of Pike's Hounds. Or had been one of Pike's Hounds. And Pike kept Stotts informed on who was working in the city.

"I don't know."

"Do you know why he's here?" Stotts asked.

"He has some sort of idea that I need someone to follow me around and look after me."

Stotts chuckled. "Why do you suppose that is?"

"Ha-ha." I tucked my chin down into my coat collar. The temperature had dropped with the rain, and holding still was making me cold. I wished I'd brought some coffee.

"So do you like having a bodyguard?" Stotts asked like it didn't matter what I answered, which meant, of course, it did.

"No."

He glanced over at me. "Huh."

"Why would I want someone to watch every move I make? I got a lifetime of that being the infamous Daniel Beckstrom's daughter."

"Not your thing?"

"Not even close to my thing."

"Do you need me to tell Silvers to back off?"

I opened my mouth, shut it fast. I had not expected that. Stotts pulling the cop card on my behalf. For some reason it always felt like Stotts and I weren't quite on the same side. But with just that one statement I realized he'd be willing to step in and help me, just because it was the right thing, the lawful thing, to do.

"No," I finally said. "I'll talk to him. He's a good kid doing what he thinks is right."

"Stalking?"

"It's not like that. Pike decided too many Hounds were being hurt Hounding without a safety net. He set up a buddy system. One person Hounds, and another Hound volunteers to stay back and keeps an eye on things. Calls the police if something goes wrong, but otherwise doesn't get involved."

"When did you tell him you were taking this job?"

"I didn't. He has a lot of free time on his hands and is too curious for his own good."

Stotts turned and leaned his back against the railing, his arms crossed over his chest. If Davy could hear us, and he might be able to—Hounds were known for having acute hearing—with Stotts' back turned, it would make it harder to hear, and impossible to read lips.

"I don't like outside eyes on my cases."

"I'll talk to him about it," I said again. I stood and started pacing, trying to warm up. When was Violet going to get here?

"Good." Stotts watched me pace from one side of the gazebo to the other. Neither of us looked over at the circle of ashes, as if we wanted to avoid it as long as possible.

"I'd like to continue working with you," he said. "Just you. I'd like this to be a more permanent partnership."

I stopped halfway to the railing, and looked back at him. "What?"

"I'd like to formalize this. You working with me. For me. Make it something more along the lines of what I had with Martin Pike."

"Are you offering me a job?"

"Yes. A trial period, anyway. On call. Contracted to Hound exclusively for the MERC. Monthly stipend. Proxy service. Interested?"

"Let me think about it," I said. "Is there anyone else in the running for the job?"

"Not until I hear from you, there isn't."

I searched his face for a hint of why he had picked me, out of all the Hounds in the city. I'd only worked for him once. Some of the other Hounds had worked for him more than once. Even Sid had, I think.

"Okay, I give up," I finally said. "Why me?"

He didn't answer right away. Instead, he stared off toward the circle of ash and shifted against the railing, so he was standing more than leaning, his arms still crossed over his chest.

"You aren't like the other Hounds, Allie. You see and track spells on a level most Hounds don't even try for. Plus, most Hounds who have more than three years of experience have already burned out on drugs and alcohol. They don't, or maybe can't, Hound as precisely as you can."

"Pike was good," I said. "Better than me."

"No," Stotts said quietly. "No." He pushed off the railing and stuck his hands in the pockets of his coat. He stopped right in front of me, and then just as quietly asked, "What are those marks on your hands and arms?"

I blinked a couple times. I didn't know what to tell him. Would he buy it if I said they were just tattoos I'd gotten on a wild drunken weekend?

"They have something to do with magic, don't they?" he continued. "With channeling it? Using it? Sensing it?"

I could not remember if I'd ever talked to him about the marks. Would it matter if he knew that I carried magic inside me, that I had always carried a small magic in me and after Cody Miller had pulled magic through me, that small flame had ignited into a roaring, barely controlled wildfire of magic in my bones, in my blood, in my soul?

No one else could do that. No one I knew about anyway. Holding magic in your body was a short road to death.

"It is from magic," I said. My heart was beating too fast. I felt like he'd just caught me, found out the secret I'd been trying to hide. Not that I could really hide metallic whorls of color that spread over my face and arm.

"Magic marked me," I exhaled. Why was it so hard to tell him this?

Because you know it's wrong, my father's voice whispered in the back of my mind. *He shouldn't know. He is not one of our kind.*

"When?" Stotts asked.

"I don't remember when it happened," I said. That was the truth. Nola had told me how I got the marks. The coma had taken that memory from me. Still, deep in the pit of my stomach, I could feel the press and movement of magic, like a sleeping thing curled inside me. I felt the memory of when it had burned through me, pain and pleasure. I felt the memory of when it had first taken root in me.

"After the coma, that's when I first remember seeing it."

"And does it enhance magic use? Does it make things more clear?"

I realized I could not look away from his eyes. He wasn't using Influence on me, but he had a presence, an intensity. As if he were really counting on me to tell him this. To do the right thing. And if I looked away, he would know I was lying.

"It makes using magic more painful." It came out straight. Even. And I meant every word of it.

He pressed his lips together. "I saw you use magic. When you Hounded for me last time for the kidnapping, I cast Sight, to watch what you did."

"I thought you were keeping an eye out on the thugs in the neighborhood."

"I was. When you drew on magic, those colors on your hand, on your face, glowed."

I nodded. "I don't know why that happens. I don't know why this is the way it is. Why I am the way I am."

He studied me and I did not look away. No deceit. I truly did not understand why magic had marked me, nor why I could hold it in my body while others could not. But that was all I could give him, all I could tell him. I didn't know how much Stotts knew about nonstandard things about magic. Or how much he knew about the Authority.

Nothing, my father whispered. *He is not our kind.*

Okay, so maybe now I did know how much Stotts knew. But here's where the trouble started. He was the law. And I was working for him. I was also about to be trained by people who used magic illegally.

Ancient magic use is not illegal. It is only unknown.

"Have you talked to anyone about it?" he asked.

I tipped my head to the side, hoping my dad would just shut up so I could concentrate on one conversation at a time. Because I thought I was missing something here. Stotts was digging for a response from me. But I didn't know what.

"Not really. I talked to Nola about it before the coma. Or at least she told me I talked to her about it."

"I mean, since you've been back. Back in the city."

"Is there someone I should talk to?" I asked, shifting the focus of the question so I could gain some ground. "Do you know someone who might be able to tell me more about this?" I held up my right hand, wiggled my fingers.

He didn't look away from my face.

"The city is full of people. All kinds." He emphasized the word *kinds* just like my father had, and I worked hard not to show him how that hit me. "Charlatans. Pushers, users, cons. You know the type."

"Yes. I do."

"I want you to know you can come to me. Anytime. For any reason. And my . . . resources will be at your disposal."

"Even if I don't take the job with you?"

"Even if we never work together again."

"Thanks," I said. "That's nice to know."

My father pushed somewhere behind my eyes, and I tasted leather and wintergreen at the back of my throat. I also sensed his displeasure. He didn't like Detective Stotts. Probably didn't trust him. And while I wasn't sure that I trusted Stotts either, I did find myself liking the man.

Not that I was childish enough to make friends just because my dad didn't approve of someone.

Okay, yeah, I was that childish.

"Just wondering," I said. "Did Nola put you up to this?"

He smiled. "You don't take anyone at face value, do you?"

"Not even a newborn baby."

He chuckled. "That's too bad. No, Nola didn't ask me to do anything for you. But if she did, I probably would have done it."

Was he telling me that he liked her? That he maybe already felt something toward her? I wasn't sure what I thought about that. Nola lived a small-town life in a place where magic could not touch her. Stotts was in the middle of a city crawling with magical crime. Opposites might attract, but that didn't mean they didn't also explode on contact.

"That's good to know too," I said.

The sound of a car engine broke off our little heart-to-heart.

We both took a step away from each other. I, at least, was surprised we were still standing that close together.

A Mercedes-Benz drove up and parked on the side of the street, behind where Davy still stood, hunched-shouldered beneath the tree, probably soaked through anywhere his coat didn't cover. Why didn't the kid just get in his car and out of the rain, or come on over here and take shelter in the gazebo? That boy made no sense.

The car engine turned off, and Violet's bodyguard, Kevin, got out of the driver's side. Kevin had to be my height or so, but carried himself like a man who was used to getting lost in the crowd. Blond hair, brown eyes, and a face that most resembled a puppy dog, eyes too big, jaw too soft, he didn't look like the killer he was. Nor did he look like a man who was good—very good—at using magic. He was part of the Authority, and Violet knew that because she was my father's widow, and apparently Dad didn't mind telling her about the secret society of magic users.

Not that I was bitter about it or anything.

Violet was just a beat behind him, sliding out of the passenger's side, and wearing a full-length wool peacoat as blue as a stormy ocean, the wide hood pulled up. Her figure was still trim.

They walked over to the gazebo, side-by-side.

Stotts waved to them, and Violet waved back. They strolled up the gazebo steps, Violet in front, Kevin behind her.

"Hello, Detective Stotts," she said.

"Mrs. Beckstrom, Mr. Cooper." Stotts shook hands with both of them. "Thank you for coming out."

Violet pushed her hood back and put on her glasses. "I didn't know you'd be here, Allie."

In the gray light, Violet's hair seemed to have a warmth of its own, the fiery hue of autumn leaves. I found myself unable to look away from her, unable to exhale, as emotions that were not mine poured through me in a river of heat.

Images flashed behind my eyes, memories, of Violet. And with those memories came emotions.

I wanted to take her in my arms and hold her. I wanted to feel her heartbeat against my own. I wanted to touch her. Love her.

Holy shit. I took a step back, away. Away from Violet. Away from the emotions raging in me. Emotions that were not my own, but my father's.

It was only a second, a hot, vivid second of wanting

her . . . as a man, as my father wanted her, but it freaked me out.

I didn't know if I should be sick or angry. Angry was easier.

Get the hell out of my head and leave me alone, I said.

The presence of my father did not dim, but he did something to lower the intensity of his emotions. There was some sort of curtain between us, a curtain that dampened his feelings.

My apology, he said stiffly. And here's the weird part—I knew he meant it. Really meant it. The primary emotion that filtered through the curtain now was embarrassment. He didn't like sharing his emotions with me—never had when he was alive, still didn't now that he was dead.

I wasn't overjoyed about it either.

"Allie?" Violet asked.

"Hounding," I said, brushing right over my little meltdown by striding over to the circle of ash. "For Detective Stotts." The sooner I got this job nailed down, the sooner I could get out to Maeve's and get rid of my dad.

I just needed to keep my cool.

"This," I said, "is what's left of a Conversion spell. No trailing line, no signature, nothing but this circle."

Violet knelt next to the circle. "Is this what you saw before on the farm?" she asked.

I assumed she was talking to me. "I don't remember what I saw before, but I'm pretty sure this matches what Nola described to me. It is very familiar. I know I've seen something like it before."

"Huh." She pulled a small vial and something that looked like a tongue depressor out of her purse. She scooped up some of the material and tapped it into the vial. She dropped that in her purse, then walked around the circle and knelt again.

"There are no other lines in the center?" she asked.

I looked down. There clearly weren't. But she wasn't asking me.

"No," Stotts said.

His gaze was unfocused, his feet spread as if he were holding up a weight. His right hand was held palm forward, in an old-fashioned "stop" motion. And though he held still, I knew, because I could smell it, that he had cast a variation of Sight.

Right. I forgot that even though he called people like me in to Hound cases, it didn't mean he couldn't use magic to see things himself. Hounds could just see it, taste it, smell it, and track it better than any other magic user.

"Nothing on any of the standard spectrums," he said.

Correction. He used magic very well. My opinion of him went up a notch.

He put his hand down, releasing the spell, and shook his wrist out. "It looks like a circle of ash. I wouldn't think it had anything to do with magic if I hadn't seen it fall when Allie broke the Conversion spell."

Kevin, who had walked across the gazebo to stand with his hands harmlessly in his pockets while he stared out at where Davy stood, suddenly stiffened. His puppy dog gaze slid over to me. That was it. No other reaction. But I knew he didn't believe Stotts.

As well he shouldn't. It wasn't a Conversion spell I had broken. I sucked at anything along the lines of spells traditionally meant for medical use, and breaking a spell took just as much skill as casting a spell.

"Do you have any idea who is involved in this?" Violet asked.

Stotts shook his head. "Nothing here. No one. Just the spell, reported by some dog walkers whose dogs wouldn't get anywhere near the gazebo, and who reported getting sick the closer they came to look at it."

Even I could tell that didn't sound like a Conversion spell. Violet pushed on her knees to stand, and Kevin was suddenly beside her, catching her hand and helping her up. "Thank you," she said with a smile.

He made it look like business as usual, but my dad, behind my eyes, focused on the two of them and would not look away.

Stop it, I pushed at him.

But he did not stop it. With a force of will a dead man should not have, he stared at Violet's smile, at the softening of Kevin's expression, then followed Kevin's hand to where it lingered just a second too long, too gently, too damn much in love, on Violet's hand.

My father's hatred burned chemical hot in my brain and everything went white for a second.

Violet, strangely enough, did not seem to notice Kevin's barely concealed attentiveness. She was all business, a scientist with her thoughts on the problem at hand, not the people around her.

"I do think it is the full discharge of magic one of the disks could carry," she said.

"Which leaves us with several more still out there." Stotts said.

"Several?" I asked, leaning against my dad, like he was a door in a hard wind that refused to close. I wasn't gaining much ground against him. I—or rather Dad—could not look away from Kevin, could not see anything but the man who had touched Violet. My Violet. My wife.

Holy shit. I pushed harder.

"We are unsure how many disks were stolen," Violet said. "There was a fire in the lab that destroyed evidence from the break-in. But we think at least one was used to cast that spell at Nola's."

I frowned.

"The circle you don't remember seeing. A circle like this was left behind at Nola's farm. This"—she pointed at the ring on the floor—"is similar to what we saw in lab tests. I'll double-check of course, but I'm comfortable saying this is the discharge of one of the disks. And as far as we know, no one but Daniel—" She visibly swallowed, then nodded to herself, accepting her own verbal slip. "No one but me knows how to recharge the disks."

"So they're worthless?" I asked. "Once they're used, no one knows how to reuse them?"

"An unloaded gun is still a gun," Stotts said.

"Someone could crack the code," Violet agreed. "Get lucky and correctly interpret the combination of glyphs and tech . . ." She took a couple steps along the edge of the circle. "Are you sure it was a Conversion spell?"

"Yes," I lied.

Dad pushed harder, the pressure of his will like a dull-edged blade sinking into the back of my eyes. He wanted to say something—he wanted to make me say something more to her. I clamped my back teeth down and pressed my lips together.

"Interesting," Violet said. I couldn't tell if she believed me or not. "Is there anything else you need from me, Detective?"

"The test results, when you have them."

"I'll get that to you this afternoon."

"Thank you," he said.

Kevin walked forward to stand beside Violet, just slightly too close. No, he stood much, much too close. He reached out to take her hand again.

My father's anger built to an unbearable pain. My vision flashed white again.

"I need to talk to you, Violet," I blurted out. A flash of heat poured over my face and chest. I didn't know if that was me or my dad talking.

Kevin frowned, his eyes suddenly narrow. Those weren't puppy dog eyes. Those were the eyes of a bodyguard, a killer. And a well-trained member of the Authority who knew something was terribly wrong with me.

Smart man.

At his look, my father in me stilled. Not because he was afraid. No. All I felt from him was burning hatred and betrayal.

Stop it. You're dead. You have no say over what Violet or anyone around her does. I concentrated and pushed on him mentally. Pushed him farther back in my mind.

He has no right, my father's voice rang in my mind. Not loud, like he was yelling. Very softly, in almost a lullaby tone.

Which meant he wasn't just mad; he was crazy, killing mad.

I rubbed my fingertips over my eyes and forehead, forcing my eyes to close so I couldn't see Kevin, so my father couldn't see Kevin or Violet.

"Allie?" Violet asked, concern in her voice.

"Sorry." It came out a little shaky, but it was all me. "I'm a little tired." I took a short breath and mentally shoved at my dad as hard as I could.

I wanted him out of my head. Away, gone. Back behind his curtain. Farther back, if I could manage it. Back where I could no longer feel him. Back until he was no longer a part of me.

Yes, I was angry. And yes, I knew magic couldn't be used when you were in a state of high emotion. But I wasn't using magic against my father. This was nothing more than sheer willpower, determination, and stubbornness of who wanted control of my head and body more.

Believe me, it was me.

"Do you need to sit?" Violet asked.

I still had my eyes closed, my fingers rubbing at my forehead. I knew I had to answer, knew this shoving match with Dad was taking too long. Fine, if I couldn't push him away, I'd shut him out. I willed a wall between my father and me, a black, thick wall of granite to replace the curtain between us.

For a brief moment, I saw him, dressed in a business suit like he was always dressed, but younger and stronger than I remembered him. His hair was black with no hint of gray, the lines on his face smooth. Death, apparently, did good things for one's complexion. He scowled at me and raised his hand, as if to cast a spell—

I mentally took a step back, thinking, *Wall, wall, wall, I really need a wall between us.*

"Allie?" A touch on my arm. I opened my eyes.

Stotts raised his eyebrows but didn't take his hand off of my arm. "Are you sick?"

"Tired," I said. Wait, I'd already said that. Great. "Sorry. It's the Hounding. Proxy headache," I lied again. I had to stop living the kind of life where it was better to lie to the secret magic police than to tell the truth. "Are we done?" I nodded toward the circle of ash.

"I'll need your report on what you Hounded."

"Right." I stepped back, and he let go of my arm. The wall in my head sat like a real weight, as if I'd put on a hat made out of concrete. But the good thing was I couldn't hear my father's voice, couldn't see him, and he wasn't pushing at me. I could feel his emotions, but they were not nearly as strong. He was still angry, still betrayed, but with the Mt. Everest of don't-give-a-damn between us, his motions were only a whisper of what they had been just a moment ago.

I took a breath and tried to get my feet under me again.

"Do you want me to come down to the station to give my statement?" I asked Stotts.

"Yes. But we need to wait until the cleanup team arrives."

"How long is that going to take?"

"Ten minutes. Are you in a hurry to get somewhere?"

"Maybe." I braced myself to look over at Violet, to be ready to fight my dad's reactions to seeing her and Kevin again.

At least he didn't know she was pregnant. And if I had anything to do with it, I wouldn't think about that any time that he could hear my thoughts. Like when I was dreaming. Or when he was trying to mutiny in my brain.

Violet stood next to Kevin, staring pensively at the circle as if she was trying to get the right answer out of an ink blot test. She and Kevin weren't touching, but Kevin radiated that overly protective bodyguard vibe.

Dad didn't do anything. Or at least nothing I could feel.

"Violet?"

She looked up.

"I do need to talk to you. About the business."

"Now?" she asked.

Frankly, here, in the rain, hell, in the driving ice and snow, would be fine with me, because at this moment, I had control over my dad and could tell her I wanted her to run the company instead of me without him getting all grabby with my brain.

As if on cue, the wind picked up, whipping rain into the gazebo, and stirring the ashes that refused to blow away.

"Is now good?" I said.

"I'd really like to get this sample back to my lab," she said. "How about dinner tonight instead?"

"Sure," I said. "When? Where?"

"If you don't mind coming over to our—to my place, maybe around eight?"

I had to see Maeve today, but it wasn't even noon yet.

And I didn't have anything else to do other than catching up with Nola to try to help her with Cody, which I still might be able to swing. I didn't know how I was going to fit it all in, but I'd try. And if Maeve helped me get rid of my father, I wouldn't have to deal with him in my head while I was around Violet.

"I can do that," I said.

"Then I'll see you tonight." She smiled. "Kevin?"

They walked together, step in step, past me.

I caught a hint of her perfume, and sadness filled me. *Bought in France, an anniversary gift. She laughed when I gave it to her, telling me it was too much, too good. I never told her what she meant to me.* I pushed that unwanted thought and the ghost of a life I had not lived back behind the wall in my head.

"You sure you're okay?" Stotts asked.

"Yeah," I said. "Why?"

"You're crying."

Startled, I wiped the tear I had not felt off my face. "It's just the wind," I said.

I don't know if he believed me, but he didn't say any more as I watched, helpless hands deep in my pockets, as Violet and Kevin hurried through the rain to their car, got in, and drove away.

Chapter Six

"I'm going to go talk to Davy before he catches pneumonia," I said to Stotts. It was as good an excuse as any to get out from under Stotts' notice. Plus, Davy looked miserable out there.

"If you need me—"

"I'll be right over there. If I need you, you'll know. But I won't. Davy's a nice kid." I headed down the gazebo stairs.

"Even nice kids do bad things," Stotts said.

I ignored him and took a deep breath. The sharp, wet air filled my lungs and hurt a little. It felt good. Cleansing. Too bad I couldn't inhale with my brain.

Davy didn't move as I approached, which was a little weird. I wondered whether he was asleep on his feet. I hurried, and was just a few feet away when he spoke.

"What is it with you and Hounding in the rain?" he asked.

"Nobody told you to stand in it," I said. "You could just sit in your car. You did drive over, right?"

"Yeah." The way he had the hood of his coat drawn up, I couldn't make out more than his chin, lips, and the tip of his nose.

"What are you doing here, Silvers?" I asked.

He finally moved, tilting his head so the low morning light could cast gray pallor over his skin.

"My job." He smiled slightly, then winced like it hurt. As well it should. There was a reason he was hiding his face. A black and red bruise spread across his right cheek, and his eye was swollen shut.

"What happened to your face?" I asked. "Start a brawl at the pub last night?"

"I don't start brawls; I end them." He tried the smile again, but thought better of it. "But no. I caught up with Tomi last night." He shrugged, like that should explain everything. Problem was, I didn't know very much about his ex-girlfriend except she was a Hound who didn't like the buddy system Pike had set up. Oh, and she hated me.

"And?" I prompted.

"We didn't agree on a few things."

"What things?"

"Me having depth perception for a few days."

I blew out air, exasperated. "Davy. Don't make me pull this out of you. Did she do this to you?"

He hitched one shoulder, uncomfortable. "We . . ." He paused, looked off at Stotts, and I swear I saw fear cross his face.

"What, Davy?" I said, softer now, trying to coax it out of him nice-like, and resisting the urge to just yell at the boy until he told me what the hell was going on. "Tell me what she did, okay?" I could Influence him. It would be easy. A word, a tone, and a little magic, and he'd tell me anything I wanted to know. Would do anything I wanted him to do. But Influence was one of my dad's favorite moves, and I didn't want to be my dad any more than I had to be.

"What were you talking to her about? Your breakup?"

He sniffed and rubbed his hand down over his lips and chin.

"It wasn't about that. We never—she never—wants to talk about that. It's over, you know?"

"So why did you go talk to her?"

"She's been mixed up with a guy. I think. And I think he's using her. She says she Hounds for him . . . but she's—she's a cutter," he said, and I nodded to let him know I'd already figured that out.

"She's doing it more. Worse." He sniffed again and looked out into the rain. Then, finally, back at me. "Something's wrong. She's different. Ever since she started doing things, Hounding for him, cutting for him, she's just not. Not the same."

I'd seen this before. It was why I'd never gotten into a relationship with a Hound. Using magic meant it used you back. It caused you pain. Most Hounds could not afford to use a Proxy service, which meant most Hounds had to endure the pain of magic use. That led Hounds to a desperate search for pain relief. Booze, drugs, cutting, self-mutilation, food, exercise. Everything in excess. Anything to get away from the pain. Chronic pain management changed people. Then it left them dead.

"Do you want to talk to Stotts about it? Maybe get her into a program and checked out?"

He laughed, a short, hard exhale. "Right. Mr. Dot the i's and Cross the Police Procedures? It doesn't work that way. There isn't a program for Hounds. Rehabs won't take her—they don't take anyone who won't give up Hounding. And me telling her she's screwed up didn't work out how I pictured it." He gave me the painful smile again.

"Listen," I said. "I'm done with this job except for filing my report. Why don't you go home? Get some sleep. Take some aspirin for your eye. Call me when you're feeling better. I'll take you out for lunch or something. We can talk about Tomi if you want. Try to come up with some ideas to help her."

"I wasn't looking for your pity. . . ."

"Oh, for cripes' sake, Davy," I said calmly. "I don't pity you. If you're dumb enough to hunt down your ex-girlfriend and tell her you think she's screwed up, while you were drunk—and no, there is no way you sobered up between the time I left you and that evening; I'm surprised you could even walk to find her, and I hope to hell you didn't drive—then you should have known she would try to deck you.

"But you are my right-hand man in the pack I am now the leader of—thanks to you. You really are a meddler, aren't you? Don't answer that. And being my right-hand man means I get to tell you what to do, and you do it. So. Go home, Davy Silvers. Sleep. When you are conscious, call me."

"And where does *listen to tedious lectures* fit in my job description?" he asked.

"Right after *stop being a smart-ass.*" I smiled, and so did he. Probably one of the stranger working relationships I've had, but then, no one before Pike had tried to organize the Hounds into any sort of group. And Pike mostly just made sure they kept tabs on each other. I had other things in mind for the Hounds. Especially with Beckstrom Enterprises' money behind me.

"Fine." He pushed away from the tree, carefully, I noted. If I had to guess, I'd say Tomi got in a few other hits besides the one to the face. Girl wore steel-toe boots, and she looked like the type who wouldn't mind getting in a few kicks to the ribs, if the opportunity presented itself.

"Anything broken?" I asked. "Do you need to see a doctor?"

"Naw. Just bruises." He grunted as he bent beneath a low-hanging limb.

Just bruises, my ass.

He pushed his soggy hood back and ran a hand through his short hair. His face was pale behind the vivid bruise, and moisture that might have been sweat covered his forehead. Kid was in pain but too damn stubborn to admit it.

Come to think of it, that was another trait you needed for Hounding. A colossal sense of denial.

"Well, don't be stupid about it, okay?" I said. "If you need to get checked out, I'll cover the bill."

"Wait—you're paying me now?"

"You'd have to actually *work* for me to pay you."

"I'll take that as a yes and go get some sleep like you told me to. On the clock." He tugged his hood closer to his face. "See ya, boss man."

I stepped back and he walked off toward the street, holding a hand up over his shoulder to acknowledge Stotts, who was strolling over to me.

"Take care of the kid?" Stotts asked.

"For now."

"Anything I should know?"

"Not unless you have jurisdiction over teenage love affairs gone wrong."

"That might be a little outside my expertise," he said.

A big white box van rumbled up to the curb, then slowly

rolled over it and came down the park path. The van parked a good distance from the gazebo, and all the doors opened. Stotts' MERC crew—or at least the members of his team I had met, two men and a woman—stepped out of the van. They each carried a backpack slung over one shoulder and had on some variation of jeans and dark coats, but that was where the similarities ended.

Garnet, the tall, aging hippy, was probably the oldest of the crew and wore a crocheted rainbow-colored hat over his balding head. He squinted in the pale light like a mole in the middle of summer sunshine.

Next to him and twice as wide strode Roberts, the woman on the team. Built like a shot-putter, she had the look of a weight lifter from the Eastern Bloc. Her cheeks were flushed red beneath her startlingly wide brown eyes. The hood on her coat wasn't up, leaving her short dark curls free to catch a frost of rain like misty cobwebs.

Julian, the driver, was the shortest of the bunch, about five foot two, and he carried himself with the confidence of a business executive. He wore a tailored black wool coat with a scarf tucked around his neck. He had to be the youngest of the group, fit, good-looking.

"Detective," Julian said when the three of them were close enough to us. "Ms. Beckstrom."

I nodded my hello.

"What have you got?" he asked Stotts.

"Spent spell. Physical remains." Stotts started walking, and we followed. "Dead animal in the bushes over there. Might be someone playing vampire. You know the drill. Pictures of everything. Map the residual of the spikes in magic use off the grid out a hundred feet square. Scrub it down to zero impact—this is a public park and we don't need the environmentalists on us for sloppy cleanup."

"Got it covered," Julian said.

I glanced over my shoulder. Garnet busied himself plunking down orange traffic cones that blocked the path-way to the gazebo, and then farther off, blocking the path along the bushes and trees. Not that anyone was out in this weather at this time of day, but it was probably a good precaution. In Portland, if you aren't willing to go outside in the rain, you never go outside.

Roberts walked along the path where concrete met the grass in front of the gazebo. In each hand she held witching rods. I hadn't seen those since college. The two narrow lengths of metal were bent and held loosely in each hand; they could be used to detect the presence of water and other energies. They had also proven to be helpful in tracking the natural flow of magic beneath the ground.

I wasn't close enough to see, but I bet those rods were glyphed up the wazoo, and it was magic, not water, she was searching for.

"You can see for yourself where the spell was located," Stotts said as we climbed the stairs to the gazebo.

Julian whistled. "What was it?"

"Might be Conversion," Stotts said.

"Might?"

"It dissolved before Allie could get a strong read on it," Stotts said.

Julian arched an eyebrow and looked up at me. "Is that so?"

"Fell apart when I touched it." That was almost the whole truth.

"Do you need anything else?" Stotts asked.

"Nope." Julian slipped off his backpack and pulled out a pair of leather gloves and a spray can.

"Then keep the spell use to a minimum," Stotts said. "We're already up against the wall with Proxy costs this month and I don't want to fight with the suits to justify an overage."

"Tell them to cut us a bigger budget." Julian shook the can and began marking a circle around the entire inside parameter of the gazebo.

Stotts just grunted. "I'd rather not lose any more men."

Julian shook his head. "Speaking of which." He held up the spray can. "You might want to step back."

Stotts nodded at me and we both walked out of the gazebo, passing Garnet and Richards on their way up the stairs.

The three of them recited a mantra, and the air suddenly felt a lot heavier.

I paused, but Stotts pulled me forward so I couldn't watch anymore. I could still feel the magic they were using. The air was heavy with it, the rain so thick that for a second I wasn't sure there was enough air between drops for me to inhale. Then they cast the spell—a spell I'd never experienced—and the rain broke free, a cloudburst, colder than natural rain, with a disinfectant smell to it.

"They clean up after magic by using more magic? That's a smart idea." I could not keep the sarcasm out of my tone. Probably because I didn't try to.

"Funny," Stotts said, "you don't seem like the kind of person who should tell me how to do my job."

"Don't I?" I blinked innocently. "If that's a problem, you might want to reconsider that job you offered me."

We'd made it to the car by now. "I might. Get in." He didn't even wait for my reply before opening his door and sliding in out of the rain.

I took another sniff of the air, sneezed at the soapy chemical stink that filled my nostrils. No fireworks, no flash or sound came from the gazebo. I hesitated a moment more, heard what sounded an awful lot like a handheld vacuum cleaner whir to life. A vacuum cleaner? To clean up unquantified and possibly dangerous magical residue? Seriously?

Today was just full of surprises.

I pulled the door open and got in out of the rain.

Chapter Seven

Instead of taking me to the station, Stotts let me give him my statement in the car while he drove me home. Which was good. Because it hadn't stopped raining, I hadn't eaten since this morning, and the coffee at the police station wasn't fit for human consumption. Using magic always made me hungry, and I was tired. Plus, that Disbursement I'd set to pay for Hounding the spell—a nice juicy headache—was in full force.

Stotts dropped me off in front of the building with a promise to contact me if he needed further information. I promised him I'd think about the job offer and let him know soon.

I trudged up the three flights of stairs to my apartment and paused at the top of the third-floor landing. A whiff of onions and beef and bacon made my mouth water. I didn't know which of my neighbors was cooking, but I seriously considered tracking them down and inviting myself in for a bite.

I stopped at my apartment door, put one hand on the smooth surface, and without drawing on magic, listened for movement. It was a habit I picked up thanks to my less-than-calm last few months in the city with a variety of magic users trying to kill me.

More than movement. I heard singing. A woman's voice. Nola.

Duh. I had company.

I unlocked the door, feeling like I'd jumped on the idiot train a day early, and walked into my home.

The delicious smell was stronger here, and my heart did a happy little leap in my chest, even though it made my head hurt more. Nola had been cooking!

She stood on tiptoe on a chair at the round table in my living room, her back to me. Her hands were full of vines from the potted plant that was now draping over my no-longer-plain vinyl blinds and white sheers.

On the other side of the wall-sized window was a bushy tree-plant thing—did I ever mention that I do not have a green knuckle in my body, much less a thumb?—which took up the empty space in the corner.

There were other touches that told me she'd been busy. A couple candles, three new throw pillows, and all the roses that had been in the kitchen sink now arranged and placed throughout the house in every vase, mason jar, and wine bottle I owned, plus a few more containers I could only guess she'd bought today.

I didn't want to startle her, but wasn't sure if she'd heard me come in. So I made some noise opening the door and shutting it more loudly behind me.

"Welcome back," she said without turning. "I heard you come in the first time."

I laughed and hung my soggy coat on the back of the door. "I didn't want to send you tumbling to your death," I said. "How was your day?"

"Good. I did some shopping. Hope you don't mind." She finished adjusting the vine, some kind of philodendron, I think, over the valance, where it obliged her, as all green living things seemed wont to do, by draping in a perfect waterfall of leaves like an interior-decorating magazine photo shoot. "You really needed some living things in here."

"You didn't pay for all this, did you?"

"It's not that much," she said as she stepped off the chair, flashed me a smile, then walked far enough back so she could look at her handiwork. "I found a nice secondhand store just down the street for the little things."

"They were selling plants?"

"No. But the flower shop around the corner was. Think of it as payment for putting me up on such short notice for a few days. Soup's ready. Did you have lunch?"

"Didn't have time. I'm starving." I headed into the kitchen, where I found on the stovetop soup filled with veggies, and bread wrapped in a dish towel on the counter beside it. Heaven. I filled a bowl, took a couple pieces of bread, and headed back into the living room.

"How did the job go?" Nola asked. She sat on the couch, and I sat at the café table. Nola had opened the blinds enough to let in the dull afternoon light. And with the cascade of green leaves in the corners of the room, the light no longer seemed as dreary.

"Good," I said around a mouthful of the best beef veggie soup I'd ever put a spoon to. "Any luck with Cody's stuff?"

She folded her hands in her lap, and I realized I had rarely seen her that still, no knitting in her hands, no bills to pay, no charity items to sort, no chickens to tend, alfalfa to bale, heck, not even her dog Jupe's big head to scratch.

It was the first time I'd really thought about how lonely her life might be.

"I went down to talk with the supervisor. She wasn't available, and no one else seemed to have any information except that he was in the care of a psychologist for tests he needs before he can be released. They said that's customary with cases that deal with the handicapped and their misuse of magic."

"The forgeries he did when he was younger? Or him being used as part of my dad's murder?" Cody hadn't been the one behind the scheme to kill my dad, though he had been a part of forging my dad's signature on the hit on the kid in St. Johns, and my signature on the hit on my dad. As far as the law was concerned, James Hoskil was the brains behind the crime.

But the law did not know about a lot of things going on in this city, like the Authority, and weird half-dog men running around. Even I didn't think James Hoskil was powerful enough to take down my very powerful father.

My dad fluttered behind my eyes. I ignored him.

"I don't know," Nola said. "They won't say more than that. I'm guessing it's from the most recent crime. He was in custody before that. Those records, of why he was jailed for a short time, I can't find. I've tried looking up newspaper articles, courtroom documents, but there are no reports in the news. It's strange. The courtroom documents aren't even public. I don't understand what all the cloak-and-dagger stuff is around this poor kid, and I'd like to know what crimes he committed before I take him in."

I took another bite of soup. The Authority was probably behind the secrecy. They had put the hush on the circumstances of Lon Trager's death, Frank's dark magic shenanigans, and my dad's stolen corpse. None of those ever hit the news. Maybe the Authority had pull, or people, in the courts as well.

Nola didn't know much about the Authority, and I was inclined to keep it that way for now. Telling her about the secret society of magic users meant putting her at risk.

I refused to do that.

"I'll ask Violet if she knows anyone that can help us with this," I said. "Are you going to call Detective Stotts and see if he can help?"

She twisted her fingers together. "I think I will. What do you think about him?"

I sipped the remainder of the broth out of the bowl. "I only met him a couple weeks ago. He seems to be a good police officer. Dedicated to his job. Determined. Said he grew up in the Northwest. Raised by his mom mostly here in Portland. Has good taste in coffee, so that's something in his favor." I smiled.

"I didn't know his wife had passed away though. I thought the ring . . . well, you know."

She nodded. "He could be lying about that."

"How very suspicious of you," I said approvingly. "But I don't think so. He didn't smell like he was lying. Oh, one more thing. He's cursed."

I took a huge bite of bread, white with a hint of garlic and Parmesan. Delish.

"What?"

I talked around the mouthful of bread. "Cursed. Hounds who work for him die very unusual deaths. Weird, huh?"

"My God, Allie. How can you joke about that?"

"I'm not joking. People really think he's cursed."

"Do you?"

I took another bite of bread to give me time to think. Stotts could prove by numbers and odds why Hounds tended to die when they worked for him. But a small, suspicious side of me wasn't buying it. I didn't think foul play was involved. I did think Stotts had a knack for being around when Hounds pushed too hard, made the wrong choice, or finally gave up all together.

"I don't know if it's a curse. I don't believe in curses. But . . ." I rubbed my fingers back through my wet hair and slouched in the chair. "Something. If nothing else, he's a magnet for bad luck."

"And you are working for him because . . . ?"

"I'm bad luck?" I grinned. "Because I made a promise to Pike that I would look after the group of Hounds he was leading. Make sure they checked in with each other, keep track of who was working with the police, with Stotts, so we'd know who was alive and who was dead."

"Sounds kind of lonely and grim," she said.

"Not really. It's a support group, I guess."

"And you're leading it?"

I couldn't parse her change of tone. "Yes?"

She grinned. "I can't believe I heard that out of your mouth. You, taking responsibility for others. Good job."

"Thanks, Mom," I drawled.

"No, really." She leaned forward, a twinkle in her eye. "I didn't think I'd ever see you step up like this. So respectable."

"Forget I said anything."

"No, it's good. And you must have really cared for Pike to promise to look after everything for him."

"Not everything. Just the Hounds. Have I talked about Pike much?" I asked.

"No. You've mentioned his name a couple times. What was he like?"

"Sort of what I wished my dad could have been. Not that he was the nicest guy around. But he was . . . fair. He always told it to me straight. Didn't lie. Even when he knew I wouldn't agree with him."

"I'm glad he was in your life," she said.

Which was just what I needed to hear, because I was glad he was in my life too. I'd just never been able to say that to anyone. See how great best friends were? Even if they were also incredibly annoying.

Someone knocked on the door. I straightened, dug my thumb in a circle at my temple, waiting out the spike of pain. I should have taken some aspirin. "Did you invite someone?" I asked, trying to remember if I had locked the door after opening it the second time.

"No."

"It's probably Zayvion," I said. "I have a . . . meeting to go to today."

I recited a mantra and walked over to the door, clearing my mind. I wasn't going to call on magic unless I had to.

The locks were not set. I leaned forward and looked out the peephole.

Zayvion Jones stood there, staring right back at me as if he knew I was watching him. He had traded his slick leather jacket for that ratty ski coat thing, had a forest green beanie pulled tightly over his dark curls, and his jeans had been worn down to threads and a couple holes in the thighs.

Street drifter, Zen master, killer, magic user, Zayvion Jones.

I let go of the breath I'd been holding and opened the door. "Hey."

"Afternoon." His gaze took me in, from wet hair to soggy shoes. "Are you ready?"

"Almost. Come on in. I need to change. Do you want some soup?"

"Smells fantastic." He stepped in and shut the door. Then he purposely set the locks, holding my gaze with that calm, Zen look of his.

Yeah, yeah. Let's see you go through my day and remember every detail, smart guy, I thought. "You have something to say?" I asked.

"No."

"Good. Have some soup." I wandered down the hall, stopping in the bathroom to take one or three painkillers. I listened to Nola and Zayvion's pleasant greetings as I walked into my bedroom and dug for dry clothes.

What did one wear to the first class of secret magic training, anyway? Nonflammable jammies, perhaps?

I doubted it much mattered. So new jeans, a gray sweater, and black boots. I brushed my hair back and put a hat over most of it, then strolled out to the living room.

Zayvion sat at the table, in the same chair I'd been in just moments ago. He was slouched back a little, his long legs stretched out, smiling that shy-boy smile at Nola. He looked comfortable there, at my table, in my home. Sexy.

An electric tingle warmed my stomach. I liked seeing him here, at that table, my table. I like the idea of being with him. But with my dad in my head, Hounds to babysit, and secret magic classes to attend, it seemed like the chance for that, for us, was still a long way off.

"Hey." I tried for bright and cheery, but it came out a little too soft. Like maybe I'd just realized I'd lost something.

Zayvion straightened in his chair, and Nola, on the couch, looked over.

"Ready?" I asked.

"I am." He stood. "Thanks for the soup. It was wonderful."

Nola stood too, exposing the old-fashioned manners she'd been raised with.

"It was great catching up with you again." Here she shot me a mischievous look.

"Wait a minute." I scowled. "You two weren't talking about me, were you?"

Zayvion shrugged into his coat. Zipped it. "Your name might have come up."

"Have a good meeting." Nola gave me a quick hug. I shot Zayvion a questioning look, over her shoulder.

He blinked and poured on the Zen.

"Promise I didn't tell him all your secrets," Nola said.

"Better not. Two can play that game, you know."

"What? With whom? Oh." A rosy blush fanned across her freckled cheeks. "You're horrible," she laughed.

"Remember that," I said with a straight face. "You do not want to play boyfriend chicken with me, missy. I aim low."

I tugged my wet coat off the back of the door, rolled

the locks, and opened the door. "I should be back in a few hours. I have a dinner date tonight with Violet, and I'll talk to her about Cody. Don't worry about cooking."

"Is her number around here in case I need to get a hold of you?" she asked.

"On the computer, in the address book." I so had to get a new cell phone. Kevin had told me he might have a suggestion for a phone that would work longer than fifteen minutes, and Zayvion had said the Authority might be able to supply me with something. I pulled my notebook out of my coat pocket, flipped to a blank page while I was walking out the door, and scribbled *Ask Kevin/Zayvion about cell phone.* I clipped the pen on that page, so that every time I put my hand in my pocket I'd know there was a note waiting for me to take care of it.

Zayvion paused, still one step inside my apartment, and said something so quietly to Nola even I couldn't hear it, before he walked out the door behind me.

Nola shut the door, and I slowed my pace until I was sure I heard her set the locks. "I didn't realize you two were such good buddies," I said.

Zayvion tipped his head but did not drop the Zen act. "She and I had some time to talk," he said evenly. "When you were in the coma." He said the last part quietly, as if there wasn't quite enough air to fill in the words.

"You like her?" I asked.

"Yes."

We didn't say anything more as we tromped down the stairs to the parking area behind the apartment building.

Zay unlocked the passenger's-side door, and we both got in the car.

"Dinner with Violet?" he asked once we were on the street and heading northwest.

"I need to talk to her about a couple things. Business things," I said, "and about Cody Miller."

"What about Cody Miller?" Zay suddenly seemed very interested. Odd.

"Nola's trying to foster him out on her farm. Away from magic. She's running into red tape. Something about psych tests."

Zayvion was impeccably calm. Blank. Zen.

"You already knew about this, didn't you?" I asked.

"Yes."

"Whoa. A straight answer. Are you feeling okay?"

"I've been worse."

"So, about Cody?" I asked.

"The Authority is involved with clearing him so that he can be fostered by Nola. I haven't been . . . updated on the details."

"Now, there's the obscure, subject-dodging man I know," I said. He gave me a look I pointedly ignored. "What should I tell Nola?"

"You can tell her that you found out Cody should be released soon. As soon as the psych eval is done."

"Psych eval? Is that the story?"

He took a deep breath and let it out. "Allie, if you are going to become a part of the Authority, you are going to have to learn how to keep a few secrets. So, yes. That is the story until we hear otherwise."

"And that's all the story you're telling me?"

"Yes."

"I don't think I like that."

"Too bad."

I scowled at him. I not only didn't like being in the dark, I didn't like that he was comfortable keeping me there. "Is there a list of who I can and cannot talk to about the Authority? I work with the police on occasion," I said. "Can I talk to them?"

"The police don't know about us. Detective Stotts shouldn't either."

"Shouldn't?"

"We are fairly sure he doesn't know about the Authority."

"Why?"

"Because he hasn't done anything to try to stop us."

"You know, that makes it sound like you're on the wrong side of the law."

"You can talk to Violet if you want."

"Way to avoid my observation," I said.

"She knows about the Authority." He continued like I hadn't even spoken. "But she doesn't know everything.

And there are some things that would be best not to tell her. Things that would put her in danger. Like Cody being under evaluation with us."

I rubbed at my face. "I give up," I said into my palms. "One slip of conversation and someone's going to get hurt? How do you keep track of it all?"

"Spreadsheet."

"Right. So how do you know who knows what?"

The clouds grew darker the farther north we headed to the Fremont Bridge. He was silent awhile, maybe thinking about how to explain it to me, or maybe just paying attention to navigating the thicker traffic.

By the time he turned onto the bridge, it was raining steadily. The windshield wiper squeaked. "It's not that difficult," he finally said, picking up our conversation once we had merged with I-5 traffic. "The majority of people in the city, in the world, do not know about the Authority."

"And why not? Why not just come out and come clean so we can all move forward with the same information?"

"The older uses for magic, the ancient spells, are far more dangerous than the simple magic approved for release to the masses. The older uses for magic—dark magic, light magic—have always been hidden from the world. The few times in history those magics have fallen into the wrong hands, wars and worse have nearly destroyed mankind."

"Wait. Magic was approved to be released?"

He glanced at me. "You didn't know that?" He shook his head. "Your father . . ." He left it at that, then went on. "When the technology reached such a point that the common man could access magic safely—"

"Relatively safely," I interrupted.

"Relatively safely," he agreed, "and not without price or pain. When that technology was released, only certain magics, glyphs, spells, were 'discovered' and tested by the pioneers in the budding field of magic.

"And all of that happened under the control of the Authority," he said. "Mostly."

"So the Authority has been hiding magic for hundreds of years?"

"Thousands."

Wow. "What changed?"

"Your father and James's father, Perry Hoskil, invented the technology to channel and access magic. And they brought it to market, released the notes on their study of uses—spells and glyphs that allowed the users to make magic bend to their will."

"My dad started this?" I mean, I knew he was one of the driving forces of the Beckstrom Storm Rods, and had found a way to draw magic out from the deep natural cisterns where it pooled. I guess I'd never really thought that he was more than a driving force behind the way to make money off it. I'd never thought of him as an innovator. And certainly never thought of him as the beginning of the common man's access and awareness of magic beyond superstition, religion, or the things conservative people always wrote off as esoteric nonsense.

"Yes," Zayvion said, "your dad started this."

"And the Authority was okay with that?"

Here Zayvion smiled. "That's one of the things I like about you. You know the right questions to ask. No. The Authority was not okay with what he or his partner, Perry Hoskil, were doing. But there are divisions in the Authority. Lines and boundaries that limit how much high-level magic users can influence and interfere with one another's experiments and studies.

"Even though it is an ancient field of study, not everything about magic has been discovered, tested, proved. Like space, like the oceans, like the human body, there is still so much we don't know about it. So much to learn."

I couldn't help myself; I smiled. That man had a hunger for knowledge, a respect for it. I'd always gone for the intellectual types. Well, not always. There were those years in college where brawn, not brains, got me in bed, but it hadn't taken me long to get tired of the pretty-on-the-outside, empty-in-the-head guys like that.

"By the time what Beckstrom and Hoskil were doing was discovered, the damage had been done. Magic was no longer a secret. Magic was now in the hands of the untrained masses."

"Why didn't the Authority go public then? They could

have established themselves as experienced managers, or at least educators."

"From what I am told"—he raised an eyebrow, maybe to remind me that he wasn't around thirty years ago when this all happened—"there were worldwide gatherings of the Authority to discuss a course of action."

Traffic slowed. Maybe an accident. More likely congestion from merge lanes and exits. The rain drew a veil of evening over the afternoon light.

"The argument to go public," Zayvion continued, "and reveal the mastery of magic was strongly championed. And so were many other arguments, factions of the Authority taking sides, for and against, including the ancient Order of the Aegis, who adhere to the oldest written laws that magic should never be revealed to the uninitiated. Never. Your father came very close to being Closed when the vote was taken to allow his transgression to stand or to remove him. Magic was very nearly erased from common use."

That was a lot to take in all at once, but the painkillers and soup were giving me a little of my brain back.

"Oh, come on. People wouldn't willingly give up magic once they had a chance to use it."

"I didn't say willingly. But enough engineered failure in the budding technology would prove magic was a wildly unmanageable, unsafe, and, if the members of the Authority did their jobs correctly, perhaps even an unreal resource."

"Engineered failure," I said. "Do you mean deaths?"

"That was one option."

Holy shit. These people really did play for keeps.

"Instead it was agreed to allow magic, the safest form of it, to be accessible to the common man. There was money to be made off of it, and like you just said, members of the Authority were in the perfect position to educate, train, and manage the change in the world."

"So it all ended happily ever after."

He frowned. "When magic is involved, there is never a happily ever after. You know that."

And the way he said it, chills washed down my skin. He was right. I knew that. Magic could lick the happy out of a lollipop.

"There are still members of the Authority who disagree with the decision to allow magic to go public. Your father's actions were the crack in the ice, and ever since then the Authority has been fracturing, splitting apart. If some of the factions have their way, there will be a war. The Authority will shatter."

"And that's bad, right?"

His lips pressed into a grim, flat line. "You have no idea."

I dug around in my head a little, expecting a comment or reaction out of my dad, but he was silent as a shadow. If I didn't know better, I wouldn't think I was possessed. The last time he was this quiet was when Zay and I had been at dinner.

Interesting.

Traffic, which had been crawling, growled back up to freeway speeds. We crossed the Columbia River and within a short while were on the opposite shore in Vancouver, Washington. Zayvion turned east along the river.

"Is it far?" I asked.

"We're almost there."

I don't know what I expected Maeve's place to be like. Where would secret classes that taught the secret ways of magic be held?

Another fifteen minutes or so and Zayvion slowed and took a road south, toward the river. We crossed the railroad tracks into an abandoned industrial area, and pulled up alongside a long building with identical rows of windows that lined the upper, middle, and ground floors. It sat parallel the length of the train tracks and the river.

I could feel magic radiating like a subtle warmth from the place.

About a half dozen cars were parked along the far chain-link fence that separated this lot from a scrap metal collection site next to it. There were no parking places near the building, which was strange since there was room for several. Instead, big raised boxes and whiskey barrels of plants and flowers took the lion's share of the parking space, green even in January, filled with sturdy bushes with red and white berries dotting twigs.

"Talk about out-of-the-way," I said as we parked.

"Used to be right in the middle of everything," he said. "It was a railroad boardinghouse and inn. Train used to go right through here."

"It doesn't anymore?"

He shook his head. "When the Flynns bought the place, they lobbied to have the spur discontinued. No real train business down here, and they didn't want to risk that kind of attention to the well." He unbuckled his seat belt and opened the door.

"Well?" I got out of the car. The wind and rain smelled of fir trees and river algae and the dusty grease of the rusting scrap metal next door.

Zayvion tipped his head to one side. "Can't you feel it?"

I tucked my chin down into my coat collar and calmed my mind. I felt the air, rain that was thankfully a lot lighter, heard the call of crows on the breeze. I paid attention to the ground.

Magic beneath my skin turned and twisted, reaching out for and not quite connecting with the massive pool of magic that radiated a strange heat of its own deep, deep beneath the soil and stone under the inn. I opened my mouth and inhaled. Magic was so concentrated here, I could almost taste it, a faint, fuzzy warmth, like electricity from a thunderstorm, but sweeter, thicker on my tongue.

The well.

The cool metal taste of iron and lead that I always associated with magic, since magic was channeled through conduits of the material, was strangely absent here. Here, in this pocket between two cities, I could almost forget magic was on the grid, controlled, tamed. Here magic roiled in a deep, dreamlike rhythm just below my conscious awareness.

"Wow," I said.

Zayvion wrapped his arm around my shoulders, a solid warmth that brought me back to my surroundings. Good thing too. I'd stopped walking and was just standing there getting wet.

"Let's go in," he said.

I didn't pull away, preferring to linger against his body and soak up the heat of him.

He started toward the inn, shifting so we were shoulder to shoulder as we walked up the wooden steps to a covered porch that stretched along this side of the building and corner to continue across the front, riverside of the building.

A wooden sign next to the door read FEILE SAN FHOMHER and beneath that, WELCOME.

Zayvion lifted the door latch and pulled open the door, the old hinges giving out a mewl of metal on metal.

The scents of sage, butter, bread stuffing, and baked apples filled my nose and mouth as we entered the high-ceilinged, open-raftered main room of the inn. A lunch counter to the right of the room traced a round-edged square in white marble countertop. Only a few people sat in the walnut T-backed stools around the counter, a mix of old and young, suits and jeans.

Rows of round tables filled the space between us and the lunch counter, and square tables tracked along the windows all the way to the end of the building.

A smattering of people sat at the tables. A group of gray-haired men who looked as if they didn't have a penny between them were working their way through heaping turkey meals. At a table by the window, six teen girls chatted and laughed. And at other tables I saw executives holding business lunches, moms with shopping bags at their feet and children in high chairs, a set of couples, some construction workers, and more than a few loners, men and women, eating lunch, talking, reading papers, drinking coffee while the waitstaff—a couple girls, at the moment—connected them all through service and smiles. Several people behind the lunch counter kept busy cooking and cleaning. The overall atmosphere was a nod to the past, when transitory people gathered and socialized in the comfort of a home away from home.

"Zayvion, Allie." The voice had a lovely Irish lilt to it, and I looked away from the tables to the woman walking across the room. Maeve wore jeans and deck shoes and a dark green sweater layered over a cream turtleneck. Her red hair was pulled back in a bun and tendrils of it fell free to curl in soft reds and gray around her face. Her eyes were green with wicked intensity, her smile welcoming, if not exactly warm.

What was it Zayvion had said at dinner? My father

killed her husband? I suddenly wished I'd asked him more about that.

"Any luck?" she asked Zayvion.

He shook his head. "Still hunting."

Maeve turned toward me. "I'm glad you made it. Let me take your coat. Then you and I can get started."

Zayvion tensed. "You don't want me there?"

"Not this first time. I want to see what Allie can do on her own." She strode off, talking over her shoulder. "You can stay out here if you'd like," she said. "I don't think this will take long."

I picked up the pace to keep up with her as she beelined between tables, smiling at her guests. She led me back to a wide hallway, where wall lanterns cast the wood in warm tones, then past a white wooden staircase that square-railed up and up. We strolled through a doorway into a small sitting room done up like an old-fashioned parlor.

Plush love seats and chairs big enough for two filled the room. Beside each chair was a small table. In the center of each table was a clear glass bowl, lined with lead.

Magic conducts through glass and lead, if the right glyphs are worked into both. I also noted the wallpaper that at first looked like gold and forest green flowers in a repeating pattern were actually magical glyphs. I caught Shield, Ward, and several other negating glyphs around the room before Maeve had crossed to a dark door that did little to call attention to itself.

She lifted the chain at her neck and caught up a key that she used on the door, before letting the chain fall back beneath her sweater.

"We'll start in here, since it's nearest the center."

Center of what? I didn't ask because the door distracted me. Wood, but with lead and brown glass worked into it to look like the finest beveled stained glass. The lead and glass were glyphs, but so natural they looked like ribbons in the wood grain.

Holy shit, I'd never seen a magic so artfully carved. I couldn't resist it; I dragged my fingers across the door. Magic shivered beneath my fingertips, licking at my flesh, pooling in the whorls of my fingerprint.

"You can shut the door, Allie," Maeve said patiently.

Like a kid caught dipping into the cookie dough, I pulled my hand away and closed the door behind me.

Magic pools beneath the city naturally. There are some points where magic is the most concentrated. Wells. Spring, summer, autumn, winter. The wells are heavily guarded gathering places among the Authority. Never revealed to outsiders.

I rubbed at my forehead. My dad was back and more talkative than ever. How great was that?

With the door shut, it completed the outer spells of Illusion and Blocking, and a half dozen more I was sure I didn't recognize. I could feel the concentration of magic in the room. It burned like a sun trapped beneath the floorboards, filling me up, scraping through me, pressing, pushing against my skin and bone. I held very still and worked hard to hold it all in.

"Did your father tell you about wells?"

"Not really." It came out calm, not like I was clenching my teeth and trying to breathe evenly so the magic would quiet, settle, and stop shoving at me.

Maeve was across the room, hanging my coat on a simple hat rack. Unlike the parlor, this room had sparse decor. A red oriental rug took up most of the whitewashed wooden floor; the walls were polished slabs of birch jointed together with diamonds of glass and outlined with lines of lead. Pale beaded board with lines of lead and glass running through it made up the ceiling. A small brick fireplace complemented by a grill worked in something way too gothic grounded the corner.

There were no windows. Instead, an aged copper wall fountain took up the space where I'd expect a window to be, and the other window had been converted into a bookcase where hardbound books were stacked in rows. As for furnishings, they were all deep browns and reds, and easy-to-clean surfaces: a couch, four chairs, and a table with a pitcher of ice water and lemon slices next to the fireplace.

Maeve crossed the room toward the pitcher of water. "Did your father tell you anything at all about the Authority?"

"We didn't talk much. He was gone a lot. And as soon as I was old enough, so was I."

She poured two glasses of water, floated a lemon round in each. "I see. Then let me explain that magic naturally occurs deep within the earth." She nodded toward the chairs, handed me a glass of water. I settled on the couch as she continued.

"I've always thought of it as hundreds of rivers and streams. In some places magic flows more swiftly; in others it is sluggish, or spread out and swampy. The network of conduits and lead and glass lines your father invented did wonders to mitigate and standardize the flow of magic. That made it safer for the common user to tap into it."

I took a sip of water, and it felt good going down my throat, trailing cold all the way to my stomach. Magic eased in me a little.

She took a sip too, then set her glass on a table and folded down into one of the plush armchairs.

"Those rivers of magic split, join, knot, and pool together. A lot like those marks on your hand."

I did a good job of not hiding my hand in my pocket, and instead nodded, like this was the most normal conversation I'd ever heard.

"The wells, and there are many of them, some weak, some incredibly strong, are where magic concentrates and regenerates. Most populated areas are within the range of at least one well. This house, this room, is over a well of magic."

"I can tell."

"Really? It is very carefully Blocked and Shielded."

Should I tell her? That I felt magic all the time? That I held it within me, something no one else could do? Could I trust her?

Did I have any choice? It was either trust her or have the Authority Close me, take my memories, maybe even take my ability to use magic, though that would be a pretty trick since I had magic down to the bone.

"I—"

Killer. Betrayer. The words rushed through my mind like a winter storm. *She is dangerous, devious. Do not trust her.*

A headache stabbed at my eyes. A headache named Dad. I coughed to cover my gasp.

Shut up, I thought.

"I do feel magic," I said. "Not as strongly as I'd expect, since this is over a well."

She held very still, that green gaze roving over me like she could see beneath my skin. I resisted the urge to just get up and walk out of there.

Which was probably good, since it was probably not my urge.

"Have you experienced any residual effects since your father used your mind?" she asked in the firm tones of a doctor or schoolteacher. "Dreams, memories, thoughts?"

No, no, no, he raged.

"Yes," I said, a little too loudly, since I was trying to drown out his voice, even though I was the only one who could hear him. Then, quieter, "I've experienced all those things."

The flutter behind my eyes turned into blunt fingers trying to rub their way out of my head. It hurt, but I'd endure a lot more pain than that to get rid of my dad. Besides, I was pretty sure my father and I were at cross-purposes. We'd always been at cross-purposes. I'd long ago learned that doing the opposite of whatever he wanted me to do was generally in my best interest.

"Are you experiencing them right now?"

I have never felt my father's raw fear before. It was just a flash, a moment. Then I could not sense him at all.

"I was," I said. "Not right this second."

"I need to look in your mind." She sat forward, her hands clasped loosely at her knees.

She'd done this once before. I didn't know why my palms were suddenly sweaty, didn't know why my mouth was so dry.

"Like last time?" I asked, stalling.

"Exactly the same. You might feel it a little more, though. Since we are so close to the well, I will be able to look more deeply than I did before, to see if it is just residuals of your father's thoughts and spirit, or if it is something more."

"Okay." I was pretty sure it was something more, like

maybe his entire disembodied/reembodied spirit, but I'd leave that assessment to the expert.

Maeve placed her hand on my left wrist—the part of me closest to her.

No glyphs, no chanting. She just closed her eyes and took a deep breath.

This time, I could sense the magic rising from far below us. The magic flooded through her—something I'd never seen anyone try—then settled like a cloak or aura around her. And even though magic is fast, the way she called upon it, it was slow and I could see the white and blue shimmer of it with just my bare eyes without calling upon Sight.

She opened her eyes, shockingly silver, shadowed by shots of her normal forest green.

With magic around her, Maeve looked *into* me.

Magic in me flickered, burned too hot along my right arm, too cold along my left. I did not want to use it, did not want to cast magic. But like fire jumping a line, it ignited, filled me.

Maeve blinked, tipped her head to the side. "Allie?"

"It's okay," I said as I recited a mantra. Just the first two lines of "Twinkle, Twinkle, Little Star" over and over. "Give me a sec."

How was I supposed to get rid of so much magic when there was so damn much magic filling the room?

Maeve stood, and I would have worried about that, but I was a little busy trying not to explode and burn the place down. I had a feeling they wouldn't let me come back to school if I killed the teacher on the first day.

Magic burned, squeezing my bones. I bit my lip to keep from moaning and twinkle-twinkled with all my might.

Something cold and heavy dropped into my lap.

Like blowing out a candle, the magic in me went dead.

Okay, this time I moaned, not from pain, but from relief.

Maeve was standing next to me, bent a little. She studied my face. "I can't believe it. I never thought . . ."

I blinked, looked down at the heavy thing in my lap. A rock. A plain black and gray river rock, smooth and oblong, about the size of a loaf of bread.

"Here," she said.

I glanced up and took the ice water she offered me.

"Thanks." I drank, and when I was done, she set the glass back on the table. "Really nice rock," I noted.

Maeve sat on the coffee table in front of me and put one hand on my knee. "How long have you held magic inside of you?"

"You could tell?" I asked, probably stupidly.

"Not before now. I knew magic had marked you. From the outside . . ." She leaned back a little and her gaze wandered over me, her eyes still silver, but with a lot more green in them. "From the outside it does not show." She shook her head. "Are you Shielding?"

"No. Mostly I just try not to let it burn me up."

"But you have used it? Drawn upon the magic within you and successfully cast spells?" I couldn't tell if she was excited or worried.

"A lot. I Hound for a living, remember? Why? Is that a problem?"

She laughed, but it came out a little shaky. "I wouldn't call it a problem. It's just so unheard-of. How long have you been able to carry magic?"

"All my life. Just a small bit, enough to work one minor spell. It always took a while to fill back up."

"You were born with it?" She pinched the bridge of her nose and took a deep breath. When she exhaled, she muttered something that involved my father's name and a couple curse words. "No wonder he never brought you to us, never let you learn." Maeve's hand dropped to her lap. Her eyes were almost all green now, and she looked resigned. "You hold much more than a small amount now, don't you?"

I nodded.

"And that changed when you received those marks on your hands? Positive"—she pointed at the wild whorl of colors up my right arm to my temple—"and negative." She pointed to the solid black bands around each of the knuckles and the wrist of my left hand. "Classic natural representation of the give-and-take of magic. Pleasure and price."

"Yes, it changed when I got marked."

"When did that happen? How?"

I didn't want to tell her. Didn't want to be vulnerable, exposed. Have I mentioned I have trust issues?

"Do you really need to know that?"

"If you want me to stand as your advocate at the testing ground, yes, I really need to know that."

"Testing ground?"

"In three days, your control of magic will be tested in front of the members of the Authority."

This must be the test my dad kept talking about.

"Is that when you decide if I deserve to use magic? If you should just erase all my memories about the Authority and put limits on what I can do?" It came out angry, which was no surprise since it pissed me off that someone else thought they could tell me how to live my life.

Yes, I knew that wasn't the worst thing they could do to me. Zayvion had told me they could go so far as try to kill me if they thought I was too much of a danger or risk to myself or others.

Of course, I wasn't going to just stand around while they threw rocks at me, or whatever they did to get rid of people they didn't want in their little club.

Maeve stood and sat back in the plush chair. "It may not seem fair, or lawful in the ways of the modern world. It is an ancient custom. A test to discover your abilities, your limits; your control. Things that can mean the life or death of those you would stand beside. It is necessary. Every person in the Authority has gone through it."

"So I don't have to like it, but I still have to do it?"

She nodded. "Tell me when magic claimed you with those marks." Woman was all about getting down to business.

I did some quick thinking, something I hadn't done enough of lately. Since I didn't want to bring undue attention to Nola, I decided to skip the part where I explained I didn't actually remember getting the marks, and tell her instead what Nola had told me I told her. Confusing, but hey, when you have a memory with more holes than a pair of hand-me-down fishnet stockings, you make do.

"I was trying to get a man to the hospital. He was injured, and when I tried to help him, he reached through me and connected to magic. Then he . . . um, pulled magic through me and into me. It fed the magic I already carried, made it stronger so that it burned"—I thought about that, nodded to myself—"burned these marks into me."

"And where did this happen?"

"Over in St. Johns."

Maeve's eyebrows shot up. "Are you sure?"

I thought back on it. I was sure Nola told me I had found Cody down by the river in St. Johns. I'd been running from gun-toting Bonnie at the time, but was slowed by trying to carry Cody and his cat. I'd told Nola that Cody was nearly dead when I found him. But she said by the time Zayvion had driven Cody and me out to her farm, his wounds were gone.

"I'm sure. St. Johns." I suddenly realized why she looked so surprised. St. Johns was off-grid. A dead zone. There was no naturally occurring magic there, and Portland hadn't seen fit to budget in a network out into the fifth quadrant of the city.

Which meant I should not have been able to pull on that much magic like that there. Which meant Cody should not have been able to pull on that much magic like that there either. "Who was the man you were helping?" Maeve asked.

"I wasn't formally introduced—"

"Allie," and there was tangible weight behind her words and a familiar honey taste. "Tell me the name of the man you helped in St. Johns."

"Cody," I said, under the spell of the Influence she'd just used on me. "Cody Miller."

Maeve didn't ask me anything more. All the color washed out from beneath her skin. She traced a circle in the air and drew her finger across it in a slash, breaking the Influence she'd used on me.

I hated Influence. "I would have told you without the push," I said.

"I'm sorry. It was—it is—very important." She wasn't looking at me anymore, but instead over my shoulder at the middle distance there. She sounded distracted, her voice thin.

"Maeve?"

She cleared her throat and visibly pulled herself together enough to give me a small smile.

"Thank you for your honesty. I won't Influence you again—it is rude. Most people don't notice it, though," she said. "Tell me how you're feeling. Is the stone helping with the overflow of magic?"

I took quick inventory. I felt great, actually. A little tired, but a lot less pushed around by magic. As a matter of fact, even my headache was better. I felt light, like someone had just pulled a lead blanket off me.

"Better," I said. "What kind of stone is this?"

"A void stone." At my look, she waved her hand dismissively. "Some stones have the right combination of chemical compounds and exposure to magic that they actually become void to it and are able to project a calming or negating effect on magic."

I looked over her shoulder and around the room and noted several more small, round river stones in grays, greens, browns, and blacks scattered among the tables and shelves.

"How much does this thing cost?"

Maeve's smile, this time, was genuine.

"That one stays here. Most stones are much smaller. I'll see if I can find something for you, if you want. Now, on to the matters at hand. I need your permission to look into you again."

I nodded. "You have my permission."

Maeve placed her hand on my wrist and did her silver-eye trick again. This time I felt the press of magic filtering into my mind, and I leaned back, away from Maeve. I could not look away from her eyes. The white magic around her cast red shadows against the back of my eyes like a flashlight pouring light toward the back of my brain.

"Breathe," Maeve said gently, without Influence. I realized I'd been holding my breath. I exhaled. While I was at it, I loosened my death grip on the rock in my lap.

"That's good. You're doing fine." Maeve, Magical Proctologist.

I didn't know if the wall I'd built between my dad and myself was still standing. Found that I couldn't really turn and assess anything in my own head. Not while magic and Maeve's gaze held me still.

But I could still feel my head, could still think. Something, like a small, many-legged thing hiding from the light, scrabbled across the back of my skull.

Nauseating. As comforting as a tapeworm.

Maeve looked a moment longer, then closed her eyes. When she opened them again, they were green—just green—and the magic around her was gone.

"More water?" she offered.

"No. Did you see him?"

"I saw something that needs to be looked at by someone more familiar with the transitional magic of life and death. It's not my expertise," she said apologetically. "Jingo Jingo should be by this evening. I'll have him look into it as soon as he's here."

As if on cue, a short, sharp set of knocks rapped on the door. Maeve flicked her fingers, releasing, for my benefit, I realized, the Ward she'd put on the room when we had entered. A Ward I hadn't seen her cast, even though I'm usually good at paying attention to those sorts of things.

Okay. That was spooky. If she was always that smooth with magic, she was a hell of a lot more dangerous than she looked.

Maybe my dad was right about her.

Fantastic.

The door opened and a kid—okay, he looked a few years younger than me, maybe twenty-one—stepped into the room. Thin as the pages of a fashion magazine, he wore black head to toe: black hair in ragged edges around his pale face, black T-shirt over a black long-sleeved thermal, black fingerless gloves, black pants with dull silver buckles running down both legs to the black tips of his combat boots. He gave off a sort of goth mixed with reluctant rock star vibe.

The only shot of color on him was the shock of green from the large potted plant he carried.

"Ready, Mum?"

"I think so. Come on in." She waved at the other chair next to her. "Sit."

His boots muffled across the rug, as if there was very little weight behind each step. He folded down into the chair next to Maeve, graceful but elbow-y, a long-limbed marionette with too much string. He plunked the potted plant on the floor next to him. The plant was so tall, the leaves were level with his shoulders. I expected him to adopt that I-don't-give-a-damn slouch, but he sat on the edge of the chair like a man ready to pony up to a bet. He leaned over the coffee table and extended his left hand toward me.

"Shamus Flynn," he said. "Everyone calls me Shame. You're Beckstrom's daughter, aren't you?"

"Allie." Shaking his gloved hand made me wish I had my own gloves on to cover my markings.

Shamus smelled of cigarettes, booze, and hot cloves.

"Nice," he said, tipping my hand to catch the light before letting go. "Sorry your da was such a prick." He settled back like a man used to casually dodging a fist to the face. "But damn, he was powerful. Guess it gave him rights to be a prick, eh?"

"Not from my point of view."

"Grew a mind of your own?" he asked. "Bet that disappointed him."

"You have no idea."

He raised his eyebrows, once, quickly, and grinned. "Might be I like you, Beckstrom."

"You should probably hold off on that."

"Got yourself a boyfriend?"

"Yes."

"Jones? That bucket of ice water? Isn't that a surprise?" he said, like it wasn't a surprise at all. "Don't you think that's a surprise, Mum?"

"No," she said. End of conversation. "Allie, place the void stone on the table, please."

I so did not want to do that. I did it anyway. She was my teacher, and I apparently only had three days to learn a lifetime of magic.

Magic began filling me again, a warm, tingly rise from my feet upward.

"Are you comfortable with the level of magic in the room?"

I nodded.

"Good." She stood and moved behind the chair, pacing to the center of the room. "Come stand here." She pointed at a position about four feet in front of her.

I did, and to my relief, magic continued to fill me but did not try to break free of my control. I wondered if I could smuggle one of those stones out of here.

"Shamus, stand here, please." She pointed at the space beside us, effectively creating a human triangle on the ornate red and brown carpet. "Close enough to touch her if you need to."

"Don't I know? Not like I haven't done this." He picked up the plant and lugged it with him, muttering, "Stand there, Shamus. Don't bother the new girl, Shamus. Don't back-talk me when I'm teaching, Shamus."

Maeve raised her eyebrows. "Don't back-talk me even when I'm not teaching, Shamus," she said.

He set the plant down between himself and his mother. He was standing, I noted, close enough that he could touch me if he stretched his arm full length. He gave his mother a smile that I bet worked on the girls, but wasn't having any effect on her.

"So, Beckstrom," he said, not looking at me. "You ever done a face-to-face Proxy?"

I had, twice, in college. It was required that you understand just how much pain you could put someone through by making them pay your price for using magic. You had to cast a spell and watch your Proxy sweat, cry, and/or puke right in front of you.

Good times.

"Yes."

"Often?"

"No."

"Won't this be fun, then?" He slapped his hands together, the knit fingerless gloves softening the sound. "All right, Mum. Name the poison."

"Allie, I want you to cast Proxy to Shamus." She stood across from me, both hands at ease at her sides. The rest of her body language was alert, taut, like a watchful cat.

Shamus angled toward me. "Give me all you got, girl, an' don't be shy. I can take it. Twice as hard as Jones."

"I don't Proxy to Zayvion," I said as I mentally intoned a mantra—the jump rope jingle *Down by the river where the green grass grows . . .*

"No, he Grounds you. Says you're more than a sweet handful. Says he likes doing you that way."

Okay, now he was pissing me off. I had enough sense to suspect that was all a part of the test. Could I keep my mind on the job when someone was dicking around?

I traced the sharp, pointed glyph of the Proxy into the air in front of me. Even though I couldn't see it, I caught at where the bottom corner should be, reached out, and touched Shamus with it with no more force than necessary—see how controlled I was?—and pressed it into his skin while I held the shape of it, the intent of it, clear in my mind's eye.

Corporations hired a bevy of casters to do these sorts of spells, and were supposed to Offload their magic use to the legally accepted outlets like prisons and the regulated Proxy pits.

There were also people who made their living freelancing as full-time Proxies. Short, high-paying career if it didn't kill you. Some people were into that kind of pain and abuse.

Shamus looked like he might be one of those people.

His lips were parted and he held the tip of his tongue between his teeth. I hesitated, wondering if the Proxy had connected. It had been a long time since I'd done this. He nodded slightly, letting me know we were okay so far.

"Good," Maeve said. "Now access as much magic as you can from the well beneath the room. Cast the strongest Lightning spell that you can."

Oh, she had to be kidding. "I'll blow the walls out."

"I'd like to see you do it." She really did sound curious.

"No. It would kill him."

"I won't let that happen," Maeve said firmly. "Now cast Lightning."

She didn't look worried. I noted she had both hands held at ready to cast—probably Cancel or Hold or some other negating spell. Hells, maybe she had a pocket full of rocks she could throw at the spell if she had to.

Okay, fine.

Back to the jump rope song, back to clearing my mind. I traced a glyph in the air in front of me. A very different glyph this time. Lightning wasn't as pointed as Proxy. It flowed in a series of broken lines and arches.

Magic rolled in me, painful, sharp. But that was just the magic that I held inside of me. The other magic, the magic in the deep well beneath us, I had been very careful not to touch.

I took a short breath, braced for the torrent, and tapped into the well. Magic stormed through me like heat through a lightning rod, riding my bones, my blood, my flesh. I burned with it, shook with it, tasted the scorched earth of it thick and hot at the back of my throat. I held my focus, directed the magic pouring through the colored whorls down my arm to my fingertips, fingertips that glowed neon blue with an afterimage of soft rose, into the glyph I continued to trace. Magic spun from my fingers.

The corners of the room fell into shadow. Lights dimmed, went out. The spell raged against the room, burning and arching against the Blocks and Wards and glyphs worked into the walls, floor, ceiling. Wild electricity struck and was sucked into Shields and Wards that were deeper and more complex than I'd ever seen.

And still more lightning poured from my hands.

Shamus groaned, swayed, taking the full painful price of my using so much magic. He did not fall. That man was tougher than he looked. Magic exacted an equal pain for power. This strong of a spell should have knocked him unconscious.

Now I understood why there were no windows. Now I understood why Maeve had wanted to teach me here, have me access power here. This room was built like a vault. What came into it stayed in it.

Even my spell.

Magic poured through me, feeding the spell, growing it larger and larger. I think Maeve and I realized at the same time that while the spell was going to stay in the room, if it continued to grow, to feed on itself, there wouldn't be room for the rest of us in here.

There wouldn't be any room to breathe.

I was trapped, suffocating. My heart pounded. There was no room to breathe.

Hello, claustrophobia. I wondered when you'd get here.

I met Maeve's gaze. The walls shook, assailed by a thousand fists. The floorboards creaked, trembled.

We were in trouble.

"Close it," Maeve said, her voice strong, pitched loud enough to carry over the din of the spell.

"I don't know how." And that was true. I had never cast with so much magic behind a spell, had never really cast this spell, as there isn't that much use for Lightning in Hounding.

And yet I had cast it perfectly. As if I'd done it a thousand times before.

Child's play. It was only a whisper, but my dad's voice was the loudest thing in the room. Although I was pretty sure I was the only one who heard him.

It is easy, Allison, he breathed. *So easy. Inhale, exhale. Relax.*

Sweet hells. Of all the time for my dad to kick up and try to Influence me, he had to do it now. I fought to hold my focus, to not fall beneath his words.

I never had a chance.

He had full control of my mind, of my hands. I was pressed, not unconscious, but simply away from myself, my body. I felt daydreamy and drifty and didn't even see it as my father used my hand to trace a new spell.

End, he said. And my daydreams were filled with his memories of using that spell in hand-to-hand combat, canceling spells other magic users threw, canceling his own spells and changing them into new, wicked blades to throw at his enemies.

The air flashed hot, cold. The spell in the room extinguished. Lights crackled to life; the lingering scents of roses and apricot and ash filled the air.

My ears popped from the pressure, and I inhaled greedily as I came back to myself, like someone had been holding my head underwater.

Shamus fell to his knees next to the plant. His fingers

spread and sunk in the soil, his head bent, hair hiding his pale face, back heaving with each heavy breath. I was amazed he was still breathing.

He grunted and rocked back the rest of the way onto his heels, one hand still in the plant that now looked shriveled, dried, dead. Drops of sweat, blood, or tears made small *plick* sounds against his jeans.

"Are you okay?" I thought I could get it all out, but my voice was hoarse and I had to take a breath between each word.

"Allie," Maeve said softly. Or at least I think she was talking quietly. It could also be that my eardrums were blown.

Come to think of it, I wasn't feeling so great myself.

"Fuck it all," Shamus muttered, his words nasal and stuffy. He lifted his free hand to his face. I noted his hand was shaking as he wiped at his eyes and nose.

Maeve had not moved. "Allie, I need your attention right now. It is very important."

I didn't know why she wasn't worried about Shamus. He was her kid, after all, and that spell, my spell, had just kicked the holy hell out of him.

I looked up at her.

Maeve was a tower of authority, twice as tall as I'd last seen her, red hair flowing like a river of flame in a wind I could not feel. Her skin glowed so bright it was like she had swallowed the moon. Only her eyes, deep, earth-holding green, showed a speck of her humanity.

I had had this kind of vision before, had seen Zayvion covered in silver whorls and glyphs, his skin burning with blue-tipped black fire.

But if Zayvion had been night and the edge of magic and ebony heat, Maeve was the pale, cruel light of dawn.

"Come to me," she commanded.

"Hey." I exhaled, inhaled. "You told me you"—pause for breath again—"wouldn't do that." It probably wasn't Influence she was using right now anyway.

Still, I started toward her. Okay, four feet had never felt so much like four miles. I didn't so much hurt as feel very, very drained. I was empty and beyond tired.

Maeve reached out one impossibly long arm. Her cool white fingers tucked under the right side of my jaw—the side marked by magic. She tipped my face so she could look into my eyes.

And I mean *look*. Just like before. And just like before, my father skittered away somewhere in the back of my head, quiet as a rat.

She drew the index finger of her other hand across my forehead, and I sighed at the cool relief that brought me.

"How did you know End?"

"I don't know," I mumbled. "Think Dad knew it, maybe, used it, maybe?"

Okay, I wasn't thinking too well right now. Right now, all I wanted to do was sit on the floor and take a nap.

"Yes," she said. "He did. It is a dangerous spell, very old, rarely taught. I'd rather you not use it again without training."

She let go of my chin and took a step back. She looked normal again, her red and gray hair piled in a messy bun, her skin creamy and freckled, her eyes green. Just green.

"Sure," I said. "Sorry. It's my first day."

A sound halfway between a snort and a choked laugh rose from where Shamus sat.

"She's right, Mum." He tipped his face up. Black hair fell back, revealing the livid bruises across both eyes that were nearly swollen shut, and the bloody smear of red from under his nose and across his cheek.

"This is only her first day. Give the poor slacker a break." He laughed again, then rubbed his forehead. "I'm going to need a lot more to drink if I'm going to make it through her second day. So. You, Beckstrom, give a man a hand, eh?" He held his hand up toward me.

I walked over to him, my energy slowly coming back—whatever Maeve had done with my forehead had helped—and took his hand. I hefted back as he rolled up onto his feet. He rocked a little too far forward, putting his mouth close to my ear. "Holy fuck," he whispered. "No one throws that much power untrained. Impressed the shit outta Mum. Good for you."

He straightened, though he rocked a little precariously on his feet. "Call it a night?" he asked.

Maeve exhaled and seemed to let go of whatever it was that was bothering her.

She's afraid, my dad said. Smug.

Hells. Me too. I so needed a drink.

Maeve reached over and touched Shamus's face, studying the blood and bruises. She drew her finger across his forehead, and he sighed happily. The bruises around his eyes faded just a little. Maeve made a *tsk* sound. "Next time we'll have a Grounder here for you."

Shamus stiffened like she'd just told him she was going to dip him in fire.

"Not Terric," he said, a tinge of panic in his voice.

"No, no. Of course not Terric," she soothed. "Maybe Sunny. She works well with you."

Shamus relaxed.

"All right, then," Maeve said. "I think we can all call it a night. This wasn't exactly what I had planned for your first day, but we've done well enough. How are you feeling? Any headaches? Pains?"

I shook my head. I mean, I was still tired, but I felt more awake by the moment. "Shamus took the brunt of the spell." I hated watching someone else pay the price for a spell I used. And seeing Shamus take an ass-kicking just to prove to his mother that I didn't know what I was doing irritated me. "He did a good job."

Maeve's eyebrows shot up. "Of course he did. He's a Flynn. He knows his way around magic, not that you could tell by his manners. Or choice in clothing." She gave him a wholly disapproving motherly look. "Out now." She flicked her hand toward the door, and made it obvious she had released the Lock and Ward set there. "Allie, I want to see you tomorrow at ten. You too, Shamus." She marched out the door ahead of us.

"And Shamus, eat a decent meal. Then I don't care how drunk you get."

"You'd think I was a bloody child," he muttered beside me. "She never lets up," he whispered, loud enough his mom was sure to hear. "Personally, I think she needs to get laid."

Maeve lifted her hand over her shoulder and made a little waving motion that somehow also managed to level the threat of a particularly uncomfortable spell—something in the line of an embarrassing rash—at him.

"Love you too, Mum," he called after her as she walked through the adjoining, empty room out into the restaurant area.

He paused and touched my arm.

"What?"

He patted his pockets for a cigarette, pulled one out, and offered me the pack.

"No, thanks."

He nodded, lit up, and took a hard suck. "Balls, woman," he said, exhaling smoke with every word, "you pack a punch. Where did you learn to throw magic like that?"

"On-the-job training."

"Well, don't let my mum fool you. She was impressed."

"She didn't look impressed. She looked angry." The memory of her standing tall, pale, and burning above me flashed behind my eyes.

"Naw, not angry about what you did. Just pissed she was wrong about you."

"Oh?"

"She argued against you getting trained. 'Cause of what your da did to my da—not a lot of forgiveness in the Flynn blood. She said you were too old, too stubborn, too likely to be the sort of person your da was—a prick," he added, in case I'd forgotten what he thought of my dad.

"But Z-Jones—" he explained, "wouldn't give up on giving you a chance. He pushed hard for you, took it all the way to the top—and I mean the top. Wouldn't be surprised if he didn't have to pay something for that."

"Huh," I said rather ungracefully.

"Do you like him?" he asked.

"Who?"

"Zayvion."

I focused on Shamus, his body language—leaning against the wall like he was just being casual, but the smell of fatigue mixed with the cigarette smoke told me he was leaning there because keeping his feet wasn't going so well. Shamus was no slouch. He had Proxied a lot of pain. A hell of a lot of pain. And since I didn't know what he thought of Zayvion, I didn't know what answer would do Zayvion the least harm. Especially since I'd just found out Zay might have put himself in some sort of debt to get me training.

It was like the frickin' magic mafia around here. I didn't know whom to trust.

I went with the truth. What else?

"I like him. And that's none of your business."

Shamus pushed his hair away from his face and smiled. "Aren't you the sweetest? Now I see why he has it so bad for you. Tough on the outside and sweet in the middle. Well." He shoved off of the wall. "Good on you both, and I mean that with all my cheating little black heart. It's about time Mr. Somber had some fun in his duty-unto-death life. And watching my mom eat crow hasn't been half bad either. As a matter of fact, for that alone, I'll buy you a drink." He pushed away from the wall, found an ashtray, and ground out his cigarette.

"What's your pleasure?"

"I don't care," I said. "Anything."

He walked through the door, and I followed him.

I felt the tingle of a Mute spell slide over my skin as I passed through the doorway.

The noise of people talking came on suddenly. The entire room was full now, every table occupied with people eating, drinking, talking. The light outside the windows was diving into evening. I'd been back there with Maeve and Shamus for hours. No wonder I was so tired and hungry.

"Pick it up, Beckstrom," Shamus said.

I did so, and followed as he wove his way between tables. He was aiming at the lunch counter, although in the dim light I didn't see any available seats there either. Just suits, fancy dresses, T-shirts, and jeans. A mix of Northwest just-off-work and out-for-the-evening. Shamus made his way through the noise and down the length of the counter, then turned left, where eight or so stools held the end of the lunch area.

Two of those seats were free. Shamus slid down into one and was already yelling over the loud conversations for the attention of one of the girls behind the counter. The stool next to him, toward the wall, was open. And in the seat next to that was Zayvion.

He was partly turned, his elbow resting next to a half-empty glass of beer on the countertop, his back toward me.

Being six feet tall gives me some advantage. One is I could look around Zayvion and see whom he was talking to.

A woman, about my age, brown hair cut in straight bangs across her forehead and pulled back in a single long braid. Her face reminded me of a movie star's—wide, catlike eyes, high cheekbones, and lips most women would mortgage the house for. She had on a black tank top, over which she had thrown a long-sleeved plaid flannel shirt, black jeans, and boots. No makeup—and she didn't need it.

She looked over Zayvion's shoulder at me, and her eyes were sapphire in sunlight.

"Allie?" Zayvion said—had been saying, I realized. I hadn't heard him over the din. Well, that and I was still thinking a little slow.

"Sorry." I looked over at him. "Kind of loud in here."

His Zen was on full strength, making his face a dark, unreadable mask. But his gaze held some worry as he searched my face.

I smiled to let him know I was okay.

"This is Chase Warren," he said.

I stepped around Zayvion enough to shake her hand. Calluses on the girl. Strength. She obviously worked for a living.

"Nice to meet you," I said.

"So, you're *the* Allie Beckstrom," she said. "Zay's said a lot about you." She gave me the oh-so-female up-down appraisal that made me want to grind my teeth. Really, I didn't care what she thought about me, my faded jeans, or my sweaty, messy hair. And I smiled at her to let her know it.

"That's nice," I said to cut this little convo short. I took the only seat between Zayvion and Shamus, and leaned both elbows on the bar.

Shamus had finally managed to snag the attention of one of the girls behind the counter and she stood there, a small pad of paper in her hand.

"What are you buying me, Shame?" I asked.

"Beer. Wait. Bet you're a wine girl."

"Beer's fine," I said, even though I didn't like beer much, "dark." Then to the waitress: "Could I get a glass of water, burger, and fries, please?"

She nodded and headed off.

"Nice shiner," Zayvion said to Shamus. "How did she do?"

Shamus leaned back so they could talk behind my back.

"She's sitting right here, you know," I said.

"Fucking amazing. I can't believe the amount of power she pulled on—and you were right—she took it in her body, right through it. Got my mum's panties in a knot, seeing all that. Might even make your bullshit about you two being Soul Complements a little easier for the Authority to swallow."

Zayvion made a little *huh* sound, then took a drink of his beer, hiding his smile. He was exceedingly pleased. It rolled off him in waves.

"Did your mother actually say she was impressed?" Chase, who had leaned forward so she could see around Zayvion, asked. I caught a whiff of her vanilla perfume.

"As much as."

"That's a no, then." Chase gave me a hard, flat look, and I wondered what the hell I'd done to piss her off.

Maybe it was just hate at first sight. Lucky me. 'Cause that's what I needed—another person who didn't like me.

I turned away from her. "What do you mean 'bullshit about Complements'? We are, aren't we?"

"Not without Authority sanctioning you're not," Chase said.

This time I looked at Zayvion. "I thought you said we were."

Shamus laughed. "Oh, sure. If I had a dollar for every

time a man used that line to get a woman in bed, I'd be richer than your daddy—wait. Richer than you, Beckstrom."

"Shame," Zay said, "you talk too much." He leaned in toward me and the hops smell of beer mixed with his pine cologne. "It isn't easy to quantify. Soul Complements are rare. So rare it is hard to prove."

"But there is a way to tell. Some kind of test?"

"Yes. There is a way."

"Let me guess, it's dangerous?"

"Yes."

Great.

"And if we don't do it?"

Zay pressed his lips together. I noted Chase, behind him, suddenly stiffened. "That's a choice we make. It's a practical choice. A safe choice. It's the choice people who are afraid to risk it all take."

Chase swore. She dug money out of her pocket and threw it on the countertop next to her empty glass. Her pale cheeks were washed in red.

"But?" I asked.

"Safe doesn't get you anywhere in life," he said.

Chase, now standing, tipped her head up and groaned loudly. "Give it a damn rest."

"Problem?" Zayvion asked her while still looking at me.

Chase, behind him, looked back down. The smile she wore was not pretty—no easy feat with a face like hers.

"With you?" she said. "Plenty."

"Will you two shut the hell up?" Shamus said. "This is supposed to be the beginning of a beautiful friendship. Hot new girlfriend meets hot ex-girlfriend, both get along like twins separated at birth, there's probably at least one drunken three-way, and voilà, happy all around."

"Girlfriend?" I said before I could bite back my surprise.

"Shame," Zayvion warned.

Shamus laughed. "Priceless. You didn't tell her? You are such an idiot."

Zayvion gave me a pleading look while Chase scowled death at Shamus. I leaned back, and Shamus swiveled his stool completely around so that both his elbows were on the counter and his back leaned against it. He flashed Chase an innocent smile and held up his middle finger like he'd just discovered he had one.

"Allie," Zayvion started.

"I just want my burger and beer," I said. It came out calm, considering the thoughts spinning through my head. Normally I would be pissed off that Zayvion had put me in this kind of social situation without telling me he used to date her. If I'd known they were lovers, I would have handled this totally differently.

Or maybe I wouldn't have. In the long run, I didn't think it mattered.

See? I can be practical about these kinds of things. I mean, I knew he hadn't been saving himself for me all his life.

And besides, he and I were together now, even though he didn't look quite as sure as I was about that. His Zen slipped and he looked an awful lot like a man who realized he might have made a big mistake.

Chase leaned full body against Zayvion's back, wrapping her hands up under his arms so she could splay her palms over his chest.

He tensed, and it wasn't love in his eyes. Not quite anger either. Maybe tolerance. Maybe denial. It got me thinking about those scars he said he had on his heart. It got me thinking maybe she had put them there.

Chase tipped her head down to Zay's face, her perfect lips so close she wouldn't have to move an inch to lick him. "Fuck you, Zay." I didn't actually hear her words over the noise in the room, but I was plenty close enough to read her lips.

Shamus, who must also be pretty good at lip reading, laughed again.

"Good night, Chase." Zayvion did not move, but it was like he suddenly drew a wall of ice between himself and her.

She tipped her head and rested her chin on his shoulder. She smiled at me, and for the life of me I could not figure out what kind of game she was playing.

Have I mentioned I have always sucked at all the bitchy backstabbing games women play? Consider it mentioned.

"Enjoy," she said.

I nodded. "I will." Simple. Honest.

I guess that wasn't what she was hoping for. She stood, turned off her smile, and strode out the door on this side of the building.

"That. Was. Awesome," Shamus declared.

Zayvion rubbed the back of his neck. "You," he said, spearing Shamus with a look, "talk too much."

Shamus chuckled. "And you are too easy to rile up, but you'll forgive me anyway."

"No," Zayvion said, "I won't."

From the tone of his voice, it was clear he liked Shamus. Maybe the way a person likes paying their taxes, or hanging out with an annoying little brother.

Zayvion put his hand on my upper arm. Since I had planted my elbow on the counter and was cupping my chin in my hand, willing the waitress to bring me my burger, I leaned my head sideways to look at him.

"What?" I asked.

"I feel like an explanation is in order."

My willing must have worked. The waitress appeared with two plates on her arm and glasses in her hand. Sweet heaven, it was about time.

She set the burger in front of me, and the beer and water, then deposited a plate of what looked like chicken, mashed potatoes, gravy, and corn in front of Shamus.

The overpowering aroma of the food reached my nose, and my stomach cramped in hunger. Using magic made me hungry. And Shamus wasn't kidding, I'd thrown a hell of a lot of magic around a few minutes ago. The nice thing? Whatever his mom had done when she brushed my forehead had totally wiped out my Disbursement headache.

"Go ahead." I got both my hands around my burger and bit into it.

"I didn't know Chase was going to be here tonight."

"Mmm-hmm." I took a swig of beer to wash down the burger, and tore into the fries.

"She and I . . . we were . . . we did date. Well, not date, but we had . . ."

"Sex," Shamus offered helpfully. "You and Chase had

hot, screaming sex. A lot," he added, with a serious nod to me.

I stopped chewing. I didn't know if I should tell him to shut up or just laugh. He was shameless.

"Shame," Zayvion said in a voice that wasn't even close to Zen.

"Sex everywhere, all the time," he continued, with a wicked glint in his eyes. I noticed he had pushed his plate away and dusted off his hands, as if in preparation for a fight. "One time during training, I actually had to carry bags of ice around and lob them at the two of them to keep them from spontaneously fucking."

Zayvion was up out of his chair so fast, the only thing I had time to do was duck. Zay towered over me, caught Shamus by the shirt, and had him in a headlock before he could squirm away.

"Tell Allie you apologize for your mouth and your manners," Zayvion said.

Shamus made a horrible choking sound.

"Hey, hey," I said, figuring I better break up this little testosterone hug before someone got hurt. Then I realized Shame wasn't choking, he was howling with laughter.

"Tell her. Tell her you are incapable of telling the truth, because you are an immoral ass." Zayvion calmly squeezed just a little harder.

"Can't . . . breathe," Shamus wheezed.

Zayvion squeezed one last time, then released him. "Remind me why I keep you around?" He glowered.

Shamus tugged on his shirt to straighten it, and brushed his hair back down over his eyes, covering the bruises, then raked it back to one side.

"My good looks, quick wit, and, best of all, my connections," he said. "Need I say more?"

"No," Zayvion said. "You need say less. Much, much less."

They both settled into their seats again.

"Well, see, I may not have morals, but I do have a conscience." Shamus pulled his plate back in place and took a bite of mashed potatoes. "And I know when to speak my mind. Not at all like you, Jones. Silent. Shifty. Temperamental. Sullen. Morbid."

"How long have you two known each other?" I asked.

Zayvion shook his head. "Exactly one hour too long."

Shamus made a rude noise. "You said that three hours ago."

Zayvion lifted his beer and flashed me a quick smile before taking a drink. "Several years," he said. "Long, painful years."

"Grew up together," Shamus added around a mouthful of chicken.

I took a drink of my beer. During the hubbub I'd managed to get through half my burger and made a serious dent in the pile of fries. The food did a decent job of clearing my head and settling my mood.

I was feeling a lot better. "Well, then, I'm sorry for you both."

Shamus coughed and laughed, and Zayvion's faint smile spread out into a grin. He looked good when he smiled. Looked like someone should be kissing him for it.

I guess some of my thoughts showed in my expression. Zayvion raised one eyebrow and pushed my knee with his knee, swiveling my stool toward him. I was now mostly facing him.

"How was class?" And even though he was relaxed, a hint of a smile still playing on his lips, he spoke a little more quietly, privately, and somehow that made it easy to hear him, only him, over all the other voices and people in the room.

He was concerned about me.

How sweet was that?

"I learned a lot. There's um, still some question about my dad."

He nodded. "She say anything about that?"

"She wants someone else to look into it. I think Jingo Jingo?"

Zay's smile faded away.

"What? Is that bad?"

"No. No, not bad. He's very good at what he does."

"He's a freak is what he is." Shamus finished off his beer and tapped the counter for a refill.

"Shame," Zayvion said.

"Sure, you go ahead and deny it. You know it's true."

"What does he do?" I asked.

"It's not what he does."

Shamus snorted, and Zayvion gave him a silencing look, then leaned in a little closer to me so he could lower his voice.

"Death magic. He is Liddy's second, and deals hands-on with the dead. It makes sense Maeve wants him to see . . . what your father may have done." He pulled back, his gaze searching my face for understanding.

And I was absolutely positive he didn't find a single stitch of it.

"What the hell?" I asked. At his look, I lowered my voice and leaned closer to him. "Death magic? I'm not letting anyone use death magic on me. Besides, it's illegal."

"Just because the law doesn't know how to use something doesn't make it illegal."

Wow. There was a concept I didn't want to think about.

"Isn't that the magic Frank used on me, on the kidnapped girls in the warehouse?" I couldn't remember much of what happened there, but I knew my dad's corpse had been there, that was where he had possessed me, and that was where the girls had been tied down and killed.

"He abused it, twisted it. Used more than just death magic. He used dark magic. Forbidden. Jingo Jingo is one of the Authority. Sworn to use magic in the ancient ways."

"Frank wasn't part of the Authority?"

"He was. A faction. Part of the splitting off, the breaking that has been going on. But he wasn't even near the same level of ability or responsibility as Jingo Jingo."

"Is that your comforting speech? Because I am not feeling the comfort," I said.

Zay rested his palm, warm and heavy, on my thigh.

"Jingo is the best person to deal with this. I'll be there with you, if you want."

I suddenly wanted that very much. "I'd like that." I slipped my fingers between his.

Two glasses of beer descended slowly between us, held

with the tips of fingers wrapped to the second knuckle in black fingerless gloves.

Shamus, standing next to us, held drinks in both outstretched hands. "More drinking, less flirting," he said. "Or so help me God, I'll throw ice at you."

Zayvion gave Shamus a withering glare. "You just don't know when to keep your mouth shut, do you?"

"Nope," he said cheerfully. "A toast."

I took one of the beers, and Zayvion leaned back, let go of my hand, and took the other beer.

"To what?" Zay asked.

"To the only thing worth drinking to. Love."

"That's not what you said last week," Zayvion said. "Last week you were toasting magnificent breasts, if I remember correctly."

Shamus grinned. "Also lovely, but I've matured since then. To love." He lifted his own glass and took a long drink.

Zay looked over at me. "To love," he said quietly.

"To love," I said. And joy, I also blushed like mad, my face washed with heat from that look in Zayvion's eyes.

"You," I said to Shamus, to have an excuse to look away from the raw intensity of Zayvion's gaze, "are a trouble maker.,

"Aren't we all?"

"No," Zayvion said. "Some of us are trouble enders."

Shamus chuckled. "Like hell."

And he toasted us again, drained his glass, then patted Zayvion on the shoulder. "My friend. Be well. I need a smoke."

"That's gonna kill you someday," Zayvion said into the rim of his beer.

Shamus nodded. "I could only be so lucky." Then to me: "Tomorrow, love. Ten o'clock. Don't be late. The mum has the temper of a demon with a diaper rash."

He lifted a hand in farewell and walked across the room, weaving his way between tables, until I couldn't see him anymore.

Chapter Eight

I finished my burger and fries, but not my beer. Zayvion sat with me, pulling his Zen moves, patient, silent.

I finally pushed my plate away. "Mind if I get a ride home?"

"I was hoping you'd ask." He stood and offered me his hand.

Like I said, old-fashioned.

I took it as I stood, then we walked out through the door nearest us, which opened onto the wooden porch that paralleled the river. The cool, dark scents of moving water filled my nose and lungs. Night had settled into the cracks of day, and only the yellow lanterns lining the old inn held it back.

There was no one in the parking lot. We walked down the porch steps and out into the clear night—wonder of wonders, it was not raining. I looked up at clouds broken by patches of stars.

Nice.

"You and Chase used to date?" I asked as we made our way across the parking lot.

"No. But we were lovers."

Okay, even though I liked his honesty and had said I was adult enough to deal with the fact he'd had other relationships, I cringed a little. Chase was gorgeous, and they'd obviously known each other for a lot longer than Zay and I. And it was highly likely she didn't get involved with weird Necromorph things, lose bits of her memory, or carry a dead relative around in her head.

Speaking of which, I hadn't felt my dad since I'd been sitting with Shamus and Zayvion.

"We trained together," Zay said.

"For?"

"Our jobs. The Authority. She's a Closer too."

"Is that what I'm training to be?"

"I don't know. None of us know. When you are accepted into the Authority, you are tested to see what your natural abilities are and which branch of magic they can best be used with."

"Like the test Maeve gave me in there?"

"No. Your real test will be done with several members of the Authority in attendance. Three days from now. Maeve was just gauging what you already know, and what preparation your testers will need so you don't harm yourself or others during it."

"And figuring that out takes more than one day?"

Here he smiled a small smile. "Not generally."

Yeah, well, that made sense. I couldn't imagine Maeve really wanted me to blow the walls out of her room again. No wonder Shamus ducked out early. If he was going to stand as my Proxy again tomorrow, he'd need the sleep.

No, I wouldn't let him do it. I could Proxy my own magic use, and Maeve would just have to deal with that.

"So you and Chase trained together," I pressed, bracing myself for the rest of the story.

He nodded. "The Authority is insular, private—it has to be to survive. And the organization is very, very careful about the people it allows in. Only a few people a year are even tested for it, and most don't make it. During most of my . . . training . . ."

I noted his pause, but didn't ask about it.

". . . I was alone. Sometimes Shamus and I were allowed to train with the same teacher, but Shamus isn't a Closer. When Chase came to the Authority, and when she was approved to train, she was taught by my teacher, Victor."

"Have I met him?"

"Not while I've known you. Maybe before then, although with how much your father kept you in the dark about this, I'd say it's doubtful. There are five disciplines of magic the Authority teaches: Life, Death, Faith, Blood, and Flux. Each discipline has its strengths, its abilities. Life is the oldest way of magic. There are some who say it is the only way of magic, and all other branches are wrong to be practiced separate of it and each other. When the Order of the Aegis first began thousands of years ago, it was only Life magic that was known, understood, and practiced. All magic as one."

We reached the car and he unlocked the door for me.

"But magic is one thing," I said. "There aren't different kinds of magic underground."

He nodded. "True. But there are different ways to tap into that magic, different ways to cast spells, different approaches to make magic do what you want it to do."

"Like that chanting thing you did."

"Exactly. Death magic is in many ways the balance, the opposite of Life magic. It is just as old, but its ways were once practiced only in secret. Those were dark days before Death magic was legitimized, recognized, and taught so that users among the Authority could cast it with some manner of safety."

I opened the door and got in while he walked around the car and slid into the driver's side.

"Over the years, hundreds of years, Blood magic and Faith magic have been defined and practiced. With your father's integration between magic and technology, the fifth magic, Flux, has been recognized and practiced."

"Which magic is the strongest?"

Zayvion shrugged. "Ask a hundred people and you'd get a hundred answers."

"Okay, let me put it this way: who's running the show? Who is the boss of the Authority and which magic do they practice?"

"Currently?"

"Sweet hells," I said. "Does it change hands that often?"

"More often than you'd think. For the last twenty years and currently, it is Sedra. She practices Life magic. The first."

Having nothing to relate that to, I decided that sounded

good. The main magic, the original magic, was the magic used by the one woman calling the shots. I wondered if I'd ever meet her.

"Before that it was Mikhail. He practiced Death magic."

"And Mikhail's dead?" I asked.

He gave me a strange look. "Yes."

I looked over at him. "My dad told me."

"When?"

"Recently. In a dream, actually."

Zay started the engine. "Maybe I should take you to Jingo Jingo now."

I yawned. "Don't. I have dinner with Violet at eight. So, do you and Chase and Shamus report to Victor?"

Zay started the engine. "Shamus isn't a Closer."

"Blood magic like his mom?"

"No." He glanced over at me. "Shamus works Death magic. He reports to Jingo Jingo."

"Whom he doesn't like," I dot-to-dotted.

Zayvion nodded. "Shame isn't shy about his opinions. But we don't get to choose our teachers. We just have to do our job."

I leaned my head back into the headrest of the seat and watched the streetlamps go by. We were driving parallel to the river. There were few businesses here, which made it feel farther away from civilization than it really was.

I don't know if it was the beer or the testing, but I was suddenly very tired. I closed my eyes and half-drifted until Zayvion parked.

We were in the parking lot behind my apartment. I must have fallen asleep for a few minutes.

"Want me to come up?" he asked.

I rubbed at my eyes and tucked my hair back behind my ears. "No. I'm just going to take a nap before I see Violet." I opened the car door. Cool air mixed with the warmth from the heater. I paused, one boot on the pavement. "Do you still love her?"

He turned in his seat, leaning his head against the window of his door. "Chase? What we had was good. It was strong. But it wasn't love. I know that now. I think she knew it even then."

That was not exactly a straight answer.

"Were you the one who called it off?"

He tried to smile, didn't make it, and settled for that Zen bit. "She left me for someone else. A man named Greyson. She thought he was her Complement. Maybe even Soul Complement."

"I thought you said that was rare."

"So is lightning striking in the same place twice. Yet it happens."

"Are they still together?"

"He was killed three months ago," he said. "Jingo Jingo found him dead just after your father was killed."

No wonder Chase was pissed at me. Three months isn't long enough to grieve, isn't long enough to recover. At least it wasn't for me.

"I'm sorry." And though I probably should have, I just didn't have it in me at the moment to ask him how he had died.

"Good night, Zay."

"Good night. See you around nine o'clock tomorrow morning?"

"For?"

"Coffee before I take you back to Maeve's?"

Right. Maeve's. I had class tomorrow. Wow, I was so totally out of the swing of morning living. I'd been Hounding jobs, mostly at night, for long enough that nine in the morning sounded obscenely early.

"Sure," I said. "That would be nice."

I shut the door and strolled to the back entry of the building. Zayvion started the engine, but didn't drive off until I had opened the door, waved, then stepped into the building.

I made my way to the stairs and couldn't help but shake my head at the bottom. Why in the world had I decided a walk-up was the kind of place to live in?

Maybe because even the sound of an elevator door opening, that rigor-sweet bell, was enough to make my palms sweat. Claustrophobia was a bitch, but I guess it meant I got my walking in every day.

I headed up the stairs, taking my time to listen to each

floor of the building. I caught the drone of a television, music, laughter, an argument, a baby crying, one sweet tenor raised in an operatic chorus, all muffled by the walls and doors of apartment living.

Then I was on my floor and it was silent, which wasn't that unusual. My neighbors and I did little more than nod hello when we ran into one another. Most of the time we kept to ourselves, and I liked it that way.

Out of habit, I paused at my door, pressed my fingers against it, leaned in, and listened. There was movement in there. I figured it was Nola.

I unlocked the door and it opened—which meant she hadn't set the chains.

I stepped in and shut the door behind me, turning the locks and setting the chains. It sounded like she was in my bathroom or bedroom. Probably hanging more plants.

"Hey," I called out. "I'm home. You forgot to set the chain on the door."

It was the kitchen that tipped me off. One, nothing was cooking, baking, and not even the smell of brewed coffee touched the air. Whenever Nola was in a house, there was always the comforting smell of food present.

Two, every cupboard in my line of vision was open.

Three, every coffee cup had been removed from my shelves and was now stacked, one on top of the other, on the stove.

What the hell?

I recited a mantra, set the Disbursement—more aches—and traced the beginning of a Shield spell. Maybe the smart thing would be to call 911. Tell them a cup-stacking intruder was in my home. Of course, since I had just yelled that I was here, maybe the smartest thing was to leave the apartment and come back when the police showed up.

Decisions, decisions.

Without drawing magic into my sense of smell, I inhaled, breathing in the scents of the room.

It smelled like my apartment, except there was a heavy odor of wet dirt, stone, and moss, like rain on a hot summer sidewalk. Maybe from all the plants Nola had put around the place. That would explain the dirt smell anyway. But hot stone wasn't anything I could place.

Screw it. I did not want to get jumped tonight. Time to go find a phone. I put my hand on the chain, quietly slid it loose. I was just turning the lock when someone walked into the living room.

Okay, not someone. Something.

I gasped, which was better than the yell I felt like belting out, but loud enough in the silent room that the thing turned its wide stone head toward me.

Big as a Saint Bernard, I recognized the gargoyle immediately. It was the one I'd accidentally broken, or as was now obvious, set free outside the restaurant the other night. The carved collar still circled its neck and three stone links of the chain hung free there.

It tipped its head to the side, as if working to see me better, and then, I swear this is true, it smiled, pushed up on its hind doglike legs, and waddled over to me, wide stone wings spread for balance.

I pressed up against the door and poured magic into the Shield spell I'd started.

The gargoyle stopped, tipped its head the other way, then lowered onto all fours, moving much more smoothly and slowly over to me. It sniffed its way down the hall, up to the edge of the spell I had cast. Then it stuck its snout into my spell and past my spell—pushed right through the Shield like it wasn't even there. Impossible.

Yep. As impossible as a living, breathing gargoyle sniffing me in the middle of my apartment.

It snuffled at my boots, then my jeans, and finally touched its flat stone snout against my outstretched hand.

I had expected it to be cold, but instead its nose was warm, and so was the air that blew out from its nostrils and mouth. I let the Shield spell drop, because, seriously, why pour magic into a spell that wasn't doing a damn bit of good?

The gargoyle made a glasslike clacking sound, like someone stirring a bag of marbles. It smiled again, revealing all three dozen of its teeth. Yes, I counted.

He—I decided it looked more he than she—blinked his big round eyes and twitched his wings.

I got the overwhelming impression he was waiting for me to do something.

"If you want me to cast magic for your entertainment, you are going to be sorely disappointed."

He dipped his head down and rubbed his face under my hand.

Like a dog who wanted to be scratched behind the ears.

"You have got to be kidding me." I rubbed at his head—stone, not as smooth as marble, but soft and warm, like heated tile. His wings spread and folded neatly down his back. He made the marbles-in-a-bag clatter sound again.

I stopped rubbing his head. He stood up on his hind legs and waddled back into my apartment.

"Are you a joke?" I asked as I carefully followed behind him. "Is someone here? Who's making you do this?" Did they make remote-control gargoyles?

I mean, Zayvion had told me the gargoyles were just statues. Carved by a master Hand, infused with a small amount of magic, but just statues.

Currently, the statue was pulling the seat cushion off my couch and balancing it on his head.

"Hello?" I called out. "Anyone here?"

The gargoyle held the cushion on his head with one hand and called out too, a sound somewhere between that of a soft vacuum cleaner and a muted pipe organ.

"Not you," I said. "I know you're here."

He clacked, which I decided was his happy sound, and got busy trying to balance an additional cushion on his head.

"If you ruin those, you'll have to pay for them."

A cool breeze whisked down the hall from my bedroom.

It was a small apartment. Other than the kitchen and living room, the only other places for someone to hide were the bathroom and bedroom. Both of which had windows. One of which, the bedroom, wasn't painted closed and was large enough for a person to crawl through.

I started down the hall.

The gargoyle clattered behind me.

"You stay here."

He tipped his head and lost both pillows. He took a step toward me, on all fours this time, silent.

"Stay."

He held still, waiting for me to turn, then took another step. Okay, fine. It was crazy to think he would understand me and do what he was told. He wasn't a dog. He was a statue, for cripes' sake.

The door to the bathroom was open. I looked in. Nothing.

The door to my bedroom was also open, and I could feel the cold night air stronger here.

I turned on the light and walked into the room. The window was open, my curtains fluttering in the breeze. My bed was unmade, but I think I'd left it that way this morning. I looked around the bed, under the bed. I even looked in the closet. No one else was there.

Meanwhile the gargoyle had decided it was some sort of game. He followed behind me, mimicking everything I did. He looked out the window, looked under the bed, even looked in the closet. Having human hands meant doors were not a problem for him.

Yes, that worried me.

"Did you open the windows?" I asked.

He stopped in front of me, crouched, wings spread, round eyes waiting for me to do something. Like cast magic. He stretched his neck out a little more, offering an ear for scratching.

"This?" I pointed at the open window.

He looked at it. Clattered at it, then waddled on two legs over to the window. He stuck his head and shoulders out the window, his wings tight against his back so he could fit his barrel chest in the space. His face was inked by the blue of night, only the barest brush of yellow from the light in my room outlining his comical features. He could crawl out through that space, I realized. Just the way he had probably crawled in through it. All on his own.

Even though I was on the third floor.

Holy shit.

He blinked his big round eyes and crooned into the night—the strange vacuum cleaner pipe organ in B flat. Pigeons startled and flew off the roof. The muscles down his back bunched as if he too wanted to take wing. I wondered, as he hung there, more out the window than in, if his wings were big enough and strong enough that he could fly, or if he'd drop like a rock.

He's just a statue, I told myself. *Statues can't fly.*

He pulled his head back in the window, and used those very human hands to pull the window shut, careful not to catch the curtain. Then he turned and made himself busy with the things on top of my dresser.

Statues can't fly, can't walk, can't make noise, and can't stack loose change on people's dresser tops.

And statues did not dig through your underwear drawer.

"Stop it." I yanked one of my favorite camisoles off his head before he pulled it the rest of the way over his snout and stretched it out. "Out." I pointed to the open door. He looked at the door, clacked. Then he went down on all fours and trotted out of the room.

Sweet hells. What was I supposed to do with this thing?

Technically, he was not my property. I hadn't stolen him or anything, but I had sort of broken him and set him free. I wondered if the restaurant had a you-break-it-you-have-a-new-roommate policy.

The water in the bathroom sink turned on and off. I strolled down the hall and leaned in to watch him.

He turned the water on, watched it drain down the sink, turned it off. The pipe gurgled. He clacked at it, and turned the water on again. Turned it off. Pipes gurgled. He clacked at the pipes and turned the water back on, childlike and content.

I should call the restaurant. Tell them their statue was messing around with my plumbing.

Sweet hells. I pressed my fingers against my eyes. They'd have me committed.

What I needed was coffee. Then I'd be able to think.

"Don't break anything," I said to Pet Rock Extreme.

In the kitchen, I found the note Nola had left for me on the coffeepot.

It said she and Stotts were working on the Cody case and not to wait up for her. The little smiley face made me think it was more than just a business appointment.

Well, good for her. Maybe one of us could have a normal date with a normal person and not have to come home to overzealous architecture messing up the place.

I started the coffee, putting a little extra grounds in, because I had a feeling I was going to need it. While the coffee brewed, I put the stacked coffee cups back in the cupboard, closed all the doors, and made myself busy cleaning.

When the coffee was done and the already clean kitchen even cleaner, I poured myself a cup and took it out into the living room.

The gargoyle was there, standing very still in the corner of the room. He had piled the curtains and vines on his head. They were still attached to the curtain rods, so it just looked like he'd stepped into a waterfall of fabric. I guess it looked a little like the waterfall stuff at the restaurant, though he had been crouched beneath a bush when I found him. Who knew? Maybe gargoyles liked being half hidden by falling water.

Or cheap curtains.

I picked the cushions off the floor and put them back on the couch. Then sat down.

"What am I going to do with you?" I asked. "Do you have a name? Fido? Rock? Quasimodo? Stone?"

He tipped his head and cooed.

"You like that? Stone?"

He clacked, walked toward me, the curtains stretching out behind him, over his thick shoulders, catching on the arc of his wings, then down his broad back and haunches, flowing away to pool against the wall. He stopped next to the couch, sniffed at me again, then lowered himself at my feet like a huge coffee table. He rested his head on his crossed arms and stared, unblinkingly, straight ahead.

He didn't close his eyes, and he didn't move. I put the toe of my boot against his side, and he didn't seem to mind.

I drank coffee, while the gargoyle sat there like a gargoyle.

Gargoyles are not real. If I remembered the stories right, gargoyles were alive at night, and sunlight turned them back to stone every day.

Well, Stone was already made out of rock. I didn't know how much more stone he could get. Maybe the sun made it so he couldn't move. Put him to sleep or something.

I'd only ever seen Stone at night, at the restaurant and now. Maybe he lost all his magical locomotion once dawn rolled around. Maybe that's why the restaurant had him chained down in the first place; otherwise he would have wandered off and messed with their sprinklers or something.

And if he did turn into a statue—an unmoving statue—in the morning, it might be easier to get him back out to the restaurant that way.

Except they were going to think I stole him.

Hells, I had money. I had my dad's whole company. I could buy the statue from them. Tell them it was a misunderstanding and throw enough money at them until they saw it my way. I'd seen my father use that tactic more than once.

Speaking of which, I needed to call Violet about our dinner plans.

I stepped over Stone, who watched me cross the room but did not follow.

I picked up the phone—a landline and therefore less inclined to die on me—and dialed Violet.

"Beckstrom residence," a man, Kevin, said.

"Hi, Kevin. This is Allie. Is Violet available?"

"Let me check. Just a second." He put me on hold and I got the soft strains of one of Bach's symphonies. My dad had a thing for Bach, and it sounded like Violet didn't mind keeping it on the system.

"Hi, Allie. How are you?"

It still surprised me how young she sounded. It shouldn't surprise me, since she was younger than me by a couple years, but I still couldn't understand why she would like my father. And she obviously liked him enough to get pregnant.

My dad, who had been silent since I'd sat with Zayvion at the bar, stirred in my mind, and I did the mental equivalent of shoving my fingers in my ears and humming while I worked very hard not to think about Violet's pregnancy.

"I'm fine, thanks," I said before the pause became too long. "Yourself?"

She sighed. "Tired, which is to be expected, I guess, with how . . ."

Please don't say pregnant, *please don't say* pregnant, I la-la-la'd.

". . . things have been going," she said. "But well."

"Good. Say, listen, I know we were going to have dinner tonight, but I'm beat. Would you mind if we push it out an hour and maybe just make it coffee and dessert?"

"Sure. Do you just want to come over here?"

My dad's condo? "I'd rather not."

"Do you want me to come over there?" she asked.

My heartbeat elevated and it wasn't me doing it. The sound of Violet's voice was agitating my dad. He'd pushed me pretty hard back at Maeve's. I wasn't up to fighting him again so soon. And I didn't know what he would do if he got control of my body, of my voice.

Stone stood and padded over to me. He growled like gravel being crushed. His head tipped up, and those round eyes were staring at me like I might be something worth eating.

Hells.

I pushed on the fluttering behind my eyes, trying to get my dad to settle down. Stone's ears flattened and he showed me some teeth.

My dad went still and Stone's ears pricked back up, but his fangs were still showing.

"Uh, no," I said. "Place is a mess. How about we just meet somewhere close to you? Maybe Tchaikovsky Coffeehouse?"

"Perfect. I've been craving chocolate. See you there in a couple hours."

"Okay. Bye." I couldn't get off the phone fast enough. "Easy, boy," I said to Stone. "It's just me."

He inhaled, a long, chest-filling draw of air, as if he were scenting me. Or scenting something in me. Like my father. Wouldn't that be great? A gargoyle who could sense the undead.

Well, since he wasn't exactly all alive himself, maybe that made some sense. He blew the air out through his nose, then tipped his head to the side and raised his pointed bat-like ears and pointed batlike wings. No more teeth. He looked happy again.

Crap. "Remind me to never piss you off, big guy. You ready to leave?" I walked into the bedroom and he followed like a big stone puppy behind me.

"Ready to go? Wanna leave?" I opened the window and pointed at it. "There you go. This is the way out. All those buildings out there. Or, if you don't like buildings, you can head to Forest Park. That place is so big, they'd never find you in there. Just think of it: you could start up some big-foot sightings."

He trotted over, quiet for something that weighed enough to make my floorboards creak. He stuck his chin on the windowsill, his bat ears two triangular peaks.

"That's right," I said. "There's your city, boy. Go get it!"

Stone clacked like a big, dumb bag of marbles, pulled his chin off the sill, and reached up to the window. He very carefully closed it, making sure the curtain did not catch in it.

"Fine," I said. "But I'm not so sure this living arrangement is working for me. If you change your mind, you know the way out."

I yawned. Okay, a little sleep, hope the gargoyle didn't eat me, then off to Violet for dessert. Maybe in the morning, sunlight would to turn him back into a statue; then I could take Stone out to the forest where he could frolic among the ferns, gurgle at streams, and make friends with the other interesting rocks.

I kicked off my boots and crawled into bed, pulling the covers over me without bothering to get undressed. I also set the alarm for eight o'clock.

Stone padded over to the side of my bed and tipped his wide head, studying me with round, intelligent eyes.

Kind eyes, I thought.

I reached out and patted his blunt nose. "Good night, Stone."

His ears peaked, then relaxed. He settled down on the floor, between me and the door, resting his head back on his arms again and staring straight ahead at the window. I had no idea if he was going to sleep, or even if he did sleep, but he knew where the window was. If he needed to go, he knew how to leave.

Good enough.

I closed my eyes, and fell, gratefully, asleep.

Chapter Nine

The bad thing about being exhausted after using so much magic is that you not only don't hear your alarm wailing away for fifteen minutes, you also don't notice that the half-ton gargoyle who has wandered off and is no longer in the apartment left your window open and let the nearly freezing air in.

I shut my window, then pulled on my boots and dug a hat out of my drawer. I checked the apartment for Stone, who really did seem to be gone. I would have thought I dreamed him up, if it wasn't for the neatly piled stack of throw pillows with a single empty coffee cup on top teetering on the table in the living room.

I picked up the cup and walked into the kitchen, half hoping Nola would be home, so I could talk to her about everything. But it was only 8:30, and she was apparently still having a good time out.

Stotts better treat her right.

I left her a note saying I was at Tchaikovsky Coffeehouse with Violet and would be home in an hour or two. I considered warning her about Stone, but instead went through the apartment and made sure all the windows were locked.

By the time I was down the stairs and out on the sidewalk, I had about twenty minutes to get to the coffeehouse. Plenty of time.

It wasn't raining, so I started off walking, and flagged down a taxi just a couple blocks from my place. He dropped me off in front of Tchaikovsky's.

Inside was warm and candlelit. Every wall was painted a different color, with art hung on nearly every square inch. A few plants were wedged up in the corners of the place. The floor—wood, with a scattering of carpets on which velvet couches huddled—was original to the building. Squeezed between those were tables of various shapes. Right in the middle of the room was a small raised stage, just big enough for the guitarist strumming away. Even though the whole thing should have come across as a crowded mess, it somehow looked and felt energetic and fun.

I grabbed a menu from the TAKE IT AND SIT DOWN box, and wandered into the hubbub. It was busy, but unlike Maeve's place, where I felt the need to keep up my guard, this felt like the kind of crowd I could lose myself in. I smiled, slid past people who made eye contact and smiled back. A server threaded the crowd with a plate of chocolates and strawberries that made my mouth water.

Even the guitar music was good.

It had been a long time since I felt this relaxed out in public. A long time since I'd done something just for the fun of it. Ever since my dad's death, my life had been intense.

And not in a good way.

I finally spotted Violet, because she waved and called my name—yes, I was being that observant. She and Kevin had secured a purple velvet love seat with an armchair snugged up against it. I made my way over to them, and pulled off my coat before taking the chair.

"Hey," I said. "Ordered yet?"

Violet held up her menu. "Waiting for you. I would kill for the mocha fudge pot de créme and a good cup of coffee."

I glanced at the menu. The vanilla sin almond torte with kumquat drizzle sounded really good. That, and an espresso. "Ready." I glanced at Kevin. "You good to go?"

He nodded.

The three of us held our menus up over our heads. Silly, yes. But standard in this place, and the server showed up in a remarkably short time. She tucked an empty tray beneath one arm while she took our orders and menus, gave us a smile, and was gone into the crowd.

The guitar guy switched to something a little more upbeat, with Latino influences.

"So." Violet leaned forward enough to fold one leg under the other. "Is this about your position in Beckstrom Enterprises?"

"I'm that easy to read?"

"It's been three months since Daniel died," she said in that matter-of-fact way of hers. "There are still a lot of details that haven't been settled. We need to take care of the business before people get too nervous."

"I know. My schedule has been really hectic and it's only going to get worse. I'm considering a job Hounding on retainer for the police."

That got Kevin's attention. He stopped looking like he wasn't scanning the crowd and instead looked at me.

"Which department?" he asked.

Yes, he was Violet's bodyguard, and no, I didn't owe him any answers. But he was also a part of the Authority and a hell of a magic user. I figured he had ways to find out who I was working for, so why keep it a secret?

"Detective Stotts."

His sandy eyebrows notched up, but that was all the reaction I got out of him.

Violet nodded. "I think that's a valid choice. I've looked into your files."

"Nice," I said.

She winced. "I'm sorry if you feel like I've crossed a line, but we don't know each other that well, and . . . your decisions about his company could change my life and my research in the most drastic of ways. Did you know your father kept detailed reports on you?"

"Yes," I said.

"As I said, I went through them and I noticed you don't have any self-defense training."

"What?"

"Self-defense. I'm surprised you never took any training. No martial arts, no sidearms training, no basic self-defense classes. Not even in college."

"I can handle myself just fine."

She stared at me for a long, uncomfortable moment.

Finally, "In the very short time I've known you, you have been chased, shot, robbed, stabbed, drugged, and attacked by magic."

"I'm still breathing, aren't I?"

Our dessert and coffee showed up. The server caught on quickly that chatty banter was not going to work at our table. She set everything on the small coffee table in front of us, and walked away a little quicker than before.

Violet picked up her coffee and took a moment to appreciate the leaf design worked in the foam. She held the cup in both hands and closed her eyes, inhaling the aroma.

The flutter behind my eyes kicked up again, and I felt a wash of memories push through me. Different times, different places, all Violet, holding a simple cup of coffee like it was treasure, savoring a plain moment like it was gold.

Go away, I pushed at my dad. Where was that wall when I needed it?

I looked away from Violet, which helped some, then took a drink of my coffee and a bite of the torte. The burst of flavors in my mouth pushed everything else aside. Violet, Kevin, the crowd, and my annoying father would all just have to wait while I ate half that torte and drank half that coffee.

Violet, however, was a multitasker.

"Yes, you're breathing. I think you should take steps to avoid injury in the first place. You need self-defense training, and I've put together a list of people you can check into."

She dug in the purse at her feet and put a manila file on the table. "Contact information, profiles, photos, classes, and costs are there. Beckstrom Enterprises has an employee wellness program set up that will cover any one of these. I'd like you to seriously consider it."

I settled back in my chair, taking my coffee with me but leaving the file where it was. "I'm not an employee."

"No, you're not. You're an owner. And the members of the board all voted to hire a bodyguard for you."

"Oh, absolutely not," I said. "I will not have someone breathing down my neck every second of the day."

"Then take the training."

The woman was relentless.

"And if I don't?"

"Beckstrom Enterprises will take appropriate steps. Allie"—she pressed her glasses up on the bridge of her nose and folded her fingers together—"personal preferences have to be put aside when you are dealing with a corporation this large. There is a lot riding on you and your majority share. The stockholders have some say in how you live your life. I'm sorry if you don't like that, but it's true. For years, your father was able to keep that pressure off you while you grew up, went to school. But he's gone now. Now you have to step up to the realities of living a public life."

"Gee," I said, "I know I brought enough money for dessert and coffee; does the lecture cost extra?"

Violet smiled, which I hadn't expected. I bet she was the head of her debate team in school. "You are so like him. I know that doesn't win me any favors. Still. It's true." She took another drink of her coffee. "Stubborn, sarcastic, annoying." She flashed me a smile. "But funny."

Funny? My dad? The flutter behind my eyes scraped and scraped. I rubbed at my forehead and tried to will him away.

I picked up my plate again and finished the torte so I had an excuse not to look at Violet.

"Have you thought about your role in the company?" Violet asked.

"Yes," I said. "Well, mostly I've thought about how much I don't want to have any role in the company."

"Really." She didn't sound surprised, just curious. "So you don't want to take a major position?"

"What, like CEO? No. I'd like to have some say in what happens, but I don't want to bother with the day-to-day decisions. Or paperwork. Or boardroom meetings. I'd like some money set aside that I can access for myself and for causes I am sympathetic toward. Maybe that money could be sheltered so my decisions on how to use it don't reflect poorly on the company."

"Why? Are you going into smuggling? Drugs? Weapons?"

"Worse. I'm thinking of creating some kind of insurance

plan or resource for the Hounds in the city. I know Dad never approved of what I did."

Violet took a drink of coffee and shrugged. "I think he wanted better for you. A safer career. Something more certain. But I don't think he was ashamed that you are a Hound."

"Yeah, well, I have my own opinion on that."

"I know," she said. "I'm comfortable with your interests being associated with Beckstrom Enterprises. But this is something we should have the lawyers work out. Would you be willing to meet with someone?"

"When?" I asked.

"I'll have to contact everyone and see when it would work. Hopefully in the next week or so."

"Okay," I said. "Oh, and what do you think about me giving you the CEO position in Beckstrom Enterprises?"

"Huh." It came out like someone had slapped her hard on the back and she'd lost her breath. She frowned and took another sip of coffee. "Let me think about that. You know your father's will left me comfortable financially, and I own the condo and many of his other assets."

"This isn't about the money," I said. "Well, I mean, it is about the money, but that's not the only thing it's about. I think you and I would work well together, even if we don't always agree."

"I'm not so sure. . . ."

"And," I cut her off before she could protest any further. "That will keep the business in the family. For the, uh, future. You know."

"You mean for your brother or sister?"

And all that scraping and fluttering in my head went dead still.

"Yeah," I said, because it was too late to deny it now. "For that."

"I'll think about it," she said again.

Somewhere in the center of my head, Dad jerked on something. It felt like he had a rope around my neck. He pulled so hard, I inhaled. Everything went black for a second, but I heard my own voice say, "I love you."

"What?" Violet said.

Kevin choked on his coffee, then cleared his throat.

Oh, sweet hells.

I pushed against the wall of my dad blocking me from control of my own mouth. He didn't fight me; maybe he was too weak to fight me. I stumbled back into my conscious mind like I'd missed the last stair. Which is to say, not very gracefully.

I stood, because it was time to get out of here before my dad did something worse.

"I'd love you to think it over," I said.

Nice save. Go, me.

"Call me when you decide, and let me know when you want to meet with the lawyers."

I pulled on my coat.

"Okay." She sounded a little confused. "And you'll tell me which self-defense instructor you choose."

Kevin pointedly handed me the manila folder, which I shoved in my pocket.

"If I choose one," I said.

"I'll know if you don't."

"Not sure that I care," I said with a smile. I tossed my share of the tab down on the table. "See you soon."

"Good night, Allie."

I strode away, but not before my Hound ears picked up Violet's last comment. "I don't think she understands the danger she's in."

And Kevin's reply. "She will."

Chapter Ten

I was restless, wanted to be on my feet, moving, thinking, doing. My apartment wasn't exactly within walking distance; still, I walked a little while before catching a cab. Halfway to my apartment, I decided I wasn't ready to go home yet. I asked the driver to drop me off about six blocks from my house and got out. I stood there on the sidewalk for a moment, trying to decide if I wanted to just walk home and let the cold, damp air clear my head, or if I wanted to go out for a while, get away. Maybe spend some time in the comfort of Get Mugged.

It didn't take me long to decide. I wanted warmth, light, and a crowd around me. Get Mugged it was. I started down the hill. The air was bitter cold, the light of dawn hours off. Most of the bars were just getting going this time of night, but I wasn't about to go wandering through dark alleys or unlit parking lots. I stuck to the streetlights, to the bus lines, and kept a good pace.

Just as my muscles were beginning to warm enough that I could really stretch into the walk, and I was actually a little more relaxed and a little less restless, I heard the sound of footfalls behind me.

Someone was following me.

I took a deep breath, searching for a scent.

The smell of blackberry burned down to a bitter, thick tar, the jarring scent of bubble gum and booze, and the dark heat of copper. The same smells from the Necromorph in the alley. The same smells from the job I Hounded for Stotts.

The wind shifted just enough to bring the smell closer, stronger. My heart skipped a couple beats.

That thing, that man-thing was here, on the streets. Stalking me.

Holy shit.

Panic drew delicate fingers through my stomach and legs, leaving behind a weak, watery sensation. I didn't know how to defend myself against that thing. I didn't think I could outrun it. Zayvion had been very clear that I should not throw magic at it.

Think, Allie, think.

Camouflage, my dad whispered in my mind.

Holy hells, I had forgotten he was there. I don't know how I had forgotten, since I was still pissed at him for taking over my mouth, but right now, I was glad he was with me.

How screwed up was that?

Cast Camouflage, he said again. Along with that came the memory of the butterscotch-and-rum spell Zayvion had thrown around us in the alley.

That was a great idea. Terrific, really. Camouflage had kept us hidden before I messed things up.

Only problem? I had no frickin' idea how to cast that spell.

I can talk you through it, Dad said a little louder, a little stronger, the presence of him growing bigger in my head. *I can teach you.*

And while, yes, warning bells went off in my head—I did not trust my father, had never trusted my father—that thing trotting between buildings behind me was possibly worse than my father. Maybe even probably.

Not by much, but the devil you know and all that.

Fine, I thought at him. *What do I need to do?*

Put a wall to your back. A strong building, not abandoned.

I didn't know that it mattered what kind of wall was behind me, but magic, especially spells I've never cast, can be tricky the first time. If Dad said I needed a good wall, I'd find a good wall.

I picked up the pace to a jog, falling into a rhythm of

breathing that helped clear my mind. I didn't know if that thing could smell fear or panic, but just to cover my bases, I decided I was not going to panic.

I jogged past plenty of buildings. How hard could it be to find a strong wall?

It was impossible.

All the buildings along this block were either separated by fences, or because of the slope in the hill, were too far above me.

There—a five-story stucco jobber with wide, fancy framed windows. Even better, the streetlamp poured enough light on the building that I should be able to get to the wall without stepping on homeless people or barging into the middle of a drug deal or something.

No, too much light, my dad said.

The creature was gaining on me. I could hear it closer, louder every few yards I ran, and my dad was critiquing my choice of hiding places.

How fandamtastic was that?

Up ahead was a one-story cedar-shingled shop huddled between two higher buildings. It was set back from the sidewalk a couple yards, but seemed to be in good repair. No light reached the walls and the windows were dark. Perfect crack house.

This one? I thought.

Perfect, he said.

Lucky in every way. That's me.

I jogged down the short brick walkway to the door and ducked into the shadows there, pressing my back against the wall.

The thing was close. Its snarl echoed from a block away, and I shivered from the sound of it. Not human enough to be a man, not animal enough to be natural.

What do I do? I thought as calmly as I could.

The snarl came closer, maybe two buildings back. Tracking me.

Clear your mind, he said.

I thought calm thoughts like my life depended on it. Which, strangely enough, it did.

I recited a mantra, the Miss Mary Mack rhyme, until my

racing heartbeat and thoughts slowed, became calm as still water.

Very good, he said with the strangest tone in his voice. Approval, I think, but I wasn't sure. I'd never heard him use it before.

Let go of your hands, and I will use them to trace the spell.

What? Use me? My body? Oh, hells no.

I stay in the driver's seat, I told him. *Just tell me what to do.*

There is no time. He pressed outward, spreading like a heavy ache, reaching into places in my mind I was positive I didn't want him touching.

No, I pushed back at him, trying to picture him trapped in a small corner of my head, a small room where he could not get out, could not touch me, could not make me do what he wanted me to do for him. A place where he could talk to me, maybe do charades through a window at me, but not touch me, or take me over.

If you fight me, he will see me—see us, he corrected.

Just tell me how to cast the damn spell, I said. Because he was right. We were out of time. The thing, the man-dog thing, had paused, right out there on the sidewalk where I'd been standing a moment ago.

The wind was blowing toward me, which meant he might not be able to smell me. For once luck was on my side, but I didn't know how long it would hold.

Tell me how to cast Camouflage, I said again. *If that thing kills me, you aren't going to have anyone's mind to hide in anymore.*

It is too complicated. And this time it wasn't approval in his voice, it was anger. And fear.

Yeah, well, welcome to my life.

The creature hunched his far-too-human shoulders, hung his head, and scented the wind. He moved toward me, on all fours, human hands curled under so only the knuckles touched the bricks, body a tragedy of bone and sinew and maggot-white skin. He looked bigger than before. Stronger.

If you don't give up, I said to my dad, *we're both going to be dead.*

I felt him pause, still, as if he held his breath. Felt him decide. *You are right*, he said quietly.

And while I would have crowed in victory at that admission when he'd been alive, staring down my own certain death sort of dampened the thrill.

My dad reached out into my mind and yanked that damn cord again. Pain rushed over me in a wave of fire. The wave, my father's will, crashed down over me so fast and so hard, I didn't even have time to exhale my scream.

Both of my arms raised, palms forward—even though I was not the one moving them.

Back off, I said. I pushed at my dad, built brick walls between us as quickly as I could, but it wasn't working.

No. Stop. I won't let you do this to me, I said.

You have never known when to fight, Allison, he said. Without my consent, my fingers traced an intricate glyph pattern. All I wanted to do was puke. Watching someone—worse, feeling someone—use me, puppet me around, control me, brought nightmares screaming through my mind.

Oh, hells, no.

I pushed at him. It was like shoving a mountain of sand—lots of movement, and none of it did a damn bit of good.

You have never known the right thing to fight for, he said, his voice growing stronger in my mind, his willpower blasting apart the walls I scrambled to build, leaving nothing but dust behind. His hands, my hands, traced magic into the air to his bidding. His will sucked at the magic in my bones.

And you have never known what is worth losing to get what you want. With that, he shoved me so hard, I felt like I'd just fallen down an elevator shaft. My body jerked, hit the back of my head against the wall, but I felt it only distantly, as if I'd been huffing nitrous oxide. Dad was doing something to screw with my vision. I couldn't see anything but blackness. But even at the bottom of an elevator shaft I could still hear, and I could still smell.

The scent of butterscotch and rum filled my nostrils and slid down my throat—the Camouflage spell.

If my dad could shove me out of my own conscious mind, take over my body, and cast a spell, I was on the hard end of a screwing.

Fine. I may not like my father, but that didn't mean I was stupid. He had the upper hand for the moment, and since it was in his best interest not to let his current ride, aka me, get killed, I hated to admit it, but letting him cast that spell was probably saving my ass. The butterscotch-and-rum meant the spell was in effect. All I had to do was keep my mouth shut and let Dad hide us until the beast moved on.

The thing was close. I could smell the foul rot of flesh and death and blood from it.

I held very still, wrapped in darkness, breathing butterscotch, and straining to hear anything, any hint of it walking away.

"Daniel." The word was low, a growl. "I know you. I smell you. I see you," it said. "You cannot hide. Your death calls me."

"Go on your way," I heard myself command. I could feel the honey twist of Influence my father brought to bear behind those words. "Or I will undo you."

He was using my hands. He was using my eyes. He was using my magic. And now he was using my mouth.

That pissed me off. My dad was using my lips. My dad was using my tongue.

Nobody used my tongue but me. Nobody.

Fuck him. Even though I was shoved down here somewhere in my own head, I could still feel magic inside my body. All I had to do was find a way to get to it and a way to cast it.

"You are my way, Daniel Beckstrom," the creature growled. "Living, undead, you hold the key to the dark and light. The key to open the gates. And then I will have my revenge on those who betrayed me."

The back of my head hit the wall again, and I was aware, distantly, that my shoulders hurt. Also, I tasted blood. That was not a good sign.

Closer, in my ear, the beast shouted: "You are mine."

Light slid like a blade of electricity between my eyes. Blackness flashed strobe white, blinding me again.

No! My Dad, inside my head.

"No," my own voice echoed.

I didn't know which one of us had control of my body.

We were mixed, too much of one person and not enough of two. The weight of the beast hit my chest—for the second time—and I crumpled to the ground beneath it.

I opened my eyes—*my eyes*. Oh yeah. Go, me! I was in control again.

Fangs hovered inches from my face, and dark black eyes burned ebony into my own.

Shit.

"You are mine now, Daniel Beckstrom," the Necromorph growled.

The Necromorph opened his mouth, unhinging his jaw, and breathed out. Dark magic poured over me like ice, magic that chilled the air. Magic I could not see, could not smell. I inhaled and deathly cold tendrils of magic slipped into me, into my lungs, into my mind.

"Come to me," the thing growled. "Death nor life, I killed you once. You have done much worse to me. I will no longer wait here in the in-between, denied both life and death."

What the hell? Killed him once?

And then the Necromorph inhaled. The darkness inside me cinched tight around something in my head.

My father moaned, twisted to try to break free of the hold that the Necromorph had on him. It was like my dad was a speck of dirt and the Necromorph was a vacuum. The Necromorph sucked in again.

I gasped in shared pain. Memories washed through me. My dad's memories. Of a man holding his hands behind his back while a gun dug into his temple. Terror and fury washed me in cold sweat.

Because even more frightening than the memory of the gun to Dad's head was the memory of the man in front of him. A man who cast magic. A man who had disks in one bloody hand, a knife in the other, and the same eyes as the beast that was tearing into my head.

Holy shit. This thing, this Necromorph, was one of the men who killed my father.

They thought James Hoskil was behind it all. And James' mother had even named him. But it never made sense for one man to sneak into my father's office, past his Wards, past his protections, and kill him. My father had been one of the most powerful magic users in the city.

But this man had killed my father.

And he wanted to do it again.

Through me.

The cold burned, and something in my head twisted and popped like a tooth being pulled out by the root. I yelled.

Ohcrapohcrapohcrap.

No, my father said again. Then, a whisper to me, *Help me. Allison.*

And sure, I hated my dad and hated him being in my head. And even though I didn't want to just stand by while he was hurt, there was one ugly truth staring me in the eyes.

This thing had killed my father. Killed someone a lot more skilled in magic, someone who was still a lot stronger than me, even when he was dead. There was no way in hell I could fight this thing and win.

I don't know how, I thought to my dad.

Cast, he whispered, his voice nearly gone now, as if caught by a winter wind. *Cast magic.*

Right. The thing had me flat on my ass. My arms were pinned beneath its corpse-cold grip. How was I supposed to cast a spell?

"Come to me." The Necromorph's words were a chain around my dad that dragged him up and up.

I felt his terror. His pain.

And there was nothing I could do to save him.

Nothing magical.

I pulled my legs up. Shoved my boots beneath the Necromorph's thighs. Pushed as hard as I could.

He stumbled back. Rose up on his legs, face contorted in fury. And roared.

A dull metallic glow radiated at its throat. A circle. A disk. Embedded deep into his neck.

The disk stank of burned copper. The Necromorph stank worse. I scrambled to get on my feet. My boots slipped on wet bricks. The Necromorph twisted his neck to look down at me, hiding the disk beneath his chin.

"I will kill her to have you." He lunged, nails clawing,

tearing at my coat. I threw my hands up to protect my face, and traced the fastest, easiest spell I could think of.

Light.

Light flashed, too bright in the night. The Necromorph growled, blinded.

Problem was, I was blinded too.

I finally got to my feet, but there was an entire frickin' house at my back. I had nowhere to run.

Fine. I wasn't planning to run anyway.

The murderer rushed me. I pivoted. Fangs sank into my shoulder, a dark, burning pain on top of the cold.

I yelled. From pain, yes. And because I was really angry. All I had wanted was a frickin' cup of coffee. Couldn't a girl go downtown without having to deal with undead mutated murderers on the way?

Forget mantras. Pain did plenty to clear my head. I didn't even bother with a Disbursement. I didn't care what magic was going to make me pay for this. I reached into my bones, into the raging magic there, and pulled it up through me so fast and hard, all my senses snapped into hyperfocus.

I could smell the beast's hatred. Could smell his fear and pain. Could see dark spells burrowed into him, long, fat tendrils hanging off his twisted, emaciated body like leeches buried belly deep, down to his soul, sucking the life, sucking the soul out of him.

Around him a crowd of dead lingered, the Veiled, bits of dead magic users, looking like they always looked—pale watercolor images of people with holes where their eyes should be—sucking at the ends of the spell, leeches, drinking the beast down.

The horror in front of me couldn't register through my anger. It sucked to be him, but hey, we all have issues.

I wove the glyph for Fire and poured magic into it.

Flames exploded in the air, blew outward, heat carrying to the sidewalk. It was a good thing it had been raining a lot lately. What plant life there was in the area was so wet I doubted a blowtorch could get it to smolder.

But the murderer wasn't a plant. He took the full brunt of my fury face on.

Idiot.

He didn't try to block. Didn't wag one creepy finger to deflect.

Allison, my dad warned, a little stronger than he had been. *Don't.*

Yeah, like I'd listen to him.

My right arm burned too hot, magic flowing and curling in multicolored strands down my arm and pouring out my fingertips. My left hand was cold, numb, and the numbness crept up to my elbow, hurting as it rose higher and higher toward my heart.

Positive and negative. Me using magic, and it using me. The joy and the pain.

I broke the Fire, and cast Sight so I could see through the darkness.

The Necromorph hadn't blocked the spell because he didn't have to. He just drank it down. The fire, the magic, everything. All my Light magic fed him. And all the leeches hanging off him got longer and fatter, and the Veiled sucking on them moaned.

Okay, here's the thing. I had not woken up thinking I was going to be facing down certain death, nor the creepy Rastafarian dog-man from hell.

Which is probably why one look at the squirming mess of magic leeches writhing over him made me stop and stare instead of pay attention to other things, like, say, the Veiled who had suddenly decided to pay attention to me.

Shit.

The Veiled rushed. Fast. Too fast for any living thing.

And the Necromorph was right behind them.

The Veiled's fingers clutched my coat, my hands, my arms, pressed under my skin, hooked magic out of me, and drew it into their mouths with huge smacking gulps.

Dad had protected me from them before. But he was silent. Inert as a lump of lead.

I was on my own.

And if I wanted the Veiled not to eat me, I had to stop using magic.

Which meant I had nothing but my fists as weapons.

Violet was right. I so needed self-defense training.

There was no way I was going to get out of this unbroken. But I damn sure was going to get out of it alive.

I dropped the spell, dropped the magic. Like a dark curtain falling on a bright screen, the real world came back.

I was breathing too hard and hurting everywhere. My head, my bleeding and possibly broken shoulder, my chest, my skin. There had to be a weapon I could use, but all I had was the journal in my pocket.

That would do. I put my hand around the book, ready to pull it out and throw it at him, or maybe jamb the pointed corner into his eye.

"For innocence to remain," the Necromorph said, "no price is too high." It was strangely soft, more man than creature.

And I swear, it sounded like an apology.

Nice, but a little too late.

He lunged at me.

I twisted at the hip, aimed the book and my fist at his face with everything I had.

And slammed my hand into a rock wall. I think I broke a finger. Or five.

A roar filled my ears. Not my own. Though I yelled too.

No, this sound was huge. The murderer was howling in pain.

That was no rock wall I'd slammed my fist into. That was a gargoyle.

Stone tore into the murderer with hands and fangs. Four ground-shaking blows from Stone sent the Necromorph to the ground, bleeding black. He was broken. More than that, he was pulverized.

I thought it was over.

I think Stone thought it was over too.

But even without holding Sight, I could feel the magic gathering beneath my feet. Feel it pooling, growing, and pouring toward the murderer.

I traced a quick glyph for Sight.

Holy shit. It wasn't magic, or at least it wasn't magic as I had ever seen it before. It was like a shadow of magic, indigo, violet, bloodred, dark and seeping. Rising up through the soil and pushing into the Necromorph's body while the disk in his neck pulsed and glowed the same shadowy colors as the magic.

He twitched. Jerked. Stood back up.

Holy shit. He was dead. Had been dead. But he was not dead anymore.

I pressed against the wall. Stone growled. The Necromorph looked at me.

"You will not stop me." Then he took off running, bleeding, fast and fluid and silent, a slice of moonlight in the shadowed night, despite the wounds Stone had given him. Stone was right behind him, just as fast, but each footfall landed like a heavy engine shaking the night.

Yes, I could have stood there and watched the rest of the gory details. But I was going to get the hell out of there while the getting was good.

I ran uphill toward my house. I didn't care if that would be the first place anyone would expect me to go. I needed to get away, get out of there, run, run, run before the nightmares caught up with me.

I was halfway home when I heard footfalls behind me. Human footfalls. Running.

"Allie?"

I knew that voice. Davy Silvers. Hound. But I couldn't stop, wouldn't stop. Not for him. Not for anyone.

Davy had two things on me. Legs and youth. He caught up to me before I reached the doors to my apartment.

"Wait," he said. "Wait. Hold on." He tugged on my sleeve and it hurt like hell. It took everything I had not to punch him in the nose.

I stopped, spun on him.

"What is your problem?" I yelled.

He stumbled back several steps and held up both his hands. He was sweaty, his face too pale in the streetlight. "I heard you scream. Heard the fight back there. Then you were running, but there's nothing behind you but me. You have blood on your face."

Maybe. I had anger too. "How many times do I have to tell you to stop following me around?" I said. "You could have been killed."

He folded his arms over his sweatshirt and tucked his

hands in his armpits. "You're hurt," he repeated stubbornly. "Do you want me to call an ambulance or take you down to the hospital myself?"

"Listen," I said, trying to calm down, trying to pull my wits back on, one word at a time. "A guy jumped me. I hit my head on a wall fighting with him. I'm fine."

Davy was a Hound. One things Hounds are good at is spotting bullshit.

"Okay, we can go with that for now," he said. "At least we both agree you're hurt. Ambulance or front seat of my car?"

"Neither. I'm going home."

I started toward my apartment a block up the hill. Davy followed me. Out of swinging range.

Smart boy.

"Go home, Davy." The adrenaline was wearing off, leaving me shaking and tired.

"I am. Just not my home."

We walked a distance from each other all the way up to my building. By the time I reached the stairs, every ache, pain, and scratch was reporting for duty.

I hurt inside and out. And magic was pointing a headache at my brain that already made my molars ache. The wind was too cold, even with my heavy coat on. That meant I had a fever. Great.

Still, if I showered, took some aspirin, and slept for a month or so, I'd probably come out of this with only minor scars. I stopped in front of my door.

"Davy—" I looked over my shoulder.

Davy's face was washed in the blue light of his cell phone, which he closed and stuffed in his pocket. "Yes?"

"Who were you calling?"

"Zayvion Jones."

My brain tried to figure that one out, and came up empty. And I mean static-on-the-TV empty.

"What?" I said. "Why? How do you even have his number? Why are you still following me?" My voice rose up and up with each question, even though I didn't want it to.

It's called panic. I'm good at it.

"You're hurt, and you stink of so much used magic, it's

like you rolled in a pile of shit and spells. Some of them are . . . stuck to you. I don't know how to fix that." He shrugged. "Zayvion did things for you back in the warehouse. He did things I've never seen a doctor do. With magic. So if you're not going to let me take you to the hospital, I'm going to get someone here who can help. Help get the magic off you, or help me pick you up and shove you in the trunk of my car so I can take you to the emergency room. Either way." He shrugged again.

I tipped my face up to the sky and exhaled. "You can't tell me—"

A movement at the roof level of the building—a head poking over the edge and looking down—caught my eye. Stone gripped the edge of the building and tipped his wide head sideways, considering me for a minute before pulling his head out of my line of vision.

I didn't know whether he was still chasing the murderer or whether he was crawling down the side of the building to open my bedroom window and give Nola the scare of her life.

If Stone was still on the hunt, I wanted to stay the hell out of his way. And there was no way I was leaving Davy out on the street where the Necromorph might be looking to get a few new licks in.

"Zayvion gave me his number when you were in the hospital. Well, before that. Before you went to the hospital, but after the . . . after the warehouse."

He was still talking? Hells.

"Fascinating. Tell me about it inside where it's warm." I opened the door as quickly as I could—speedy as a snail in glue. My fine-motor coordination was set on suck mode. Still, I got the door open, stepped into the lobby, and closed the door behind Davy before anything jumped out of the shadows and tried to eat us.

Now all I had to do was get up the stairs and save Nola.

Well, get up the stairs and get into my apartment before Stone let himself in the bedroom window, if that's what he was doing. Or maybe he had crawled down the building and was back on the street. Or maybe he had found a nice garden to be a statue in until the dawn.

If he actually went inert in sunlight.

What was I doing? Oh yeah. Climbing the stairs to the rescue.

I started up the stairs, and maybe six whole steps into it, my head really started pounding in earnest. Holy hells, I hurt.

Davy, behind me, was chatting away. Kid was awfully talkative for a Hound. I didn't catch half of what he said; the thrum of my own heartbeat, rough breathing, and internal bitching was too loud. It wasn't until we got to the second floor that I realized he had called my name. Repeatedly. And I only heard him because he somehow got around me on the landing between flights and stood in front of me.

"What?" I panted. Hells, I was so worn out, I felt sick. Too hot, too cold, I was covered in a slick sweat that made me really want a shower. And a toilet to barf in.

"Zayvion wants to talk to you." He held his phone out for me.

I took it. Look at that—there was blood on my hands. I wondered whose it was.

"Hello?"

"Allie," Zayvion said. "I'm almost there. Davy said you were mugged."

"Yeah," I said.

"Was magic involved?"

"Yeah."

"Was your father involved?"

"Yes."

"Anything else?"

"Y-yes."

There was a short pause. I could imagine him frowning, going through options. "Don't use magic until I get there, okay?"

And I don't know if it was just that the events of the night had finally all stacked up or what. But I was so done with being bossed around.

I hung up on him.

Yep. On Zayvion. Probably the only person in the city who knew, one, about the Necromorph; two, that I had a renter in my brain; and, three, how the two were related, which they obviously were. And he was probably the only person in the city who was actually on his way to help me.

I handed Davy the phone.

Because now I was worried. If Zayvion had some sort of idea that I shouldn't cast magic, then he must know something else I didn't know. Like maybe what kind of danger I was in, or, what worried me more, what kind of danger the people around me were in. Violet's words came back to me. If she had known I was in this kind of danger, was she a part of it? A part of that thing having the disk?

I did my best to pick up the pace.

Ow.

"Someone," I panted to Davy who walked next to me, "might be breaking into my apartment. With magic. Nola might be in there. My friend. She doesn't cast. Do you know how to set Proxy on someone?" I asked.

"In theory. I've never done it before," he said.

"Just like setting a Disbursement on yourself. Project it onto the other person. Onto me."

He laughed. "Right. You're barely standing."

"Fuck you. I'm so very more than standing. I'm climbing. And talking. And thinking."

We'd made it to the third floor now. I didn't hear any screaming, growling, or anything else, really. Everything seemed normal.

Well, except for the hallway being all blurry at the edges and the sparks of silver fog that lit up at the corner of my vision whenever I turned my head too quickly.

I turned to look at Davy and had to spread my feet so I wouldn't fall over. Wow. The price of casting all that magic, probably the magic I cast and the magic my father cast, was really kicking in.

"Listen," I said in the most reasonable voice I could muster. "I can't cast right now. You can. Proxy me so you can stay clearheaded and help Nola."

"Like I can't pay to play?" He actually sounded offended.

As well he should be, I guess. I'd basically just told him he wasn't strong enough to cast magic. Wasn't strong enough to endure the pain. But that wasn't even close to what I was worried about.

"Course you can," I said. "I know that. But you might need a lot of magic in a hurry. I'm wiped. One of us needs to stay clearheaded. 'S gonna be you, Silvers."

I put out my right hand and got back to that walking thing, dragging my fingertips along the wall. I wasn't getting anywhere fast, but I was getting somewhere slow.

"Wait," Davy said beside me. "What kind of magic?"

We had reached my apartment door. "Any good at Hold?"

"I can do it."

"Great. Get ready to hold back a tank."

I tried the door. Locked. I was pretty sure I was happy about that.

Davy muttered something, a rhyme, a poem, that I couldn't quite catch the words of, his mantra to clear his mind for casting.

While he did that, I pulled my keys out of my pocket and turned the lock. I opened the door as quietly as I could.

The apartment was dark except for the wan light of streetlights seeping down through the windows in the living room. Everything seemed to be exactly as I had left it. I walked in, glanced over the half wall to the kitchen. Nothing in there moved, but that didn't mean something wasn't crouched down in the dark.

Davy glided behind me, damn quiet for someone who showed no sign of shutting up just a minute ago. He had that kind of wolflike grace, his young face set in a calm but fierce determination, his body language aware but not tense.

I pointed at the kitchen and Davy walked into it, leaving the lights out.

I snuck into the living room as well as I could. I was beginning to feel more than a little dizzy. I checked the couch, the corners, and down the hall. Nothing. No one out of the ordinary. No Nola on the couch. I wondered if she'd gone into the bedroom.

I switched the light on in the bathroom. Nothing but bathroom. Then I knocked gently on the bedroom door, which would tell whoever was in there that I was out here, but barging in on Nola, spells a-blazin', didn't make any sense either. And if something was in there, I didn't think I had the element of surprise on my side anyway.

Davy came up behind me, a yellow-haired shadow, and put one hand on my shoulder.

Pain rushed through me, hot enough I could hear my blood pounding in my ears.

Holy shit, that hurt. I pressed my lips together and tried not to make a sound. That, apparently, was the shoulder the creature had bitten. Good of Davy to bring that particular pain back to my attention.

But he wasn't just poking at my wounds. He moved closer so I would have to step out of the way and let him go first.

I glared at him, and he glared right back and held up his right hand. The tips of his thumb and ring finger were touching, the end point of the Hold glyph he'd probably traced. Since I wasn't pulling magic into my sense of sight, I didn't actually see the glyph he held.

Right. I'd told him he'd have to take point on this. Best to get out of the kid's way and try not to faint when the Proxy hit me.

Davy opened the door.

"Nola?" I said quietly.

Someone behind the door put something heavy down. It sounded like the bat I kept under my bed.

"Allie?" Nola pulled the door the rest of the way open and turned on the light while standing in the doorway.

Wearing a rumpled cow T-shirt and a pair of sweats, it was obvious she had just crawled out of bed. Her hair was unbraided, and falling in messy waves around her face.

Her confusion turned into anger at seeing Davy in front of her.

"Sorry," I said from behind Davy. I was pretty sure I was still behind him anyway. Everything was getting jumpy, the whole room skittering side to side with each pound of my pulse. Just to make sure my head wasn't going to fall off my shoulders, I leaned it against the wall. The Sheetrock felt cool beneath my cheek. I closed my eyes, and had to fight to open them again.

Did it too. Go, me.

"Thought there might be something . . . one . . . breaking in." It came out almost all slur, and I hoped they'd gotten the gist of it because I sure as hell wasn't going to say it again.

"Nola Robbins," I heard her say in the brisk matter-of-fact way that made her sound like my mom instead of like my friend who was the same age as me.

"Davy Silvers," he said. "She got jumped on the street."

There was some moving around going on, the room switching from the slide step to a bouncy little cha-cha.

"I got you," Nola said. "Take another step for me, honey. Good."

That was when I realized that she was talking to me. And it wasn't the house jumping around, it was me walking, or more likely, being dragged somewhere.

I opened my eyes. When had I closed them?

"Can you get her boots?" Nola asked.

"Yup." That was Davy.

"Wait," I said, except it came out all air and nothing else.

"We got you, honey. Now you're going to lie down."

I swear the woman shoved me. Nice job, Nola. That push made the whole damn room circle the drain, and I was caught in the vortex.

"The thing," I tried to say. The beast. The murderer. The gargoyle. The bite on my shoulder. The blood on my chest. The dad in my brain. The disk in the throat. The Veiled. The leeches. The magic not being magic. But none of it came out.

In the distance, Nola and Davy discussed hot water, stitches, and butterflies, all of which seemed strange.

I tried to listen, but their voices faded into the ocean thrum of my heartbeat, and soon that was all I could hear, all I could feel, until silence finally found me.

Chapter Eleven

I didn't dream of my father. I didn't dream at all. One second I was falling into a static darkness; the next my eyes were open.

It happened so fast, my heart tripped in my chest and stuttered hard before it caught up again.

"Morning, Sunshine." Zayvion Jones, that dark Adonis, leaned down above me, his usually calm expression warmed by a smile.

"Mmm," I managed. My tongue was stuck to the roof of my mouth. There wasn't any spit left in me. I tried to swallow, felt like I hadn't drunk in years. And tasted mint. Lots and lots of mint.

I knew the taste of that mint. Zayvion was Grounding the hell outta me. Which must mean I was using magic. While sleeping?

He drew his hand up my bare leg, cupping the back of my calf, up the smooth, warm inner arc of my knee, then over the lean muscle of my thigh, his thumb trailing the inside of my thigh, until he reached, much too soon, the fold of blanket draped over my hips, stomach, and chest.

He pulled the blanket down over my exposed leg, and looked me straight in the eye as he tucked me in, proper as a priest.

"Water?" he asked.

I nodded, which shook my headache loose. I groaned a little.

"Aspirin?" I asked. It came out sounding a lot like *ass spoon*, but Zayvion seemed fluent in mumbleze.

He handed me water and a pill from my bedside table.

I elbowed up (elbows working, check; stomach muscles working, check; heart and lungs still on duty, check; head hurting like a three-day bender, check) and sat against the headboard. My shoulder still hurt like hell. I closed my eyes and took a second to breathe. Zayvion rested his free hand on my thigh and warm, soothing mint washed over me like a blanket of morphine.

Yums. Even though I wasn't using magic, I felt burned inside, raw. And the Grounding helped.

"Okay." I opened my eyes, got lost for a soul's breath in the deep brown and gold of Zayvion's gaze before he gently let me free by breaking eye contact.

"Water," he reminded.

I took the water this time and looked at the pill in my palm. Not the white aspirin that I kept in my medicine cabinet. This pill was blue and had a tiny little glyph carved into it. Magic medicine? How did that work? Did they put glass and lead in the pill to contain the magic?

"What is it?" I asked.

"Painkiller. Prescription."

"The glyph?" I asked.

He shook his head. "It's legal. I can get you the bottle to look at, if you want. I'm surprised you Hounds don't eat this stuff like candy. The small bit of magic in the pill is capsulized in sodium chloride crystals. Won't hold the magic for long, so that gives it a very short shelf life, but enhances the painkiller. And when the pain is because of magic . . ." He shrugged. "It's a lot better than aspirin."

I swallowed the pill and drank the rest of the water.

"How's your shoulder?" he asked.

"Good," I said. I shrugged my shoulder to see if it still worked. A shot of pain cramped my neck and I hissed and rubbed at my shoulder, trying to work out the knot.

Then Zayvion's hands were there, thick, heavy fingers, still surprisingly gentle as he moved my hand away. He kneaded the muscle, working it until the cramp eased, and I sighed.

"Better," I said. I shrugged my shoulder again. A little sore, but it seemed to move more fluidly.

I don't know if it was the painkiller, the relief from him working the cramp out of my shoulder, or the fact that in order to reach my shoulder at the right angle, Zayvion had to sit on the bed next to me and lean full body over me, but whatever it was, my mind was no longer on pain.

No, my full attention, every last flick of every last nerve, was on the man sitting above me.

"Tell me what happened." He dragged one finger under the edge of my jaw, fingers catching there, just like in the restaurant, and I inhaled the familiar pine scent of him.

"I—" I swallowed like it was hard to breathe enough to get the words out.

The truth? I hurt. My lips were swollen, sore. My head still hurt, though the meds were starting to kick in. I figured that pill probably had two to four hours worth of painkilling in it.

I intended to make the most of my pain-free time.

Zayvion frowned, braced with one arm on the far side of me, the other still holding the edge of my jaw in his fingertips, as he looked worriedly into my eyes.

"I—" I whispered.

He leaned in a little closer to hear me.

Perfect.

I lifted my right hand, which was bandaged across several knuckles, and dragged my fingers up his side. He was wearing a sweatshirt, and I wished I had the coordination to actually get my hands under that and on his skin, but I was still clumsy.

Zayvion raised his eyebrows as I dragged my palm over the hard muscles of his chest and rested my hand there.

"Yes?" he asked.

"I want you. I want us."

Zayvion went so still, if I hadn't had my hand on his chest, if I hadn't felt every steady thump of his heart beneath my palm, I would have thought he were just an incredibly handsome statue.

Or a dream.

Please don't let him be a dream, I thought. I reached up, stretched my fingers, and traced the fullness of his lips. He closed his eyes, and I could see his Adam's apple bob as he swallowed.

His lips opened for my finger and he caught the tip of it with his teeth, held it there, and slowly dragged the tip of his tongue across it. He opened his eyes and exhaled, releasing my finger like a man hesitant to give up something so sweet.

"You are hurt," he began. "You always want . . . this . . . when you're hurt. Or afraid. I want us to be more than that."

Well, I might be a little bruised, but I wasn't scared. Even though I probably should be. The Necromorph was still loose. He knew my dad was in my head.

If I wanted to get Zayvion into bed with me, this was not the time to bring this stuff up. But he wanted more than trauma sex. So fine. Let's see how he handled honesty.

"The Necromorph," I said.

"Yes?" Zayvion went very, very still.

"Last night. He tracked me. My dad, in here?" I pointed at my head. "Cast Camouflage. With my magic. The Necromorph knew it was my dad. I . . . lost control of my body. Dad took me. Used me to try and fight him." Wow, admitting I'd been used sucked. Tears stung my eyes.

I hadn't allowed myself to think of it that way, couldn't think of it that way out on the street. But I'd been violated. By my father. From the inside out.

Zay leaned back just a small amount, giving me a little more room to breathe. Waited.

It took me a while to swallow back the tears, but I did it. Mostly because I was really angry at my dad, and I refused to let him make me cry.

"The Necromorph," I said, my voice steady, "said he killed Dad. And I saw memories, Dad's memories of a man with a knife and disks. It was the Necromorph before he changed. He killed my dad, and he has a disk, stuck in his neck."

I took a breath, held it, keeping my calm.

"So, listen. I'm probably always going to be hurt. Some way or another. Hounding means I use magic, and using magic means pain. And wanting you might have something to do with hurting. But that's not all. That's not the only reason I want you."

Zayvion looked away, past me, at the wall above my head. I could feel the heat radiating off his body, but I did not touch him. The decision was his to make too.

Finally, he looked down at me. He didn't say anything, which was strange since I'd just given him what I assumed was pertinent information about the Necromorph he'd been hunting, and had also declared my true feelings about us. Seemed like either one of those things would be worth commenting on.

I found I could not read the look in his eyes. And that frightened me.

Wordlessly, he bent to me, his mouth searching for mine. He parted my lips with his own, gently kissing, coaxing. This, I understood. My lips were swollen and sore. I opened for him, wanting to taste him, needing to feel him inside me.

His hands slid behind my back, easing me away from the wall while his tongue dipped like honey, liquor, sex, in my mouth. I kissed him back, fumbling in my need for him. I gripped the back of his sweatshirt with my good hand and tried to pull. It hurt too much to make a fist with my right, so I scooped my hands beneath his sweatshirt instead and dragged my hands, fingers wide, up his back, so I could brace myself closer against him.

He caught the weight of me in his arms, then shifted, standing slowly, still kissing me as he helped me lie back down. He pulled away and straightened. For a moment, he stood there, almond eyes burning with gold, lips parted, nostrils flared. I wondered what he was waiting for.

I licked my lip and tasted blood.

Oh.

"Have you been tested?" I asked.

He nodded. "I'm clean."

"It's been a while since I have," I said honestly. "I think I'm good. But things have been weird." The bloody needle Lon Trager had stabbed in my thigh. Pike's blood pouring into my open wounds as he lay dying in my arms. I'd had a lot of dangerous fluid transfer lately, and hadn't asked if the doctors ran all the tests.

"God." I threw my arm over my eyes. Blood in the bedroom wasn't anything to rush into. I didn't care how many medical advances there were. I didn't care how many spells could extend a life—for a price. The kinds of diseases blood could transfer were deadly.

Zayvion pulled a tissue out of the box. "Here," he said quietly.

I pulled my arm off my face. Zayvion stood there, holding a tissue for me. But I wasn't looking at the tissue. He had taken off his shirt and held it in the other hand.

Sweet holy hells, that man was built. Thick chest, wide at the shoulder and narrower at the waist, muscles that moved beneath his mahogany skin as he offered the tissue to me again.

I took it, though I could not keep my hungry gaze off his body. "If you're trying to torture me . . ." I began.

Zay didn't even smile. "Yes?"

"Just don't," I said miserably. "Put your shirt back on." I dabbed at my lips, my blood catching in the paper. It wasn't a lot of blood. But it was enough. Too much.

"Think you can keep your mouth off me?" Zayvion asked.

"What?"

"Nola patched you up. You're not bleeding anywhere else. The punctures in your shoulder are bandaged. So are your knuckles. And that headache is from a lump on your head, but not a cut."

"So just my lips?"

"Just your lips."

That list of wounds brought something else to mind. "Have I had a shower?"

"Do you want one?"

"Yes."

"Going to let me help you with that?"

I met his gaze. There was a challenge there. Maybe a little bit of anger. I couldn't tell what he was angry about. "Yes."

Zayvion tossed his shirt at the foot of the bed. A casual, natural gesture, as if his clothes always belonged at the bottom of my bed. I pushed the blankets away, took his hand, and stood. The room spun a little. He put his arm around me and we walked down the hall to the bathroom.

My bathroom is small, and I don't like tight places to begin with. But here, right now, in the darkness of predawn, I liked having Zayvion with me in this tiny space, in this tiny room.

He shut the door and locked it, which I thought was sort of strange, but that was okay. I liked a careful man.

I pulled back the shower curtain and turned on the water, adjusting it until it was hot, but not hot enough to burn.

Okay, now I needed some graceful way to get out of my sweater, undershirt, bra, jeans, and panties. With a bum shoulder, swollen knuckles, and bad equilibrium.

Joy.

Zayvion stepped behind me and spread his hands flat against my stomach.

"Can you do this?" he murmured against my neck.

My mind spun with a thousand ideas of what he might be asking me to do.

"Can you get undressed on your own?" he clarified.

"Maybe," I said. Then, honestly, "No."

I expected him to be quick to get me naked. But no. He took his time, drawing his fingers beneath my sweater and undershirt, across the soft skin of my lower stomach, just above the waistband of my jeans. I licked my lip, tasted the copper heat of my blood there, and bit the inside of my cheek instead to keep from making any sound. He traced a sideways figure eight, the symbol of infinity, across my stomach.

I wondered if it meant something, but then his hands were gone, catching the hem of my sweater. He moved to one side, gently pulled the sweater and sleeve over my good shoulder, the right, and then he was on the other side of me. I tried to help get my arm out, but he shushed me and pulled the sleeve and sweater off over my head, then down my arm without me having to move my shoulder at all.

He glanced at me, and I smiled.

"Smooth. You get a lot of practice undressing wounded girls?"

"It's come up."

I would have said something about that, but one look

at his smile, and electric heat caught fire in my belly. The weight and need for him pressed at my chest, and dragged delicious warmth down my stomach to pool between my legs.

Next went the undershirt. Painless. After that, he moved behind me again and unhooked my bra.

I gasped at the warm, moist air that licked my skin as he pulled the strap off first my good arm, then down my bad arm. Once the bra was gone, he stood behind me again and brushed his fingertips slowly up my stomach, then my ribs, which I could feel on the right, but lost track of over the numbness of the scars on my left.

Hadn't I worried about my scars? About if Zayvion would find them ugly, me ugly, because of them?

But he did not pause over the scars, did not pull away. His fingertips traced the curve beneath my breasts, lifting the weight of me. I leaned into the warm hardness of his bare chest and stomach and closed my eyes. I could feel his heartbeat, pounding, hard, strong. Still, he barely touched me as he traced gentle circles around my nipples. An aching sweetness bloomed beneath my skin. I arched my back and rolled my hip against his, wanting more. Wanting him. All of him.

He made a soft, deep sound, his body responding to my invitation, and plunged his fingertips down my stomach to the warmth beneath the waistband of my jeans.

He kissed the side of my neck, licking along the mark of magic at the curve, then sucking until fire and magic rose through me, answering his touch.

I got my good hand on the button of my jeans, but Zay's hands were already busy, unbuttoning, unzipping, his fingers slipping down my panties.

Oh. Yes.

But my jeans weren't loose enough for much more than that. Zayvion pulled his hands away and caught at my belt loops. He knelt behind. As he lowered my jeans off my hips and down to my thighs, he followed with his lips, kissing the small of my back, the side of my hip, back of my thigh, behind my bare knees. Each wet, soft press of his mouth against my skin rolled a shock of heat through me, and left me aching for more.

He paused.

"Zay?" I breathed.

"Lift your foot."

What? Oh, right. I lifted one foot, stepping out of my jeans, lifted the other. Zayvion pushed my pants across the floor, out of our way.

From his kneeling position, he caught the edge of my panties and tugged them down off my hips, away from the wet warmth of me.

He didn't have to remind me to lift my feet this time.

I turned around and faced him.

Zayvion crouched, face level with my stomach, burning gold eyes, deep brown skin. The man radiated power, hunger, need. I caught my breath at the sight of him.

"I need you," I said. "Please." I dragged my good fingers though his hair, thick, soft black curls, wet with the steam of the shower. I wanted to pull him up to his feet so I could kiss him.

Wait. No kissing.

Well, none for me. Zayvion's lips were just fine. He proved it by licking across my stomach. I moaned as he worked his way up.

I arched my head back, closed my eyes again as need thrummed through me.

He rested his hands on both sides of my hips. "Shower," he said.

What? Oh, no way. Forget the shower.

"Allie."

I opened my eyes. He was standing.

"I'll be right here," he said, low and sexy. "Waiting for you." He let go of my hips, gave me a little push toward the shower. He leaned his butt against the sink and crossed his very nice arms over his very nice chest.

"I can't," I said in a voice that was all breath. "I can't wait."

He smiled a slow, dark smile. "It will be worth it."

From that look, I guessed arguing with him would only extend my wait.

I got into the shower and let the warm water stroke my aching skin. I fumbled with the soap, but managed to wash myself left-handed without dropping anything or falling over. Then I washed and rinsed my hair, which was not as easy as it seemed. My right hand was bandaged, sore, and I didn't really want to put soap on it. My left shoulder, however, hurt every time I raised my arm, so that pretty much counted out my left hand. Still, this wasn't the first time I'd had to take care of my battered body. I managed.

I even turned off the water on my own.

I pulled back the curtain.

Zayvion still leaned against my sink. He held a towel in his hands.

I stepped out, took the towel, and wrapped it around me without bothering to dry off.

"I'm done." I leaned full body against him, warm, naked, and slid my good hand down to the button of his jeans. I pressed my palm there, cradling his warmth. He grunted, and I grinned. Oh, I liked what I could do to this lovely, lovely man.

I thumbed the button through the button hole, letting my knuckles press against his stomach. He needed me, wanted me, that much was clear. But instead of unzipping his jeans, I stepped away.

I unlocked the door and didn't care how cold it was in the hallway as I swayed off to my bedroom. I didn't hear him behind me. Of course, I never heard him. But I could feel him. His need so strong, it was like a second pulse beneath my skin. I stopped next to the bed.

I pulled off my towel, let it drop to the floor, and heard the door close behind me.

I turned and watched as Zayvion unzipped his jeans and pulled them off. He stood naked before me—dark, intense. A condom appeared in his hand, and I was glad he remembered. I wasn't sure I had any in the house.

I wanted to savor him, touch him slowly, taste his body, his soul. I held my arms open for him and he stalked over to me. We pressed together, folding into each other's embrace. His hands slid down to the back of my thighs and he lifted me.

He lowered me gently onto the bed and held himself above me, his hungry gaze taking me in before he bent his head, his lips searching and finding my breast. He exhaled, something between a moan and a sigh, my name, I think.

He leaned to one side, supported by his elbow, and drew away just enough to trace something with his fingertip against my stomach. A glyph. Infinity, again.

"Zay?" I asked.

He just smiled and kissed the side of my throat, drawing magic up through me. The glyph against my skin warmed. Magic spread through me, hot, sweet, following the stroke of his tongue, circling the glyph on my stomach, growing stronger until I had to stretch to hold it all.

Oh. Oh yes.

Magic drew a second pleasure beneath my skin, settled like a weight in my belly. I wanted Zayvion. Wanted to open for him, wanted to wrap around him, feel him hard, powerful, inside me.

I kissed the side of his jaw softly, not wanting to split my lip on the rough stubble of his skin.

He stroked his palm down my body again until his fingers slipped to the warmth between my legs.

His fingertips were cool and drew a slow, delicious circle, then withdrew.

"Please," I said.

And then there was no more talking. No more thinking. He was with me, in me, and my heartbeat was too loud. I inhaled, tasted mint, pine, threw my head back, moaned.

Magic licked fire across my nerves, aching, Zayvion pulling on magic. I reveled in the sensation of our bodies together, the stroke and texture of him inside me, stretching my senses, making me tingle, ache, burn, making me needful. I gasped, each breath short, shorter.

Heat, a deep, silken stroke took me, shaped me, shaped us, magic, every inch of my body, until I knew I could not be this any longer, could not be only myself. I wanted more. And magic could give it to me.

I called magic up through me and sent it, racing, wild, into Zayvion. He groaned. Shuddered. His eyes washed with gold.

A plunge of cool mint pressed me down. Like iron to lightning, he Grounded me, drinking down the magic that

I poured into him. Magic rolled through me, through Zayvion, then rushed back through me again. I did not know where he began and I ended. Magic and need were one, and I was lost to it. Lost beneath his hands. I closed my eyes, arching, reaching, needing more. More.

Zayvion's breathing became my breathing, his heartbeat my heartbeat. I wanted to wait, wanted him to beg for me to give him release, but I could not stop, too caught in our tempo, as we slipped up and up and up.

For a brief, bright moment, I was whole, alive, complete, hovering upon the crest of a wave that crashed through me, hot, rushing. I shuddered and trembled and clung to Zayvion, wrapped around him, not wanting to let him go.

Heat lapped over me, simmering into a languid warmth, releasing my breath and heartbeat slowly, and making every muscle in my body heavy.

Zayvion kissed the corner of my mouth, and I exhaled the taste of mint.

We rested there, sated, still embracing, unwilling to draw apart. Zayvion leaned his head against my shoulder—the good one—and I drew my fingertips lazily down the back of his head, tugged at his dark curls before sliding my fingers down the back of his neck.

I was exhausted. Tingling. I felt like I'd just taken a few hits of pure oxygen. Zayvion's strong, wide body felt so right. This felt so right.

Why had I ever doubted him? Us?

He took a deep breath and kissed my shoulder, my collarbone. I moaned softly, pulsing gently to his touch, as he gently drew away from me and shifted to lie next to me.

I rolled onto my side, toward him, my back to the door. He wrapped his arms around me.

He stroked the curve of my cheek and temple with his thumb, calling magic to rise softly, then fall like mist away from his touch. "I never want to hurt you."

It was a strange thing to say after making love.

Not knowing what else to do, I just nodded.

We lay there a while. I wanted more, wanted to make love to him again. Instead, I drifted off to sleep.

* * *

A knock at the door woke me.

"I'm going out." It was Nola. "There's breakfast in the kitchen for both of you. I'll be down at the courthouse, and later with Detective Stotts. I should be back around six."

"Okay," I said. "Thanks. Bye." I clutched my blankets like they were going to fly away.

Zayvion wiped his hand over his face and grinned at me. "You didn't forget she was here?"

And I knew I was blushing because I felt the heat of it spread across my chest and up my neck and face.

"No," I lied. "Of course not." I waited until I heard the front door close and then pushed the covers off. I felt the need to be dressed now. Just in case someone or something else decided to drop by. I found clean jeans, panties, bra, a tank, and green sweater. I managed the panties on my own. Then picked up my jeans.

"Gonna go that alone?" Zay asked.

The man lounged in my bed like a cat claiming a sunbeam, stretched out with only the corner of the blanket over his hips. I literally had to wait a second to get my breath back. It didn't help when he smiled and stretched, flexing all the muscles down his hard stomach.

Maybe all I wanted to do was crawl back into bed with him.

"You offering to help?" I asked.

"Could. Might cost you."

"So you're going to blackmail me and leave me naked?"

Zayvion sat up and pulled to the edge of the bed. "You do see where it might be in my best interests to do so."

"I can get into my own damn jeans," I said.

"You didn't ask what it would cost."

"And I'm not going to." I held the waistband, got one foot in, pulled the jeans up, reached my good hand across to get my other foot in, pulled the jeans up. Getting them over my hips was a little trickier and involved a lot of shimmying and wiggling.

I even zipped and buttoned the button. "Ha!" I said triumphantly.

"Very, very nice." Zayvion lifted his gaze from my chest, a wicked grin on his face.

I wasn't wearing a shirt. Or a bra. I'm sure I'd just given him quite a show.

"Bastard."

"Worth it," he said. "Need any help with your shirt, or would you like to prove it's better if I stay out of your way with that too?"

"Get out."

He stood, the sheet dropping completely away, then stretched before finding his boxers.

Okay, I really didn't want him to leave.

I pulled my gaze away from his fine body and worked on getting into my bra. I got both straps over my shoulders, but couldn't twist my arm backward to fasten the hooks.

Zayvion silently made his way up behind me.

"Hands off, flyboy," I said.

"Promise I'll be good," he said. "Just use a couple fingers and a thumb." He did just that, only one knuckle brushing my spine as he hooked my bra. Then he stepped back. "How's that?"

"Nice." I turned and wrapped my arms around his waist, resting my head against his shoulder. So much for the tough-girl act.

He held me, waiting to see where I would take this. I had all sorts of ideas of where I wanted it to go, but my stomach rumbled. If I was going to be using magic today at Maeve's class, I'd need food.

I let go of Zay, gave him a small smile. We both wordlessly went back to getting dressed. I managed the tank on my own, but by the time I found my sweater, I was tired and my shoulder was sore.

"How bad is my shoulder?"

Zay pulled his shirt down. "It's healing. You have a couple punctures."

I held out my sweater for him. He took it, and without a smirk, without a single smile, he helped position it over my head, and held the sleeves so I could push my arms into them.

"Anyone call a doctor?" I asked.

"As I understand it, Nola called her physician back home and asked him if he thought you needed medical care. He didn't seem to think so. Do you want me to take you to the hospital?"

"Right now, I just want some of that breakfast I smell."

Zayvion and I explored the kitchen together and discovered sausage, eggs, and pecan-maple French toast. We moved well together, comfortable in each other's space. I liked that. It had been a long time since I had someone around me, this close to me, who made me feel good.

We also discovered a note from Davy that said, *Hound meeting 7:30, same place.*

A phone started ringing, and I got up from the table to answer it. Except it wasn't my phone.

Zayvion pulled a cell phone out of his pocket. I didn't think he had a cell. This thing looked more like a Victorian card case, with metal swirls and gears and beveled glass and tinted mirrors. It took me a second, because I guess I was just slow today, but I finally recognized a Shield glyph etched into the case.

Heavily Warded didn't begin to describe that thing.

"Yes?" he said.

Whoever was talking on the other line was quiet enough I couldn't hear them, not even with my acute hearing. Either that or the phone had some sort of Privacy or Mute spell worked into it too.

All I know is the man before me went from a happy lover to a blank wall of Zen.

"Yes." It was one, stilted word. The answer of a man having to fulfill an unwanted duty. I wondered who it was on the other line and what they had asked him to do.

He hung up and pocketed the phone.

"Nice gizmo, Batman," I said.

He frowned, and it was strange to see him try to figure out what I was saying. That call must have shaken him up more than I thought.

"The phone," I said. "It's neat. All magical and stuff."

He nodded. "I need to get you one like that. You said your cell keeps dying, didn't you?"

"Yes."

"That's because of how much magic you use. Hold in you. The Wards on it help with that."

"Great," I said, feeling like he and I were talking around whatever was really going on. "Is everything all right?"

He rubbed at the back of his neck. "It is." At my look, he said, "It's just a job. I need to take care of something. I thought I had the rest of the day before . . . before I had to go."

He went silent and somber. I tried to lighten things up. "No rest for assassins." I caught myself on the last word, and Zayvion gave me a sharp look.

"You aren't going to kill someone, are you?" See how understanding and supportive I could be?

"No," he said. "Not today. Not this job." He gave me a hard smile, and I had no doubt that he had killed in the past. And would kill again.

Hells. Now, that was a way to blow all of the fun out of the room.

Still, that's what Zayvion was—an assassin, a magic user, a Closer. He was also a lover, my lover, and someone who had done his best to help me, and other people in the past. I wondered whether one thing balanced the other.

"Is there anything I can do?" I asked.

"No. It's fine. I know . . . it's fine." He took a breath and let it out again, pulling his Zen back over the top of the killer.

"Do you want me to pick you up here?" he asked.

"Why?"

"To take you to Maeve's today."

That's right. I'd forgotten about class again. Ten o'clock or she'd get demon diaper rash or something.

"Sure," I said. "Around nine thirty." I gathered up our plates and coffee cups and took them to the kitchen sink. I walked back to the living room.

Zayvion stood at my window, curtains back just enough so he could see the street below. It was six o'clock, and false dawn was beginning to polish the edges of night.

"Huh," he said.

"What?"

"Nothing." He let the curtain drop, picked up his coat, and put it on.

"Good luck," I said, not knowing what else to say. "Be safe."

"I will." He touched my arm. "Be careful."

With that, he walked out my door.

I stood there, not doing much more than staring at the walls and thinking about too many things. A lot had happened in a day.

Which reminded me. I was seriously behind in my journaling. I pulled my book out of my coat pocket, and the small manila envelope that Violet had given me fell out onto the floor. I was surprised I hadn't lost that in the fight.

My self-defense list. Might need to make a few calls on that before Violet sent the Beckstrom Enterprises henchmen out to get me.

I took the envelope and journal with me back to the living room and tossed the envelope on the table. That could wait. I found a blank page in my journal and quickly recapped everything that had happened in the last day.

Just reading it made me tired.

I got up and pulled back the curtains, looking outside just like Zayvion had. I didn't recognize anyone on the street. The city looked normal. I looked across the street and up. There, on the rooftop opposite my building, sat a hunched and familiar form.

I doubted anyone except Zayvion would even look up and see the gargoyle sitting on the roof of the building, his wings pressed against his back. Not because you couldn't see him in front of the heating vents. But most people did not look up as they went about their daily motions.

Stone's head was tipped so he looked not out over the building like most gargoyles in architecture, but down at the street. Specifically, down at the street in front of the door to my building.

Well, it looked like I had myself a big ol' watchdog.

I stared at him for a bit, but he did not move. I didn't know if that was because dawn was coming on, turning him to inert stone, or if he was pulling the immobile-statue bit for his own reasons.

Either way, I liked the thought of him being out there. Sort of like a big, dumb pet rock guardian angel.

The memory of him tearing into the Necromorph flashed

behind my eyes. Correction: big, dumb, deadly pet rock guardian angel.

I let the curtain fall, and straightened the living room and kitchen—not that either needed much cleaning. Nola visiting had some extra advantages. I tried reading one of the several paperbacks I'd been picking my way through, but didn't have much luck. After reading the same page three times I gave up and opened the manila envelope.

Violet knew how to do her research. Five brochures fell out, each with a photo of the instructor and staff, and a note card with her list of pros and cons attached.

I scanned them. Put two back in the envelope just because the instructors looked too damn smug, and spent some time comparing the remaining three. Two male instructors, one female. All offered a variety of training, from weekend self-defense classes to lifelong fighting disciplines. Not having much to go on, I decided to just call all three and make appointments to meet them.

But before I could dial, the phone rang.

I picked it up. "Hello?"

"Allie?" The voice was young, a woman. I couldn't quite place it.

"Yes?"

"This is Tomi."

Davy's ex-girlfriend, the cutter Hound. The one who had kicked the shit out of him. The one who was running with a rough crowd. The one who hated me.

"Hey, Tomi," I said. "Are you okay?"

I think the question surprised her. I could hear her catch her breath, could hear the sound of traffic in the background as she paused.

"Tell Davy to leave me the hell alone or I'll get a restraining order for him."

"Have you told him that?"

"Yes. He won't listen to me. It's over. It's so fucking over."

I rubbed at my forehead. She sounded angry and sad and a little afraid. Hells, I hated breakups.

"He's worried about you," I said. "About who you're with and that maybe you're hurt. Tomi, if you are hurt, or if you've gotten in a bad situation, you know the Hounds are here to help you. I know some doctors, lawyers, who would help straighten things out for you if you needed it. I'd make sure they got paid, so you don't have to worry about the money."

She paused again, inhaled, held her breath. I could almost feel her thinking it over Finally: "Tell Davy to back off or they'll kill him."

And then she hung up.

I stood there with the dial tone buzzing in my ear while I tried to think this out. I could call Stotts, tell him Tomi was mixed up with someone who wanted to kill Davy. Of course, a lot of new boyfriends want to kill old boyfriends, so it might be an empty threat.

It hadn't sounded like an empty threat. She sounded afraid.

But Tomi was a Hound, and Hounds did a lot of things to manage pain—drugs being one option. She might be high and hallucinating, for all I knew.

I hung up the phone. Stotts already knew I had scented her at the job yesterday. I assumed he was following up on that, so there was a good chance the MERC's had their eyes on her.

Which meant what I should do was try to find Davy. I didn't have his number or address. *Note to self: get phone numbers of Hounds.* But I could still make the meeting at 7:30 and see him there, or get his number from someone else.

Since my last attempt to walk the street had ended with me sporting a raft of new cuts and bruises, I called a cab, waited for it to drive up before I left my building, and took it down to Ankeny Square.

The driver dropped me off at a corner with a light. It was cold out but not yet raining. I put my head down and walked as quickly as I could, not looking right or left. Not looking at the buildings or the street. Not looking at the people who hustled through here, like winter ghosts waiting for this graveyard to come back to life in the spring, waiting for the courtyard to fill with booths and music, the smell of incense, handmade soap, and food from carts.

My heart was beating a little too quickly. Ankeny Square felt like death. Pike's death.

I ducked into the building. Compared to the stark gray light outside, the light inside was burnished a warm yellow. Long mazes of halls and shops and doors that went nowhere pocketed light into corners, lost it in the rafters, and poured it against blank walls. The smell of grilled garlic, incense, and soap hit me so hard, I held my breath. The fragrances filling the building followed me all the way down the central stairs and into the barely finished basement.

Jack Quinn, thin and tough as leather, stood in the middle of the hallway, smoking.

"Morning," I said.

He nodded. "Evening." At my look, he added, "Night shift."

I opened the door to the other unfinished hallway and practiced not freaking out in enclosed places while I strode past the spackled Sheetrock to the room at the end.

The door was open, and the room, which probably had been a Prohibition hidey-hole and gambling parlor in an earlier incarnation, stank of mold and old, wet building. There was one table—a sheet of wood propped on two sawhorses—in the middle of the room, and six folding chairs against the peeling, faded floral wallpaper and bare brick walls.

Hounds, about twenty of them, only six of whom I'd actually met, one of them being Davy, thank all that was holy, stood in the room. A mix of men and women, old and young, insane and even more insane, the Hounds all stood or sat in such a way as to not come into contact with their fellow human beings.

I scanned the faces of everyone gathered, letting the sudden silence at my entrance stretch out. I'd learned years ago that she who controlled the silence in a room, controlled the room.

So far, so good. Every eye was on me.

"Morning," I said to everyone gathered. No one answered; they just stared.

Neat.

There was a chair at the table, the chair Pike used to sit

in. I guess I was expected to go sit in that chair, but my feet would not move. The idea of taking his place, really taking his place, made me want to turn around and leave.

Pike was gone. And I could never replace him.

I stepped in and leaned against the wall on the left side of the doorway so Jack could walk in past me.

"So we need to go over a few things," I began.

Davy flipped open a pad of paper on a clipboard and clicked his pen. What do you know? He really was going to be my secretary. I gave him an appreciative glance and tucked both my hands in my coat pockets, letting my body language say *relaxed*.

"Pike had a lot of hope for the Hounds. He was a smart man. He knew potential when he saw it.

"But I'm not Pike. I don't know what he had planned for the Hounds, for us. So I'm going to tell you what I'm going to do."

A few feet shuffled. But other than that, the only sound in the room was Davy's pen moving across the paper.

Tough crowd.

"First, I'm moving our meeting place to somewhere that doesn't stink." *And doesn't remind me of Pike's death*, I thought.

"I know the guy who runs Get Mugged. There's a warehouse right next to him that he's thinking about buying. I'll see if he'll cut me a deal. I'll set up a permanent meeting place with a couple couches available for Hounds who need to sleep."

It was like a collective exhale. Body language changed from angry, tense, tight, to . . . well, to less of that.

"Who's gonna pay for it?" a short, athletic man I'd never met asked.

"Me."

"An' what are we gonna owe you for it?"

"The courtesy of not burning the place down, or doing illegal crap while you're there. If you can't follow those two rules, the door will be locked next time you come calling.

"I'm also setting up a medical fund. Not just for disasters, but for regular doctor visits, pain-management counseling, legal drugs, rehab. That kind of stuff."

I can say one thing for Hounds. When they have something to say, they are not shy about speaking up. I leaned back against the wall, letting them bitch and grumble until someone actually asked a question.

"You think you can throw money at us and we'll follow you like dogs, Beckstrom?"

"Listen," I said with more calm than I felt. "I promised Pike I'd try to do good for the Hounds in the city because *he* cared about you. You don't want my help, then don't show up."

That went over well. There's nothing like a couple dozen Hounds with stares set on hate.

Yeah, well, they could bite me for all I cared.

Bea, the bubbly Hound who worked the morgues, came bustling in the door, pulling the wide hood of her jacket away from her mop of curly hair.

"What did I miss?"she asked with a grin.

I swear, I had never seen that woman in a bad mood.

Jack, an unlit cigarette in his mouth, leaned toward her conspiratorially. "Beckstrom's kicking the hive."

"Really?" Bea looked around, spotted me. "I always knew you'd be trouble." She sounded excited about it. "So, what's the buzz?"

I opened my mouth to answer, but Jack cut me off. "She's aiming for health care, free bunks, that sort of shit."

Bea's eyebrows hitched up until they got lost in her bangs. "Really?"

I spoke before Jack could. "Yes. And now I want to know who's working a job. And I want cell numbers so I can call you to let you know where the next meeting will be held."

It took maybe an hour to record where and what everyone was working, and to get non-Hounding volunteers to buddy up and keep an eye on the job and be willing to call 911 if something went bad for the Hound.

Davy handed me the notepad he'd been using, and I worked on memorizing Hound names and gigs. Between schools, retailers, hospitals, personal hires, and nonprofits, the Hounds in this room covered all corners of the city, and even some of the other nearby towns.

Strange to think there were that many people who believed magic was being used illegally against them.

Maybe stranger to think that they were probably right.

The meeting broke up a lot like the last one I'd attended. People simply filed out the door when they were done talking. Soon the only people left were Bea, Jack, Davy, and me.

"Anyone have the time?" I asked.

Jack glanced at his watch. "It's five after nine."

Which meant Zayvion was probably on the corner of the street outside my apartment, waiting to take me to Maeve's.

"I have an appointment." I walked over to the door. "Who has the key to lock up?"

Jack held up his hand.

"Good. I'll see you all next week. Davy, can I talk to you a minute?"

He had already started walking down the hallway, but stopped and waited while I caught up with him.

"Tomi called me this morning," I said as we kept walking, a little more slowly. "She said you've been bothering her."

"She's really fucked up," he said.

And what he didn't say, but what was obvious on his face, was that he still cared for her, maybe even still loved her, but he was helpless to keep her from screwing up her life.

Love sucks.

"I told her if she's in trouble we would help. She knows there are other options out there for her. But you need to give her some space."

"Space?" He turned on me and I took a step back, wondering if I'd have to block a punch. Instead, he leaned against the wall and swallowed hard, his hands in fists at his side.

The light hit his face so I could see his bruised eyes were puffy and red. It looked like he hadn't shaved for a couple of days. His sweat and breath smelled of beer and cheap whiskey.

Kid was in a world of hurt. His girlfriend dumped him; the man he looked up to, Pike, had been murdered. He was beat, inside and out.

"She's not going to make it," he said, so quietly I wondered if he was talking to me or himself. "She's slipping away. And she won't listen.... Won't let me help... You know how crazy that is?"

I felt a strange twinge in my chest, sorrow for him. I knew what it was like to lose everything. If we were somewhere alone, I might even talk to him about that, give him a sisterly pat on the shoulder or something. Instead I placed my hand on his upper arm.

He couldn't have looked more shocked if I'd hit him with a Taser.

Have I mentioned Hounds don't do contact?

"If she won't take our help, then we'll get her pointed in the right direction to help herself."

"Like that's going to work," he muttered.

"Maybe not. Lots of Hounds fuck up and die. But Tomi's pretty smart. And she's strong. A survivor."

He nodded, watching me, and not doing a very good job of hiding how miserable he was and how much he really wanted to believe there was some hope left for her.

"Do you know who she's with?" I asked. "That guy you said she was working for, cutting for?"

"She calls him Jingo."

"What?"

He shrugged one shoulder. "Mr. Jingo. I looked. There isn't anyone in Portland by that name. I figure it's just what he's told her."

Bea and Jack came strolling down the corridor. "One side," Jack said as they neared. Then, "After you, Beatrice."

Bea smiled and walked past us. "See you later, Allie, Davy," she said.

Jack just gave us a short nod, and then both of them were out the door into the building proper.

Jingo. Not nearly a common enough a name for it not to be Jingo Jingo. But what would a member of the Authority, a teacher of Death magic, want with a Hound? Maybe he wanted what anyone wanted from a Hound—someone to track magic. Or maybe he had taken her on as a student, like Maeve had taken me on.

"Have you ever met him?"

"No."

"Okay. Let me look into it. I'll see if I can track him down. You just stay away from her for a little while."

He glared at me.

"She said she'll get a restraining order on you if you don't."

"Like that matters," he said.

"It does. I'll pay medical bills, but I'll be damned if I'm going to post bail for you, Silvers." We glared at each other. I won.

He looked down at his shoes.

"She'll come around," I said. "Just give her some time."

"You don't know Tomi," he said. "She never comes around."

"Just promise you'll stay away from her until she cools off," I said again.

He blinked and gave me a disinterested look.

Fabulous.

"I have an appointment to keep." I started walking to the door. "You going to be okay?"

"Sure." He didn't move away from the wall. He just leaned his head back, clenched his hands into fists, and closed his eyes.

"If you need anything, call," I said.

He didn't respond. I felt bad leaving him alone in the hall, but I really had to get home if I was going to make it to class on time. And I had some new questions I needed to ask Maeve.

I strolled back out into the building and took the stairs that exited to street level.

It was raining. Hard. I paused under the dubious cover of the building's overhang and dug my knit hat out of my pocket. Hat on head, I strode across the street, not waiting for the light to change. I caught the MAX light rail train instead of waiting for the bus.

I made it to the bottom of my hill and started up. I finally spotted Zayvion's car, parked a block away from my apartment.

More walking in the rain. I was soaked, cold, and the wind was picking up. Still, instinct told me to slow my steps before getting too close to Zayvion's car. Something was wrong. By now he should have at least acknowledged that he saw my approach.

The back of my neck tingled and magic, deep and hot within me, pushed to be released.

Danger, danger, danger.

A moth-wing flutter on the back of my eyes reminded me that my dad was still there. Not exactly comforting.

I paused beneath an overhang in front of a glass shop, set a Disbursement—a headache again—then drew the glyph for Sight with my fingertip and poured magic into it.

The street filled with the ghostly multicolored ashes of old spells, many dissolving and regenerating—business spells set on cycles or loops as the magic pulsed into them—the price for the constant refresh going off somewhere to Proxy pits and penitentiaries.

A dozen Veiled, men, women, wandered the street, so far uninterested in me. Time to get a move on before they changed their minds.

I used Sight to look at Zayvion's car. No new spells wrapped it; no ashes of old spells clung to it. It looked like any other magically unenhanced vehicle. And when I looked a little closer, past the car to the single occupant inside, I did not see traces of Wards or traps or trips there.

It took me all of ten seconds. And in that time, the Veiled turned and shuffled toward me.

I hurriedly dropped Sight, breaking the spell and ending the feed of magic into it. The street snapped back into rain and traffic. I took a couple deep breaths, letting go of the adrenaline rush. I did not like having to worry about the Veiled attacking every time I used magic.

I could show you how to block them, my dad's voice whispered through my mind.

Do you really think I'd trust you? I thought at him.

We could do so much for each other.

Too late for that. Much too late.

I strode the rest of the way to Zayvion's car, but kept an eye out for nonmagical threats. All I needed was for some whack job to jump me for my wallet.

Nothing and no one stopped me. Even though all I

wanted to do was rush into the shelter of the car, I bent and looked through the passenger's-side window before so much as touching the door handle.

The car was empty except for Zayvion, who slouched in the driver's seat, his shoulders angled so that his face was pressed against the window. His eyes were closed. I bit the inside of my cheek and watched. His chest rose, fell.

He was still breathing.

The door was unlocked, so I let myself in. Zayvion didn't stir as cold wind blasted into the car.

"Zayvion?" I touched his arm.

He jerked awake. His eyes, normally dark brown, were flooded by rivers of gold. He'd been using magic. Lots of magic. The whites of his eyes were bloodshot, and his dusky skin was a shade too gray. He looked sick. I smelled the bitterness of exhaustion and the powerful metallic odor of spent magic mixed with his pine scent.

"Allie?" He straightened and rubbed at his face with hands that shook. "Sorry. Tired. Ready?"

I might have said yes if it hadn't taken him two tries to hold the keys tightly enough to start the engine. This man was in no shape to drive.

"You are not driving."

He frowned. "Why?"

"Because I value my life." I got out of the car and didn't hear his reply.

I jogged in front of the car and opened his door.

"You're being ridiculous."

And I might have believed that if he hadn't slurred his words.

"Doesn't matter. Let's go."

Maybe it was the tone of my voice. Maybe it was the look in my eyes. Whatever, Zayvion squinted up at me, then fumbled with his seat belt and finally got it off. He grabbed the doorframe and used it as leverage to get his legs out of the car.

He paused there, breathing hard.

"Shit," he said softly.

"What happened?"

"Just." He swallowed. "Bad day at the job."

"What is that supposed to mean?" I reached down and gripped his arm to help him get out of the car. "Is this from magic? Did you kill someone? Close someone?" The memory of the Necromorph who had cornered me, and then the strange shadow magic that had brought him back to life, rushed behind my eyes. I literally shivered.

"Did something attack you?"

"No," he said. "Sleep. Just need sleep."

"Well, you're in luck. My bed's upstairs. Come on, big guy," I said as I pulled back to get him up on his feet. "Time to go for a walk."

I tugged his arm toward me, ducking to put it over my shoulder.

"Walk?" he muttered.

"Walk," I said, pushing a little Influence behind it. "You need some sleep, so we're going up to my place. Ready?"

"Influence doesn't work," he grunted as he took a step, "on me."

I'd forgotten that. "Well, how about, 'Please don't argue with me, because I can't fucking carry you up three flights of stairs'?"

He took a deep breath. Exhaled while he spoke. "Since you asked so nice."

I led us to the apartment door, keeping his arm over my shoulder and my arm tight around his waist. "Are you hurt?" We paused by the door so I could dig the key out of my pocket. "Were you attacked?"

"Just tired. Should pass in an hour or so. Heavy lifting." He didn't say *magic*, but I knew that's what had exhausted him.

"There's this new thing on the market. Called a Proxy," I said. "Maybe you ought to try one sometime." I pushed open the door.

"Did," he said. "You don't know. It's . . ." He lowered his voice to mitigate the echo in the lobby. "I am the only one who can do it. Closing. Closed. Like that."

Well, at least now I knew what he'd done.

"Does it always hit you this hard?" I asked as we walked over to the stairs. "Closing?"

"No. He. This one. Complicated."

"Who's complicated?"

He looked over at me, gold eyes too gold, too red. Exhausted. Maybe feverish. Very quietly, he said, "Cody. I closed Cody. Took his memories, his magic away."

It was like a razor-sharp finger dragging down my spine.

"What in the hell?" I said, low, vicious. "He's an innocent."

"No." Zayvion shook his head sadly. "He's never been innocent. Powerful. Hand." He blinked and seemed to realize where he was and what he was saying. He clamped his mouth shut and glared at the stairs.

"Shit," he said quietly. "Not here. I need to rest. Then." He lifted one foot and set it down on the first stair.

"Then you'll tell me what you did?"

"Then," he agreed.

"Promise?"

"Word." He put a few more stairs behind him and added, "You have mine."

Man was barely able to walk and make sense at the same time.

So we climbed the stairs, not saying much. Me, fuming. Zayvion, less winded than I expected him to be. I wondered if the fatigue, if the price he was paying for Closing Cody was already fading.

He was going to have to come up with a hell of a good reason to convince me taking Cody's memories away was a good thing. That kid already had enough going against him without dealing with people like the Authority. Like Zayvion.

By the time we got to my door and I checked and listened before opening, Zayvion was moving a little better than he had at the bottom of the stairs. But as we walked into my apartment, he stumbled, and I leaned back hard to correct his balance.

"How much do you weigh, Jones?" I groaned.

"Sorry." He swayed a little and put his hand on the wall.

"Do I need to call someone?" I asked.

"No. I'm sleep." He let go of me and walked a straight line into my living room. "Gonna couch. Okay."

"Couch is fine." I threw my wet hat on the half wall between the foyer and kitchen and glanced into the kitchen. No one there, and no note, which meant Nola hadn't been back yet. Just in case, I checked the bedroom and bathroom too. No Nola.

The phone rang.

Zayvion was off the couch in one smooth motion. He stood slightly crouched, hands spread in front of him, ready to cast, eyes startlingly alert. If I had ever doubted it before, it was very clear just how deadly this man was.

"Hang on, hero," I said. "Don't kill the phone."

Zayvion straightened, rubbed his hand over the back of his neck. He blinked and looked around, trying to get his bearings, then sat on the couch.

I picked up the phone. "Hello?"

"It's Davy," Davy said. He sounded out of breath. Strained, like he was running. "I'm at Cathedral Park. Can you get here?"

Cathedral Park was in St. Johns. "What are you doing there?"

"Following a Hound. I need your help."

"Who, Davy? Which Hound are you following?" He hadn't volunteered to follow anyone at the meeting today. "If you're in trouble, call the police."

"Forget it," he said. "I'll handle it."

And then he hung up.

Great. Just what I needed. A lovesick idiot kid out getting himself killed.

I swore softly. Davy wasn't thinking straight. I'd put money on it being Tomi he was following. And I'd bet money he was about to get his ass kicked again.

Or worse. Tomi had said they would kill him if he didn't stop bothering her.

Hells.

"Okay?" Zayvion mumbled. He was lying down again, on his side, since my couch wasn't wide enough for his shoulders if he lay on his back. He had a pillow bunched up under his head. His eyes were closed.

"It's fine," I growled. I pulled a blanket out of the linen closet and brought it over to him.

"Should take you to class," he said.

I pulled the blanket over him. "I can get to class on my own. I'll call Maeve and let her know I'm going to be a little late." And buy myself some time so I could take a trip to St. Johns and drag Davy home, in chains, if I had to.

"Mmm." He was snoring before I made it back to the phone.

I had Maeve's number in my book. I dialed.

" 'Lo, you've reached the Feile San Fhomher," a familiar male voice answered. "How may I help you?"

"Shamus?" I asked.

There was a short pause. "Allie?"

"Yes. I need to talk to Maeve."

"Right, right. Well, you can't. She's . . . busy."

"Can you take a message for me?"

"Sure." There was a little shuffle sound like he was digging out a pen and paper. "Shoot."

"Tell her I'm going to be late for class. Two hours, maybe."

He let out a hoot. "Oh, no, no, no, darling. Don't do that. She hates it when students stand her up."

"I don't have a choice, okay? I can get there in about two hours."

"Hmm. And what will you be doing in those two hours?"

At my pause he said, "Allie?" dragging the sound of my name out, like he knew I was hiding a naughty secret. "Are you up to something?"

"No." It didn't even sound convincing to me.

He chuckled. "What have you gotten yourself into? Come on, now. You can tell me."

Annoying. And Zayvion's best friend. Fine, if he wanted to know what I was dealing with, he could deal with it too.

"Zayvion was supposed to drive me out there, but he"—I paused, not knowing what Shamus knew and how much I should say—"he's passed out on my couch."

"Is he breathing normally?" Gone was the laughter. Gone was the teasing. Shamus was deadly serious.

The turn of conversation made my stomach flip with panic. I looked over at Zay. He was still snoring.

"Does snoring count?"

"Good enough." Shamus sounded relieved. "How did his eyes look?"

"Gold. Really gold. And bloodshot."

"Was he talking clearly?"

"Not really. He did climb three flights of stairs."

"Idiot," he muttered. "Okay, here's what you're going to do."

"Whoa, back up," I said. "I already know what I'm going to do. I have a friend who's in some kind of trouble. Zay said he just needed an hour to sleep it off."

Shamus grunted and exhaled with a click that told me he was sucking on a cigarette. "And you believed him? Fine. You go take care of your friend. I'll see that Z is on the mend."

"You're coming over to my apartment? I have company. . . ."

"Your friend Nola? I know. Just tell her to let me in when I come by."

"She's not here."

"So leave her a note."

Truth was, I didn't like the idea of Shamus coming over to my apartment. Didn't like my privacy invaded. I had lived alone for a long time. I didn't like it when other people thought they could move through my space.

Who was I kidding? I might have been that private, closed-off person before, but in just the last couple days I'd had my friend, a magical detective, my boyfriend, and a gargoyle in my living room. Not exactly the life of a hermit.

"I'll let her know," I said. "Knock loud. If she's not back by the time you get here, you'll have to get Zay to open the door."

"Don't worry, love," he said. "I know how to wake Jones."

"Tell your mom I'm going to be late," I reminded.

"Right. Later, then."

"Bye." I hung up and then wrote a note for Nola, letting her know Zayvion's friend Shamus was going to be over to sit with him until he woke up. I also mentioned that Zayvion was okay, just exhausted and needed a place to crash.

I left the note—which I hoped was innocent-sounding enough that Detective Stotts wouldn't get suspicious if he was with Nola—on the coffeepot, grabbed my spare knit hat off the hook behind the door, and left, locking the apartment behind me. I paused out in the hallway and considered setting a Ward on the door. I never used them, but good Wards could at least warn the person inside that an intruder was coming.

No. A good Ward took more time and concentration than I had right now. And all it was likely to do was set off when Nola came home, freak Zayvion out, and cause a ruckus.

No Wards for the door.

Interesting, though, that I had wanted to set one. That I had wanted to do something to make sure Zayvion was safe. Even though he'd told me he had just taken away Cody's memories. What did that say about how I felt about him?

And what would Zayvion feel about me when he found out I was stealing his car?

Chapter Twelve

Tracking someone in a city the size of Portland isn't easy. But I had a few things on my side for a change.

One, I knew Davy, knew his scents. I also knew Tomi and her scents. It was a pretty good guess that she was the trouble he had gotten himself into. Where I found one, I'd find the other.

But unless they were using magic, I couldn't track them by magical means. Or at least I couldn't if I didn't have something personal of Davy's.

And I had the notebook he'd been writing in during the Hound meeting. Lucky for me, he'd also been in a state of higher emotion. That always left a better impression on the item, especially since it had so recently been in his hand.

Back in college we called this kind of tracking work swamp-walking. The impression left on an object gave a hint of where the person was, but the trail rarely held out long enough to actually lead to the person. Still, it was a point in the right direction.

I got in Zayvion's car, locked the doors, and cleared my mind. I held the notebook in my left hand, added a little more pain onto that headache that was going to kick my ass in a couple days, and traced the glyph for a version of Sight that allowed a more subtle energy trace.

The notebook flickered with faint lines of energy—not like the hard-carved glyphs of magic; these lines were fading and fading fast.

The lines trailed off at the edges, rcaching out as if they

followed a slight wind, or magnetic pull, toward the north, toward St. Johns.

Good enough.

I let go of Sight, breaking the glyph. I hadn't seen any of the Veiled when I used magic this time. Of course I hadn't looked around for them either, and I was quick at swamp-walking.

I started the car and eased out into traffic, getting the feel of Zayvion's car. It was strangely like him. Smooth, lots of power, and geared a little tight.

It took some time to get there, traffic being heavier than normal at this hour. We got a lot of rain in Portland, but when a really good downpour decided to open up over the city, sane drivers didn't go faster than their windshield wipers could move.

I drove over the St. Johns Bridge and down into the lazy little broken-down neighborhood. I don't know what it was about St. Johns. Every time I came here, my shoulders relaxed and my mind cleared. Coming back to St. Johns always felt like coming home.

Sure, the neglected neighborhood showed signs of wear. But there was an honesty to the place. No fancy magic spells to make a business look like it was made of marble and gold. No fancy magic spells to keep the flowers blooming out of season. St. Johns was unapologetic.

I loved that.

I didn't know where Davy was, and I didn't know what kind of trouble he was in. So I decided to stay out of Cathedral Park's parking lot. I stopped the car behind a warehouse on North Brandford Street. Out of the way of curious eyes but still within running distance of the park.

I got out of the car, locked it, and made sure I had the keys in my pocket. Then I crossed the street to a soggy patch of trees on the edge of the park. Time to find Davy.

I cleared my mind, chanted a mantra, set my Disbursement. Drawing on magic here in the fifth quarter, on the other side of the railroad tracks, was difficult. But now that I carried magic within me, even in a dead zone, there was enough magic to power a dozen spells. Maybe more. I'd never really tested how much I could use magic without the constant refill from the city.

I hoped I wouldn't have a reason to find that out any time soon.

I drew the glyphs for Sight, Smell, and Sound and poured magic into them.

St. Johns might not have magic going for it, but the few spells that were at work here stuck out like a sore thumb. Mostly, I saw spells wrapped around people who had bought cheap magical vanities that never lasted long, to try to improve the look of their cars, clothes, hair.

I ignored all those petty spells, my Hounding instincts drawn instead to the flicker of magic in the shadows beneath the bridge.

Indigos, bloodreds, burnt copper. All the colors I'd last seen bringing the Necromorph back to life shimmered under the gothic arched pillars of St. Johns Bridge. I couldn't make out the spells from this distance—they were too tangled, too dark, caught with the scents of blood and shadow—but I could catch the slightest magical scent of Davy, cedar and lemons and pain, and of Tomi, strawberry bubble gum and blood.

Davy was there. In the park. In that mess of magic.

Stupid, stupid, stupid, I thought as I dropped the spells I'd been using. What did Davy think he could do? Follow Tomi around all day, and convince her he wasn't crazy?

Stupid.

I wound through the strip of trees, not wanting to use the footpath that was out in the open. My jeans were wet halfway up my calves from the tall grass, but I kept going, heading downhill toward the river.

The wind shifted and the smell of the river came to me, greens and wet soil and the slippery scent of fish. I'd been through this part of town plenty of times, smelled the river plenty of times. This time a memory rode the scents of the river. Dread settled in the pit of my stomach. Something bad had happened to me here, alongside the river.

I searched my mind but came up blank. Still, the emotional knowledge that something terrible had happened here was so strong, I broke out in a sweat.

Losing my memory made a lot of things feel like a half-remembered nightmare. And I hated that. Hated going into a situation with such an obvious blind spot in my experience. It made me feel like around every corner someone—or something—was there, waiting to jump me.

And it probably was.

I followed my gut toward the bridge. The huge green expanse of the St. Johns Bridge arched overhead at least three stories, spanning the river with gothic arches that ended across the river in Forest Park.

I didn't see anyone walking the concrete trail around the park. Still, I couldn't see the whole thing. There were too many hills and valleys and trees to get a good view of the place.

I set a Disbursement again and drew Sight. A bloodred trail of magic pulsed like a vein through the air, tracing the natural curve of the land along the water and knotting just twenty yards ahead of me, where the hill took a sharp downward curve into a gully, hidden from most of the park. The spell pulsed there, bright as copper lightning from the sky.

The traces of Davy's signature were clearer there. He was either part of casting that spell or he was a victim of it.

I jogged closer, as quietly as the wet grass would let me. I probably should have contacted the police or Stotts or, hell, even told Shamus I was coming out here. But I figured Davy was mixed up with ex-girlfriend-fistfight problems, not giant-dark-crazy-magic problems.

And, hey, maybe it really was just fistfight problems.

Yeah. Right.

Tomi seemed like the kind of girl who wouldn't mind using magic to torture her ex. Or on the woman who was trying to rescue him.

I didn't have a gun. I didn't even have a cell phone. But I had magic. If someone was hurting Davy, I could at least Hold them and get Davy away. I could probably knock them unconscious with magic, if I had to.

Just in case, I traced a Hold spell and held it pinched between my forefinger and thumb, but didn't pour magic into it yet.

I took the curve of the hill and came over the crest.

The full smell of the spell hit me as the scene spilled out before me. Davy was crumpled on the ground about twenty feet away. Blood poured from the side of his head onto the concrete path. Blood trailed away from him and connected to the edge of a circle of black ash that was as glossy as crow feathers, and burned finger deep into the grass.

Standing on the other side of that circle was Tomi. Too pale, too thin, wearing too many layers of black with too many bruises and scratches mucking up her skin. She looked like hell had sucked her up warm and spat her out dead.

She had a knife in her hand. A very large knife. With a lot of blood on it.

"Tomi?"

She didn't say anything. She just stared into the empty space between us. I didn't think she even realized I was standing there. Shock?

I crept forward. She didn't move, didn't so much as blink. I bent next to Davy, keeping my eye on her. His skin was warm, but his breath came out in uneven gurgles. Maybe a punctured lung. Or worse.

"Tomi," I said again. "Are you hurt? Do you know what happened?"

'Cause, yeah, asking the crazy chick with the big bloody knife if she was up on current events was a great idea.

Nothing.

Davy wasn't breathing well enough for me to wait around for her answer anyway.

I had to get him out of here. To the hospital. I bent and picked him up, swore at the pain in my injured shoulder that shot down my back. I tried to lift him as carefully as I could, which is to say, not very.

He made a moaning noise.

Tomi blinked. Focused. Looked over at me.

"I told you they'd kill him," she whispered. "See what happened? See?"

She gestured with the knife and blood fell from the blade into the circle of ash. The magic in the circle, in the spell, rippled with shadows of indigo and bloodred.

"Tomi, listen. Davy's not dead. I need to take him to the hospital. Put the knife down and come with me."

Tomi just stared at me and jerked the knife in a couple haphazard strikes through thin air. No, not strikes. Drawing. She was working Blood magic, casting a spell. Oh, this was not good. Not good at all.

I didn't think I could get him up into a fireman's hold, so I pulled his arm over my shoulder, which also hurt like hell. It was good he wasn't a heavy-built guy. Still, deadweight is deadweight.

I gritted my teeth and grasped him by the waist, then started to sort of half drag him back along the path to the car.

I thought about putting him down so I could tackle Tomi and drag her butt along with me, but I didn't think Davy had that much time, and I sure as hell didn't have the strength to haul them both back to the car.

"Tomi," I called. "Follow me. Let me help you."

She looked up away from the circle of ash, her expression blank. "Me?" She shook her head. "You don't understand. He's coming," she said. "He'll kill him. Don't . . . don't let him hurt him."

The circle in front of her seemed darker, more shadowed, and filled with flashes of things that moved.

Shit.

Tomi went back to casting the spell. I saw yellow eyes in that circle, fangs.

I moved as fast as I could, across the park, through the trees. Not easy, not fun.

I so needed to start going to the gym.

Davy kept right on breathing. Jerky, slow, but breathing. And that was all I could ask for.

Well, that, and maybe for Tomi to snap out of the crazy and stop casting magic. That chick was messing around with dark magic—something she should not know about. No wonder Davy said she was different.

I picked up the pace and made it to the car. It was raining and I was shaking from fatigue and anger. I unlocked the back door, lay Davy half in the car, ran around to the other door, and pulled him by his armpits the rest of the way across the seat.

Davy's breathing wasn't doing so hot now. I needed to stop Tomi, save her, but Davy didn't have any time left.

This pissed me off to no end. I couldn't go back to save Tomi, and I would not just drive away and let her die.

Then I remembered I had friends in low places. Time to call in a favor.

All I needed was a phone.

Something moved at the edge of my rearview mirror. I looked up.

Creatures ghosted across the grass, dark, transparent horrors of indigo, midnight, blood, low to the ground, nightmare beasts like the Necromorph but compact, muscled, all claw and fang and burning yellow eyes. Running my way.

"Shit, shit, shit!" I gunned the gas.

The creatures were fast. Too fast. Before I was even out of the parking lot they were behind me, beside me, then past me, silent as poison, spreading out, half a dozen or more, into the streets, the rain.

Crap. Nightmare creatures chasing me was bad. Nightmare creatures loose on the street was worse. Maybe they were what had hurt Davy. Maybe they were the "him" Tomi was talking about.

Maybe I didn't have time to find out.

I pulled up in front of Mama's place, a two-story brick and wood building with a diner on the bottom floor and some living space on the top. I ran up the stairs and pushed open the door.

Boy, the one who was always behind the counter, didn't bother to pull his hand away from the gun I knew he kept hidden. As a matter of fact, he pulled out the gun and casually aimed it at me.

Oh, how fandamtastic was that?

"Where's Mama?" I asked. He lifted the gun, just in case I hadn't noticed it the first time.

"Out," he said.

Yeah, we had history. The bad kind.

"Give me your phone. There's a woman hurt. In the park. She might be dead."

He didn't seem very impressed with the news. And I supposed if you'd grown up in this part of town, the report of a dead person in your backyard wouldn't exactly hit the headlines.

"Give me the phone, Boy. I've got a kid dying in my car."

Mama stormed out of the kitchen, five feet not much of street and attitude. She stopped, obviously surprised to see me.

"Allie, girl?"

"I need your phone," I said.

And that, I knew, was very familiar. I'd told her the same thing just a few months ago when I was still Hounding for her and trying to get her to call 911 for her youngest, Boy, who had been hit by an Offload from my father. Well, not my father, but at the time I'd thought it was his spell.

Instead of arguing with me, she handed me the phone from where it hung on the wall next to the kitchen. That was new.

"Is it bad?" she asked as I dialed.

"I think so."

She nodded and waited, watching me.

I dialed Detective Stotts. He would be the one they'd call in on the case anyway, because there was no way that was a run-of-the-mill magical crime.

After one ring, he answered. "Stotts."

"This is Allie Beckstrom," I said. "You need to get to Cathedral Park as soon as you can. There's a woman hurt there. Tomi Nowlan. Magic is involved."

I noted Mama tensed at that, and I was not about to give him any more details with her listening. "I'm on my way to the hospital with Davy Silvers. If you need me, you can find me there."

I hung up before he had a chance to ask me anything.

"Police are on their way," I said to Mama. "Detective Stotts. He'll know what to do. Lock the doors and keep Boy, your youngest, off the street for a while, okay?"

She bit her bottom lip and nodded. Her hands were laced together in front of her, her body language saying she was trying hard to hold something back. I didn't know what she wanted to say to me, or do to me, and sure as hell didn't have time to find out.

I straight-armed the door open. Just before it closed behind me, I heard her say, "Good luck."

And I hoped she meant it in an innocent sort of way, and not in a she-knew-more-about-what-was-going-on-than-I-did kind of way.

The whole thing in Mama's had taken a minute, tops.

I jumped back in the car and tore off toward the hospital as fast as I could, hoping I hadn't taken one minute too long to save Davy.

Chapter Thirteen

I was amazed I didn't get pulled over by the police on my way to the hospital. It all went by so fast, and yet every pause, every second I had to brake or work my way around someone in traffic, felt like a lifetime. I raced up to emergency, and ran inside to get help.

Two people rushed out to the car with me, and between the three of us we got Davy moved onto a gurney that was wheeled into the ER.

My heart pounded so hard, I was breathing as if I'd run the entire way.

I followed Davy, but was stopped by a petite nurse.

"Are you a relative?"

"No. Friend."

"Do you know family we should contact? Insurance information?"

I didn't. I had no idea at all. I wasn't even sure how old he was. "No. We've just started working together. He's a Hound."

She nodded and motioned for me to follow her to a desk. "We found his wallet. Do you know if he's allergic to anything?"

"No." I should have taken medical information from the Hounds at the meeting today. How stupid could I be?

"That's all right," she said. "We'll see what we can pull up on him. If he's been in a hospital in the last ten years, we'll have something on record. Why don't you have a seat? I have a few more questions."

I sat across from her, but didn't have any more answers.

Note to self: start a Hound medical information data bank.

She finished entering my lack of information into her computer, then gave me a sympathetic smile. "You can wait right out there. There's coffee at the far wall if you'd like some."

I mumbled my thanks and walked over to the coffee station, pouring myself a cup and then walking woodenly back to one of the banks of lima-bean green chairs in the waiting room. There were several people in the waiting room whom I hadn't even noticed until now.

I paced for a little while, held the coffee between my hands until it was cold, then finally took a seat near the door. I wasn't sure whether I was sitting there for a quick escape or whether I was keeping an eye out for monsters.

Either way, it took some time for the adrenaline to wear off, and when it did I realized I was really tired.

My thoughts were jagged and random.

Somewhere out there monsters roamed the street.

Zayvion said he Closed Cody.

Where was Nola?

I was late for class.

Tomi was using dark magic.

She might be dead.

Was Davy going to be okay?

Had taking the time to make that phone call killed him?

What did Jingo Jingo have to do with this?

And what the hell was that spell anyway?

Did Tomi have a disk?

I don't know how much time passed before Detective Stotts came walking in, wearing a trench, a maroon scarf, and a frown. But he brought two cups of coffee with him.

"Allie." He sat down next to me and offered me one of the cups.

This was the good coffee from the mom-and-pop shop close to the police station, not the overcooked canned coffee the emergency room provided.

I put down my cold Styrofoam cup and held the larger,

warmer cup in my palms. Was it strange that I couldn't feel the heat against my skin?

"How's Davy?" he asked quietly.

I shook my head. "They haven't told me."

He took a drink, and so did I. The coffee was black, hot, and rich. It felt like heaven going down. And it somehow made the world feel real again.

"Did you go to the park?" I asked.

He nodded.

"Tomi?"

"We couldn't find her."

I lowered my head and pressed the coffee cup against my forehead.

"What happened?" he asked.

A sick feeling rolled in my stomach and I put the coffee down because the smell, the heat, was suddenly too much. "Was there anyone . . . else?"

"No. The circle was still there."

"Did you get rid of it?"

"Not yet."

I stared at him, confused. Then my brain kicked in. Right. Procedure. He'd have someone Hound it, get photos, take samples, all that before they cleaned it up. It could take days.

I stood. I needed to talk to Zayvion. Or Shamus. Or maybe Maeve. Find out if any of them knew anything about Tomi. Find out if she was hurt, dead. Find out if I needed to get her to the hospital too. "I have to go."

Stotts stood slowly. He put his hand on my elbow. "Where?"

"Out. Away. Find out if anyone else, if people, if Hounds know anything." Wow. I was not thinking straight. Really, all I wanted to do was sit down in a quite room for maybe a century. The idea of losing Davy, when I'd promised Pike I'd take care of him, and that Tomi was probably hurt, maybe dead, made me crazy.

So I did what I usually do when I'm afraid, or worried. I got angry.

"I have people to take care of, okay?" I said.

"I understand that. One of them is in there." He pointed at the double doors that led to the emergency room.

"And the rest are out there." I pointed at the door, and turned to storm off.

But the door had already slid aside. And through it walked the Hounds Jack and Bea and Sid.

"We heard about Davy," Bea said, her normally smiling face worried.

"Davy wasn't working for you, was he, Stotts?" Sid looked like the sort of guy you'd expect to program computers, not Hound. He was dressed in his usual tan slacks, button-down shirt, sensible loafers, and wire-rimmed glasses.

He was smart too. I hadn't even thought about Stotts using Davy. Stotts was cursed. More Hounds died working for him than for anyone else in the city.

Stotts blinked once. "Yes."

"What the hell?" I said loud enough that half the emergency room looked over at me. "You asked me to work for you. Not him. Not Davy. Didn't I answer you fast enough? You had to go out and find someone else to kill?"

"That," Stotts growled, "is enough. He was already working the job before you and I talked."

I glared at him. He glared right back at me.

Sid, next to us, just sighed. "It's done," he said tiredly. "Neither of you have ground to fight on. Leave it be and let's move on."

To my surprise, Stotts backed down. "Do you know if he has family here?" He was all business and police procedure again.

Sid rubbed at the bridge of his nose, then pushed his glasses back in place.

"I don't know much about his personal life. He never mentioned family. I always thought he lived somewhere out southeast. Thought he went to PCC. But I'm not sure about that either."

Note to self: once all this settles down, if it settles down, get some kind of basic information on all the Hounds in the city. If nothing else, it will make it easier for the police to notify the next of kin.

Bea spoke up. "So, who's taking the first shift?" she asked.

"First shift?" I said.

"Waiting to hear if Davy's going to be okay," she said. "I'll stay for a while."

Jack motioned to one of the empty chairs. "I've got some time," he said. "You and I can take first shift, all right?"

Bea nodded and sat down where I'd just been sitting. Jack exchanged a look with Sid, and I remembered they had buddied for Sid's job tonight.

"I'll get someone else," Sid said.

Jack nodded and settled down next to Bea, his elbows on his knees as he started a mundane conversation about what kinds of corpses she'd been sniffing lately.

"I need to know what you saw, Allie," Stotts said.

"I didn't see much," I said.

"If you'll excuse me," Sid interrupted, "I'm going to the coffee shop in the main lobby. Anyone want anything?"

"No," I said. "Are you staying?"

He shook his head. "Have a job in a few hours. Just a look-see at the library for some shenanigans with the books. Someone thinks a few books have had offensive passages 'spelled' out of them."

"I don't care if you're Hounding a newborn. You need a shadow." I hated sounding like an overprotective mother, but right now, even the library sounded like a death trap.

"I'll get one," Sid said. "I have the list. I'll see who's available and give him or her a call."

He headed off to the coffee shop.

I told Stotts what I'd seen. Well, not all of it. I mentioned Davy, Tomi, the knife, the burned circle of ashes, and the shadowy magic. I did not tell him about the nightmare creatures loose on the street. As far as I knew, Stotts did not know about those kinds of things. About the dead walking among us, the Veiled, the Necromorph, the nightmare creatures. As far as I knew, those were the sorts of things, Death magic things, dark magic things, that the Authority worked very hard to keep out of the notice of the rest of the citizenry.

Including the secret magical police department.

Of course, I could be wrong. No one had given me a damn spreadsheet to keep all the secrets straight.

"And that's it?" he asked as he wrote down the last of my statement on the pad he'd pulled out of his pocket.

"That's all I remember," I said.

"Okay." He put the pad and pen away. "I have some things I need to take care of. Are you going to be okay here?"

"What?"

"I'm beginning to like this buddy system you have worked out. Do you want me to call someone for you? Nola, maybe?"

Wow, and how strange was that? Mr. Police Detective had Nola's number and was looking after me like I was trying to look after my Hounds.

"Do you know where Nola is?" I asked.

"She said she was going to do some shopping, maybe catch a movie." He glanced at his watch. "She might be at your apartment now."

"I'll give her a call and let her know I'm on my way home."

"Do you need a ride?"

"No," I said. "I got it."

He hesitated for a second, which made sense, since I usually didn't have a car. But he nodded. "Call me. Anytime. For anything. Okay?"

"I will." *Anything I can tell you about*, I thought.

I checked with the nurse on duty but she said they didn't have an update on Davy yet. This was where a cell phone would really come in handy. Instead I gave her my home phone number and asked her to please call me as soon as they knew anything.

Then I gave my home number to Jack and Bea and made them both write it down. When Sid came strolling back with an energy drink and two sandwiches, I told him my number too.

"I know your home number," he said around a bite of pastrami. "We'll call as soon as we know. And if any of us get tired sitting down here, we'll call someone else to take over."

"I'll be back soon," I said. And I planned on that being the truth. I also planned on hunting down those nightmare creatures and sending them back to wherever they came from.

And to do that, I'd need the help of Mr. Zayvion Jones.

Chapter Fourteen

So here's something I never thought I'd see. My apartment with three people in it, laughing without my being there.

I tried to open the door, but it was locked. And I was glad about that.

I knocked. Who should open the door (after ample time to look through the peephole to see who was on the other side) but Zayvion.

He opened the door wide and stepped aside with a warm, relaxed smile on his face. "Welcome home," he said.

My heart caught at the sound of those words on his lips.

"You and I have issues," I said.

"Apparently," he said.

Nola and Shamus were laughing in the living room. Something about dogs, and Nola going on about Jupe's disastrous skunk-hunting expeditions.

"What's wrong?" Zayvion glanced down the hallway behind me, then shut the door.

And when all I could do was shake my head, he took the three steps necessary and wrapped his arms around me. I should have pushed him away. I was still angry at him for hurting Cody. But he held me, my face tucked into his shoulder, didn't say anything. Didn't ask anything. Just afforded me a little time to pull myself together for what I knew I had to do.

Nola walked out of the living room. "Allie? I was just going to pour us all coffee. Do you want a cookie?"

That's what I smelled—homemade oatmeal cookies.

"No." I pushed away from Zayvion and smiled for Nola. "It's been a bad day. I found Davy Silvers—he's one of the Hounds in the group—hurt over in St. Johns."

Nola's face shadowed with concern. "Is he okay? Do we need to take him to the hospital?"

"I already did." I looked at Zayvion, who watched me with a dark intensity. "There's blood in your backseat. Sorry."

"Are you all right?" he asked.

"Yes."

"Is he?"

"I don't know yet. Some of the Hounds are at the hospital, waiting to hear if he's going to be okay."

"Should we go down there too?" Nola asked. "How was he hurt? Was it an accident?"

"No. It was magic."

Zayvion didn't move, but Shamus, who had been sitting in my living room with his feet on my coffee table, stood up and strolled over.

"Well, it's been a fine afternoon," he said to Nola. "And a pleasure meeting you, Ms. Robbins." He shook Nola's hand. "But it's getting late, and I see that you have things needing your attention. I hope we'll get a chance to see each other again before you head out of town. Maybe catch a pint out at O'Donnel's."

"I'd like that," Nola said.

Shamus turned to me. "Good afternoon, Allie."

I nodded.

Then he slugged Zayvion in the shoulder. Zayvion didn't so much as flinch. "See you soon, won't I?" he asked.

"Of course," Zayvion said with smooth Zen calm.

I had a feeling they had both just said a lot more to each other than was obvious.

And then Shamus let himself out. I could hear him whistling down the hallway and down the staircase.

Nola was no dummy. Even though she didn't know a lot about magic, she knew when the mood in the room had suddenly changed.

"Do you two need some time in private to talk?" she asked.

Can I just say that I loved her? Honest. Down to earth. No bullshit Nola. Loved her.

"If you don't mind," I said.

"I'll be back in the bedroom if you need me." She walked off, and Zayvion and I both stared at each other until we heard the bedroom door shut.

"Tell me why you Closed Cody," I said.

"Because it's my job."

"Don't," I warned. "I am so not in the mood."

He held still a moment, considered me. Finally, "He's been a part of the Authority for a long time. But he wasn't Closed. Someone put a hit on him, years ago, when he was turning witness for those magical forgeries he was involved in. We don't know who did it, but they broke him, his mind. And just a few months ago James used him to work Blood magic, Death magic, dark magic, to kill your father and hurt you. . . ."

Zayvion took a deep breath, looked away. His gaze finally returned to my face. When he spoke, he was very calm. "The Authority approves of Nola looking after him. And Sedra . . . she thinks living away from magic will be the best thing for him. Might even give his mind some time to heal, if it can heal. But before he could be given into Nola's care, he had to be Closed. The traumas and the memories of how to use magic taken away. So no one can use him again."

"So you just erased the parts of his life that you didn't think were good enough? That you didn't think he could handle? How kind of you to make that decision for him."

Um, yeah. Sarcasm. I had it.

"I don't need your approval to do my job," he said, flat, cold.

We spent a little time glaring at each other.

"Are you going to tell me what happened to Davy?" he asked.

I didn't know whether the change of subject was a peace offering. But it was common ground, maybe better ground, for both of us.

"I found him half dead in Cathedral Park. Tomi Nowlan, his ex-girlfriend, the Hound, was there with a knife and a burnt circle of ash."

"The disks," he said.

I nodded. "She was working dark magic, I think. Shadowed colors in indigo and red. And then things, creatures came out of the circle."

"She opened a gate."

"And that's bad, right?"

He nodded. "The creatures are called the Hungers. They exist only on the other side of magic, in the realms of death."

"Well, I think they're setting up a vacation home in Cathedral Park."

He spared me a brief smile. "I need to go."

"Are we going to hunt them?" I asked.

"No. *We* aren't going to do anything," he said. "Shamus and I will take care of them. It's what we're trained to do."

"No," I said. "Hell, no. You are not going after those things alone. I am going with you. I have to learn how to kill a nightmare sooner or later, right?"

"Allie . . ."

"Consider it on-the-job training."

"Bad idea."

"Why? Keeping me in the dark about these things will not keep me safe," I said. "Not anymore. Not if I'm going to be a part of your world."

"Nola?" I said over my shoulder.

Zay caught my wrist. "Allie, listen. The disks are involved. The only person out there that we know of who has a disk is the Necromorph. He knows your dad is in your head. And he is willing to kill you."

"I can handle myself."

"That's not my point."

"Then point," I said.

"Did you ever think that hurting Davy, involving Tomi, and calling you to the park to watch Tomi release the Hungers might have been planned? Might have been a way for the Necromorph to draw you to him?"

"That's crazy. If he had wanted me there, why didn't he show up?"

"I don't know. Maybe something didn't go the way he expected it to."

I thought about Tomi's shock. How she had seemed really out of it. So much so that even her spell casting had been jerky. Maybe she was the weak link in the Necromorph's plan.

"He doesn't want me, Zay," I said.

"No, he wants your dad. And you're giving him to him."

Nola came out of the bedroom. "Did you call me?"

"Yes," I said. "We're leaving."

"Going to tell me what you're up to?"

"We're going to go Hound the place where Davy was hurt. I gave a bunch of people my home number. Two men Hounds named Sid and Jack. One woman Hound named Bea. And also the nurse at the ER. I asked that they call me if they hear about Davy, or if they need someone to sit down at emergency, waiting to hear about him. Do you mind handling phone duty?"

"I can do that. But first." She strode into the living room and then came back. "Take these with you."

I don't know what I expected. Maybe a cell phone. Or a gun. Nope. Nola dropped two palm-sized cookies in my hand. Oatmeal chocolate chip, and still warm.

"Come home safe," she said.

I took the cookies. "Lock that door and do not open it for anyone but us. Call 911 if something funny happens. Call Stotts too, if you need to. Be careful, okay?"

"Me?" she said. "It's not me who's mixed up to her eyeballs in magic."

I gave her a quick smile and then headed out the door, not waiting for Zayvion to catch up to me.

"What?" I asked him once he was striding alongside me.

"Aren't you going to share those?" He pointed at the cookies.

I bit into one of the warm cookies. Delicious and moist and buttery. "Absolutely not. You probably already ate a dozen of these."

"Your point?"

We jogged down the stairs. "So, how hard is it to take care of these Hunger things?" I asked.

"It's not easy. Hardest to do it so no one notices. I think you should stay here."

"Not on your life."

We hit the lobby at a fast walk. "How hard will it be to find them?"

"We know how they move."

"And what, exactly, do they do?"

"Hunt people and magic. Then consume. Kill."

Comforting. "Car's this way." I dug in my pocket and tossed him the keys. He caught them and we strode out the door to the back parking lot.

I realized last time I'd been in this building with Zayvion, he'd been nearly passed out from exhaustion. "You are feeling okay, right?" I asked as we hit the cold late-afternoon air.

"I'm fine," he said. "Shamus has his uses."

"Oh? Like what?"

"Like mitigating burn-out. He's really quite good at what he does. Just don't ever tell him I said that. I'll deny all knowledge that this conversation ever took place."

I shook my head. "You like him, don't you?"

"Like the brother I never got around to killing." He flashed me a bright smile, and I couldn't help but smile back.

"Killing?" Shamus walked out from behind some bushes in the parking lot. "You mean the brother who has saved your sorry ass a hundred times. A little respect, here."

"That was respect. You're still alive. Do you have everything?" Zayvion asked.

Shamus pulled one hand from behind his back. A strange collection of leather and silver and glass dangled between his fingers. "I'm always ready with the ass saving, now, aren't I? Apologize."

"Sorry you can't stop thinking about my ass."

Shamus grinned. "True. It's just so tight and muscular. Want me to shove these in your trunk?"

"I'd rather you put them in the car." Zayvion opened his car, and motioned for me to get in the passenger's side while Shamus put the contraptions in the trunk. Zay walked around and stood by the open trunk with Shamus, like two men comparing guns or tackle boxes or something.

Satisfied with the inventory, they slammed the trunk

shut, and Shamus crawled in the backseat while Zayvion got into the driver's seat.

"There might be some blood back there," I said.

Shamus shrugged one shoulder. "What's new?"

Zayvion took a moment to adjust the seat for his legs, and the mirrors. "Safety first," he said.

"Always," Shamus agreed.

Zayvion started the engine and turned the car toward St. Johns.

"So, tell me what to expect," I said.

"Blood, death, horror." Shamus sat forward so he was nearly between us. "The usual." He pulled out his cell, hit a button.

"Who?" Zayvion asked.

"Who do you think?" He sat back and answered the phone. "Chase, darlin'. Want to do a job?"

At the mention of Chase's name, Zayvion tightened. It was only for a second before the Zen took over and he looked relaxed, calm again. But I could tell it was an act. That woman bothered him.

"Should I be worried?" I asked while Shamus kept right on talking behind us.

"About the hunt?"

"Yes. And Chase."

Zay stopped at a light. Even though it felt like the longest day ever, it wasn't even dark yet. It was three or four at the latest, and as light as a cloudy day in Oregon could be. To the west, a patch of blue sky opened up, and sunlight shot down in liquid gold, painting the wet city in van Gogh fire. It seemed strange to be going out hunting nightmares in such nice weather.

"Chase is a Closer," Zayvion said. "She's good at her job. You don't have to worry about her." The light turned green, and Zay moved along with traffic, angling north toward the St. Johns Bridge.

Why did I not believe him?

"The hunt isn't something I want you to be involved in. At all," he added, like maybe I hadn't heard him before. "If we're dealing with Hungers, they are creatures that have crossed through the gates from death to life."

"Like the Veiled?"

Zay shook his head. "The Veiled are the thoughts and memories and bits of magic users' souls impressed on the magic that runs beneath the city. They aren't so much dead people as a recording of people who were once alive."

Recordings with burning fingers that like to eat magic.

"What did the Hungers used to be?" I asked.

"Some say they are failed spells from the ancient days when magic was first used by mankind. Some say they are the fears, the panics, the horrors of all the world's tragedies, the nightmares of mankind's dreaming mind. Some say they are hunters, killers, creatures that dwell in the world beyond the gates, hungry for the blood and magic of the living world." He shrugged. "Your basic denizens of death."

"Huh," I said.

"What?"

"I was just trying to remember the last time I had a conversation with someone who used the words *dwell* and *denizens of death* in the same breath."

"Your point?" he asked.

"You are a seriously strange man, Zayvion Jones."

That got a surprised grin out of him. "You don't know me very well, then."

Well, well, look at who had gone all Mr. Tough on me. It looked natural, easy on him. I had a feeling there was a side to Mr. Jones that I hadn't seen yet. The bad-boy hunter side. And I liked it.

"So, the Hungers?" I prompted.

"Right. Cross over from death. It happens, but not very often, and usually only one at a time. You saw more than one?"

"Six, I think."

"That's a large crossing. It would have taken a lot of power behind the spell to crack the gate that wide."

Maybe that was why Tomi looked so exhausted.

"Is Davy being hurt a part of it?" I asked.

"Yes. Death magic takes a sacrifice. It doesn't have to be a life, just an exchange of energy. But the old ways, dark ways, always use a sacrifice."

"You said those ways were forbidden."

Shamus, who was done with his phone call, laughed. "They are. But first someone has to catch you doing it. Death magic is hard stuff to Hound."

I didn't know that. I wasn't sure if that made me feel better or worse, knowing there was a kind of magic less detectable to Hounding.

"There's something else," I said. "Davy said Tomi mentioned a man named Jingo. Is she part of the Authority?"

They both got quiet. Finally, Zay spoke. "Not that I'm aware of."

"Told you he's a freak," Shamus muttered. "Gonna be a fuckin' war."

The muscle of Zay's jaw tightened. "Maybe," he said. "Or maybe we'll find a way to fix this first."

Shamus snorted. "Optimism does not suit you, my friend."

"So is Jingo Jingo using Tomi some other way?" I asked. "For Hounding? A little light on the subject would be nice."

"I don't know what to tell you," Zayvion said. "I don't know if Jingo Jingo is involved with Tomi at all. There are . . . people who would plant his name. Make false trails to cover their own tracks."

"Backstabbing and double-crossing? Fantastic show you're running," I said.

"There's a lot of unrest among magic users right now," Zayvion said. "Especially since your father's death. A lot of finger pointing, blame of magic and knowledge being improperly supervised, leaked, used.

"But right now, we need to deal with the Hungers," Zayvion said, changing subjects.

I still wanted to know what Jingo Jingo had to do with all this, but for all I knew, Shamus was more than his student. He could be his spy.

Where was that secrets spreadsheet when I needed it?

"Do you still think they're in St. Johns?" I asked.

"Probably. There's a reason the gate was opened there. There isn't magic in St. Johns. Nothing is piped in, nothing natural beneath the ground. I think Tomi didn't want us knowing the gate had been breached. It's possible the

Hungers are waiting for nightfall to slip into the rest of the city."

"And once they're in the city, what do they do?"

"They kill," Shamus said.

"So why haven't I heard about this on the news? Dead bodies? Rampaging nightmare creatures? That's got to be good enough to at least hit the morning shows."

"You don't hear it because we are very, very good." Shamus grinned.

"No, if someone dies, it's noticed," I said. "By a neighbor, a friend, a coworker."

"We don't hide the bodies," Zayvion said, "when there are bodies. We just make sure the cause of death never points toward the magical."

"That doesn't sound easy," I said.

"After years and years of training?" he said. "It's not."

"Crap," I said. "Training. Shame, would you call your mom and tell her I'm going to be late—later? Please?"

He just shook his head. "You're gonna owe me for all this sugar I'm pouring on her." He dialed, and spent several minutes explaining exactly what we were going to be doing.

Finally, he hung up. "Says she'll consider it extra credit, but no getting into the middle of anything really dangerous. Thinks I'm gonna look after you."

"I can look after myself," I said.

Shamus nodded. "Of course you can."

I was demure enough not to flip him off with both fingers.

We drove past the park. Police tape closed off the parking lot, but North Bradford Street was clear. Zayvion parked the car several blocks away, tucked down a one-way gravel and bramble dead-end road, then popped the trunk.

Shamus jumped out and started rummaging through the gear in the trunk.

"I don't suppose I could talk you into staying in the car?" Zayvion asked.

"No."

He didn't look surprised by my answer. "Did your father teach you any of the Closing spells?"

"No."

"Attacks?"

"What? No."

"Allie . . ." He rubbed the back of his neck and tipped his head down.

"Listen," I said. "I don't have to be the one who kills these things, but I do want to see how they are killed. I'm here to watch and learn so the next time one of my Hounds gets attacked, I'll know what to do. I'll stay out of your way. Think of me as a job shadow."

He stopped rubbing his neck. "I'd like to think of you as a lot more than that. Alive and safe, for one thing."

"How about stubborn and smart enough to look after myself?"

"Mmm, that too. But I'm still going to go with alive and safe."

He leaned toward me. I met him halfway. We kissed, and delicious warmth spread through me, filling me. The taste of him—a little smoky and sweet, along with the scent of pine that would forever remind me of him, of his touch—poured through me and made me want him more.

He pulled back and rested his forehead against mine. "Please. Please take the keys and drive home," he said softly.

I leaned away, just enough that I could see his eyes. Just enough that I wouldn't fall into needing to do what he said. Not because of Influence or anything magical between us. But because I hated to hear the worry in his voice.

"Just tell me what to do if one gets too close to me. I promise I am not going to get close to one of them."

He licked his bottom lip, and I wondered if he could still taste me, taste our kiss.

"Shield will work against them," he said. He was all teacher now, all Zen. Calm. Reassuring. Matter-of-fact. Like he hunted nightmares every day.

Which, come to think of it, he probably did.

"Camouflage works too. If things get hot, back off and back out. Most of the defensive spells—Hold, Sleep—won't do a thing. The Hungers absorb anything thrown at them. So your best defense is to not attack. Try to blend in, try not to smell like magic or give off the sign that you use magic."

I rolled my eyes, and he nodded. "I know. But try. Blocks will work on you, not on the Hungers."

He searched my face, his gaze dropping to my lips, then back up to my eyes. "Allie—"

"—tell me later," I said with a little too much cheerfulness. "When all this is over and you and I are sitting on the couch, drinking a glass of wine."

"Stubborn," he said.

"Middle name," I agreed. And before we could say anything else, before I lost my nerve, I got out of the car.

Shamus bent over the open trunk, humming a tuneless song and smoking a cigarette.

"Need any help?" I strolled over, my boots crunching in the wet gravel. I stuck both my hands in my pockets and was grateful I'd put on a hat. It wasn't raining or very windy right now, but the air was bone-bitingly cold and damp.

"Sure," he said without looking at me, "hold this." He handed me a leather rope that looked a lot like a short-handled bullwhip, but with silver glyphs worked down the length of the leather and a blade of glass at the tip.

I held it, leaving the length curled in the trunk among the other weapons—a couple sheathed machetes with glass and glyphs worked into the hilts, more leather whips, some plain rope, a few stained glass boxes that looked like they should hold jewelry, sheathed knives, and several glyphed and Warded cases that looked like the right shape and size to carry guns.

And with all that to choose from, Shamus, who was still wearing his black fingerless gloves, was instead carefully unwrapping silk handkerchiefs off of four small round medallions. The medallions were lead and glass like everything else in the armament ensemble, but each was loose. He opened one of the stained glass boxes and pulled out four leather cuffs. He pressed the medallions into the leather cuffs, and I could feel, rather than hear, a low thunk as they snapped into place.

Zayvion got out of the car, paused to assess what I was

holding, then got busy on the other side of Shamus, sorting small bits of glass, leather, lead, and steel.

They each took one of the leather cuffs and snapped them into place on their bare wrists, medallions pressed against their skin.

"You think?" Shamus asked, holding up a leather band with one of the medallions in it.

Zayvion nodded and took it from him. "This," he said to me, "is for you to wear. We'll each have one on. They allow us to sense where the other person is. If we're injured. If we're unconscious. If we're alive."

"Do they let us read each other's minds too?"

Shamus chuckled. "Trust me, you don't want to know what's going on in Jones' mind."

"No," Zayvion answered.

"Which arm?" I asked.

"The right, I think."

I pulled back my sleeve and he wrapped the leather around my right wrist. The medallion fit like a warm, silky disk against the inside of my wrist and pulsed with two distinct beats. I raised my eyebrows.

Zayvion lifted my hand to his chest and pressed my palm there. I could feel the beat of his heart under my hand and echoed in the medallion at my wrist. And when I took a second to think about it, I could somehow tell that he was well, confident, and a little excited.

"Shame?" he said.

"Right." Shamus sucked the last of the smoke out of his cigarette, threw it to the wet gravel, and dragged his shoe over it. He stepped up, and I put my hand on his chest. His heartbeat matched the second rhythm on my wrist, and touching him gave me the sense of his state of mind. He was exhausted, worried. Two things I never would have guessed, looking at him, and I was good at reading body language. He was also determined, like someone who had been working a hard, long shift and was willing to roll up his sleeves and work for however long it would take to get the job done.

He grinned, and the worry shifted to amusement.

"Okay," I said. "Do you need to touch me?" I asked.

Shamus wiggled his eyebrows. "If you insist." He lifted both hands—curled, not flat—and reached for my chest.

I took a step back.

"Shame," Zayvion growled. "Knock it off."

Zay took my arm and stood half between us, turning his back on Shamus. "We use these all the time. We're attuned. As long as you're wearing that, we can sense you without touching."

"Maybe you can," Shamus said, "what with the whole Soul Complement thing you two have going on, but I might need a little feel."

"No." Zayvion did not look at him. "You don't."

The conversation stopped as a car drove down the gravel road and parked behind us. For a second I worried that we were all standing there in front of a weapon-filled trunk. Then Chase got out of the car.

She wore black combat boots, black jeans, and a blue-and-black plaid flannel coat zipped up so that just the turtleneck of her gray sweater showed. Her hair was back in a single long braid, and her eyes, beneath the straight, thick bangs, were wide and sapphire blue.

She made flannel and combat boots look as though they belonged on a Parisian runway.

"Hello, boys." She nodded toward me. "Why are you here?"

"On-the-job training," Shamus said. "Plus, we think the things like her. She's our in."

Her pretty face settled somewhere between curiosity and disgust as she gave me the full-body once-over. "You saw the Hungers?"

I stuck my wrist with the band on it in my pocket. I don't know why, but I didn't want her opinion of me wearing the band that connected me to Zayvion and Shamus. "I saw them. I use Sight a lot when I Hound."

"You were Hounding the Hungers?"

"No, just looking for a friend."

She bit the corner of her lip, like she was trying to decide something. I honestly didn't care what it was.

"Heads up." Shamus tossed a leather band to Chase, and

she snatched it out of the air and clipped it on her wrist. As soon as it closed, I felt a third rhythm tapping at my wrist.

Apparently, she felt it too.

"You're joking, right?" She looked between Shamus and Zay. "She's not coming with us, is she?"

Zayvion zipped his coat and made quick work of pulling things out of the trunk and attaching them to his body.

"Yes," he said, "she is. She needs to touch you, Chase. This is her first time."

Chase camped back on one hip. "You Read?"

"Sure." I walked over to her. "Doesn't everybody?" I placed my right hand below her neck, palm resting flat against her sternum. She was annoyed, a little jealous. That, I could have told just by looking at her. But the last emotion I picked up from her was fear.

Okay, maybe I should turn in my degree in body language. She didn't look afraid at all on the outside.

"Done?" she asked.

"Uh, yes." I pulled my hand away, stuck it back in my pocket where I could rub my thumb over my fingertips to try to wipe away the emotions I had sensed. But rubbing at my fingers wasn't doing me any good. With each of their heartbeats tapping gently at my wrist, I found that if I thought about one of them, I could not only tell that they were breathing and conscious, I could also sense a hint of their mood.

Move over, lie detector tests. These suckers were good.

Shamus had taken his turn stuffing things in his coat pockets. I glanced over to see if the machetes were still in the trunk. They were not. Which meant Shamus and Zayvion had three-foot blades strapped onto their bodies somewhere.

In broad daylight. In the middle of the city.

"Should I take anything?" I asked, as Shamus slammed the trunk shut.

"A healthy sense of self-preservation would be good," he said.

Zayvion reached over and wrapped his hand around my wrist, his fingertips pressing the medallion closer to my pulse. And I could tell that at this moment, he was intent and focused on nothing except me.

"Stay out of the way, out of reach. Use your defense spells if you must. Run, if you must. Just stay safe." He pressed the hilt of a sheathed knife into my hand.

I knew that knife. It was the one he had given me when Pike was still alive. It was the only weapon I had ever killed someone with. It knew my blood, Zayvion's blood. And it knew the blood of my enemy.

"Chase and I will take point," he said, drawing his fingers away but leaving his heat behind. "You and Shamus will handle cleanup."

Shamus was in the middle of lighting another cigarette. He gave me a quick wink and exhaled smoke. "Nothing but glamour, this job."

"This is done." Zayvion made it sound like a ritual, an ending, a prayer.

He motioned for us to walk away from the cars. There was enough room on the road that we could all walk shoulder to shoulder. Next to me was Zayvion, then Chase, then Shamus. As soon as we were a yard away from both cars, all three of them flicked their fingers, like flicking away a bug or, in Shamus's case, tapping ashes off a cigarette.

With that one small motion, they each set a spell—I couldn't tell which one—but I could tell exactly what it did. Instead of looking like three people armed for war, marching around in broad daylight, they looked . . . normal. Average. Zay was his ratty-jacket-wearing, street-drifter self. Shamus passed for goth poser, and Chase looked like the kind of woman who chopped her own firewood, grew her own food, and didn't take any flack.

None of them looked like they were carrying weapons, and I couldn't even smell magic on them. I took a deep breath and all I smelled was Zay's pine, Shamus's cigarette smoke and cloves, Chase's vanilla perfume, and the wet, green, rain-drenched soil and trees around us.

"Might want to put that away," Shamus noted.

"What? Oh." I belatedly tucked the knife I'd been holding like my life depended on it—ha, not funny—inside my coat, where it fit pretty well behind my belt and lay against my hip.

Zay turned to face the cars for a second. He wove a spell and knelt. His middle finger and thumb were pressed together. He opened his fingertips, and pressed his fingers into the wet gravel. I smelled the wash of a spell, slightly buttery and sweet. Then the cars were covered with leaves, and looked like they'd been there awhile, like maybe they were one of the neighbor's cars or belonged to someone staying overnight.

The amazing thing about that simple spell was that it not only gave a visual camouflage, but it also gave off an emotional ping—that the cars belonged there and weren't anything for anyone to take much note of. Subtle and natural, no one—not even the best Hounds—would think there was magic going on here.

"Wow," I said.

Zayvion stood and gave me a short nod. "Thank you."

We walked to the end of the road and turned toward the park. It wasn't far, but before we got there, Shamus touched my arm.

"Let's get some coffee while they start," he said.

"Don't you need me to show you where I saw the gate and the Hungers?"

"No," Chase said.

I looked at Zayvion. "We can tell. It's about midpark, isn't it?"

I nodded. "But I saw them while I was driving out of the parking lot."

"We'll go to the origin point," he said. "Close the gate. Track out from there."

"You mean the gate might still be open?" It had been hours since I'd been there. If the gate had been left open this entire time, there could be dozens, hells, hundreds of the Hungers on the street.

"Gates don't Close on their own," he said. "Someone always has to Close them."

He and Chase continued walking, and Shamus tugged on my elbow again. He started walking uphill into the neighborhood and toward the main street. "Let them do this part. You and I can scout to find the Hungers' nest."

"They nest?"

Shamus shook his head. "Your da, he didn't tell you a damn thing about magic, did he?"

And it was strange, now that we were a good distance away from Chase and Zay, I could feel the weight of my father in my mind again. Could feel the scratch behind my eyes that was going to drive me bat-shit crazy pretty soon.

"No." I pressed at the bridge of my nose to keep from rubbing my eyes out. "Want to give me a quick rundown on procedures?"

"Easy. Z and Chase will stroll into the park clothed in Camouflage spells. Zay will close the gate—he's the guardian; closing gates is his shtick. There are specific cancellation spells that you use for gates. They are hard as hell to cast and take a shitload of training and magic to work. Good Closers can use some of the magic that is suspended in the gate itself to fuel the spell, but still, it takes balls to shut those things out here in the dead zone. Probably another reason Tomi cast it out here. Harder to close.

"But as you intimately know," he added, "Jones has balls. When it comes to magic."

"Do you even listen to yourself?" I asked.

"And ruin the surprise? Once he closes the gate," he said without breaking verbal stride, "the Hungers will know it. That's where you and I come in. The Hungers should be nested, waiting for dark. We kind of hit the shiny side of luck with that one. If these things cross in the night, there's no nesting. They're everywhere. Get your workout trying to run one of these bastards down. Coffee?"

We'd made it up a couple blocks and a coffee shop was just across the street.

"We have time?"

"How fast can you drink?"

"Let's do it," I said.

Lucky for us, there wasn't anyone in line. I ordered a cup of house brew, black. Shamus ordered half a cup of house brew. Then he proceeded to fill the cup up the rest of the way with milk and sugar. Lots of sugar.

"Sure you got enough milk in your sugar?" I asked as we strolled out of the shop and headed south.

He flipped me off. "You drink your coffee your way, and I'll drink my coffee the right way."

And we did. Quickly. My cup was almost empty and my throat almost burnt by the time we reached the end of the next block. We threw our cups in the garbage, and kept walking downhill toward the river and Cathedral Park, the St. Johns Bridge to our right.

"What do we do when we find the nest?" I asked.

"Kill them. As many as we can. You know how to set a Drain, right?"

"Let's pretend I do."

"Okay, in that case, you stand back like Zayvion said. I'll set the Drains. Too bad you and I haven't cast together before. If we were Complements or Contrasts, you could pour magic into the spells I throw."

"We could try now," I said. My dad, behind my eyes, fluttered and scratched. I don't know what he was all worked up about.

"Why not?" Shamus ducked into the mouth of an alley and leaned against the wall. "I'm going to weave a simple Light spell, right?" He did so, quickly. Watching him made me feel like I was all thumbs. "A little magic." He exhaled, and the Light spell glowed soft white in an orb the size of a golf ball.

Even though I was watching, I was pretty impressed with his reach. Magic did not pool naturally beneath St. Johns. He had to access it about five miles out, over on the other side of the train tracks where the city had stopped laying the networks and lines.

"Now you," he said, "make it bright."

The spell was tiny. Even if my way of casting and his completely clashed, the worst we'd probably get would be a flash and then nothing. Like fragile wire, the glyph he cast wouldn't hold very much magic before it self-destructed.

I cleared my mind, set a Disbursement, and thought about how I could best feed magic into his spell.

Like this, my father said. And I knew the way to cast the magic, almost with a flick of my wrist, so that the magic would catch and wrap naturally, matching the pulse of Shamus's spell.

And sure, I could have ignored my dad. Could have decided he was just trying to screw me up. And sure, I thought about it.

Stubborn, my father sighed. *I have not always tried to make your life miserable, Allison. Far from it.*

I ignored his comment. If I were ever going to listen to him, this seemed like a fairly harmless time to do so. The light would either get brighter, or it would go out. No lives on the line with this spell.

So I cast magic the way he had shown me, pulling just the barest amount of it out of my flesh and bone and into Shamus' spell.

The orb glowed brighter, doubling in intensity, but did not burn out.

"Sweet," Shamus said. "Might be Complements, you and I."

"I thought I was Complements with Zayvion."

"Soul Complements, maybe, that whole rarest-of-the-rare, only-one-for-the-other thing. There are other degrees of magic use that complement one another. That aren't as powerful and are still fairly rare. Mostly, there's Contrasts or nothing. Course, you and I might be that too."

"Contrasts?"

"Means our magic blends, sometimes perfectly, sometimes not so much. Do the same thing twice and get different results. Never know when it will work and when it won't."

He unwove the spell, then traced a new orb of Light into the air in front of him.

"Here's the same thing I just cast. You do your part again. Exactly the same. Let's see what happens."

I cleared my mind, set a Disbursement, then drew magic through me just as my father had showed me, just as I had done the last time, and added it to Shamus' spell.

Instead of growing brighter, the orb sizzled, filled with black specks, then went completely black. It snapped like a firecracker and was gone.

It happened so quickly, neither Shamus nor I had time

to flinch away from it. I felt the failure of the spell like a quick headache behind my eyes that was gone almost as soon as it registered.

I dug my left thumb into my temple.

Shamus nodded. "Give you a pain?"

"Yes."

He rubbed his hands over the thighs of his jeans, as if trying to wipe away sweat or pain. "Thought as much. We're Contrasts. That means you keep your magic to yourself, missy."

I gave him a sour look. "Like I'd want my magic mixing with yours anyway."

He chuckled. "Ooh. Spunky. I like. No time, unfortunately. Z and Chase should be done digging at the gate. Ought to have it closed anytime. Which should flush the Hungers from their nest."

"And how, again, do we find them?"

"We don't. They find us. Me," he amended. "They find me. You stay quiet and don't call attention to yourself."

He headed down the sidewalk. "We need a side street, alleyway, abandoned building. Best would be a spot out of sight—especially since it's still light out—but open enough we have room to maneuver." He tipped his chin toward the left, where a broken-down metal shed that might have once been a workshop or warehouse huddled behind half of a rusted chain-link fence. Next to the shed was a patch of dirt and weeds.

Here, huddled between the rise of the bridge to our left and the untended bushes and scrub of the empty lot, we had everything Shamus had said he was looking for. Enough area to move in, and privacy from prying eyes.

He strolled through the gap in the fence and then over to stand beneath a sickly hemlock. I followed him.

"You'll want to be over there." He pointed at the rusted shed.

"Couldn't you have said that before I walked all the way over here with you?" I kicked my way through the wet weeds that slapped at my shins. I put my back against the shed.

"And?" I asked.

"And don't use magic. At all. Period. Not even Sight. Nothing. Got it?"

"The first time."

He flashed me a grin, then shook out his hands and held them up, chest high, palms facing outward. He pulled on magic. Not just a small amount to fill a spell; Shamus accessed enough magic that I could taste it, feel it on the back of my throat like hot peppers when I swallowed.

He chanted, or at least I think he chanted. His lips moved and he was half whispering, half humming words I could not understand. A glow, something that didn't look like anything more than weak sunlight through the storm clouds, surrounded him. That was not sunlight. It was magic.

The heartbeats against my wrist changed. The one I knew belonged to Shamus slowed and pumped harder, like he was falling into his stride in a marathon. But the other two rhythms, Zayvion and Chase's hearts, suddenly quickened. I turned my thoughts toward Zayvion's heartbeat and could feel his strain as he drew magic toward him, from the stores out past the rail line, from the stores on the other side of the river, and then could feel him focus all of that magic into one place.

A rush of heat flooded my body—it felt like I was blushing from head to toe. I swayed and took a step to right myself. Hells, he was pulling on so much magic, I could feel the drain in my bones. I bit the inside of my cheek and recited my Miss Mary Mack jingle to keep my head clear.

The heat rushed out of me. Zayvion's heartbeat skipped, paused, long enough that I wondered whether his heart would beat again.

Chase's heartbeat continued on, strong, heavy, almost as if she were trying to make up for the lack of his. I felt Shamus' heart and I felt Chase's heart. But not Zayvion's.

The only emotion I could feel from Shamus was a sort of grim patience. When I focused on Chase's heartbeat, I could feel her anger, her worry.

I opened my mouth to say something, and then I couldn't move.

They had arrived. Nightmares, monsters. The Hungers I

had seen running through the edge of the park loped up to the broken chain-link fence. And paused.

They looked more solid than when I had seen them in the park. They had killed, fed, devoured.

But if I had not been staring at them—if I had not been *expecting* them to be there—I would not have noticed them. They were silent. I couldn't hear their breath, couldn't hear their paws on the concrete. I breathed in, caught no scent other than the rain and green of the nearby river and the slight meaty tang from the sewer processing plant.

My senses said that they should not be there, that nothing but shadows hovered beyond the rusted gate. But a chill down my back raised every hair on my arms.

I looked into their eyes and knew I was gazing into death. It took everything I had to look away from them. Away from their eyes. It took everything I had to look instead at Shamus, softly glowing, chanting, with his feet spread wide, his face tipped up to the sky, eyes closed, as if caught in some sort of exaltation.

And it took everything I had not to run as the nightmares, the creatures, pushed through the gate—all of them just solid enough that they could not pass through the chain links, but instead had to squeeze through the hole between two fence posts. Silent, even in the wet, tall, noisy grass. Silent as only predators could be. Silent as winter's killing cold. As death.

They ignored me, drawn to the magic Shamus was using.

Shamus did not move. There were a dozen of them, all bigger than a Saint Bernard, all muscled and thick. Tanks. Killing machines. They spread out, half stalking around behind Shamus, the rest in front and beside him, keeping equidistant and in a circle, maybe three yards between themselves and him.

They paused, tasting the air. Scenting their prey.

Every nerve in my body told me to run. And if not that, then to cast magic, to fight. To save Shamus before these things jumped him and tore him to shreds. But he had told me to hold still and not use magic, not smell like magic, not even look like I'd ever been around magic.

The Hungers stepped closer to Shamus.

Shamus pulled on more magic. The yellow-white glow didn't grow bigger, but it brightened enough that I thought it might catch the eye of a casual passerby.

I glanced at the road, didn't see any cars or people walking by.

Still, I thought Zayvion said they knew how to do this in daylight. I thought they knew how to do it without being seen. And I certainly thought they knew how to do it without leaving Shamus all alone to face down every nightmare that had crawled out of death's hole.

Except, of course, that calling the nightmares was exactly what Shamus wanted to do.

The beasts crouched, stepped closer, closing the circle. Two yards out. Four feet.

Shamus tipped his chin down. He was no longer chanting. He was grinning, his arms spread wide as if welcoming the beasts in for an embrace.

His eyes burned with black fire. Literally. He lowered his head just enough that his hair fell forward, hiding his eyes. Then he pulled his hands together, as if in prayer, against his chest.

Zayvion's heartbeat abruptly struck with bruising pain against my wrist. I sucked in a raking breath. My heart stung, beat on beat, in time with Zayvion's pounding pulse.

Ouch, ouch, ouch.

I pulled my wrist up to my chest, pressing it close, trying to ease the ache behind my ribs.

Zayvion was alive.

Shamus chanted, a soft singsong whisper that reminded me of a lullaby.

Even though he was singing a lullaby, things were going to hell over there. The beasts' mouths gaped, muscled shoulders bunched, ready to jump, rip, devour. I couldn't understand why they didn't attack. And then I knew. Even without Sight I could tell they were draining the magic out of the spell he was chanting. Draining him.

The nightmares grew more and more solid, and Shamus stood there, head bowed, hands at his chest, humming a childhood song, while his heart pounded a slow, almost meditative beat. He was enduring the drain of magic. Enduring the pain, just as he had endured the Proxy I'd set on him.

The Hungers were no longer translucent at all. They were solid, slathering beasts, heads too large for their compact bodies, skin mottled with scales. Thick veins snaked beneath the mottled skin.

Magic, no longer just shadowed, but now black and thick as tar, pulsed through those veins. Magic that Shamus had just fed into them. Magic that pounded Shamus' body and mind. Magic that punished him, drained him. And made the beasts stronger.

The beasts moved forward. Shamus swayed. Another step. Shamus' song faltered. He licked his lips and sang on. Another step. Sweat or maybe tears dripped from the edge of his jaw. Even from across the field, I could see him tremble.

I couldn't just stand there and watch him get eaten. I took a step away from the shed.

Just then, Shamus looked up. But not at me. He stared at the beasts in front of him. Then smiled and opened his hands, palms upward like he was pushing something up to shoulder height.

He stopped pulling on magic.

The beasts lunged.

"No!" I yelled.

I traced a glyph for Sight, filled it with magic, and drew the glyph for Hold so I could throw it at the beasts and stop them, even though Zayvion had told me not to use magic at all. I threw that spell at three of the beasts tearing at Shamus. As soon as I cast Hold, I remembered Zayvion had said it wouldn't work.

Hells.

Shamus was still standing, still grinning, though I could not fathom how.

Hold hit two of the beasts. It locked down on one of the Hungers, clamped like a black-legged spider that latched on and pulsed, injecting the paralyzing venom of Hold into the beast's flesh. For a second, I thought it might work. But instead of freezing, the Hunger stretched and absorbed the Hold spell like a gutter sucking down rain.

The beasts turned. Three of them. Toward me.

Bigger, faster, more solid. Their eyes widened, burning with unholy, bloody fire.

Right. Screwed up. Big time. Wondered if I'd live long enough to apologize to Shamus about it.

The Hungers charged.

Camouflage, my father said.

In that second, with that one word, I saw the lines it would take to cast the Camouflage glyph. Where the beginning and ending twisted back to parallel one another, so the spell fooled the eye, ears, senses.

Screw the Disbursement. Screw trying to clear my mind. I drew the glyph for Camouflage as fast as my fingers could move and poured it full of magic, as much magic as I could get my hands on, as much magic as I had in me.

Hot, sweet, slippery, the taste of butterscotch stung my eyes to tears, snapped at the back of my throat and burned.

Still the beasts ran. Three yards away, two, one. I pulled the knife out of my belt and shifted my stance to brace for impact. I was really wishing I owned a gun right about now. Or, yes, that I'd started those damn self-defense classes Violet insisted I take.

No time to worry about that. Not while the bulldozers of gonna-fuck-you-up bore down on me, butterscotch coating and all.

Screwed, screwed, screwed.

A solid wall appeared in front of me and blackness slammed down. I yelled at the sudden absence of light and jerked back. I couldn't see anything but blackness. I also couldn't smell the creatures, couldn't hear the creatures.

I was about to die, and I'd gone blind.

This sucked.

The wall reverberated with three heavy impacts that shook the ground like small earthquakes. The creatures, I think, slamming into the wall again and again. I stepped backward and traced a Blocking spell blind, from memory alone. I didn't know how long before the Hungers pounded their way through that wall of darkness.

But before I put the last twist on the Blocking spell, the

pounding stopped. For a second I stood there, wet, panting in the dark, too silent, too cold, too hot. Too damn blind. The heartbeats on my wrist thumped, three different drums in three different beats.

Then the wall exploded into smoke. Standing in front of me was Shamus.

He was pale. I didn't know white could get that white. Through the heavy hang of his hair against his face, I noticed he had freckles I'd never seen before. His eyes burned green, carved beneath and above by black smudges. But he was not bloody or bruised. He just looked really, really angry.

"Didn't I tell you not to use magic?" he growled. "'Get back,' I said. And did you? No." He shoved my shoulder—my injured left one—so hard I yelped and stumbled. He palmed me ruthlessly toward the rusted metal building. "Stupid. Stubborn. You're fucking trouble. Fine, if you want to die on your own. There's fucking four of us out here." Another shove, and my back hit the metal wall.

"I—"

"Shut it. Watch."

He faced me, so close I could smell his sweat, feel the heat rise off his body. He kept his back to the open field. The way he stood, it was like he was a wall between me and the beasts. And since I had not let go of Sight (which was amazing, considering. Go, me) I could see the low glow of light caught in the folds on his clothes where only shadows should be. The air around him seemed thicker, as if glass stretched out to either side of him.

The grasses and weeds at his feet were already yellowed by winter, but the longer he stood in one place, the browner they became. A slow-creeping circle of dead grass and weeds extended out from his boots as he sucked life in to feed the exchange of magic.

Death magic, my father whispered. And I caught a hint of him being impressed by Shamus' skill, a hint that he hadn't thought the boy he once knew would ever sacrifice enough to become a master in the art.

Shamus very calmly pulled a cigarette out of his jacket pocket and lit it, letting the match fall to die in the wet, brittle grass. When he slanted me a look, his eyes burned a green so dark, it was almost black.

That boy was pulling in some heavy magic.

Master indeed.

I didn't know how he did it, but he really had become a wall, and was accessing a hell of a lot of magic in this magicless part of town to hold it in place. I briefly considered pouring some of my magic into his spell to support it, but we were Contrasts, unpredictable and explosive when mixed.

I looked past his shoulder. Zayvion, in his ratty blue ski coat and black beanie, strolled through the middle of the field, heading uphill and toward the base of the bridge. His head was bent, his hands loose at his sides. He looked like a transient, watching his feet and hoping to find a discarded miracle lying in the dirt and weeds.

But with Sight I saw not only Zayvion the street drifter, I also saw Zayvion the warrior.

Seven feet tall, his body was alight in a symphony of black fire and silver glyphs that whorled like tribal tattoos down his arms, torso, back, and legs. The black fire flickered with silver blades of light.

The beasts followed the light and darkness that was Zayvion, as if they could taste the magic he held, caught by his fire, his shadow, hungry, but just wary enough to stay several feet away from him.

I took a step forward. I wanted to be a part of that fire too, wanted to feel his hands on me, his magic in me. Wanted to be a part of whatever he really was. Wanted to know what he could be, maybe even what we could be together.

Shamus clamped his hand on my shoulder and pressed down until it hurt. The pain—normal physical pain—did wonders for clearing my mind and stopped me from walking after Zayvion.

"Beauty, isn't he?" he said with just a hint of longing in his voice. "Guardian of the gates." He nodded. "No one but Jones can handle that and come out of it breathing. And sane. Magic from Life, magic from Death, light and dark, Blood, Faith, and Flux; he's got it all, uses it all. Some of them doubted him. Not me. Not once. Just have to look at him to see it. He's more than any of us. Scary. But disciplined. Controlled. No matter what kind of shit he's in. No one doubts him now. Not even Sedra." He sucked on the cigarette, his eyes narrowing for a second while he considered me. "Well, until you came along."

"Me? What does this have to do with me?"

"If you're his Soul Complement, you're just like him. One finger in each kind of magic. Light and dark. Able to break open or close the gates between our world and death. Maybe a lot more than that. You worry people, Beckstrom. I think you even worried your all-powerful da. I think that's why he didn't want you using magic. I think that's why he kept you out of the Authority."

"Trust me," I said, "You don't have to worry. If I could do half of what Zay's doing, I wouldn't be standing here with you. I'd be over there taking care of those things."

Shamus just stared at me and sucked on his cigarette. Not exactly a vote of confidence. But not a dismissal either.

"Should we help him?" I asked.

"We should do nothing but stand here. Chase has him covered. I'll do cleanup. You'll do nothing. Nothing." He exhaled smoke into the wet air. "If you so much as twitch, I'll knock you out and hold you down until this is done."

"You could try," I said.

That got a tight smile out of him. "I bet you even worry Jones."

The way he said it, I didn't think he was joking.

The Hungers that I knew were solid, monstrous nightmare creatures now looked like dogs, sniffing around in the dirt, trotting at Zayvion's heels. It was an Illusion, and a very clever one at that. I squinted at the shadow of the glyph that maintained the Illusion. The lines of the spell floated in the air toward the sickly hemlock tree.

Chase leaned against the trunk of the tree, one knee bent, the heel of her boot propped behind her. She didn't look any different from the last time I'd seen her, flannel and black jeans. Tough, pretty, strong. No amazing transformation like Zayvion-on-fire. Her hands were shoved in her flannel overcoat, one of her shoulders hitched toward her ear. To the casual observer, she was watching Zayvion, waiting for him to join her under the tree and out of the lightly falling rain.

To the not-so-casual observer, like maybe someone with her back against a wall using Sight, it was clear she was maintaining the Illusion and had made the pack of monsters look like a pack of dogs.

To the not-so-casual observer, she was throwing around magic like it was as easy as breathing, like it cost nothing. I wondered whether people in the Authority Proxied their spells. If I had to guess, I'd say Chase did. I wasn't sure about Zayvion. And I'd guess Shamus took the pain for casting his spells. Maybe even liked it.

Chase lifted her chin and met my gaze. I was pretty sure Shamus' wall blocked us from the creatures' senses, but that didn't make us invisible. Chase's mouth quirked, and there was challenge in her eyes. I was not about to take that challenge. Sure, I was good at magic, but as people seemed to be pointing out to me, I was largely untrained. Watching Chase manipulate the Illusion filled me with a burning desire to learn more and fast. Then the next time she gave me that condescending, dismissive look, I could smack a spell up the backside of her head.

Zayvion started whistling. Soft, swaying, the song was an old folk or country tune, something that brought to mind half-remembered words of a man wanting to waltz with a woman but ending up dead, his lonely ghost calling her name and wandering the land.

At the end of the chorus, Zayvion stopped, turned. He pulled the machete out from beneath his coat. Chase had an Illusion for that one too. To the nonmagical eye, he was doing nothing more than stretching.

But the beasts saw him for what he really was. A seven-foot-tall, burning black and silver god of a man wielding a wicked steel and glass machete glyphed to a killing edge.

The beasts leaped. Zayvion caught the first one through the chest with the tip of his blade. He pulled the blade free and pivoted, swinging the machete more like a billy club than a sword, putting the strength of his body into it. He sliced the next beast in half. Both sides of the creature fell to the grass and quivered.

I blinked, lost my focus on Sight for a half second, and the scene changed to Zayvion standing there, lighting a cigarette while the dogs wandered aimlessly around him and eventually made their way into the shadows under the bridge and out of sight.

Note to self: Chase can kick some serious Illusion ass.

I concentrated on Sight again. The glyph was still there, still working.

And Zayvion was still fighting. Silent, even in the noisy grass, he took the next beast through the thick head, the blade wedging and not coming free. He abandoned the machete, and a string with glyphed blades at the end appeared in his hands.

It didn't look like a formidable weapon, and frankly, I was trying to figure out why he didn't just pull a gun. Zayvion said a word I didn't hear—maybe Chase was working a Mute spell too—and the string burned with wicked fire. Magic dripped like flame down the edges of the blade. He swung the string in a tight circle and folded it against his chest to shorten and change the string's direction. The blade whipped out and cut off the front legs of the creature nearest him. A second strike through the ribs, and the thing moved no more.

This time I saw the Hunger's muzzle open in a howl.

But I heard nothing. Definitely a Mute spell. Zayvion probably didn't use a gun because Mute, even a really strong Mute, still allowed some noise to escape. And it was harder to hold an Illusion and Mute spell at the same time, doubly so in the dead zone of St. Johns. But a machete and rope—pretty easy to mask the sound of their strikes.

And apparently, the howl of undead, unliving beasts.

The rest of the creatures seemed to finally figure out that Zayvion was going to finish them off in short order. As if a cue had been sent, they took off running, fast, fluid, disappearing beneath the bridge.

Zayvion swore—that I heard—and Chase and he set off after the Hungers, their heartbeats tapping fast at my wrist.

Shamus flicked his cigarette to the ground and rolled his

boot over it. He also dropped whatever spell he had been using to hold up that wall.

He coughed a couple times and spat.

"Shouldn't we follow them?"

"No." He wiped his mouth on his sleeve, but not before I noticed the blood at the corner of his lips. "I'm going to clean up. You can watch if you want."

It really bugged me to just stand around while other people were working, but I'd said I only wanted to come so I could learn. So I could keep my people safe from those creatures. So I would know what to do next time. So I never had to haul Davy's broken and bleeding body into the hospital again.

All I'd learned so far was that it took at least three people to handle the Hungers. And a certain knowledge with weapons.

Which meant, if I really wanted to know how to fight these things, I had a lot of learning ahead of me.

Shamus must have taken my silence for agreement. He walked off toward the dead—at least I hoped they were dead—bodies of the Hungers.

I put the knife back in my belt and followed, noting the circle of dead grass where Shamus had stood had grown to six feet in diameter.

"Bet you suck at gardening," I observed.

Shamus shrugged. "It's all about energy exchange. It could always go the other way, me feeding a plant instead of drawing the life out of it."

"Do that often?"

Shamus looked at me over his shoulder. "No."

"Why not? Have something against plants?"

"No, but I haven't met a vegetable good enough to sacrifice a year of my life for."

"What?"

"Energy exchange. Death magic is all about transition, transfer, mutation, change from one state into another." At my look, he rolled his eyes. "Oh, come on. This is the ABC's. I can draw the life energy out of a living thing, like a plant, or I can give my life energy to a living thing, like a plant. Once that connection is set, it is a carrier for magic.

And that carrier—say it with me: Death magic—shifts how magic responds when it is cast into glyphs."

We stopped above the inert creatures. They were reduced to a strange collection of torsos, limbs, and body parts. Zayvion's machete stuck out of the skull of one of the things, hilt toward the sky, with just enough blade showing that it caught silver in the light. Fluid, thicker than blood, oozed black from every wound. I still didn't smell any kind of scent from them.

What had Shamus said? Death magic was hard to Hound?

"So, yeah, I like my vegetables. Don't love 'em enough to die for them." He knelt and poked a finger at one of the Hungers. His finger disappeared to the last knuckle inside the flesh, like he'd jabbed a stick into sand. He pulled his finger back. It came out clean.

Not so much creepy as sort of barf-inspiring.

It didn't seem to bother Shamus. "I'm going to stay here and retrieve the rest of the energy they fed on—since a lot of it was mine. Give me your word you'll stay out of trouble."

"Scout's honor," I drawled.

"Close enough." He traced a spell, one I did not know, into the air above the creature nearest him. The Sight spell I had cast was gone now, and I'd promised not to use any more magic, so I had to settle for the very normal sight of Shamus kneeling over four butchered nightmares.

He tipped his head back a little and closed his eyes. He whispered something, a single liquid word. Then a look of rapture crossed his face. His heartbeat slowed, and when I turned my thoughts to how he was feeling, I was surprised at the slick, lazy euphoria that filled him. Apparently, this was the upside of using Death magic.

The Hunger nearest him began to fade. Within two minutes, it was gone, all the remaining energy that made it solid absorbed by Shamus, leaving nothing, not even black blood behind.

Shamus sighed. Maybe it was my imagination, but he didn't look quite so pale. Without opening his eyes, he whispered that liquid word again. The next beast began to fade, and a second, stronger rush of euphoria took him.

If I stayed in touch any longer with his emotions, I was going to get a friggin' contact high.

The wind picked up, pushing the misty air around and reminding me that it had been a long day. I was cold. Tired. Wet. I tucked my chin into my collar and exhaled, my breath doing little to warm me up. I wondered if Zayvion and Chase were done running the Hungers down. I glanced over the way they had gone, didn't see any movements there. Of course, Chase was pretty good at Illusion.

"Daniel Beckstrom."

I spun at the voice behind me.

The Necromorph crouched on all fours in the shadows behind the metal building. I had no idea how long he'd been standing there, but he was thicker, stronger than when he'd jumped me. I think he'd been feeding well too.

Shit.

The wind shifted. I smelled death and blood and burnt blackberry—him—and then strawberries and bubble gum. Tomi's scents. The murderer shifted up and back, jerking his hand as if he were pulling a rope tight. I heard a very human whimper behind him.

Tomi stumbled forward into the tepid light.

I sucked in a breath. Every inch of exposed skin was black and blue or covered in blood.

"Shame," I said.

Shamus didn't move. Not an inch.

I took a cautious step back and shook Shame's shoulder. He was too caught in the rapture. I didn't know how to break whatever spell he was using.

Inside my head, my dad had gone very, very quiet. He didn't seem afraid of the murderer. No, he seemed terrified. And angry. Bad combination for a powerful dead guy who could run my body on remote control.

"You betrayed me," the Necromorph growled quietly, but not too quietly for me, not for my Hound ears. I could hear him across any distance. "And now your death will free me."

The murderer turned, lost again to the shadows.

I heard a high, muffled scream.

Shit, shit.

Quick mental calculation: Shamus zoned out. Zay and Chase running down the Hungers. I could feel their heartbeats, still fast, still alive. They might even be done killing them by now. They might be back any minute.

Shit, shit, shit.

Tomi didn't have time for any minute. I strode around Shamus. Careful not to touch the Hungers, I pulled Zayvion's machete out of one of the remaining creature's skull.

Black ichor clung to the blade and then was absorbed, the faint ribbons of glyphs worked into the steel sucking away the blood.

Time to find out what this thing could do to a Necromorph.

I held the machete low against my side and jogged to the back of the building. I sang my Mary Mack song. I needed to keep a clear head. A cool head. And a Disbursement. Needed one of those too. I decided on body ache, afraid to add any more to the headache and push it up into deadly levels.

Dying was not in my plans for the day.

If you have a suggestion, I thought to my father, who had been too silent for too long, *I'd love to hear it.*

He surprised me by answering. *Let him kill the girl. While he feeds on her, he will be vulnerable and you can kill him.*

No.

The price of one life is nothing to destroying that monstrosity.

I will not stand by and let one of my Hounds—hells, let anyone—die just so I can get a clear shot at that thing, I said.

Allison, he warned.

No. Done. Final.

I slowed and walked down the narrow path behind the shed, brambles as high as my head forming a wall uphill to the left of me, the shed to my right. A pile of discarded wood—two-by-fours and broken pallets—made the footing tricky. There was no room here to swing the machete. I traced an Impact glyph—something strong enough to blow that thing off his feet—with my left hand and held it there, pinched between my fingers, ready for me to fill it with magic.

All it needed to do was buy me some time so I could get in better machete-swinging range.

One metal panel on the back of the shed was rusted and bent open. I glanced in. There was just enough light fingering through cracks at the roofline and seams of the wall panels that I could make out the figures in the otherwise empty building. The Necromorph stood on all fours, rocking side to side, his head low. Tomi sat beside him, her arms extended to chest height, fingers spread wide, shaking, but poised to cast magic. Even in the low light I could see her eyes were wide and blank.

My heartbeat kicked into fight-or-flight, but my mind went totally clear. I could do this. Take that bastard down and save Tomi. As a matter of fact, I was looking forward to this.

We could end this. End him. He could be the proof that dark magic is too dangerous, even in good hands. The end of those who seek to open the gates and bring Mikhail back. You and I have the power to change which magic is used and how. We could rule the Authority, if we so wished. My father was a cold fire in the center of my head, raging, babbling.

Tell me later, I said. *When I'm not busy staying alive.*

I stepped quietly into the shed, holding to the shadows alongside the wall, the machete's blade raised so I could swing quickly.

The murderer growled, and Tomi whimpered again.

First, throw the Impact to knock him out. Next, go in swinging.

It wasn't a big plan, but it was simple. I liked simple.

Allison, my dad said. *Wait for him to feed on the girl. He will be vulnerable.*

Like hell, I said.

The thing sunk fangs into Tomi's shoulder and she yelled, her blood pouring down her arms to her hands. Hands that wove a spell for him.

I poured magic into the Impact glyph and threw it at him with everything I had.

No!

But I wasn't listening to my dad. I ran, covered the distance between me and the murderer with half a dozen pounding strides.

The Impact hit its mark and the beast toppled. Tomi crumpled, unconscious. The Necromorph only stayed down for a second before he turned, faced me.

And smiled.

Block. Block! Dad yelled in my head.

I tried. But it is impossible to trace a glyph at a full run, with a clear enough mind to do it correctly, and fill it with magic when your frickin' dad is yelling at you.

. The Necromorph lunged at me.

Oh, shit.

My dad, all cold fire and hate in my head, pushed past me. Shoved me out of the way. A wave of vertigo spun the room. I was chanting, only it wasn't me chanting. It was my father. Using me. Using my body, my mouth. Again.

For the love of all that's holy, he had to stop doing that shit.

He raised my hands, tracing something with my left that made black fire—fire a lot like what I saw Zayvion wield—drip down the blade of the machete.

The Necromorph jumped, slammed into me. I went down and knocked the back of my head against the ground. I knew it hurt, but it was a distant sort of pain.

My dad angled the blade, thrust it at the Necromorph.

The Necromorph dodged out of the way, standing back on two legs.

I, or rather my dad, scrambled up onto my feet. I wasn't even breathing hard.

"Tell me who owns you," my father said with my mouth. "Tell me who hired you to kill me. Tell me, or this will be your end, Greyson."

Greyson? Chase's ex-boyfriend? The man she thought might be her Soul Complement? The man Zayvion said was dead?

Holy crap.

"There is no end for me." Greyson stretched his neck so the disk implanted in his flesh shone a sickly green. "Not anymore. You have seen to that. You and your technology.

But there is still revenge for me. And I will have it through you, Daniel Beckstrom."

Greyson opened his mouth, his jaw unhinging so that I could see all of his serrated teeth. He inhaled, and I could feel him drawing like a hard wind in my brain.

My dad yelled. I had never heard him yell like that before, had never heard myself yell like that before.

I knew he, we, were in excruciating pain. But I didn't feel it.

I pushed to regain control of my body, willing him to move out of the way, to step aside so I could be in the front of my own mind.

With that thought, I was fully in control of my body, and could feel every aching inch of it. I think I broke a rib.

It was too damn easy to take control of myself. And I knew why. Greyson somehow had a hold on my dad's soul and was sucking him out of my head.

My dad still screamed, but not from inside my head.

In the dim light of the warehouse, I could just make out the watercolor image of my father wavering in the air between Greyson and me. Dark business suit, gray hair, and eyes too much like mine, his face contorted by agony. He yelled, but even as I watched, he was fading, becoming less and less solid, his screams quieter and quieter as Greyson breathed him in.

Greyson drank his soul like the Hungers had drunk down magic. The disk at his neck pulsed with magic.

I was beginning to dislike those damn things.

With each heartbeat, my father faded, and Greyson slowly changed from the beast he was back into the man he had once been.

Long black hair fell around his rugged, long-featured face—one a model would kill for. He was taller than me, wide in the shoulders, his beastly form shifting into the scarred and muscled body of an athlete, a runner.

Yes, he was naked. Yes, even with my dad screaming and Tomi unconscious and possibly dead, I looked.

Very nice in that department too.

Allison, my father whispered. *He will hunt. Violet. Please.*

Here is the problem with being left in the dark about magic and the people who use it. I wasn't sure if Greyson draining my father's soul was a good thing or a bad thing. But I did know this: my father had asked me *please* only once.

And I also knew that even if Greyson had been Chase's lover, he had also killed my dad.

That did not make us friends, no matter what I thought about my father.

Fuck.

I didn't know how to break Greyson's hold on my dad, but I might be able to stop him.

I traced a Hold spell and poured magic into the glyph. I threw it at him. Nothing.

Well, since magic didn't work, it was time to get back to basics. I ran past my father's ghost and swung the machete at Greyson's head.

A sharp pain shot across my ribs and I groaned. Yep. Broken.

My swing fell a little short, pain hitching my reach. Greyson had good reflexes. He twisted away from most of the strike. Just the tip of the blade bit flesh, drawing a deep line of blood across his biceps.

My father wasn't screaming anymore. There wasn't much of him left to scream. Only the very faintest outline of him and two dark holes where his eyes should be were all that remained of his soul. I didn't know how to get him back in my head, didn't really want him back. But swinging at Greyson had broken his concentration.

I knew if Greyson got one more sip of him, he would have absorbed my father's soul.

And if Greyson could carry around my father's soul like I could, then Dad would be awake, aware, just like he was in me.

I did not like the idea of my father, and all the spells and training he had, being at the beck and call of Murder Boy over there.

Greyson opened his mouth, unhinged his human-looking jaw.

No time to think.

I ran to my dad's ghost, ran *into* his ghost and inhaled, occupying the same space.

I didn't know how to ask a spirit to possess me. So I did my best to clear my mind and concentrate on allowing my father's soul, his mind, back into me.

I am a river and magic flows through me. Your soul is a part of that magic, a part of the magic I carry in me.

"Come back to me, Dad," I said with enough Influence, I think even my willful father would respond.

A cool breeze, soft as a sigh, washed over me. I smelled wintergreen. Tasted leather. My father's scents. But it was faint. So faint.

"Dad?"

No response.

And still no time.

Greyson yelled. That wasn't good.

I turned. Threw both my arms up to protect my face.

A massive figure charged out of the shadows and hit Greyson like a one-ton truck.

Greyson rolled, but the beast kept after him. Greyson finally crumpled beneath the beast. And it was a beast. A very familiar beast.

Stone growled. His strange pipe-organ vacuum-cleaner croon now had a primal guttural rattle. He did not like Greyson. Not one bit.

I didn't know where the big lug had come from, but I was really happy to see him.

He had Greyson pinned with one stone hand on his throat, and the other shoved in the center of his chest. Stone rocked forward, leaning a little more weight on each hand.

Greyson yelled.

So, here's the deal. I had no problem with Stone making mush out of this guy. Maybe in man form Greyson could not only feel pain, he could also die. He sure hadn't died in beast form when Stone messed him up before.

But I didn't know if my dad was in me. I didn't know if my dad was in Greyson. And the last thing Dad had asked him was who hired Greyson to murder my father. Greyson had answers to questions I wanted solved. Whether or not my dad's soul was in me, in Greyson, or finally at rest.

"Stone, don't," I said. "Don't kill him. Yet."

The breathing boulder actually listened to me and eased up a little. Not that it did Greyson much good. He was bleeding, and from the angle of his arm and leg, broken. But bleeding and broken weren't enough to make Stone let go of him.

And yes, Greyson's wounds were already healing, just like they had in the alley, though I didn't see dark magic filling him. No, just the disk that pulsed green at his neck.

A shiver ran down my sweaty back. Every instinct in my body told me the man on the floor was inhuman. Something that broke the rules of life and death.

Yeah, I know. So says the woman who keeps a dead man as a brain buddy.

Already Greyson looked less human. His face shifted into feral angles, his limbs bent and twisted into the form of the beast.

Maybe losing his humanity meant he no longer had my father's soul. Maybe it meant I still had my father's soul, what was left of it, inside me.

I'd cheer, but, really, who was I kidding? I had a couple problems on my hands here.

I shifted my grip on the machete. Cutting Greyson may not stop him, but large injuries seemed to slow him down some. And I was hankering to stab somebody until they told me what the hell I wanted to know.

"What did you do to Tomi?" I asked. "What did you do to my dad? Is he still in you? Did you kill him? Again? Did you fuck up Davy? Who hired you? Who put that damn disk in your neck? Why did taking my dad's soul change you?"

He didn't say anything. Didn't move.

Yeah, I heard it too. Footsteps coming close to the shed.

The room suddenly flooded with light. Greyson looked over my shoulder.

I did too. That was stupid. Luckily, Stone was not at all interested in the light. He stared straight at Greyson and growled again.

Chase strode into the warehouse through the same hole in the wall I'd gone through. She held an orb, the source of the light, in her left hand. The fingers of her right hand curled around a snakelike glyph that I could see even without Sight.

"Allie?" she called.

"I'm fine," I said even though I wasn't. Because, really, right now I was a little worried that the kick-ass woman behind me was going to meet her undead, half-beast murderer boyfriend and oh, I don't know, maybe the conversation would get awkward. If I understood her job description, it was a Closer's duty, Chase's duty, to Close people who used magic wrong, who used magic to hurt others. And that meant it was her job to kill Greyson.

The man she once loved.

The beast he now was.

Who might house my father's soul.

Who might know who was behind my dad's death.

Who might be impossible to kill.

Holy shit.

She strode over to me like she didn't believe a word I'd said. Good instincts.

Greyson was still sliding into his mutated beast form, the disk at his neck pulsing toxic silver-green with every beat of his heart. He didn't run, not that he could get out from under Stone's grip. He didn't raise his hands to cast a spell. He simply lay there. Watching Chase draw nearer. The rhythm of his heartbeat quickened, and the disk at his neck pulsed faster.

Pain twisted his face while contortions changed his body.

Chase caught sight of Stone and Greyson and paused midstride. She seemed to catch herself and finished the march to my side. She dimmed the light to nonnuclear levels and stopped next to me.

"Greyson?" she breathed.

"Please," he said, his voice still more man than beast, "let me go."

The spell in her right hand flickered and died, but the orb still burned, deep yellow now, like dying candlelight that caressed Greyson's face, blurring the edges until it seemed only the man rested within its glow.

She was losing concentration. Probably going into shock.

I didn't blame her, but I sure as hell wasn't going to let her shock get me killed.

"Oh, Grey." Her words caught. She swallowed, tried again. "I—I can't."

Greyson lifted one hand toward her but did not touch her, even though he could have. "Then look away. Please look away."

Chase was shaking. "No. We can help you. We can undo this."

Greyson shook his head. "No one can. Not even Zayvion."

Chase's breath caught in her throat. She pressed the back of her hand against her mouth as if she could somehow keep the sorrow behind her lips. She closed her eyes, just for a moment, but I knew she was doing mad work to clear her mind. Her heart at my wrist fluttered like a hummingbird in flight.

When she spoke, she was no hummingbird. She was steel and ice. "Tell me who did this to you."

"Daniel Beckstrom," he growled.

Chase swung on me so fast I didn't even have time to exhale. And that bitch knew how to throw a punch. I took it just below the eye, and fell. Blood poured down the back of my throat, and the dust from the floor filled my mouth. She'd put something else behind that hit. I couldn't move. Not even to pull the knife out of my belt.

I'd spun before I landed so now the only thing in my line of vision was the bent metal opening at the back of the building.

I could still hear, which was something, I suppose. I heard Stone growl and jump. I heard Chase chant and throw magic. The ground shook as Stone hit the floor and was silent. After that, I heard Greyson getting onto his feet.

"Chase?" Greyson said.

"Go."

I heard the sound of four feet running, watched as Greyson headed toward the opening in the wall.

She had let him go. She had let my dad's murderer free.

But just as Greyson reached the opening, a figure stepped through it. Zayvion, with a two-by-four over his shoulder. He swung at Greyson like a batter aiming for the far wall, and connected with his head.

Greyson flew out of my line of vision. Zayvion adjusted his hold on the board and drew a glyph in the air with his left hand. He threw the spell at Greyson. I didn't hear any other movement from that part of the room.

"Looks like this worked out to our advantage after all," Zayvion said. "Do you want to explain this to me, Chase?" He left my vision, weaving another spell, walking toward where Greyson fell.

For a second I thought Chase had left to be beside Greyson too. But she squatted down next to me, her boot inches from my face.

She tugged my chin to one side so I could see her cold, cold face. "You have screwed with the wrong woman, Beckstrom," she whispered. She pressed her fingertip into the center of my forehead.

And then everything went black.

Chapter Fifteen

It didn't take me long to decide my dreams sucked. I dreamed Zayvion and Chase were yelling at each other, angry about me, about Greyson, about Tomi. I was a little fuzzy on the details, but it sounded like Chase wanted to Close me or maybe kill me, and Zayvion was having none of it.

My hero.

A third voice spoke up. Shamus. Told them to shut the hell up. Told Chase to take care of Tomi. Told Zayvion to figure out how to move the rock. Told them he would handle Greyson. There were a lot of moving-around sounds. Some silence, during which I drifted. Then more noise.

They were talking about Tomi. About the glyphs cut into her to bind her with Blood and Death magic. Talked about whether Greyson had done this to her, or if someone was working with him. Greyson had been a Closer before he'd been changed. And they could tell he had closed Tomi's mind over and over to keep her from knowing what she was doing, how she was being used.

None of them seemed to know why he picked her, of all people, though they did begin to question why she had mentioned Jingo Jingo, and whether he or someone else in the Authority was part of this.

I heard Chase say she'd take Tomi to someone, see if her mind could be mended, her body healed.

Then someone dragged fingers across my forehead. It was nice, warm. Plus, I was awake again.

Shamus sat crossed-legged next to me. He gave me a small smile.

"Trouble."

I swallowed to say something, but could not find my voice.

"We're going to take care of Tomi. Get her some help, then take her home to heal if that's the best way to go. She won't remember any of this.

"Greyson is a bit of a problem."

I raised my eyebrows—because that was as much sarcasm as I could manage.

"We're taking him in. Have ways we can make sure he doesn't wake up for a while. Hopefully, we'll be able to get into his head and find out who he's working with. Find out who did that . . ." He swallowed, shook his head. "Did this to him. Don't know that there's a cure, but if there is, we'll find it. Fix him." He took a deep breath. I didn't think he'd been saying most of that stuff for me.

He patted his pocket, found his cigarettes, and lit up. He inhaled and pulled the cigarette away.

"But the gargoyle? Damn, girl. I'd love to know how you did that. The only Animation I've ever seen done that well was on a much, much smaller scale. It's sentient, or at least free-willed, isn't it?"

Since I couldn't talk, I just stared at him.

"Right. Sorry. We're taking it along with us. With you. Next time you wake up, you'll be at my mum's, okay?"

Somewhere behind me, I could hear Zayvion take a breath, hold it, then begin singing softly, casting a spell.

Shamus glanced up, away from me, toward where I thought Zayvion must be. He shook his head. "Beauty."

Then he looked back down at me. "Hell of a day, love. Not bad for your first day in the field. Took care of all the Hungers, in case you wanted to know. Now get some sleep. You'll need it."

He brushed his fingers over my forehead again, and, really, I did the only thing I could. I slept.

Chapter Sixteen

"Come on, now. Wake for me, Allison Beckstrom."

I didn't recognize the voice. Deep, male, almost a purr. I could not resist it. Influence, most likely.

I opened my eyes. I was lying in a soft bed, not my own, in a clean room that smelled like honeysuckle. I'd never seen this room before. Maybe a hotel?

I had, however, seen the man who sat in the chair next to the bed. He had been at my father's funeral.

Big didn't begin to describe him. He was the kind of guy who needed all three seats on an airplane. His eyes and skin were almost the same color, coffee dark, and there was a gentleness to his expression that was at odds with the intensity of his gaze. He might look like a nice guy on the outside, but he creeped me out. I inhaled and caught the sweet scent of licorice and something more chemical that tasted like death.

"My name is Jingo Jingo." He smiled, and fear rubbed fingers across my stomach. At the sound of his name, an image of candy in his pocket and little bones came to me. What was it my father had whispered to me at the funeral? He had a thing for the bones of little children?

"I am a teacher here," he said. "I understand you know my student, Shamus Flynn."

I did. And I also knew Shamus didn't like him. Shamus said he was a freak.

Shamus was a very smart boy.

Plus, Davy had said Tomi was messed up with Jingo. None of this inspired my trust in the man.

"Yes," I finally said.

"And I understand you've been hearing your father. Ever since that unfortunate happening in the warehouse."

It took me a second to place which unfortunate happening in which warehouse he was talking about. Probably the one after Pike had died, after I'd killed Lon Trager, when Frank Gordon had dug up my dad and tried to use him to open the gates to death.

Unfortunate, indeed.

"Have you?" he asked.

What were we talking about? I was tired, muzzy-headed. What the hell had Chase done to me?

We were talking about my dead dad in my head. Right.

Even though I didn't like this man, didn't trust this man, he was a teacher in the Authority, and innocent before being found guilty and all that. Even Maeve had told me she wanted him to look in my head and see if my father was really still there.

And after everything Greyson had done to my father, now would be the best time to find out if my dad was still alive, still in my head.

"I've heard him, yes," I said. Could I sound any more like an idiot?

"I'm going to look into your mind, Ms. Beckstrom. To see how much of your father is still with you. Do I have your permission to do so?"

"Do you have to have it?" Well, that was a stupid thing to ask.

"It does make this a more . . . pleasant experience."

"Okay." I hated that someone I did not know, someone I did not trust, was going to get inside me, feel around.

Sure, I tried to think of Jingo Jingo the same way I thought about having a new doctor. He was an expert. He had my best interests in mind.

I wasn't buying it.

"Just relax." He shifted so he could rest his hand on my right wrist, the arm where magic had left its indelible mark.

His fingers were soft. Warm.

Just like Maeve, he closed his eyes and took a deep

breath. When he opened his eyes, copper fire glinted in their brown depths.

He reached into my mind—a slick warmth that felt a lot like a finger going down my throat. But instead of gagging, I felt a numbing sensation follow his touch.

My vision shifted. I didn't know whether it was because he was in the middle of my head, looking around, or whether I had lost control of the magic inside me and had accidentally invoked Sight.

Jingo Jingo no longer looked like a man. Or rather he did. He just didn't look like the same man. The man revealed to me was skeletal, lean, empty, and hungry as an addict. All around him, tied by candy-colored lines, were the images of ghostly children.

He had a thing for the bones of little children.

I blinked, but the ghosts did not disappear. They shifted and moved, a fog of sorrowful faces and wide, frightened eyes.

Shamus said Death magic was a transference of energy. Did that mean Jingo Jingo, a user of Death magic, was somehow drawing upon, using, or (shudder) harvesting the souls of little children?

I wanted to look away. Wanted to unsee what I was seeing. But Jingo Jingo's thick fingers were in my head, holding me still. Pinning me down to the mattress beneath me.

"Beckstrom," Jingo said in his soft baritone, "come to me, Daniel Beckstrom."

A flutter, soft as a one-winged moth, flickered at the back of my head.

Betrayer, my father whispered.

Jingo Jingo's eyes went wide. I saw his fear.

Call me petty, but I liked the look of it.

He withdrew from my mind, pulling away from me both physically and mentally.

He blinked. The copper fire in his eyes was gone. And so were the ghostly children.

He was just a man again. Except I knew he was not.

Still, he smiled that warm smile and hid the fear in his eyes. "You are fine, Allison," he said. "Your daddy isn't going to bother you no more. He was something once, but nothing to worry about now. Just a couple echoes of his memories in you. But he's gone. He's gone."

Really? Then why did I feel that flutter in my mind again, still faint, but growing stronger? Why did I smell Jingo Jingo's sweat? His fear.

I didn't believe my father was gone. Maybe drained. Maybe broken. But I was pretty sure he was still in me. I was pretty sure I'd just heard him. And I was pretty sure that scared the hell out of Jingo Jingo.

Wasn't that interesting?

There was a soft knock on the door.

"Come on in," Jingo Jingo said. He seemed awfully happy for the interruption.

The door opened and Maeve walked in carrying a tray with a bowl and cup on it. I smelled chicken soup and fresh coffee.

My stomach growled.

"Ready for some food?" she asked.

"Please," I said.

Jingo Jingo took that as his cue to leave. "I'll leave you to your meal, Ms. Beckstrom." He pushed up to his feet, filling more space than I thought the room had.

My heart notched up at that, claustrophobia kicking in. I really needed him to go, to leave, to empty out the room and leave me with air to breathe.

Or, hells, he could stay and I'd be happy to leave. He and Maeve could have the room and spend all the time they wanted there.

I pushed the covers down to my legs, thinking now would be a great time to get out of here.

"Could I speak with you?" Jingo Jingo asked Maeve.

She nodded, and expertly deposited the tray over my uncovered lap. "Stay here. Eat."

No Influence behind it, but such a motherly command it had the same result. Before I could push away the tray, she and Jingo Jingo were out the door, leaving a lot more air and the smell of chicken and vegetables behind to remind me that I hadn't eaten for what felt like a long, long time.

They shut the door behind them, but that was okay. The room itself was large. It just wasn't large enough to contain me, Maeve, and Jingo Jingo.

I picked up the fork. It wasn't soup, but a nice stir-fry that filled the bowl. I took a bite. Salty, savory, with veggies that still snapped with flavor. I ate as quietly as I could, listening to the drift of Maeve and Jingo Jingo's voices.

Hounds don't need magic to have good hearing.

"How is she?" Maeve asked.

"Tired. Her father left some memories behind. As is to be expected with the magic Frank Gordon used to resurrect his soul. But Daniel is not in there. I'd go so far as to say he never has been. Nothing but a few of his memories left behind for the poor girl."

I stopped with a fork full of rice halfway to my mouth. Lies. He was lying to Maeve. He had seen my father in me. And even the tiniest flicker of my father's presence had made him afraid. Why wouldn't he want to tell Maeve the truth?

Was he part of Greyson using Tomi? Was he part of my dad's death? Part of the hit on Boy out in St. Johns that almost got me, Zayvion, and Cody killed?

"Thank you," Maeve said. "That's one less thing we'll have to worry about."

"My pleasure, always, Mrs. Flynn," he said.

"If you'd like dinner or a drink, help yourself, on the house."

"Thank you. But I'm sorry I have to refuse. I have a few errands to attend to before she is tested."

He said his good-byes, and so did Maeve. I got back to eating.

I don't know why she waited for so long, but about five minutes later, Maeve knocked on the door. She opened it. "May I?"

"Come in." I left my fork in the empty bowl and picked up the coffee cup. "This is your place, right? Your inn?" The food and coffee were doing wonders for clearing my head.

She nodded. "Our guest rooms are often used for people recovering from the demands of magic. Though we get our ordinary travelers through the place, too."

She walked over to the chair where Jingo Jingo had been sitting and pushed it back against the wall where it probably belonged. Then she sat on the edge of my bed. "You were listening," she said.

"Hound ears."

"He says your father is not inside you. Which is good. Removing a soul is a difficult, painful procedure. It is nice to have some good news."

I think Zayvion had told me that once. After experiencing what Greyson had done, I didn't want to get anywhere near soul removal for a while.

"So what's the bad news?" I asked.

"It has been decided by the Authority that you will be tested tonight."

I guessed I should be frightened or worried. Instead, I was tired enough to just accept it and move on. After all, I'd just faced down a half-beast ex-man who killed my father. Or at least killed most of him. Twice. I could handle a little test.

"What about my classes with you?"

"I'm afraid there's no time for that now. The things you've done on the hunt with Zayvion, Shamus, and Chase, and the things Chase said you did to Greyson, makes it too dangerous to allow you to continue using magic untrained. Or perhaps at all," she added softly. "Chase demanded you be tested or Closed. There are some who support your Closure. But more who believe we should test you. All agree we can not wait."

"I didn't do anything to Greyson," I said.

She half nodded. Not an acceptance or rejection.

So it was clear I wasn't going to convince her of my innocence. "Can you tell me what to expect?"

"The test will be held here in the lower level of the inn, where there is an appropriately Warded room. Many of the Authority will be there, including Sedra."

"She's the president of the Authority, right?"

"She is the head of it, yes. You will be asked to stand and defend yourself, magically, against one opponent."

"It's a wizard's duel? Seems like a silly way to decide who can be a part of the secret magic club."

That, finally, got a smile out of her. "It is a magic-user test. Carefully orchestrated to measure you. Both of you will be instructed to draw upon every capability at your disposal. You cannot hold back, Allie. No matter what. If you want to survive the test, you must be relentless. Show us your true colors."

That sounded familiar. My dad had told me something similar, although he'd told me to use anyone and anything I had to to survive. "I'll do what I can," I said.

"Good," she said, "I expect you to do so."

"How much time until the test?"

"It's four o'clock now. We'll begin at eight. I think it would be best if you got some sleep."

"Can I talk to Zayvion?"

"No." She reached over and took the tray off my lap. "I can send Shamus in, if you'd like."

"Okay. And I need to make a phone call."

"We can do that."

She stood, got halfway to the door.

"Maeve?"

"Yes?"

"What happens if I don't pass?"

There wasn't even time for her frown to register before it was replaced by a neutral line. "You'll be Closed."

"How Closed? Just my memories of this place? Of the Authority?" What I didn't say, what I didn't ask was, Will I forget you and Shamus? Will I forget Zayvion? Will I lose the ability to use magic? I realized my chest hitched at that thought. I didn't want to lose them. Didn't want to lose Zayvion. And I didn't want to lose this life I was living, even though this life was currently kicking my ass.

"Very, very Closed," she said softly. "You don't want that to happen, and I don't want that to happen. You belong here, Allie. You belong with us. And I know you are strong enough to prove me right. I'll send Shamus in. Then I hope you'll take my advice and get some sleep."

"I'll try," I said in answer to both her suggestions.

She left. I needed to use the bathroom, so I got out of bed. I was still in my jeans and the tank I'd put on under my sweater, but no boots or socks. My coat draped one corner of the bed and my hat dripped dry on a towel on the dresser top.

I walked across the floor, wood and waxed to a deep shine. My feet hurt. My legs hurt. Everything hurt.

Oh, right. Probably from the Disbursements I'd set. Wondered whether the headache was going to kick in too.

The bathroom was small, clean, and white. The honeysuckle smell was stronger here. I used the facilities and washed my hands. I turned my wrist to see if there was any mark left from the cuff and disk I'd been wearing. There were no marks other than the ribbons of colors on my arm. Nothing to remind me of what it had been like to feel the heartbeats of three people, to feel their emotions, to be part of them. I rubbed my thumb over my wrist, pushing away the sudden loneliness.

Pull yourself together, Beckstrom, I told myself. *This is no time to get all sappy. People out there were going to try to kill me or Close me. Take my memories away.*

I stood there, warm water pouring over hands that had been clean for at least a minute, trying to gather up the guts to look at myself in the mirror.

Stupid, stupid, stupid, I thought. *Just look. See what you've become. What you are. You can do it. You've done it before.*

I bit the inside of my cheek and forced myself to look up.

For once, I didn't look as bad as I felt. No bruises, no strange burned circles on my face. My eyes were a little dilated, and pale, pale green. The only person looking back at me through my eyes was me.

Maybe Jingo Jingo was right. Maybe my dad was gone.

Or maybe he was just very, very tired.

Yeah, that made two of us.

I turned off the water and walked out of the bathroom. Got all the way back to bed and under the covers before the knock on the door.

"Come in."

Shamus breezed into the room like he'd spent the day strolling through the Rose Gardens.

"You wanted to see me?"

"Are you okay?"

He paused and gave me a strange look before continuing on over to the chair Jingo Jingo had sat in. He dragged it away from the wall, over to the side of my bed.

"Am I okay? You're the one in bed, trying to shake off a Paralyze spell in time for the test of your life. I'd say of the two of us, I'm gold." He flopped down into the chair and stuck his feet on the bed frame.

So that's what Chase threw at me. I hoped she Proxied her own spells and was barfing from the pain.

"Honestly." I gave him a serious look.

He smiled. "I don't think you and I are close enough for *that* much honesty. You'll just have to trust that I'm fine enough."

"That's fair," I said. "How is Tomi doing?"

"The bait? She's had a bad time of it. We did what we could to take away the memories. Someone's staying with her to help her heal. There's a cover story about a hell of a bender, drugs, too much cutting. Blood magic. Bad crowd. That kind of thing. Not all that unusual for a Hound, eh?"

"No," I said. The sudden reality of what being a Closer really meant sent shivers down my back. How many times had I woken up not remembering? How many times had I blamed it on drugs, booze, magic? Was there something else I should have blamed it on? Someone else? Closers. Chase? Zayvion?

"You Close Hounds?" I asked.

Shamus tipped his head to one side. "Don't tell me this is the first time you figured that out."

"Yes. How often do you Close Hounds? Whom do you Close? Have you Closed me? Have you taken my memories?"

Shamus held up one hand, his black fingerless gloves making his fingers look ghostly pale. "*I* don't Close anyone. *I* am not a Closer. Death magic, remember?"

"Who?" I demanded. "Who Closed me?"

"Listen, love," Shamus said with a hard smile. "I don't know how to break this to you, but I have no fucking idea. You weren't even on my radar until a couple months ago when Zayvion went head over shit kickers for you. Well, I did harbor a bit of hate for you, seeing that your da killed my da. Other than that though, I didn't care you were alive, much less who might be Closing you."

I just sat there and blinked. It was cold water to the face.

These people—Shamus, Maeve, Zayvion—did things to people, made choices without the advice of law or courts. They had probably done things to me.

"Scary, ain't it?" Shamus asked when I was quiet a little too long. "This secret magic shit is crazy stuff. The things we can do to try to keep people and society safe. Most all of it is in good intention too; that's honest. If it helps any, I can ask around. You'll be on the files if you've been Closed. I can't access the files on that, but I can talk to Victor about it. See if he'll release some information."

"Do they ever tell someone if they've been Closed?" I finally asked.

"Tell someone? Darlin', haven't you been paying attention? We can do anything. Tell you if you've been Closed. When and where and why. Or—this is a possibility—give you back your memories if the person who Closed you is willing. It's not so easy as clicking your heels and everything snaps back into place, but it happens.

"You won't believe this, but sometimes people want to leave the Authority, and so their time here is Closed. Then sometimes they wander back, and their memories are Opened. Just like new." He stuck out one hand and made the so-so motion. "More or less."

"Is that your pep talk?" I asked.

"Not mine so much, no. Standard-issue. Drag it out whenever the situation calls for it. Did it work?"

I rubbed at my eyes and tried to let go of my anger and fear. If they had Closed me, I'd find out. First, I had to survive the test. I pulled my hands away from my face. "Let's pretend it did," I said. "So Chase pushed to get me tested tonight?"

He nodded, his eyes wide. "Woman is chewing glass and spitting sparks over what she thinks you did to Greyson. You remember that part, right?"

"Shouldn't I?"

"No one Closed you," he said. "By the time I got there, Zayvion and Chase were yelling to bring the roof down. Neither of them got in your head. I made sure of that."

"Thank you."

"No problem," he said. "It's a serious thing what went down there. Greyson. You."

"I didn't do anything to Greyson."

"No? Just coincidence he was there? That he used the Hound girl for bait to lure you? Made her open the gates with the other Hound, Davy, and release the Hungers? You did notice Greyson, he isn't exactly human anymore, right? Oh, and one of your da's disks is crammed in his craw?"

"Listen," I said. "He tried to kill me. Three times. Of course this wasn't a coincidence."

Shamus was good at hiding his body language, but from the subtle tensing in his shoulders, I knew that Greyson trying to kill me was news to him.

"And I didn't do anything to him. He killed my father."

"Is that true?"

I nodded.

"So you think your father implanted the disk and converted him to a Necromorph?"

"No."

"Come on, now. Don't be dense. It's your da's disk. Who else has access to the disks? And you say he killed your da. Two and two. It adds up."

I shook my head. "He was still a man when he killed my dad. He didn't have the disk in his throat." I dug for the flash of Dad's memory that I had seen, of Greyson standing in front of him with a knife and a disk in his hand.

"I find myself potently curious as to how you know this," Shamus said.

"My dad told me."

We stared at each other for a minute or so.

"In your noggin?" he finally asked.

"Yes."

"Huh." That was it, nothing more.

But my head was spinning. I had assumed the stolen disks had been used on Greyson. But Shame brought up a very good point. There were other people who had access to the disks. People like my father. And people who worked for my father. People like Violet and probably even Kevin.

So it could be a stolen disk in his neck, and stolen disks being used to open the gates. Or it could be someone inside Beckstrom Enterprises was supplying them.

Is that why Dad said Greyson would hunt Violet?

Shamus shifted his feet on the bedframe. "We do have Greyson contained. Off the street, thanks quite a bit to you. That's a problem we've been trying to take care of for months. I'm sure someone will figure how to get in his head and pull the truth out of him. Find out who morphed him."

"I don't understand why anyone would even want to do that," I said. "It's dark magic, right?"

"Very. With technology to bolster it. Bad shit."

"Why mess someone up like that?"

He took a deep breath and leaned back so he could stare at the ceiling. "I forget you haven't read the history." He was quiet a minute.

"Basically," he looked back down at me, "magic has always been around. It took mankind a long time to discover it, and even longer to learn how to access it. Lots of hints of that show up in the history books if you know what you're looking for. We, the Authority, have mostly covered up the reality of magic until about thirty years ago, when your da and a few of his cronies went public with the 'safe' technology to access magic.

"Magic is a natural part of this world. Okay?"

"Okay," I said.

"Some ways to use magic are still kept secret from the general population. Death magic, for sure. Blood magic to some degree, and lots of ways magic can be used aren't taught—dark magic especially. Those college classes that teach how to use magic for business, counseling, medicine, construction, the arts?

"Who do you think developed those courses? The Authority. Who do you think teach it in the universities? Mostly members of the Authority. See, once your da let the devil out of the bag, damage control was the best the Authority could do.

"It's worked okay. Some people who were dead set against magic being used by the general public changed their tune. Making magic available has helped the world more than hurt it. So far, anyway, and so long as the Authority keeps a close eye on what 'advances' are being released." He shrugged.

"And making someone into a beast is an advance?" I asked.

He held up a finger. "Getting to that. So magic is bright, right? It casts a shadow when it's used. And that shadow contains magic too. That shadow is a twisted version of magic—dark magic.

"Dark magic can do very bad things. That's why it's forbidden. But making something forbidden only means it gets used in secret, which is why some people think dark magic should be sanctioned, taught, and regulated. The price for using dark magic is death, so that goes a long way toward deterring users. Still . . ."

He shook his head. "People, right? Crazy. Anyway, dark magic is used sometimes. Not often, because, well, it's sort of hard to access. Like catching a shadow. But just like magic casts a shadow, so does life. Life's shadow is death. You still with me?"

I nodded.

"So for a long while, dark magic was rarely used. But your da opened the door to experimentation with the rules, changed centuries of tradition. Gave people ideas. Wasn't long before someone discovered where dark magic was most plentiful: in death. All you had to do was find a way to tap into it, and just like sucking magic out of the ground, dark magic was at your fingertips.

"Frank Gordon gave it a go, and tried to reanimate your dad's corpse to open the gates between life and death."

"Why?" I asked. "Don't we have enough trouble dealing with light magic?"

"I think it's all about control, who has the most magic at their disposal, and who can keep it that way.

"But legends say that a man who can walk between life and death will be immortal. Maybe that's what Frank was trying with your dad. Maybe that's what someone is trying with Greyson, seeing as how he isn't quite living as a man. Frank's dead, so we can't ask him. But now we have Greyson, so maybe we can find out who's been dipping their fingers in the naughty sauce, and take care of them before this blows into a war."

Shamus shifted in his seat, crossing one ankle over his knee. He was quiet, letting me absorb it.

That was crazy. Impossible. Half-alive, half-dead magic users. Light magic, dark magic, life and death. Controlling all the magic, all the time. Was I the only one who thought that was a hideous idea? And immortality? Hadn't that been what my half-alive, half-dead dad had told me he wanted?

Okay, even though it was crazy, it could also be true.

I rubbed at my eyes again, hoping this might be a dream and I might wake up and find out that my world was just a world again, that my city was filled with regular people going about regular lives with simple, regular magic that made their shoes look shiny.

"Holy shit, Shame. Are you joking?"

"Dead serious," he said, and I knew he was. "Frank was on to something, thinking your da, out of all the powerful magic users of our time, might be able to pull it off—life and death, dark and light. Might have done it too, if you and Zayvion hadn't stopped him. That was probably the one thing that got you the chance to be a part of the Authority, you and Z shutting Frank down. Well, that and Z saying you're his Soul Complement."

I didn't even know what to say about that. About any of this. Okay. Regroup. Back to the problem at hand.

"What happened to Stone?" I asked.

"Who?"

"The gargoyle."

Shamus' smile spread into a grin. He looked like a kid who'd just taken a dive into a pile of cotton candy. "Hell of a thing. Awesome. Just." He twisted his wrists so both hands spread open, palms up, fingers wide. "Magic. Don't ever get to see that kind of thing anymore. Animation is part of the old ways. Not all that useful, a parlor trick, not much taught. I thought the knack had been lost. How'd you do it?"

"He was already animated, I just, uh . . . gave him a boost and set him free." There was more to it than that.

I had used magic on him, and I was pretty sure my magic had triggered something more inside him, like oxygen to a flame. But since I wasn't sure how I had done it, I didn't know what more to say. "He's okay, right?"

"Absolutely. Well," he amended, "we couldn't have him rampaging through the house. Knows how to mess up a place. Plus he seemed pretty upset when Mum woke him. Think he was looking for you. She stuck a Grounding Stone on his head to keep him quiet while we figure out what to do with him."

Great. Now I not only had to survive the test, I needed to make sure they'd set Stone free no matter if I passed the test or not. I did not want him to be trapped here just because he'd come to my rescue.

"You should set him free," I said.

Shamus laughed. At my look, he sobered. "Sorry. Didn't realize you were serious. I don't think they'll let him free. A gargoyle loose in the city? How are we going to keep that under wraps? Plus, he's too . . . interesting, you know?"

"Anyone ask him if he wants to stay here?"

"You do know it's not really alive," he said.

"Yes. He's not really dead either," I said.

"A lot of that going around lately. That's part of what makes him so interesting." He pointed at my head. "Heard you saw Jingo Jingo. Let him look in your attic?"

"Yes."

"What do you think?"

"Of Jingo Jingo?"

Shamus nodded, his fingers now folded together, index fingers steepled against his lips.

"I don't trust him and I don't like him."

His eyes squinted in a smile. "He think your da's in there?"

"No."

"You believe him?"

"No."

We sat there, neither of us breaking eye contact. I don't know what Shamus had expected of me. For all I knew he was Jingo Jingo's ears, a student and spy.

But I didn't give a flying fig what he told Jingo Jingo.

There was no way I could feel good about a person who wore the ghosts of children like a winter coat.

"What's with all the children's ghosts around him anyway?" I asked.

Shame blinked. "What?"

"When he uses magic, if you look at him with Sight. You know, those little ghost people attached to him?"

"How hard did you hit your head?" he asked.

"You can't tell me you don't see them."

"I don't see them."

"But Zayvion? When he uses magic? Don't you see the silver glyphs, the black flame . . . ?" From the look on his face, the answer was obvious.

"I know Hounds use all sorts of things to deal with pain," he said, "and I'm not going to ask you what you're using. But you might want to back off it a wee bit."

"Never mind," I groused. My tolerance for weirdness had come to an end.

"Is Jingo Jingo going to be a part of my test?"

"He'll be there. A lot of people will be. Maintaining the Wards. While you're pushed to your limit to see where you crack."

"Nice."

"Think you're ready?"

"I'm always ready."

He shook his head. "You are so full of shit." He pulled his hands away from his mouth. "Zayvion will be there too, you know."

Something about the way he said it, or maybe his carefully neutral body language, set off my warning alarms.

"Going to talk to me about that?"

He shrugged one shoulder. "Just thought I'd mention it."

There was more to it, but it was clear Shamus wasn't going to, or maybe wasn't allowed to tell me.

"Thanks," I said.

"Sure. You should get some sleep."

"Wait. Could I use your phone?"

"If you tell me who you're calling."

"Why? Afraid I'll call the cops?"

"Like I'd care about that. Just curious."

"I'm going to ask Nola how Davy is doing. And tell her I won't be home tonight."

He raised one eyebrow. "Can't believe you're worrying about him with what you have going on in a couple hours."

"He's one of my Hounds. That means I look after him no matter what I'm dealing with. Besides, if I screw up and don't pass the test, I might not even remember him, right?"

"It's possible."

"So I take care of him now." It came out calm, confident, businesslike. I was really glad we weren't still wearing the disk cuffs, because he'd feel how fast my heart was pounding. He'd know that I was scared and wanted to get the hell out of here and never look back.

He handed me a phone like Zayvion's. Cased in metal and glass and glyphed to death. "Need privacy?" he asked.

I shook my head and dialed. Nola picked up on the third ring.

"Beckstrom residence."

Her sunshine voice sent a wave of homesickness through me. Nola had always been there for me when my life was going to hell. This time was different, though. This time I had to do it alone.

"Hi, Nola, it's Allie."

"Allic, honey, I've been worried about you. Where are you?"

"I'm at Shamus' mom's place; she runs an inn. We're talking business and investments. I'm going to stay late, maybe even overnight to finish up some things. How's Davy?"

"I got a call from Sid Westerling a couple hours ago. Davy's in ICU. He's in critical condition, but stable."

"Are any of the Hounds staying with him?"

"Sid said everyone's gone home for the day, but they're going to take turns looking in on him tomorrow. He also said they've done what they can to contact his parents; they don't live in the area."

"Okay, good. Any luck with Cody?"

"Yes. I got the call today. They've approved his release."

That wasn't much of a surprise. As soon as Zayvion had Closed him, Cody was free to go live three hundred miles away on an extremely magic-less farm.

"I'm going to go pick him up in an hour or so," she said.

"Alone?"

"Paul, I mean, Detective Stotts is going to go with me."

"That's really great, Nola," I said. "Are you heading right back to Burns?"

"Of course not! You and I have hardly had a chance to talk since I've been in town. You'll be home tomorrow, right?"

I glanced at Shamus. He didn't seem to be paying particular attention to the conversation. And since he was not a Hound, he might not have heard what Nola asked.

"Hang on." I palmed the phone. "Think I'll be home by tomorrow night?"

"Who knows?"

I drew the phone back up to my ear. "I'll try to be home tomorrow. If something comes up I'll call."

"Are you sure you're okay?" she asked.

"Yes." I put as much cheerfulness as I could into that lie. "I'm great. Just trying to take care of something for the Hounds. I'll be home soon, promise. Please ask Sid and the other Hounds to keep you up-to-date about Davy, okay?"

"I already have. Take care."

"I will. Bye." I hung up. I hated lying to Nola, but didn't want to worry her. I handed the phone back to Shamus. "Thanks."

"Sure." He tucked the phone in his pocket and headed toward the door. "Get some sleep, if you can. You're going to need all the energy you can get."

"Shamus?" I asked before he was out the door.

He turned and looked at me.

"You did this, right? The test? And came through it okay?"

"I did something like this. But you're different, Allie." He gave me a tight smile. "Lucky you." He turned out the light and shut the door.

Chapter Seventeen

I didn't think I would sleep. Too worried about Davy, about Tomi, Stone, about the dead, the living, and everyone in between. Too worried about the test.

But I did sleep, the soft darkness of the room eased by a little night-light that glowed amber in the wall outlet against the floor. It reminded me, for a moment, of the little room at Nola's house, one of the safest places in the world to me. Home of my heart.

No dreams this time, no conversations with my father.

I woke and stared at the darkness, listening to the movements of the big inn. There were people here, footsteps, and sometimes laughter. The lonely call of the far-off train filtered through the walls, but I could not hear the drone of the big engine. When the clock on the nightstand said it was seven, I got up, checked to make sure the bathroom door had a lock, and took a long, hot shower.

The vanity had a care package complete with toothbrush, toothpaste, some generic deodorant, and a comb. I used all of them. Even though my clothes could use a washing, I felt better, my muscles looser, the ache at the back of my head from hitting the floor gone. The ribs that I had sworn I'd cracked felt sore, bruised, but not broken.

Give me a hot cup of coffee and a couple aspirins, and I could take on the world.

I figured they had Wards or maybe a guard on my door, so I used the last fifteen minutes or so to clear my mind and relax. Magic filled me, rippled through my body from the ground and well deep beneath the inn. I worried that it would fail me, or worse, that I would fail to control it. I worried that the Veiled would appear during the test. If they were eating me alive, pulling magic out of me, there was little chance I could handle anything else. The Veiled hadn't bothered me when I tested with Maeve, but my father had been strong. He was the one who kept them from hurting me. Without him, I was vulnerable again.

Dad? I thought.

There was no answer. Not even a faint flutter.

If he was still with me, his presence was very, very small.

No help there.

I jumped at the knock on the door. Stupid.

"Yes?" I stood.

Maeve stepped into the room. "Are you ready?"

"Let's do it."

She walked over to me, took both my hands in hers. Her fingers were warm, strong. "You can do this, Allie. Do not doubt yourself."

"Thanks," I said. And I meant it.

She released my hands and strolled out of the room. I followed her down a white hall with walnut woodwork and old oak floors. Down to a staircase with wood that arched downward again, to another short hall, then down once again.

I don't know what I'd expected. Secret society stuff. Maybe a dungeon, torches, cast-iron braziers, pillars, weird statues. Something archaic. Mystical. Magical.

But the huge room—and I mean the room must spread out beneath the entire inn, and then some—looked more like a ballroom. The stone floors, maybe marble or granite, laid out in a glowing and subtle shift from white to gray to black all the way to the far end of the room.

The ceiling was two stories high and supported by columns carved from the walls that arced wings across the ceiling, graceful tips crossed at the center. Adding to the winged effect were thick ribbons of cast iron molded into the columns, and lead-lined glass panels that caught glittering wedges of light falling upward from the fixtures set cleverly along the walls and within the nooks and curves of the winged arches.

Grand. Beautiful. The walls were done in rich reds and browns and forest green, light scattered here and there to the room's best advantage.

It was difficult to remember this was a basement of an old inn.

The room itself was enough to make me pause on the last stair step. But the people who lined the walls of the room, perhaps a dozen or so, made me want to call a cab and go home.

No ceremonial uniforms, they all looked as if they'd just stepped out of their everyday lives and come here. A few were familiar faces. Kevin, Violet's bodyguard, stood next to Chase, and tall, stern Victor, whom I'd seen at my dad's graveside. Shamus slouched next to Jingo Jingo, and mousy Liddy, whom I'd also seen at the funeral.

My dad's accountant, Mr. Katz, stood next to a dark-eyed woman and man who looked like they could be twins, and another man who must have been a linebacker in collage.

But even in a room of magic users whom I could only assume were incredibly skilled, my attention was pulled toward one woman who stood at exact east, if the room were set on a compass rose.

There was no reason why she should stand out among the crowd. Maybe thirty years my senior, her light brown hair was pulled back into a severe bun, lending her delicate features a razor's edge. She had a wide mouth that might be pretty if she were smiling, and the kind of flawless grooming that gave her a brittle, premeditated beauty.

She wore a black, or maybe very dark blue, suit with a red shirt beneath—neither colors doing her pale complexion any favors, and both managing to downplay her figure. At her neck, a medallion caught silver and copper light.

She reminded me of someone. I didn't remember ever meeting her, but there was a frailty beneath that hard exterior that made me think of summer and blue skies. Maybe not her, but someone similar. Someone I had liked.

Weird, since she was currently scowling death at me.

If I had to make a wild guess from the body language of the people around her, she was Sedra, the queen bee of this little buzz fest.

I glanced at the man who stood next to her. Tall, with a square, unmistakable face, the sight of him was a punch to the gut. I remembered him.

Just after my coma, when I had returned to the city to find my life, my home, and Zayvion again, this man had been there. He had opened a taxi door for me and told me there was a war brewing. My heartbeat shot up, instant panic, though I didn't know why, and my palms slicked with sweat. He stood next to Sedra in the same way Kevin stood next to Violet. Like a guard.

Okay, maybe I didn't want to be tested. Maybe I didn't care if they sent a Closer into my head and yanked out my memories of this place, of these people. Maybe I didn't care if they made it so I could never use magic again.

Yeah. Right.

I was nothing if not a stubborn bitch.

I pulled my shoulders back and forced my feet to move again, to follow Maeve as she walked across the white stone to the very center of the room, where the white tarnished into the color of silver cast iron. It looked like she walked above a stormy sky.

Everyone, the men and women of the Authority, watched me. I worked on not tripping over my own feet.

Shamus, on the far side of the room, wearing black from hair to boot, standing on black stone, next to huge Jingo Jingo, winked, and I took that as a hint to maybe try to breathe.

"Allison Beckstrom," Maeve said, her voice filling the room. "Are you prepared to be tested as one favored by magic, to be forged in the ancient ways of this Authority?"

Okay, so there actually was some pomp and circumstance in the ceremony.

"I am," I lied through my teeth. Sounded good, though. And I was pretty sure the other magic users bought it.

"Let us begin," she said. She didn't smile, but gave me a grave, encouraging nod before she walked away and took her place on the slightly darker side of the room next to my dad's accountant and the twins.

I didn't know the place could become more silent. It was as if every person simultaneously held their breath. But that was not what happened. Not at all. What happened was that every person in the room drew upon magic.

Yes, they drew glyphs. Yes, I heard whispered chanting, humming. The lights dimmed and took on a deeper orange cast, which might just be good special effects, but was probably a Warded reaction to so much magic being summoned at the same time in such a suddenly small space.

Speaking of Wards, there were plenty of them, worked in the walls, worked in the tiling of the floor. Probably worked in the wings across the ceiling and every other square inch of the place. They hummed from the rise of magic in the room.

I held still, black stone to my left, white stone to my right, all my Hound senses geared up for survival. Someone in the crowd was going to fight me, push me to my limits until I broke. But no one had stepped forward yet.

To keep myself busy, I silently recited my Miss Mary Mack song.

The crowd across from me shifted and allowed a new figure to enter the room.

Tall, dark, and oh, so deadly, I immediately recognized my opponent.

Zayvion Jones.

My heart rattled in my chest. No. Oh, hells, no. Fight Zayvion? My mind spun with possibilities. If he cared for me, he'd pull his punches. No, they'd know. Which meant if he cared for me, he would hit me with everything he had. And I would have to do the same, push back just as hard as he pushed me.

Maeve had said I had to do everything in my power to survive.

Survive.

Zayvion Jones, the guardian of the gates, the go-to boy of the Authority, didn't look like he was going to go easy on me or do me any favors. Those cool brown eyes sized me up as an opponent, not a lover.

Crap. Could my dating life get any weirder?

He wore a white shirt, loose fit and open from the collar to his sternum, and black wide-legged pants, both of which looked vaguely martial arts-ish. No weapons in his hands. Not that the man needed weapons.

I was so going to get my ass kicked. But I was going to make him work for it.

I grinned at him, which made him frown. I set a Disbursement. This time, the pain would be hard and fast, but I made sure that it wouldn't hit me for a week. Plenty of time to recover from this little song and dance.

Correction: plenty of time to recover if I survived the song and dance.

I had to assume he had set a Disbursement too, and that he wasn't Offloading his use of magic to a Proxy in the room. But, hells, for all I knew, every member in the room was sharing his cost. That would give him virtually unlimited access to magic at no cost, and make him a very, very difficult person to take down.

Nothing like an impossible challenge to really wake up a girl.

I traced a quick spell for Sight, Smell, and Sound, willing to risk him canceling each of those for the chance to better observe what was going on.

The room burst into color. Magic crackled and flowed up the walls, crawling over the cast-iron ribbons and setting the winged arches afire.

Every person held a spell in their hands, or was wrapped by gossamer shifting magic, ready to cast that magic into a spell. I wanted to take my time and study them, study all the different ways they used magic, study their signatures and what that said about them, about who they were and how they perceived magic, but instead, I concentrated on not dying.

Zayvion traced a spell and threw the world at my head.

Yes. The world.

In response, magic flared in me, flooded my bones and blood, hot on the right, cold on the left. I raised my hands and drew a Block, catching the brunt of his attack. I left lines of the spell open so the impact of the magic could wrap at my right fingers. I pointed at the floor, bleeding the magic into the ground, while drawing Impact with my left hand.

It pays to learn to cast ambidextrously.

I never got the chance to throw it. Zayvion rushed me, a tower of black fire and golden eyes.

No time to duck. I braced my feet, tipped my shoulder down, arms out so he could not pin them and keep me from casting.

Paralyze rattled off my Block, then another spell I could not identify, and another.

Hells, he was fast.

My Block broke, burst into ash in front of me. I inhaled too quickly, felt that ash sting my lungs.

And then Zayvion was there, his arms around me, pulling me hard against him. Pinning me.

Not in a nice way.

I wriggled my right arm free, my left pressed into the center of his chest, palm flat against his skin.

Claustrophobia shot liquid panic through my bones. I had to get out. Break his hold.

Those gold eyes were filling with blackness. Everywhere he touched hurt.

He was draining me, draining the magic out of me. Grounding me.

Not in a nice way.

"Surrender." His voice was cold.

Yes, I was freaked out. Yes, I hurt. But I was also determined to take him to the mat.

And not in a nice way.

Instead of throwing more magic at him, which he would just Ground anyway, I used my left hand pressed against his heart to draw the magic out of him.

No, I wasn't any good at Grounding. But Zayvion said we were Soul Complements. I was going on a hunch that whatever he could do to me, I could do right back to him.

The concept of Grounding was to take the price of the other user's magic and act as a lightning rod for both the magic and the price. That meant you had to release what you were Grounding, let the magic flow back into the earth.

Zayvion's eyes widened. I drank the magic out of him. Drew it into me. Filled myself with the hot, dark, mint flame of him. Drank his magic down ruthlessly.

No, I didn't know how to let go of the magic. Have I mentioned I suck at Grounding?

I was full, every inch of me stretched and thrumming with magic, his magic. There was no room in me for more. But that didn't stop me.

My head swam. A high-pitched ringing filled my ears. I drank and drank and drank. He did the same.

Zayvion's grip loosened slightly.

I pushed down and away, broke free. I wove a spell for Hold. Cast it blind with all that magic I held inside me.

He froze. Long enough for me to cast Shield, something strong enough to surround me and keep him from touching me physically again.

Zayvion lifted his hand and muttered a word. Hold shattered like cheap glass.

So not fair. I didn't know the magic words he knew.

He chanted, drawing magic in multicolored ribbons out of the floor, singing it into a jagged ball in his hand, which he then threw at me. It hit my Shield and broke into bits that scrabbled over it like spiders trying to climb ice.

He followed it up with a wave of darkness that clung to my Shield, blinding me.

Fuck.

I'd have to drop the Shield to see. And he'd be waiting for me.

Think, Beckstrom. What did I have at my advantage? Not my father's memories or skills. Certainly not Maeve's training.

No, all I had was the magic inside me and a knack for Hounding. I also had a burning determination not to fail myself, not to lose my memories, my life again. Not even for Zayvion Jones.

I took a deep breath. Calmed my mind. Then I called to the magic in the well beneath the room. To hell with fighting fire with fire. I needed some napalm.

I dropped the Shield.

Zayvion threw everything he had at me.

Pain—hot, slicing, deep—shook me. I screamed, but couldn't hear the sound over the spell he threw.

An explosion of lights blinded me again, and all I could taste was pine, mint, and blood.

He meant to kill me. He really did. I don't know why I

hadn't believed it before. Zayvion had proven himself to be a dangerous man, a killer, a Closer. And now it was me he was going to end.

Screw that.

The magic from the well poured into me, and I knew I could hold it—could claim all of it for myself, keep it in my body and my bones.

So I did.

The pain disappeared. Everything around me suddenly slowed. I watched, from somewhere above myself, as magic spun from my fingers, from my soul, from the inexhaustible well beneath the earth. I was wrapped in ribbons of light and color and shadow. I was living, breathing magic, and I could make magic do anything I wanted it to do.

I didn't aim the magic at Zayvion. I aimed it at all the other magic users in the room.

No glyphs, no words, no songs. Just my need for magic to do as I desired. Gold threads followed my thoughts and sank deep into the chest of each user. Some of them were able to disengage, to turn the magic away before it knocked them out. A few fell.

And that's all I needed.

I threw magic at the walls. At the Wards. Magic users scrambled to reinforce them so I didn't blow the walls out and bring the whole building down on our heads.

That is what I call a proper distraction.

Now to deal with Zayvion.

Zayvion wove a glyph like a massive net and threw it toward me slowly; everything was still running in half-time.

I knew that the moment he released the spell, he would be overextended. Vulnerable. I could take him down. Take him apart. I could tell the magic to wrap around his heart, his brain, and squeeze. It would stop him. I wondered if it would kill him.

Was this test worth that? Was it worth ending Zayvion's life to save my own?

I had never been good at these kinds of decisions.

Zayvion told me once that I was not a killer. I remembered that now. Remembered him laughing, remembered him reaching out to me as a bullet tore through me. Strange, the things you think of in the last moments of your life.

I walked over to Zayvion, letting the net he cast glide over my head, then continue on to land somewhere behind me. I stood so close to him, I could feel the heat of his body.

The memory of his smile, of his body, strong, warm, naked, against mine flashed through me. He had been there for me, more than anyone but Nola. If I had the time, I would mourn the loss of that, the loss of him.

I placed my hand on his chest. Even though I was fast, too fast, and all the world was too slow, I know he felt my touch. His body tensed.

I am not a killer. Not if there is any other choice. And I was making another choice. A choice for both of us.

I reached into his mind. Just like he told me Soul Complements should not, because once Soul Complements touched mentally, they would not be able to let go. And now I understood that.

Oh, baby, it felt wonderful to be touching him like this. It felt right.

Zayvion arched his back in pleasure, and I felt his pleasure under my skin as if it were my own. Sweet loves, this was good.

I felt him laugh inside my mind, inside my mouth, echoing through me, as if we were one person, not two. Joined. Soul Complements.

I gloried in it. Never wanted it to end.

But I am a stubborn woman.

"Tag," I said. "You're it." Then I knocked him unconscious.

Zayvion crumpled at my feet.

And somebody threw a lead coat over my shoulders. All the magic in me, all the magic I was pulling out of the well, pumped out of me in a heartbeat.

I was suddenly emptied.

Whoa.

I lost my knees, fell on my ass next to Zayvion, who stirred, already waking up. Gotta love a man with stamina.

Maeve stood above us. She didn't look happy. I didn't

know what her problem was. We were both still alive. Wasn't that the point of all this?

"I am going to remove the void stones," she said like a traffic cop telling me which way to go and how. "You are not going to draw upon the magic in the well. Do you understand me?"

"Yes." Weird, but my voice came out all breathy, like I was exhausted or something.

Maeve removed the lead coat, and I got a look at it. Not a coat, but a blanket with tiny, round, black river rocks sewn into it. Void stones, like the one she'd put on my lap. Smart woman.

"This was not a test to see if you were Soul Complements," she admonished.

Zayvion moaned, swore. And yes, Maeve was angry at me, but I couldn't help but grin as Zayvion blinked up at me and realized where he was. Namely, flat on his back on the floor.

He moaned again. "I can't believe you did that." He dropped his hand on my knee, and levered to sit.

"Hey, I was supposed to use anything and everything to survive, right?" And even though I was smiling, a sick sort of dread gripped my throat. What if I had done permanent damage to him? What if I had done permanent damage to us? What if I had failed the test and now they were going to take all my memories away? My life away?

Zayvion's hand was still on my knee. "They're not going to take all your memories away."

"Did you hear me think that?" I asked.

He nodded, and in my mind I heard him say, *Loud and clear.*

His voice in my mind was not at all like my father's voice. His voice was familiar, comforting, warm.

Are you always going to be able to hear my thoughts? I thought.

We'll have to find out.

He pulled his hand away from my knee. We were close, just inches away from each other, but we were not touching.

"Think something," he said.

I thought how maybe I'd like to get the hell out of here.

He shook his head. "I didn't hear you. Can you hear this?"

I listened, strained to hear him in my mind. Nothing.

"So only when we touch?" I asked.

"Yes," he said. But he didn't sound very sure of it.

There had been a lot of noise going on around us. A lot of people hurrying here and there, a lot of magic being used, but I hadn't been paying attention to it.

Then Shamus strode over and crouched down next to us.

"You two done? Because we have a problem here." He pointed at the far, dark side of the room.

The room was in chaos. Magic vibrated in the air. Even without Sight, I glimpsed the afterimages of spells being cast, of magic being used. A hell of a lot of magic. By a hell of a lot of people.

And no wonder.

A hole, easily a yard wide and tall, and getting wider and taller by the second, was burning into the air, like a lightbulb burning through a filmstrip.

"What?" I said.

"A gate," Shamus said. "It opened when you tapped into the well. Fuck if I know why, but we haven't been able to close it."

"Here?" Zayvion said. "Impossible. It's too Warded, too safe."

"Yeah, well, your girlfriend there wreaked havoc with the Wards. Nice going, Beckstrom." Even though I was pretty sure I'd done something bad, Shamus didn't sound mad. The boy loved trouble.

"Not possible," Zayvion said again as he stood.

"Looks pretty damn possible to me," Shamus noted.

I got my feet under me and managed to stand too. The magic inside me was small, and I felt emptier than I had in a long, long time. Maybe even a little light-headed.

The hole on the other side of the room sizzled and flashed, lighting the room like a flare.

"That's your cue, Closer boy," Shame said. "Go. Fix." He shoved at Zayvion's shoulder.

Zay strode away from me, toward the hole. Between one step and the next, between one blink and the next, he became a man of black flames, silver glyphs blazing against his body.

I had seen him like this before, but I had never felt him like this.

It was as if I walked with him, felt the crushing weight of dark magic and light magic war through my body, tug at my control of sanity, singing of pleasures within my reach if I succumbed to its siren call. Shamus had said Zayvion could use all the kinds of magic, and now I believed him.

No wonder he was so disciplined, so calm. It took an amazing amount of concentration to keep sanity and reality in perspective while dark magic sang its song. Zayvion stopped, lifted his hands, and wove a spell that looked a lot like the net he'd thrown at me, only more solid.

He incanted something, or at least I thought he did. Everyone in the room was chanting or humming or singing. Well, except me.

Blocking spells, Warding spells, defensive spells; magic users moved as far from the burning gate as they could, casting their magic at the walls, the pillars, the inn itself to repair the damage I'd done. They supported the inn and guarded the well of magic that pushed up and up from the earth and rolled beneath the floor.

They, the Authority, worked to contain the magic, to support the room, and not let a lick of magic escape these walls.

Zayvion stood alone before the gate. He twisted at the hip and threw the net. Magic flared in me, wanting to leap to join his spell. I inhaled, cleared my mind, and held tightly to the magic that rushed up to fill me, afraid to let it merge with Zayvion's.

We might be Soul Complements, but we had not yet cast magic together. Now seemed like a horrible time to find out what would happen if we did.

The net closed over the gate, damping the mercury-gray light that poured through it, but the gate was still growing, still burning.

Then a voice rang out, a man's voice from the other side of the gate.

"I will not be denied."

Oh, no. This I did not want to know. There were things, people, on the other side of the gates, in death? Angry people?

Within the gate stood a dark figure of a man. Magic fluctuated across the gate and obscured the huge shadowed figure, but I could make out his hands held to either side, elbows locked, as if he could force the gate to open faster. As if he could walk through that gate and into our world.

No, no, no. That was not good.

A small part of my mind refused to believe what I was seeing. Sure, I'd seen stuff like this before—in horror movies. But this was real. This was now. I could taste the copper-hot burn of magic, could smell the sweat and fear in the room, could hear the people around me swearing, chanting, angry, calm.

This was really happening. And this was really, really bad.

The man yelled and shoved the gate wider. Now I could see behind him, slashes of fangs, bloody red eyes and claws, just like the Hungers we had hunted in St. Johns.

The man tipped his face so that shadows and magic hid his features. Except for his eyes. Blue as a summer sky, his eyes were familiar. I scoured my memory, but could not think of where I had seen those eyes before.

"Life and death are mine to wield. Light and darkness." The man flicked one hand, and as if to prove his point, dark magic, a solid tentacle of blackness, whipped out and rammed into Zayvion like a wrecking ball.

I yelled as Zayvion flew across the room. Shamus was already running toward Zay and reached him before he hit the ground.

"Sedra," the voice called out. "You will bow to my will. I will walk between life and death. Immortal."

The tentacle of darkness that had knocked Zayvion down whipped through the air and plunged into Sedra's chest.

The ice queen stiffened. She took a jerky step toward

the gate. Her jaw was set, the bone there straining against muscle and tendon as she took another involuntary step.

"No," she mouthed. She lifted one hand, traced a spell, and a shot of light pierced the man's chest.

Several people around her cast magic, trying to break the rope that held her.

Nothing worked. Dark magic forced her forward, toward the gate, even as the light seemed to force the man to lean against it to keep his feet.

Okay, here's the deal. I had no fucking idea what was going on. I mean, really. If this was how they always gave tests, it was amazing anyone survived.

But even though I didn't know what was happening, that didn't mean I was going to stand around while people were hurt.

First, stop the dude in the gate.

Right. Like I had any idea how to do that. And since I had no idea how to stop him, the next thing I could think to do was to save Sedra from his grip.

Zayvion stood again. I felt his anger, felt the calm Zen that kept his mind clear. He wove an intricate spell in the air with one hand and sang that lullaby waltz. Shamus was beside him, a bright shadow to his dark light, his hands extended in a hell of a Shield spell.

They looked good together. Like they had done this sort of thing before.

Another man joined them, Victor. Tall, lean, fit, dark-haired. Older. He took the place to Zayvion's right, and fell into rhythm with his chant, sang with him, building a spell that licked with silver light.

While Sedra marched toward the gate.

I felt Zayvion hold his breath. He and Victor threw the spell at the same time. It skittered over Sedra, past her, a wind of silver and gray, a shatter of glass that tore into the gate and burned into it like a maelstrom of silver embers.

The man in the gate looked away from Sedra, as if noticing other people in the room for the first time.

"Victor, and your favored student. Why have you betrayed me?"

"Mikhail," Victor said. "Let Sedra go. You cannot cheat

death. No man is immortal. It violates the true ways of magic."

"True ways?" Mikhail snarled. "Do you think you follow the truth? You follow the enemy among you. Light cannot be separated from darkness. I was a fool to assume the old ways could withstand the change. This—" He pulled, and the rope tightened on Sedra. She yelled, and stumbled forward again, but still didn't do so much as raise a hand in her own defense. "—This is what comes of truth. Lies. Deceit. Betrayal."

He gestured with one hand, tracing an arc from his left to his right. The burning, shattered glass tearing holes in the gate extinguished like a candle in a breeze.

"I will have what is rightfully mine." Mikhail spread his fingers, as if throwing seed upon the ground.

The Hungers behind him burst through the gate, claws scrabbling upon dark stone. And they ran straight for me.

Chapter Eighteen

Great. Just what I needed. Slathering hell beasts from the other side of death out to kill me. And me without any magical kibble.

I was so freaked out, I was flat calm. I wove a spell for Shield and cast it, while checking in to see if maybe my dad was still in my head and awake, and might want to give me a hint as to what else I could do to save myself.

No luck. Dad was silent as a tomb. Those beasts hit my Shield with the force of a Mack truck.

Plan B would be good right about now. Really great, as a matter of fact.

I concentrated on feeding magic into the glyph, to keep the Shield strong. The beasts tore at it with fangs and claws, sucking at it, draining it.

I had maybe four or five seconds before they broke through.

Zay told me throwing magic at them wouldn't work. I traced another glyph to shield me, and buy me time to think.

The nightmare in front of me sliced in half.

Zayvion was there, his machete in hand, carving through the creatures. Beyond him, I saw Victor wielding a sword that burned with silver flame. Shamus clapped his gloved hands together, and when he pulled them apart the Hunger in front of him exploded into black fire in midleap. Shamus held his arms wide, his mouth open, and drank the fire down.

Jingo Jingo was more subtle, wading out among a knot

of Hungers and grabbing them with his big hands, sucking the magic out of them with his touch alone.

Kevin moved through the room like a tai chi master, each circle of his hands, each flowing movement pouring out a wavering, glossy impact of magic that tore the Hungers in half.

Chase was there too. And what did you know, she had an ax in one hand and a hatchet in the other, magic trailing behind each strike like electric acid.

Fuck this damsel-in-distress bit. If I survived this, I wasn't signing up for self-defense classes, I was signing up for battle training.

More and more of the beasts poured out of the gate, a black wave of muscle and fang. So many, they filled the room.

My Shield broke; Zayvion pressed the machete into my hands and pulled a glass-bladed whip from out of thin air.

He looked up at the gate, half a room and fifty or more beasts away, and then turned his head sharply at the scream to his left.

The dark-eyed twins fell beneath the beasts. I scanned the room and realized there were other people missing: my dad's accountant, the linebacker. And I could not see Chase.

Zayvion swore and laid into the beasts, making his way to where the twins had fallen.

That was all I had time to watch. I hacked at the first thing with fangs that jumped at me like the mother of all rosebushes was out to kill me, and then fell into a steadier rhythm, my body catching on pretty quickly how to use this much metal.

Which was great, because I liked breathing. It was one of my most favorite things to do.

But in the heat of battle, no one could reach the gate, Sedra, and Mikhail.

I stumbled backward over a dead beast and spotted a clear path to a column. I jogged to it and pressed against its relative safety. From here, I could see Sedra.

She stood in front of the gate, looking up at Mikhail. She didn't look angry. If anything, she looked strangely happy.

The rope in her chest was gone. She had managed to cast another spell. Something that attached at the edges of the gate, trying to close it.

Mikhail stared down at her. He held up one hand, and she held up hers. Magic, dark and light, shot like caught lightning between their palms. They seemed to be caught in a stalemate. She pushed him away as he drew her closer. Her spell tried to shut the gate, but Mikhail had cast a counterspell. Neither moved.

More beasts poured out of the gate, streamed past Sedra and Mikhail, whose hands were now clasped, fingers twined.

We were quickly going to run out of room for more bodies in here.

Someone needed to close the gate.

I took a deep breath and calmed my mind. Even took the time to set a Disbursement. Then I closed my eyes. Going off of nothing but memory, I traced the glyph for End.

It was an old spell, Maeve had told me. It was, I was certain, my father's spell.

I didn't know it. Not really. I hadn't been trained in it. But I cast it with a certainty, a gut knowledge once.

I didn't aim at the gate, because that wasn't what needed to End. I aimed at Sedra and Mikhail.

And threw the spell with all my strength. End slammed into them. Sedra yelled and turned toward me, her hold on Mikhail, or perhaps his hold on her, broken.

For a brief second, I could see them both clearly. Two handsome people, filled with rage.

Not exactly a Hallmark moment.

And then Mikhail lifted his hand and tore my End spell to ribbons.

I wove it back together as fast as he unraveled it, but it was clear I was losing ground.

"Not even your father could stop me, Allison Beckstrom," he intoned, his voice so loud, the wings against the rafters trembled.

He traced a spell. Sedra stared straight at me, unable or unwilling to stop him. And I knew that spell was my death.

A hand brushed against my fingertips. I jumped and looked down.

Beside me stood Cody, or rather, a ghostly version of Cody. My brain went blank a second. Cody wasn't dead. Zayvion had Closed him, but he wasn't dead.

"Cody?" I said. "Why are you dead?"

Tact. I got it.

He seemed older somehow, his sunny sky blue eyes calm. Even though he smiled, I could tell he was sad.

"Not dead. Just . . . separate from myself. When Zayvion Closed me, my mind was already broken in two. It's been that way for a long time. But now that I'm Closed, I can't . . . reach myself anymore. It's okay. The part of me that is still alive is happy."

This was one of those moments when I just wanted to call a time-out. This didn't make sense.

"Promise me you will make this right," he said. "All of this." He lifted his hand, long, artistic fingers pointing at the room, and somehow also taking in just Sedra and Mikhail, the Hungers in the gate. "The fight over magic, over who should rule it. The light and the dark. Promise you'll make it right. For all of us." He tipped his head in question.

"If I can," I said, not knowing what I was promising. Because, hey, I had about three seconds left to live, and then I'd probably be a ghost like him, and who wanted to spend their last seconds of life making someone sadder?

"I think you can. I think you were born to do this." He nodded, solemn, as if we'd just sealed a deal.

Then he turned. Looked at Sedra, who stood silent outside the gate. Looked at Mikhail, who stood silent within the gate.

"Don't take too long, okay?"

Cody smiled.

And ran. Ran past me, past the beasts, past the people who fought the beasts. He ran past Sedra. Images of fields, of summer sunlight and kittens, flashed before my eyes. Then Cody jumped, flew, arms wide, back arched, a specter, a ghost, the soul of a broken man-child, laughing as he fell inside the gate. He somehow held himself there, between life and death, his soul outlined in silver, gold, copper magic that wrapped him in satin ribbons. Cody became fire, became magic, as he stretched to bridge the space between life and death, burning and sealing the gate, his laughter fading, fading into a childhood song.

Beyond his fire, I could see Mikhail's eyes, blue, so blue, eyes just like Cody's, wide with shock, with sorrow. I could see Sedra yell, "No!" her fingers stretched out to the flame as if she could reach Cody and pull him back to her. But it was too late.

The gate closed. Light snuffed. Ashes fell to the black stone floor.

And the room was just a room again.

Cody was gone. Mikhail was gone. The gate was gone.

The beasts fell like toys whose batteries had gone dead, faded into shadow, then nothing more.

Sedra, her hair a little mussed, but not much—I totally had to find out what kind of hair spray she used, because, damn—looked over at me.

I swear I saw tears.

Then her bodyguard rushed up beside her, and other people—Maeve, Victor, Liddy—approached. Sedra pulled the pale, brittle, beautiful mask over her face, and brushed their concerns away. She walked into the center of the room.

"Allison Beckstrom," she said, her voice soft and surprisingly musical, a little like Cody's. No, a lot like Cody's.

I might be dense, but I wasn't stupid. She had to be Cody's mother. And I bet Mikhail was his father.

Poor kid. I thought I had it bad.

I pushed away from the column, took a step. Winced. Every muscle hurt. Even the bottoms of my feet. I was so going to pay for tapping into the magic in the well.

"Zayvion Jones," she called.

Zay appeared from somewhere toward the front of the room, looking a little bruised, bloody, burned.

But whole. A wash of relief flooded through me.

We walked together but not touching, and stood in front of Sedra.

"There are no laws written to guide me in my decision of your test today, except the law that states that if a user of magic causes harm to others or violates the laws of magic, he must be Closed."

Was she kidding? We'd just fought nightmares, dealt with a whacko from the other side of death, and watched as part of her kid's spirit sealed a gateway to death. And she wanted to go over my test results? Talk about focus. Or denial.

"Allison Angel Beckstrom, you have done harm, broken the Wards, attacked members of the Authority standing witness to your test."

Holy fuck. The woman knew my middle name.

"But we are too few . . ." Her voice caught. She swallowed. "We are too few. The gates between life and death have been opened, even here where it should not be possible. This is just the beginning. I am afraid . . . aware . . . the war will now follow. We will need all who are strong to fight for this world's fate. To keep the innocent safe and magic true.

"You have shown your strength, your innate talent to use magic. Allison Angel Beckstrom—"

Would she quit using my middle name already?

"—will you accept your place among the Authority?"

Would I have gone through all this just to say no? "Yes," I said.

"We welcome you. Learn well and quickly."

She stepped back and looked around the room. The Hungers were gone, not even their black blood left on the floor. Magic and the ashes of old spells still clung to the room. Sedra gestured to several people to come to her side.

Zayvion and I were clearly not among the group she wanted to talk to. I'm not even sure the people she called to her wanted to talk to her. To me, it sounded more like they wanted to argue.

I had good ears. I heard Victor demanding an investigation to find out who opened the gate, heard Liddy tell him that was unnecessary. Mikhail's name was bandied about and so was Cody's. Someone who sounded like my dad's accountant, Mr. Katz, suggested contacting other branches of the Authority in other cities to warn them of the breach, and to make them aware other gates may open. Greyson's name was brought up, and it was decided Sedra would search his mind to see who he might be working for and who had implanted the disk. Jingo Jingo said he was almost sure it had to be someone like Frank Gordon—a doctor and magic user who dealt in Death and Blood magic.

Even my name was brought up. Was I Zayvion's Soul Complement? About a fifty-fifty split, yea, nay, on that. I was apparently a boon and a danger, and my continued training, under Maeve for a while, then Victor, Jingo Jingo, and a name I did not catch, would help them define how I fit into the organization.

Zayvion touched my arm briefly and walked toward the stairs.

I followed him.

"How badly are you hurt?" he asked.

"Nothing permanent, I don't think." Which was weird, really. I'd used a hell of a lot of magic, done things I'd never done before. And so far, I remembered all of it.

Maeve broke away from the group around Sedra and strode over to us. She still didn't look happy.

"Allie, I'm proud of you. And of you, Zayvion. Though Sedra refuses to rule on it, it is clear to me you are Soul Complements." She touched each of our shoulders. "May you live and love." It was a blessing, a wish. Not magic, but still, I could feel it echo between us.

"Thank you," Zayvion and I said at the same time.

Weird. But cool.

Maeve smiled. "You are welcome to stay here in one of the rooms and rest," she said to me.

"I'd rather go home," I said.

"Call me tomorrow, then," she said. "Your training will begin in earnest."

'Cause, you know, today had been such a picnic.

"Zayvion, we will need you soon." She glanced over at the group.

I did too. Body language spoke of screaming-mad magic users.

"Not for an hour or so, I think," she said with a sort of grim determination in her voice. "You should rest."

Zayvion shook his head. "I'm fine. I'll take Allie home."

She nodded. "Be safe." And then she strode back to the group.

I looked around the room for Shamus and Chase. Neither were to be found. Strange.

"Is Shamus all right?" I asked as we started up the stairs.

Zay shrugged one shoulder. "He left just before Sedra called us to the center of the room."

"Why?"

"Maybe he didn't want to see us. Soul Complements. Accepted."

"Why not?"

Zayvion took a deep breath and let it out slowly. "He had this chance once. Well, an actual Soul Complement test, not this. This wasn't standard," he noted.

"Shamus had this chance to see if he had a Soul Complement? With whom?" I asked.

"Someone he denied. I think he still regrets it."

Oh. I didn't know what to say to that.

Zayvion squeezed my hand gently, and I realized I didn't have to say anything.

We made it up the flights of stairs, and then finally through the inn that was quiet and cozy, all the lights low. For all I knew, it must be almost midnight now. We let ourselves out and walked across the gravel parking lot to Zayvion's car. The night was cold, the moon setting silver fire to the clouds within its reach.

The night here in the parking lot felt blessedly sane, real, normal. I glanced over at the inn that looked just like an inn, and wondered how so much magic and tragedy could happen beneath the notice of the regular world.

So much had happened today, tonight, I didn't know how to sort it all, how to make sense of it all. My thoughts kept skipping from one thing to the next, not lingering long enough for me to really think through the ramifications.

Fatigue. I was tired. Really tired.

Zayvion held the car door open for me.

"I'm sorry about the test," he said.

I shrugged. "What about it?"

"That I was your opponent. I didn't know they would choose me."

I turned so I could lean my hip against the doorframe. "Why did they? Why not send someone else to try to kill me? Chase certainly seemed willing."

He winced at that. Maybe it wasn't tactful, but it was the truth.

"Do all suspected Soul Complements have to fight each other?" I asked. " 'Cause that sounds like a stupid rule to me."

"No. But whoever is being tested must face someone equal or better than them in the use of magic." His brown eyes searched my gaze, asking me to understand things I'd barely begun to know.

"They chose me because of what I am," he said. "Guardian. They chose me because both light and dark magic are at my command. They chose me because they feared only I could stop you if it needed to be done. They know how powerful you are."

My feet hurt, my back hurt, and I really needed to pee. Yeah, I was feeling really powerful.

"I think they might have overestimated my abilities," I muttered.

"No," he said. "They didn't."

We stood there a second longer and I wondered if he was going to kiss me. Or maybe trying to kill me had set our relationship back a bit. Back to trying to decide if there was enough trust left between us to build something on.

I rubbed my eye with the cool fingers of my left hand. Then looked back up at him. Waiting. Patient. Zen.

"We'll figure it out," I said.

He exhaled and nodded. I realized he had been really worried about my answer.

We both got in the car, and Zayvion started the engine and guided the car through the parking lot.

"Would you have?" I asked.

"What?"

"Killed me?"

"They would have wanted me to," he said.

"And would you have?"

Zayvion looked over at me, his brown eyes just brown. Warm. Human. He put his hand on my arm. "No."

And I knew he was telling the truth. I could feel it reverberate in him, could feel it spread between us.

I leaned my head back against the headrest. "Good."

He drew his hand away. We were silent as Zay drove onto the access road.

"I did win, you know," I said.

"No, you didn't."

"Yes, I did. I knocked you out."

"Stunned me. I wasn't unconscious."

"Oh, please, save it for the preacher. You were out cold."

He stopped to turn onto the main road that would lead us back to the bridge across the Columbia and into Portland. He drew a breath to argue, but movement to his left caught both our attention.

A shadow. Two shadows, running in the night. Running toward us, toward Zay's side of the car.

Holy shit.

Zayvion tensed, then very calmly whispered a spell that I knew would tear someone apart from the inside out.

The figures broke from the shadows and moonlight bathed them in silver.

Shamus sprinted and threw open the back door, holding it for the gargoyle who ran beside him.

"Go, go, go," Shamus said as he jumped into the backseat behind the gargoyle and slammed the door shut. "Drive, drive, drive!"

Stone caught sight of me and cooed.

"Stone!" I twisted in my seat and rubbed his warm, marbled head. "Good to see you, big guy. Are you hurt?"

He crooned again and lifted his ears. He looked happy, and had not a scratch on him.

"What the hell, Shamus?" Zayvion said, not driving. "Tell me you did not just steal that gargoyle."

"Steal? Come on. He doesn't belong to my mum or the Authority. Can't steal something that didn't belong to them in the first place."

"You know your mother will find out," Zayvion said.

"Not if you drive fast enough, she won't."

I thought Zayvion, the responsible goody-good guardian of the gates, was going to turn the car around. Instead he put it in gear and started toward Portland. "You have a decent cover story?"

"Bulletproof. Couldn't stand to see you two get the nod for your Complement status; I went out for a smoke and a whiskey. Girls closing up the bar even saw me crying in my drink. Such a sad, sad thing I was."

I was still rubbing Stone's head, so I saw Shamus's wicked smile.

"Of course, I have no idea how the beastie shook off the Grounding stone and snuck out. Clever, though. Too bad we don't know enough about animates to have kept him properly caged."

Zayvion shook his head. "And I caught up with you?"

"You know how I am. Shadow to your light. Saw you and Allie leave, and you hauled my drunken ass along for the ride."

Zayvion chuckled. "Pretty good."

"Good? Gold. Plus, with Armageddon going on back there, I don't think they're going to worry much about a missing statue."

"Are you comfortable being an accessory to his crime?" Zayvion asked me. "The Authority will not approve of this kind of behavior."

"What crime?" I said.

Shamus grinned and sat back. "You know," he said. "The three of us could take the world apart and have a hell of a lot of fun putting it back together."

"Who knows?" Zayvion said. "We might get that chance."

Chapter Nineteen

Like teenagers sneaking a keg into our parent's basement, Zay, Shamus, and I managed to smuggle Stone into my building and up the three flights of stairs to my apartment without getting caught. Sure, we could have used Illusion to cloak him, but no one suggested it. I didn't know about the boys, but I was exhausted and had had enough magic to last me a while.

Our luck held. Nola wasn't back from getting Cody, which worried me until I realized it was only ten o'clock. Paperwork and processing can take a lot of time. And they might have stopped off for a late dinner, or, heck, gone out to a movie, for all I knew.

Once inside the apartment, Stone lifted up onto his hind legs and waddled off to the bathroom, clicking all the way. The hiss of water turning on and off was accompanied by his clicks.

"Now, that's good fun," Shamus said. "He has a thing for water?"

"Just the bathroom sink so far," I said.

Shamus headed down the hall and looked in on him. "Hey, fella. You like the sink?"

Stone just clicked and hummed. I had no idea if it was an answer.

"Do you want me to take him somewhere else?" Zayvion asked.

"Shamus? Yes, please."

He smiled. "Stone. Back to the restaurant?"

All I could think of was the chain that held him down

there, and how he had pleaded for me to release him. "I don't think he'd make a very good statue anymore," I said. "His world has gotten a lot bigger now."

Zay caught my double meaning, and nodded. He strolled over to my window and looked out. "Can't let him loose on the street all alone. Even if the Necromorph is under lock and key, there's a lot of dangerous things still out there."

"I'll see if he'll stay here during the day. Maybe let him out at night. He's been free for a few days already. I haven't heard any reports of a gargoyle loose in the city. He knows how to stay hidden. Knows how to take care of himself."

"If someone who is part of the Authority sees him, or if the police or Stotts sees him, you'll have to give him up."

"I know."

Zayvion turned. "He might not last long anyway. There isn't a lot of information on animates. A few old stories about magic users—Hands—making golems and other creatures. Those histories are more story than history, though."

"Speaking of Hands," I said. "When you Closed Cody, did you see his spirit?" I asked.

"No." Zayvion drew the word out, asking me to explain.

"I saw him. His spirit. At the gate. He was there. He made me promise to make this right for everyone. Then he jumped into the gate and closed it."

Zayvion was suddenly very quiet and very focused. "He did what?"

"Jumped into the gate."

He didn't say anything.

"You want to tell me how that is any weirder than everything else that happened tonight?" I asked.

"He's not dead," he said.

"Cody? I know. Nola just got cleared to foster him."

"Yes." Zayvion held up one hand. "Cody is still alive. But that part of him, the part of him I Closed, should have stayed within him. He shouldn't be dead."

"He said his mind was broken before and he was just half of himself. That he couldn't reach the rest of himself when he was Closed."

Zay rubbed at the back of his neck and stared at his shoes for a minute, thinking. "So Cody is alive and dead, so to speak. Your dad is alive and dead, so is Greyson, and Mikhail. This is a disturbing trend."

I rubbed my hands through my hair. Bad move. One, I was sore, so putting my hands up over my head made everything ache. Two, my hair was in serious need of brushing.

"Is that something we need to deal with tonight?" I asked.

He must have caught how tired I sounded. He walked over to me, put both his warm palms against my arms. I didn't know what he was thinking, but then I wasn't trying to.

"No. Not tonight."

Shamus strolled into the living room. "High-larious, that rock. Kind of wish he were mine."

Zayvion pulled away. "He's not, so don't get any smart ideas."

"Please. I have some morals," he said loftily. "Ready?"

Zayvion nodded. Then, to me, "I need to go back. There will be a council meeting called. I'll need to be there."

"Will I see you later?"

Shamus was already at the door, looking out through it before he opened it. Such a small gesture, but so telling. Zay was right, there still were dangerous things out there. Maybe more than I knew.

It just might be time for me to buy some decent Wards for my door.

"If I don't see you tomorrow, I'll come by in the evening," he said.

"Good luck."

That made him smile, and I liked the look of it on him.

"You too. Lock the door."

And then Zayvion and Shamus were gone, out my door, which I did indeed lock behind them.

Stone trotted out of the bathroom and sat next to me, staring at the door.

I wondered if it was going to hurt to have Zayvion so far from me. I closed my eyes and thought about him. A warmth filled my chest like a glowing orb. I had a tactile knowledge that Zayvion was alive, and a part of me in a way he never had been before, soul to soul. It was a good feeling, a gentle knowledge. It probably should have freaked me out, since I wasn't sure I was all that good at that kind of commitment, but I wasn't up to worrying about it.

I rested my hand on Stone's smooth head. "What a mess," I muttered.

Stone cooed his soft vacuum cleaner sound.

"Speaking of messes, what am I going to do with you?" I asked him. "Do you sleep?"

He tipped his head. I didn't think he understood me, but he trotted across the floor and into my bedroom, where he curled up in the corner, the curtain draped over his back, his big head rested on his arms. He didn't close his eyes. He just stared and looked very much like a nonbreathing statue.

"Close enough," I said. I thought about taking a shower and decided against it, and for coffee instead. I checked my phone messages—there were none—and looked for a note from Nola. Nothing.

As I was pouring the fresh brew into my favorite mug, the handle of my door jiggled. Then keys slipped into the lock.

Only Nola and my manager had keys to my apartment.

The door opened and I heard Nola's voice.

". . . just for tonight, okay? Go ahead, you're okay."

I walked out of the kitchen and leaned against the doorway. "Hi."

Nola smiled at me. Next to her was Cody. He looked a lot like his spirit self, thin, pale. Blue summer eyes. But behind those eyes was a childlike hesitation. He somehow looked much younger than his ghost.

He looked at the room and at me. Recognition lit his face. "Pretty."

I smiled even though I no longer had my memory of actually meeting him. I did, however, remember how I felt about him. Sad, I think. Maybe even protective.

"Hi, Cody. It's good to see you again. Would you like to see my house?"

Cody looked over at Nola, who nodded encouragingly. "Go ahead. She likes you."

Cody smiled. "Pretty." He wiggled his fingers in the air again. "Magic."

Wasn't that interesting?

He wandered into my living room, holding his hands against his chest, as if afraid to touch anything.

"How'd it go?" I asked Nola.

"Long. Difficult. But everything's taken care of. I picked up some dinner. Have you eaten?"

She wasn't carrying anything but her purse.

"Not really."

I heard footsteps and the crinkle of a paper bag. Then Detective Paul Stotts was there, two bags in his hands.

"Hello, Allie," he said.

"Hello," I said to one of the last men in this city I wanted to see right now. "Come on in."

He walked past me into the kitchen, where he proceeded to unpack cartons of Chinese food. Nola shut the door.

I probably should have panicked. The head of the MERC was in my house and so was the gargoyle who'd followed me home. But after tonight, it would take more than that to get me to jump.

From the other room, I heard Cody's delighted cry. "There you are! I missed you."

"You're staying for dinner, aren't you, Paul?" Nola asked.

He shook his head. "I can't tonight. How about breakfast tomorrow?"

"Sure." She took off her coat and hung in on the back of my door.

Detective Stotts strolled out of the kitchen and stopped next to me. "I don't have any leads on the case in St. Johns yet," he said. "Someone destroyed the crime scene. The evidence is gone. But we have some promising information."

"Oh," I said, trying to look surprised. Trying not to look like I was dating the guy responsible for destroying the crime scene.

"Have you heard anything more about Davy?" I asked.

Nola answered, "Just that he's stable. Sid said they'll call here tomorrow."

I took a drink of coffee and wondered whether I'd have time to go see him in the morning. Probably.

"Have you thought about my offer?" Stotts asked me.

Offer? I frowned. Finally remembered. He wanted me to work for him. I hadn't thought about it since my life had taken the short road to crazy town. It seemed like a really bad idea to take a job Hounding for a cursed secret magic police officer, with everything else on my plate.

Which would mean he would ask another Hound to work for him. Maybe Sid, Bea, Davy.

An image of Davy's broken, bloody body floated through my head.

Shit.

"I thought about it," I said. "And I'd like to take the job."

He nodded. "Excellent. I'll have the contract drawn up. Come by the station and we'll go over the details." He held out his hand for me.

What the hell. I shook it.

"Welcome to the force," he said. "I hope this will be a long and productive career for you."

The irony was not lost on me. "Thanks."

Stotts turned to Nola, and the whole police-detective demeanor changed. "Congratulations," he said softly.

Nola beamed. "Thank you. For everything. It would have taken me days to get through all the legal tangles."

"My pleasure." He bent and gave her a brief hug.

I suddenly felt like the three of a crowd, so I walked off, leaving them their privacy.

I found Cody sitting on the floor of my bedroom, his arm around Stone's neck, chatting away at him, like he'd just found a lost friend.

And maybe he had.

"Everything okay, Cody?" I asked.

He smiled at me. "Sleeping. That's okay. He'll be back."

That's great, I thought. How was I going to explain that to Nola?

"That's great," I said, with a lot less sarcasm. "Dinner's ready. Come on out and we'll eat."

"Eat?" His face clouded over.

"After dinner you can have a cookie with a secret note in it."

"Cookie?"

"That's right." I held out my hand for him.

He stared at my hand, then patted Stone's head and took my hand.

At his touch, magic stirred in me.

"Pretty," Cody said. "Magic. Like me."

"Think so?" I asked him. He nodded and nodded.

I led him out of the bedroom and shut the door. Nola had already set the food out on the little table for the three of us. Stotts was gone.

Once he saw the food, Cody didn't need any more encouragement. He sat down and contentedly began eating it with a spoon.

"So," Nola said, as I took my seat to one side of her. "How was your day?"

"You don't want to know." I got busy with the chopsticks, and for just a little while, pretended like everything in my life was back to normal.

Chapter Twenty

We made up a place for Cody to sleep on the couch, and Nola slept on the living room floor on an air mattress she'd been smart enough to buy.

I slept in my own bed, alone except for the gargoyle who was silent and still by my window.

When morning rolled around, I heard Nola and Cody get up. Heard them each take a shower. Smelled coffee being made. But I pulled a pillow over my head and ignored it all. I was every kind of tired that had a name. And it wasn't nearly light enough outside for me to drag myself out of my warm blankets.

A soft knock at my door, and then Nola's voice. "Allie? Cody and I are going to go out to breakfast with Paul. After that, I might get Cody some clothes to take to my place. We won't be home for a while. Coffee's fresh in the kitchen."

Then I heard her patiently coaxing Cody into his coat, and a knock on the door that I could only assume was Detective Stotts. His voice was low and gentle in greeting, and then Nola and Cody and Stotts were all gone, the door shut and locked behind them.

I pulled the pillow off my head and rolled over on my back, hogging the bed. It had never felt this good to be alone in my life.

Bliss.

Something shook the bed. That something was the size of a Saint Bernard and made out of rock, with opposable thumbs.

Stone shook the bed again. When I didn't respond on

the third try, he made himself busy opening and closing my dresser drawers, then opening and shutting the closet door. Repeatedly.

Oh, sweet hells.

I propped up on my elbows. "Can't a girl get some sleep?"

Stone twisted his head to look over his wing at me. He crooned, but did not stop opening and closing the closet door.

I moaned and got up.

"Fine. You want out? Try using your thumbs on this door." I opened the bedroom door.

He trotted over and made a happy glass-marble clicking sound, then headed straight for the bathroom.

"No way," I said realizing there was about to be a half ton of rock between me and my morning shower. "Go talk to the kitchen sink." I maneuvered around him in the small hallway, which gave me the willies and made it hard to breathe for a second. There was so not enough room in the hall for me and him at the same time.

Still, it was worth it. I made it to the bathroom first and shut the door on Stone's curious snout.

"Kitchen," I said through the door. Just in case that wasn't a word the gargoyle knew, I locked the door.

The shower woke me up the rest of the way and reminded me that I was full of aches. A headache—probably part of my payment for all the magic I'd been throwing around—started up at the back of my neck. There would be more to follow that. I tried to remember all the Disbursements I'd set. Fever, body ache. Head cold? Migraine? Too many to remember. I guessed I was just going to have to wait and find out.

I got out of the shower and took a couple aspirins. Maybe I'd go out today and buy some of those glyphwork painkillers, some cold medicine, and chicken soup.

I took my time drying off. Paid attention to my injuries and scars, a habit that was becoming a ritual. Besides the puncture wounds on my shoulder that seemed to be healing pretty well, I had a variety of scrapes and bruises.

But it was the thin silver arc beneath my navel that really caught my notice. I tried to rub it off, but it didn't so much as smear. A delicate symbol of eternity, the figure eight on its side, traced across my lower stomach, and in the light, silver touched with blue, rose, and green washed across it as I moved. It was like the marks down my arm, but different.

I traced it, and remembered Zayvion's fingers against my skin.

I wondered if it would fade, or if this new mark was a part of me now.

I wrapped my towel tighter around me and wandered off into the bedroom. I dressed, then headed into the kitchen for some of Nola's coffee.

Stone was not in the kitchen. He was, however, in the living room, his forehead pressed against the window, his batlike wings curved umbrellas over his shoulders as he stared out at the city.

I walked over, coffee in one hand and patted his shoulder. "Nice, isn't it?"

It was raining outside, but a rainy day in Portland felt comfortable as an old pair of slippers.

Stone clicked in agreement and continued to watch the people who walked the streets below.

My thoughts wandered to Davy. Maybe the city only looked nice on the outside. On the inside, it found an awful lot of ways to hurt people. I decided to call the hospital to see how he was doing. The nurse on duty wouldn't give me any information, which made sense since I wasn't related to him. She could only confirm that he was still there, still in ICU. I thanked her and hung up. I'd just have to head down there and see if I could find anything out.

But before I went anywhere else and did anything else, I needed to record the last few days in my book.

I padded, barefoot, over to my coat and pulled out my little notebook. I took it and a fresh cup of coffee back to the table and worked on writing down everything that had happened in the last few days. It took a while, even though I was fast at this. And looking back over it, all I could do was shake my head.

"I need a vacation," I muttered. And from my notes, it

was also clear I needed to call Violet and talk to her again about turning my dad's company over to her.

Better now than never.

I dialed her number. Violet picked up on the second ring.

"Beckstrom residence," she said.

"Hi, Violet. It's Allie."

"I'm glad you called," she said. "I've been thinking about your offer for me to take over as CEO of Beckstrom Enterprises."

A soft flutter brushed against the back of my eyes. Not as weak as before. Growing stronger. I had a sinking feeling in my gut that my father was recovering.

I rubbed at my eyes to try and push the flutter away. No luck.

"Great," I said to Violet. "And what did you decide?"

"To accept."

I exhaled with relief. I'd really been stressed about having to run my dad's company, or handing it over into incompetent hands. "Good," I said, trying to be nonchalant about it. "How do we make this happen?"

"Leave that to me. I'll get everything together and let you know when and how we'll handle the transfer."

"When you need me, just call, okay?" I said.

"I will. And Allie?"

"Yes?"

"I tested the material."

I had to think for a second to come up with what she was talking about. Then I remembered she had taken a sample from the ring of ash in the park.

"It is from the disks. The signature is there. But we never had these kinds of results in the laboratory. Someone has found a way to use the disks with"—she paused, thinking—"Blood magic, I'm fairly sure, and some form of magic I've never seen."

My heartbeat sped up. Of course she'd never seen the other magic. Death magic was not known to the general public. "Do you think it could just be contaminated?" I asked. "I did break the spell. I might have messed it up."

"Perhaps." It was clear she didn't think so. "I'm going

to run a few tests in the lab to see if I can duplicate the results."

"Well, let me know if I can help." I hated keeping information from her, but there were too many dangerous things going on in this town. And I wanted her, and my future sibling, to stay far, far away from them.

"Thank you," she said. "I will. And you've contacted a self-defense coach, yes?"

"I've narrowed it down," I said. "When I pick someone, I'm sure you'll know."

We said our good-byes, and the flutter behind my eyes stopped. I put on my long coat, which was dry again, and a scarf and hat. It was time to go check on Davy.

"I'm going out," I said to Stone, who still stared out the window. "Do you want out, boy?"

He looked over his shoulder, bat ears shifting back, then up into points. He clunked his head against the window again and cooed down at the street, rocking his head slowly from side to side to watch traffic go by.

"I'll take that as a no. Then how about you stay in my room? There's a window in there too. Lots of doors and drawers to open. Oh, and hey, you could go to sleep."

His ears pricked up at the word *sleep*. He waddled back from the window, tipped his head up at me, and then waddled on two feet off toward the bedroom, his marble-clack sounding like he couldn't believe it was night again already.

I chuckled. "Just while I'm gone so you don't scare Cody and Nola," I said. *Or Stotts*, I thought. He curled up at the bottom of the bed and I patted his round head. "With any luck, I'll be home before them."

I shut my bedroom door. No lock on the outside, so I left a note on the door that said *Sleeping*, and hoped for the best.

It didn't take long to get to the hospital.

I didn't see any of the Hounds there, didn't see anyone who might be Davy's parents. I talked to the nurse on duty, explained I was a close friend.

Maybe I looked worried or tired or sincere. Whatever it was, she told me his room number and pointed the way.

I paused outside his door and took a deep breath, calming myself, preparing myself for seeing him before I walked in.

It was a little darker in his room, a small window placed in just the right position to reveal a generous portion of the gray sky, city, and the hills beyond.

Davy did not move. Sleeping, maybe. His face tipped toward the window, so that I couldn't see his eyes.

"Bring me a beer?" he wheezed, just the breath of sound.

I walked around the bed and stood in front of him. "Of course. But I had to use it to bribe the nurse to let me in."

He rolled his eyes up to look at me. With some effort he rocked his head back so he could see me better. "Hi."

"Hey," I said. "I appreciate your eagerness, but you know I haven't nailed down the details on that health insurance program for Hounds yet."

He raised one eyebrow. He was still pale, his left eye swollen, the bruises on his face worse than the last time I'd seen him. "What's the holdup?"

"I've been busy." I glanced around the room, pulled the wooden chair next to the bed so I could sit. "Knitting, filing my nails. You know, baking bon-bons."

That got me a ghost of a smile. "Bon-bons are ice cream, stupid. Tomi okay?"

Ouch. How should I tell him how messed up she was? "She's okay as far as I know. I'm going to check on her later to make sure. You were right. She got into some bad shit. Bad people." And not being someone who could let an opportunity slip by, "Did you see anyone with her in the park?"

He swallowed. "I tried. I thought I'd find her. Who she was with. In the park. She said . . . " He swallowed again. "She said she screwed up. And she was sorry."

"Everybody makes mistakes," I said, surprising myself. "She has a chance to fix things. Her life. You have to let other people help her do that, Davy. Fix her life."

He just stared at me. "I can't," he said. "Can't just give up."

"Do you remember her hurting you in the park? Do you remember her doing this to you?" I asked.

He just stared at me. Belligerent.

Sweet hells. What was I going to do with a boy who was too stupid for his own good?

I swore, as soon as I nailed down health insurance, I was going to hire a counselor for the Hounds. Talk some sense into his thick head.

"I think you need to give her room to make choices," I said. "She's not alone. She has all of us, all the Hounds, to help her too. Maybe you should give her some room to try other options, other people."

He quirked one corner of his mouth up, and the fire I knew he had sparkled through the pain and pain medications. "Like you have all the answers."

I smiled. "Damn right I do. Sometimes a change of strategy is called for, you know? Getting different people involved. And besides, Hounds do not go into dangerous situations without having backup. That includes love."

He blinked, his eyes staying shut a little too long. "Sure. How's that going for you?"

"What?"

"Love."

"None of your business."

"Thought so." He was slurring now, and I figured I needed to let him get some sleep.

"I'll see you soon, okay?" I reached over, rubbed the back of his hand.

He surprised me by catching my fingers, even though his eyes were still closed. "Don't give up," he said. "It's worth it."

"What is?"

"Love." He let go of my hand. Between one breath and the next, he was asleep.

Poor kid. He just wouldn't give up on her, no matter how much she hurt him. I wanted to shake her and make her realize she was screwing up a chance to be with someone who was a really good guy. And I wanted to tell her just to leave, break it off clean and quick so that Davy could grieve and heal and love again. So he could find someone who would be good to him. But I knew Tomi was in pretty bad shape too. I just didn't know how permanent her wounds would be.

The wounded loving the wounded. How could that ever end happily?

I heard the footsteps outside the door before the person paused and pushed the door open. It was Sid, a cup of coffee and sandwich in one hand.

"Hey, Allie," he said. "How's he doing?"

"Sleeping." I stood.

He nodded. "Looks like you got hit by a shit truck. Go home."

"It's suddenly clear to me why you're not married, Sid," I said.

He grunted, a short laugh.

"Call me if anything changes, okay?"

"No problem," he said. "We've got it covered."

I left the hospital and went home to make sure Stone wasn't causing a riot. My luck held. Nola hadn't come back yet. I opened my bedroom door.

Stone stood in front of my dresser, pulling one of my sweaters on over his head. He'd already put a shirt on each leg and had stacked every shoe I owned into a precarious pyramid. The room looked like a small, overly curious tornado had torn it apart.

"You have got to be kidding me," I said. "Maybe I should give you to Shamus."

Stone crooned, only one ear and one eye sticking out of the neck hole of the sweater. I pulled the sweater off him.

"Now your foot," I said.

I don't think he understood what I wanted him to do, but I am nothing if not a determined woman. And besides, there was no way I was going to let him stretch all my sweaters out of shape. Once free of my clothing, he trotted down the hallway on all fours and started in on his second favorite pastime, conversations with plumbing.

Just what I needed: Stone, the Toilet Whisperer.

I let him mess with the sink while I cleaned up most of the disaster in my room. By the time I got done shoving clothes back in my drawers, I was thinking Stone would have to learn a few new phrases. Such as "Keep your grubby hands off my stuff" and "Windowsills are not for chewing on." So much for my cleaning deposit.

There was a knock at my front door, and I closed the bathroom door on my way by, hoping Stone would stay busy with the sink.

I looked through the peephole.

Zayvion Jones stood there, wearing his ratty blue ski coat, a black beanie pulled down over his dark curls. A warmth in my chest, more than just my pleasure at seeing him, spread out.

I unlocked the door, opened it.

"Hey, stranger," I said.

He gave me a soft smile. "Mind if I come in?" He held up a bottle of wine and a cell phone.

His eyes were a little bloodshot, and even though it looked like he had changed back into jeans and a sweater, he didn't look like he'd gotten any sleep last night.

I stepped aside so he could come in. "You do realize it's ten thirty in the morning?"

He glanced at the bottle in his hand. "Too early for wine?"

"Unless you like it in your cereal. Did you sleep at all last night?" I took the bottle from him. He unzipped his coat and pulled off his beanie, then scrubbed his head.

"No one did. We'll meet again at five tonight. Thought you should know. Maeve wants you there. Not at the meeting. But in case she needs to ask you questions." He rubbed at his face, muffling the last couple words.

"Calling someone?" I asked.

He frowned, noticed the phone in his hand. "Oh. No. This is for you. Compliments of the Authority."

I expected it to be heavy from the silver glyphs that encased it, but it was light, compact.

"Thank you," I said.

"My number's in there. Maeve's too, I think, and Shamus'." He yawned.

I could feel his exhaustion wash through me. Okay, maybe there was a downside to this Soul Complement thing.

"How about coffee?" I said.

He rolled his shoulders, nodded, then wandered into the living room. I poured coffee for both of us and took a second to assess myself. I still felt like me, just me. But with Zayvion so near, I did have an awareness of him, of his exhaustion. Maybe with practice I'd be able to have a stronger awareness, feel his emotions and mental state like when we were wearing those cuffs during the hunt.

Or maybe he would always be just a faint echo in me. Maybe that's all a Soul Complement added up to.

Yeah, I doubted that.

The water in the bathroom had stopped turning on and off.

I found Zayvion slouched on the couch. He had kicked off his shoes and stretched his legs out, propping them up, but not on the coffee table. I walked around the couch and saw Zay's stockinged feet resting on Stone. Zayvion rubbed his feet over Stone's back. Stone looked up at me and crooned contentedly, stretching to angle his shoulder for a better scratch.

I sat next to Zay, handed him the coffee.

"Want a pet rock? Give him to you cheap."

Zayvion smiled. "Oh, no. He's all yours." He stopped rubbing Stone and took a drink.

Stone belly crawled so that he was positioned on the floor between both Zay and me, and looked up at me expectantly. I kicked off my shoes and propped my feet on his shoulder, scuffing my toes against him.

Stone clacked and crooned, a happy little rock.

Zayvion exhaled and closed his eyes. He pressed the coffee cup against his chest. Hells, he was tired.

I drank my coffee, savoring the moment. Yes, there was a gargoyle at my feet, and yes, my boyfriend was mixed up with magic and people who were more dangerous than I'd ever known, and now I was mixed up in it too. And yes, my dead father was still in my head, growing stronger. Even with all that, this was the most normal and right my life had felt in a long, long time.

"They haven't found out what Greyson knows yet," he said softly. Zay had been quiet so long, I thought he had fallen asleep.

"Why?"

"He won't talk, and we can't make sense of what's going on in his head. Yet. He'll come around. We'll get it out of him. Jingo Jingo has taken over, and he's good at this kind of thing."

Yeah, so good that he told me my dead dad was not in my head.

"I don't trust Jingo Jingo," I said.

Zay nodded. "I know. You don't trust anyone. That's why I like you."

"Is that the only reason?"

"Not at all." He still had his eyes closed, but he smiled.

"How's Chase?" I asked. Even though I should be angry as hell at her, I mostly just felt sorry for her. For the chance she and Greyson never got.

"Looking." He opened his eyes, took another drink of coffee. "For clues of who did this to him. She's pretty sure your dad was behind it."

"So she and I are like this?" I crossed my fingers.

"More like just the middle finger," he said.

"This becoming a part of the Authority thing," I said. "Pretty complicated stuff."

"Smooth as glass here on out," he said.

"Really? Gonna promise me that?"

He shifted his cup into his other hand, and turned so he could better face me, his right arm long enough to drape across the back of the couch.

"Maybe. What will it cost me if I'm wrong?" He smiled, and those warm brown eyes didn't look quite as tired as they had a minute before.

He was a beautiful man. Not just on the outside. There was a strength in him that drew me in like a cat to sunlight, a calm in him that made me believe things might somehow work out if we both kept working on it. I mean, we'd done some good already. Gone on a real date, caught a Necromorph, gotten most of Cody safely into Nola's care, helped a Hound who was being used, and oh yes, closed down the gates of death and made me an official member of the Authority. Not bad for a couple days' work together.

"You have to admit I beat you," I said. "Knocked you to the mat with magic."

Zayvion sparked at the challenge in my voice. He grinned. "And if I see it differently?"

Instead of answering, I leaned forward and kissed him. I took my time, lingered over the reality of him, here, warm, alive. He tasted of coffee, smelled of pine. And felt like home.

"How about we negotiate the price later?"

"Think we'll have time?" he asked.

"I think we'll make the time."

He smiled, took my hand. And I walked him into my bedroom, intending to make it very clear to him that we had all the time we needed.

Read on for an exciting excerpt from Devon Monk's next Allie Beckstrom novel,

MAGIC ON THE STORM

Coming in May 2010 from Roc

Two months of self-defense, mixed martial arts, and weapons training did not make it hurt any less when I was thrown over my opponent's shoulder and slammed into the ground.

Yes, I should have tucked and rolled. Would have too if he hadn't kept hold of my arm and twisted at just the right instant to knock me off balance and make me sprawl like a dead jumper waiting for my chalk outline.

"Give up?" he asked.

My right wrist still locked in his grip, I stretched out my left hand and grabbed his ankle, used the leverage to pull my right arm down, and twisted. I broke his hold on my wrist, rolled up onto my feet. I got off the mat and out of arm's reach quickly.

"I'll take that as a no, then?" Zayvion Jones asked. He was a little sweaty, a lot relaxed, standing halfway across the mat from me. Barefoot, he had on a pair of jeans that, if there were any justice in the world, would not let him flex and move and stretch the way he did in a fight, and a nice black T-shirt that defined the muscles of his chest, his thick, powerful arms, and flat, hard stomach.

He was every kind of good-looking in the dictionary.

"Take it as a hell no," I said sweetly.

That got a grin out of him, his teeth a flash of white against his dark skin, his thick lips open enough that I suddenly wanted to drop this whole I-kill-you/you-kill-me act and kiss the man.

Instead, I rolled my shoulder to make sure my arm was still in its socket—Zayvion Jones played for keeps—and tried to come up with a game plan to tip the fight to my advantage.

My shoulder sore but still attached and functioning, I stepped back out onto the mat.

I could use magic on him. It might be worth ending up in bed with a fever just to take Mr. Superpowerful Guardian-of-the-Gates down a notch during a practice match.

"Is there a particular way you'd like to end up on the floor this time?" he asked as he shifted his stance and waited for me to attack. "Or do you just want me to surprise you?"

"Gee, if I get a choice, how about if I end up on top this time?" I gave him that slow blink–smile combination that always got him into bed.

He licked his lips, and a flash of uncertainty narrowed his eyes. "I thought you said you wanted to fight."

I strolled up to him and paused—out of arm's reach. I'm not dumb. "I thought you were asking me how I wanted this to end."

Zay studied me, his brown eyes just brown, no hint of the gold that using magic always sparked there. As far as I could tell, he hadn't been using magic for the past couple months. Ever since my test to see whether I could become a part of the Authority, and the craziness with the gate between life and death opening right in the middle of the test room, things had been quiet.

Things were actually pretty good. I liked that. Liked not having to worry whether I'd survive the day. And it wasn't just my life that was better for the downtime. Over the last several weeks I'd watched Zayvion change from a somber, tightly controlled, dutiful man, to someone a little surprised he was enjoying life.

Time off from his duties with the Authority looked good on him. Sexy.

"I wasn't talking about ending this," he said, and it took me a minute to remember what we were talking about. Oh yeah, the fight. "But we can call it a day. Since you're surrendering and admitting you lost. Again."

Light poured in through the windows, casting warm coffee-colored shadows beneath his high cheekbones and jaw. His hair was always short, but he'd recently buzzed his dark curls, which somehow only enhanced his beautiful eyes and strong, wide nose. The look of worry that I only occasionally glimpsed through his Zen mask had been absent for weeks. He smiled more. Laughed more.

And it made me realize how hard I'd fallen for him. I didn't want what we'd had for the last few weeks to change or disappear. But I'd lost too many people in my life—and too many memories along the way—for me to think things would always be this easy between us. The idea of losing him made it hard to breathe.

I tried to push that fear away, but it clung like a bad dream.

"Allie?" Zay was no longer smiling. "Are you hurt? Your shoulder?" He came closer and put his wide, warm palm on my shoulder.

That touch gave me the faintest hint at what he was feeling: concern that he'd torn my arm out on that last flip, which, yes, he could have, but no, he hadn't. I wasn't that fragile.

And that reminded me of what this little get-together was all about. Fighting. Training. Becoming strong enough to hold my own against anyone. Even the legendary Zayvion Jones.

I knew I shouldn't have done it. But hey, a girl has to take what opportunities present themselves, right? I had my game plan.

I stepped into him and turned my hip, sweeping his foot out from under him. He went down, rolled, but I was there, got in close, getting his arm back, my arm through it, and the other over his throat.

"Give," I said. We were in close contact, but I was too busy staying on the winning side of the tussle to have brain cells left to concentrate on what he might be thinking.

"No," he grunted.

Even though I am a tall woman, Zay still had me on sheer muscle. He flexed and managed to break my hold, twisting over onto his back, his legs scissoring to catch mine.

No way I would've let him do that.

I followed him, using his momentum to roll over him, and then behind. I huffed out air, got to my knees, and tried to keep his arm pinned.

He shifted, rolled. I ended up kneeling with him beneath me. Boo-ya! I was on top.

I had one knee planted beside him and the opposite foot braced on the other side. I decided to forget about his arm; I wrapped my hands around his throat, knuckles at his windpipe.

He pressed his palms flat against my hip bones and tilted his hands inward so his fingers stroked upward beneath my T-shirt.

I raised an eyebrow. "You do notice I'm choking you. . . ." I squeezed a little harder in case he thought I was kidding around.

He grunted.

I most certainly was not kidding around.

He shifted his grip. Tried to pull me down and rolled one hip to throw me. No chance. I braced my heel to stay out of the roll and pressed harder.

"Mercy," he whispered.

I relaxed my grip. "Say that I win."

"I win," he managed.

I tucked my thumbs against his windpipe. "What? You win? Is that what you said? I must not have heard you correctly."

"Draw," he whispered.

"Oh, sweet hells, Jones. You have got to be the most stubborn man I know. You lost."

"I agree," he said.

Huh. I hadn't expected him to give in that easily. I pulled my hands away, rested them against his chest.

"I am the most stubborn man you know," he rubbed at his throat with one hand. Grinned at me.

I smacked his other arm. "My honor's at stake here. You lost. I won. If you can't admit that, I'm not sure our relationship will survive."

He snorted, grabbed my shirt, and pulled me full on top of him. His fist, in the valley between my breasts, was a hard pressure between us.

"Nothing's going to get in the way of our relationship." His gaze searched my own, and the slightest fleck of gold sparked there. "So long as we want this, nothing can stand in our way."

Damn. Could the man get any more romantic?

I tipped my head down and caught his lips with my own, soft, thick, hungry. He instantly responded, then licked gently at my mouth until I opened for him. He tasted of deep, warm mint, and his pine scent, peppered by sweat, carried the memory of the countless times we had touched, loved.

It had been two months, and it still felt as if I couldn't get enough of him.

I want you, he whispered in my mind. We kissed again, his tongue tracing the edge of my bottom lip. I felt his desire burn through me like a hot wind, making my skin prickle with tight heat.

A rock hit my arm.

I twisted, my palms up, ready to cast a spell.

Zayvion was way ahead of me. One elbow braced beneath him, he rolled, putting me partially behind him, his right hand already outlining a glyph in the air, though he didn't pour magic into it yet.

Another rock—a wet rock; no, an ice cube—hit my hip. More ice hit Zayvion's shoulder, clattered down his chest to the mat in front of him.

Shamus Flynn stood at the door across the room, a bucket of ice tucked between his arm and chest, and a grin on his face.

"Thank God I got here in time." He tossed another volley our way. "You might have gone up in flames. Burst into sex at any minute."

"Shame," Zayvion warned, "put the ice down."

"Like hell. No need to thank me. It's what friends are for."

Zay didn't take his eyes off Shame, but he shifted so that we were no longer tangled.

"Do you remember what happened to you the last time you threw ice at me?" he asked calmly.

Shame shook his head. "Doesn't ring a bell."

"It had something to do with you not walking straight for a couple days."

Shame pulled out a piece of ice and stuck it in his mouth. He chewed it—noisily—as he strolled over to us.

I swore he had a death wish.

Shame did a fair job at that goth-rocker vibe. Black hair cut with the precision of dull garden shears shaded his eyes. A black T-shirt over a black long-sleeved shirt on top of black jeans, black boots. Even his hands were covered by black fingerless gloves. But behind all that black was a man who wasn't as young as he looked. A man whose eyes carried too much pain to be hidden by that sly smile.

"That was your last warning." Zayvion tensed, ready to pour magic into the glyph.

"Do not burn your best friend to a crisp," I said, sounding more like a babysitter than a girlfriend.

Zay just kept staring at Shame. "He won't burn long. Not with all that water on him."

Shame laughed. "Bring it on."

"No one's going to bring anything on." I stood and alternated my glare between Zayvion and Shamus. "No magic fights in the gym."

Right. As if they'd do what I said.

Time to change tactics. "How about food? Zay and I were just going to lunch," I said.

"Lunch?" Shamus said. "Is that what you kids are calling it these days? Back in my day we called it fucking."

"Shamus," Zayvion said, "may I have a word with you?" Zay let go of the spell and stood up in one smooth, graceful motion that showed just how many years this man had spent sparring.

Shame didn't have time to answer because Zay closed in

on him, fast and silent as a panther, and forced him toward the far side of the room.

I shook my head. Those two acted like brothers even though they were physically about as different as two people could get. Zay and Shame were far enough across the room that I shouldn't have been able to hear what they were saying. But Hounding for a living meant I had good ears. There was a chance I would've been able to spring into action if Shame had needed me to save his life or something.

"... ever throw ice at me again, I am going to beat you with that bucket. Do you understand me?"

"Oh, please. Like I should take you seriously. You haven't raised a finger in two months."

"Listen." Zay paused, lowered his voice. "This is different." He paused again. "I need you to respect what Allie and I have or you and I are going to have real problems."

"Respect?" Shamus asked, just as quietly. "I'm filled with envy."

"Then stop being an ass."

Shame snorted, then raised his voice, obviously talking to me. "Aren't you going to ask why I came by?"

I shrugged the shoulder that didn't hurt. "You need a reason to harass Zay?"

"Hell, no. But I'm not here to talk to Zay. I'm here for you." He strolled across the room toward me.

"What's up?" I asked.

"My mum wants to see you."

"Did she say why?" I asked.

"Officially?"

"At all."

"There's a storm coming," he said, all the joking gone now.

Zayvion stiffened. I watched as the relaxed, laughing man I'd spent the last few weeks with was slowly replaced by an emotionless wall of control, of calm, of duty.

"What kind of storm?" I asked, even though I was pretty sure what the answer would be.

"Wild magic," he said. "And it's aiming straight for the city."

Also Available
from

Devon Monk

MAGIC TO THE BONE

Using magic means it uses you back, and every spell exacts a price from its user. But some people get out of it by Offloading the cost of magic onto an innocent. Then it's Allison Beckstrom's job to identify the spell-caster. Allie would rather live a hand-to-mouth existence than accept the family fortune—and the strings that come with it. But when she finds a boy dying from a magical Offload that has her father's signature all over it, Allie is thrown back into his world of black magic. And the forces she calls on in her quest for the truth will make her capable of things that some will do anything to control...

MAGIC IN THE BLOOD

Working as a Hound—tracing illegal spells back to their casters—has taken its toll on Allison Beckstrom. But even though magic has given her migraines and stolen her recent memory, Allie isn't about to quit. Then the police's magic enforcement division asks her to consult on a missing persons case. But what seems to be a straightforward job turns out to be anything but, as Allie finds herself drawn into the underworld of criminals, ghosts, and blood magic.

Available wherever books are sold or at penguin.com